D1202878

STAND UP AND DIE!

MICKEY SPILLANE

Edited and Introduced by
MAX ALLAN COLLINS

ROUGH
EDGES
PRESS

STAND UP AND DIE!

SIT DOWN AND READ!

AN INTRODUCTION BY MAX ALLAN COLLINS

This new and definitive collection of what might be termed the "lost" fiction of Mickey Spillane gathers the novellas and short stories he wrote between 1952 and 1974 for *Cavalier* and other men's adventure magazines and the digest pulp, *Manhunt*. They are "lost" in the sense that Spillane did not collect them in pairings for a series of paperbacks (*Me, Hood!*, *Killer Mine*, etc.) issued in the mid-1960s by his regular reprint publisher, Signet (New American Library).

My professional relationship with Mickey began in 1984 when I talked him into collecting a number of the stories in this book as *Tomorrow I Die*, published by Mysterious Press in that year. The remainder of his short fiction appeared in another anthology of his work I edited, *Together We Kill* (2001). Both of those anthologies are long out of print and pricey on the collector's market.

Essentially this book combines those collections after I have excised material that is of secondary interest – a script for a Mike Hammer test film Spillane made with his cop friend Jack Stang (now a short story included with the Hammer novel *Kill Me If You Can* from Titan), a comic book "filler" story (found in *Primal Spillane* from Bold Venture Press), a non-crime/mystery tale, and a ghosted science-fiction story written at the last minute by *Fantastic* editor Howard Browne under Spillane's byline when Mickey missed a deadline. This chaff is not without interest, but the time had come to publish a new book consisting strictly of wheat.

Perhaps the most talked about Mickey Spillane mystery is not *I, the Jury*, the 1947 publication of which in hardcover by Dutton featured the first appearance of private eye Mike Hammer, making *Stand Up and Die!* part of a 75th anniversary celebration of that debut. The biggest mystery has been why Spillane did not write a Mike Hammer novel or even a Hammer short story for the ten years that separated *Kiss Me, Deadly* (1952) and *The Girl Hunters* (1962).

After all, Spillane was not just the most internationally popular mystery writer of that 1950s and early 1960s, he was the best-selling author in America, period...even if he decried the designation "author" as too pretentious. Mickey Spillane not publishing any novels for ten years would be akin to Stephen King laying off for a decade after he wrapped up, say, *The Stand*.

Much speculation has been bandied about to explain the "long wait" between Spillane novels – Mickey was suffering from writer's block *or* he had too much money coming in from radio and comic strips and movies to bother *or* his religious conversion to the conservative Jehovah's Witnesses made him swear off his sex-and-violence style *or* he was too caught up in macho pursuits like deep-sea treasure hunting, hot rod racing, touring with the Clyde Beatty circus, and sky diving. While each of those holds a grain of truth, the real reason turned up in research for the biography I've written with James L. Traylor – *Spillane: King of Pulp Fiction*, coming out in January 2023 from Mysterious Press and the capstone of this 75th anniversary celebration. And I'll reserve the right not to reveal the solution of that mystery until the biography's publication.

But I can clear up another long-mulled mystery – why did the most popular, best-selling writer in America publish his novellas and short stories in such low-end magazines? His most frequent home was *Cavalier* (again, in its men's adventure magazine days, not its incarnation as a *Playboy* wannabe) but also *Saga*, among others. The most respectable of these periodicals was probably *Manhunt*, considered then and today the successor to the legendary pulp *Black Mask*, where Carroll John Daly invented the modern private eye and Dashiell Hammett and Raymond Chandler first flourished.

But such slicks as *The Saturday Evening Post* and *Collier's* (who initially bought "Everybody's Watching Me," seen in this collection, and then reneged) considered the Spillane name too notorious for their magazine's whitebread reputation, and *Ellery Queen's Mystery Magazine* was out, as well – too many top writers in the field held Spillane in contempt, even as the genre they labored in boomed thanks to his enormous success.

Nonetheless, it would seem likely Spillane's work might have found its way into certain of the better markets – *Playboy* or its slick imitators, for example – while the more modestly paying men's adventure mags might have expected Mike Hammer's creator to be well out of their price range. Spillane, however, was a loyal friend – remember, Mike Hammer in *I, the Jury* avenged the murder of an army buddy who saved Mike's life in combat – so it should be no surprise that the Mick turned to the editors and publishers of men's adventure (in particular Marvel's Martin Goodman), who were the same ones he worked for and with in his pre-war days as a comic book writer, scripting everything from *Captain America* and *Sub-Mariner* to *Blue Beetle* and *The Human Torch*.

Significantly, in his novellas for the men's mags and his short stories for *Manhunt*, Spillane did not use his signature character, Mike Hammer. (Again, the reason for this is discussed in the forthcoming biography.) His heroes are very much in the Hammer mold, in this volume's title novella and others herein. Occasionally – in the *Manhunt* stories particularly – he drops his trademark first-person and utilizes third-person, not focusing on his usual strong, tough heroes. These shorter crime stories seem to foreshadow his novel *The Last Cop Out* (1973). The only novella written for *Manhunt*, "Everybody's Watching Me" (a four-part serial that marked the first four issues of this now classic digest), prefigures the non-Hammer bestseller, *The Deep* (1961), his comeback after nine years of silence as a novelist.

As this is a volume at least in part commemorating the

75th birthday of Mike Hammer, we are including a rare Hammer short story – "Tonight I Die." This is a reworking of a previously published story, "The Night I Died," which marked the first collaboration on a Hammer story by Mickey and myself.

While Spillane and I worked together on many projects – including three anthologies of his work, half a dozen other anthologies of assorted mystery and crime writers, the *Mike Danger* comic book, and the documentary *Mike Hammer's Mickey Spillane* – we wrote no prose fiction together. But when we were putting together an anthology for NAL called *Private Eyes* (1998), it was obvious we needed a Mike Hammer short story for inclusion.

Mickey only published a handful of Hammer stories – two condensed versions of his novels *The Killing Man* and *Black Alley* in *Playboy* and an oddball comic tale, "The Duke Alexander" (not conceived as a Hammer story) that appeared in *Byline: Mickey Spillane*, a mostly non-fiction collection from Crippen & Landru in 2002 (co-edited with Lynn Myers). (NOTE: The original version of "The Duke Alexander" appears for the first time as a bonus feature with *The Menace* from Rough Edges Press – a novelization by me of an unproduced Spillane crime/horror screenplay, another of the 75th anniversary publications).

In going through Mickey's material with him in one of his South Carolina offices, I discovered an unproduced script he'd written in 1953 for the radio show, *That Hammer Guy*. I believe it was a sort of pilot episode. In it, Mickey distilled everything about his Hammer character into one thirty-minute morsel. With Mickey's blessing, I put the script into prose narrative form, not adding much of anything – he'd provided a lot of voiceover-style narration.

That version of the story appeared in *Private Eyes* as "The Night I Died." Later I discovered longer versions of the story in TV and movie script form, and these have led to the 75th anniversary Hammer novel, *Kill Me If You Can*.

I was never entirely happy with the short story version of "The Night I Died" – I had been too "hands off" and it remains more script than prose. Since I have essentially become – at Mickey's own request in his final days – the literary executor of the Spillane estate, completing seventeen novels and numerous short stories from his unfinished manuscripts and unproduced screenplays thus far, I have taken the opportunity presented by *Stand Up and Die!* to revisit the radio script and write a more fulsome story, which appears here in this form, for the first time, as "Tonight I Die."

I believe this is the single best, most representative collection of Spillane's work in the shorter fiction field, with an emphasis on the short novel, his favorite mode of storytelling. In the stories in these pages, written during the ten years between Hammer novels, Mickey – who had emerged in 1947 almost out of nowhere as a compelling, one-of-a-kind storyteller – honed his art and became a more polished craftsman of crime fiction than ever before.

So I invite you to sit down and live a little with one of the genuine masters of American crime/mystery fiction.

M.A.C.
January 2022

Stand Up And Die!

Stand Up And Die!

I LAY on my back in the brush and watched the three buzzards circle over the ridge. "They're the smart ones," I thought. "No matter who loses, they win."

The three of them circled on a thermal, catching the updraft to the top of the rock shelf, then sliding down in formation, picking up speed so they could buzz the kill area for a quick check before picking a landing spot. They saw me, and when I waved, rode the breeze out of range and orbited until Operation Downstairs was complete.

For a second I grinned at them and wondered who learned from who. A long time ago I'd maneuvered like that over a Pacific beachhead.

But then it was different. It was honorable and noble and young. It was war and killing was righteously explained away and sometimes it was even fun to pull the trigger. Then you bragged to your wing mates about the kills, glorying in the noise and fumes and sometimes it took a long while before you realized the complete waste and foolishness of it all.

Now dying was only a few trees or a couple rocks away —and upstairs the real winners watched and waited.

Left of me there was a metallic clang of a bolt-action rifle reloading. The shrill whistle of the tree bugs stopped abruptly and I turned over on my stomach, bellying down as

close as I could get so I could see through the underside of
the brush.

I knew they wouldn't give me credit for having any sense.
To them outsiders and animals were classed together—fair
game stupid enough to get themselves treed. It made me
think of that classic line from a book, *Animal Farm...*"All men
are created equal, but some are created more equal than
others." Then I grinned again and wondered how they'd
take to having the buzzards circle their side of the deal for a
while.

The spot I had been watching for a few minutes moved
and I knew it wasn't a tree fungus. It took a minute more, I
could see the length of rifle barrel. It was angled off, so they
hadn't located me fully yet. They needed a sound, or a
movement, then all the guns I couldn't see would swivel and
zero in. They knew I had the .45 and maybe I had the two
boxes of shells. But it wouldn't matter. They had the rifles.
They could stay out of range.

Trouble was, I thought, they didn't really know the range
of a .45. They discounted trajectory. When you had to live
off birds you shot with a .45 for three long weeks before they
rescued you from that stupid little Pacific island, you didn't
discount trajectory any more.

I leveled the gun in the crotch of the brush root and
sighted it. The target was nice and white and unsuspecting.
Then I squeezed the trigger and the whole mountainside
blew up in noise and the target was a screaming, cursing
joker yelling the hillbilly version of "medic!"

Old Man Hart's voice rolled up from the gully and said,
"Who got hit?"

Then it was real funny because nobody wanted to talk
and give away his position. But not Clemson. He found
either a rock or a tree to hide behind and hollered out, "He
done it to me, Paw. It's Clem! He done..."

"How bad he git you, son?"

"My hand, Paw. He's got him a rifle someplace. He's
got..."

"He ain't got no rifle, son. He just got you. You come
down here, Clemson."

It was quiet for a second while the horror of it went

through Clemson's mind. Then he sobbed softly, "He'll get me sure, Paw. He's got a rifle."

"He ain't got no rifle, son," the old man repeated.

Clemson's voice had a wail in it. "He'll get me, Paw. I'm hurt."

My leg started to knot with a cramp and I eased my foot out. The slightest sound, the tiniest movement, and I'd have had it.

Upstairs the buzzards were at 3,000 again, circling for a complete reconnoiter.

The old man's rumbling voice said, "Mitch...you hear me, Mitch? You won't shoot my boy if he comes out to git fixed up, will you now?"

I thought, *Hart, old boy, you're a rotten one. I speak up like a sportsman, give the kid a chance and you zero in on me by sound.*

I didn't say a word. Down the hill, Clemson was still sobbing. Over thirty and crying like a baby. Maybe he knew what his Paw had in mind.

Hart said, "Okay, boy, you come down here right now and get yourself fixed up."

The sobbing was so jerky and unrestrained then. The old snake was ready to throw his son to the lions. So I wouldn't talk. Now I'd try for a kill shot and the others could zero in on that.

Clemson was hurting too hard to think. He was crying and thrashing around loud enough to cover any sound and when he broke for it and started down the slope I rolled out of my cover, skirted a pair of fallen trees and went under the brush to the spot he had left.

My shot had smashed his hand and taken a chunk out of the rifle stock besides. It lay there in a mess of blood on top of a dozen shells Clemson never got to use. While there was still enough clatter to cover me, I propped the rifle in the general direction of the old man, lit a butt to use as a fuse, and with a thin strip of shirt I rigged up a Rube Goldberg crazy invention-type deal that would fire the gun when the cigarette burned through the cloth.

When it was set, I got out, held a position far to the south and waited. Clemson made the bottom of the gully and a hard smack stopped the yelling. It grew quiet again.

Too quiet. The old man was thinking. Things weren't working out like he wanted them to. He had the wrong cat by the ears and the back feet scratched pretty deep. Of all six, the old one'd be the only one to see the picture clearly. He'd be the only one to know the shot wasn't an accident, the only one to know that the hunted could steer clear of the bait.

Those damned black buzzards dropped another thousand feet trying to determine if it was over yet or not.

Then suddenly the rifle spat out a roll of thunder and while the slug ricocheted off with a screaming whistle, every gun out there zeroed in on the spot and salvoed a full clip. A moment later it was a full barrage and nobody heard me getting out of there. Nobody at all.

They didn't even hear Old Man Hart yelling himself hoarse that it was a trick and I was laughing because the old fox had figured it right, but his line of communication had broken down.

He sat there in his wheelchair hating me with his whole face and just before I got to him he did something nobody knew or even thought he could do. He moved one hand and jerked an antique Colt revolver up and just as fast I shot it out of his fingers.

I said, "It's good you got no feeling in that hand, old man."

"I got feeling."

"Hurts?"

"It hurts," he said.

I turned and looked up the mountain. "I've seen better hill men in white shirts and ties."

"They'll git you," he told me.

When I shook my head, I was grinning. "Maybe. But I'll tell you something, old man. If I get took, I get most of them first. You too. I'm not worth fighting over."

"It's a long way out of these hills, Mitch. Long way. If I were younger, I'd git you myself."

"No you wouldn't. You'd be dead like the rest of your stupid breed will be if they get too close to me. Because an animal runs, don't figure it to be scared. Sometimes it's smart. Strategic."

"You won't get out, boy. You know it too." The old man's eyes were so blue and watery he looked dead. "Yer lost right now. Even if you got past my kin, you'd die on the hills. There ain't no way out, boy—for you. You'd be better off shot fast and proper. Even a good hill man would have trouble gettin' out if they didn't take the pass and you can't find it. The kin is back there too. You..."

Then he stopped because he knew I figured it. He was stalling. Maybe I didn't even have a second left, but I took the time to do it anyway. *You're no good if you're not mean,* I thought. *You'll never get time to squeeze out or even think unless they figure you to be as mean as they are.* I grabbed the side wheel of the chair, ripped it loose and the old man toppled out cursing.

I started to move then—and none too soon. What I expected came fast. Two of the shots kicked up dirt at my feet and another whistled right by my face. I made the rocks and the shade side of the mountain where I had at least a million-to-one chance of getting out alive and when I picked a decent defensive position I squatted and took a breather.

The wind carried their voices up to me now. Anger and chagrin pitched their tone high and over it all the old man was swearing at them. One of them, most likely Big George, would be trailing me, I knew. I sat, waited, and when I saw the swaying of the grass against the wind, picked up a fist-sized rock and underhanded it in a long arc.

Chance and circumstance play cute tricks. I didn't mean it to happen, but Big George was pulling himself up a shale face when that rock smashed his fingers to pulp and he made more racket than his kid brother when he scrambled back into the gully.

For maybe thirty seconds there was utter, complete silence. An absolute void of sound, but the wonder and awe in their minds was like an odor I could smell all the way up here. I sat back, felt the trickle of water coming out of the mountainside and decided that it wouldn't be too bad a place to die.

Luck only went so far. You were only so good...and others were good too.

Too bad. It was really too bad. I looked up the slope and knew I'd never make it after all.

With Caroline it could have been pretty nice. Beautiful even.

Now I'd never find out.

It was funny, how things worked out.

Some place in back of the ridge, she'd be tearing things up and throwing them around, wishing I was there to throw them at. She'd be hating me as hard as she could hate anything and even with all that primitive fury charging around inside her mind, she'd be lovely and beautiful. That crazy blonde hair would still be swirling soft and the gray-green of her eyes alive and hungry-looking. Because I did what I did to her she would cook a special supper tonight and for the one who fired the kill shot she'd make a special dish.

By then the three vultures upstairs would be exploring their main course—me.

Caroline. Lovely, wild Caroline.

———

SHE WAS LOOKING up with wide eyes and that luscious mouth pulled tight when I came down out of the blue. She didn't see me until I called from twenty feet up and when she saw me twisting under the chute she froze.

"Hey kid...get outa the way! Beat it...get over, will you!" I yelled.

I yanked hard on the suspension lines and spilled enough air to come in at a gentle rake. But she didn't move. She just watched. It was bad enough trying to hit the only clearing within miles from 5,500 feet without having to clobber the only broad around doing it. I could see the ground breeze that shot up the gully and before it caught me, unhooked my chest and leg snaps as if for a water landing, came in with a *swoosh*, hit the dirt and ran with it ten feet or so—right into the dame. For some silly reason the wind stopped and the chute came down around us like a tent collapsing on its centerpole and I said, "Well, hello."

"Man, man," she said, "I never did see anything like that in all my whole life."

"Honey," I grinned, "you better remember this day because you'll never see another one like it again."

Slowly, her face untightened and I had to squint to make sure it was the same girl. She reached out and touched my arm. "Where'd you come from, man?"

"From a lobster pot, honey."

"Lobster?"

"They're like crawfish but with two great big claws so big." The corners of her mouth twitched. Her eyes went over my head and I saw the beauty in them.

"From up there?"

"That's right. Up there."

"I know you're not lying, man. I saw you come. You real for sure?"

"Honey," I said, "I ought to ask *you* that. I've gone over the side before, but it was never like this."

"What?"

"When's the last time you've been kissed, honey?"

The eyes went real big and she showed white high on her cheeks. There was a strange rigidity in her body that outlined the flat of her stomach and swelled the gentle curves into taut, unbelievable contours. I took her arms, gently, pulled her to me easy, then kissed her. I did it softly, feeling that soft tension in her mouth, feeling the kiss go suddenly hot, though she barely touched me.

I should have known then. I should have been on the ball. I should have taken off like Moody's goose right then, only it was the kind of kiss I had never known before. It was all stupid and impossible. Who ever heard of bailing out to come down under the sheet with a strange blonde in never-never land?

She pushed me away and when she did, the fire burned out. Her face was cold and hard, her mouth trembling under an emotion I couldn't catch. "You want to go back, man. You go back where you came from."

Very softly I told her, "There's no going back, sugar."

Just as softly she said, "You in trouble now, man."

I flipped back the folds of the chute, threw it over our

heads and rolled it up into a tight pack. There was a hollow in the side of the hill that took it nicely, then I stowed the .45 and the two boxes of shells in the knee pockets of the coveralls and turned back to the dame.

"Where to now, girl?" She frowned at my expression. "Where do we go from here?" I explained.

"To home. No place else, is there? Not 'thout crossing the hills and we can't do that."

Out of curiosity I asked, "Why not?"

"You'd get killed."

"Oh." I grinned at her again. "What about you?"

"I could go. Not you, though."

My grin was getting hard to hold in place. "I'm important?"

She frowned again, but the meaning got through to her. "You kissed me," she said. "You kissed me a shooting kiss. You going to have to shoot for kissing me, man. I'm spoke up for. You going to have to shoot to keep me or shoot to get rid of me. You in trouble, man."

There wasn't anything I could say. Suddenly she came out with the screwiest-looking revolver I'd seen in a long time and let it dangle in her hand. "What you want to do, man?" she asked me.

I had to laugh. "Oh, hell, honey, I'm with you," I said.

She tucked the gun away in her patchwork shirt. "Then we go tell them, man. We go see Pap and the boys and tell them. You in real trouble, man, but I ain't scared." She looked up at the blue again, her eyes showing the puzzle behind them. "I used to think something like this would happen one day."

Then she looked at me and there wasn't any before or any afterward. There was only now and she was all soft and gone and in my hands she was mine and beautiful. Her mouth was a wet thing full of unexpected life that surprised even her.

It was me that pulled back and I said, "Was that a shooting kiss too?"

She nodded solemnly, strangely. "That was a killin' shootin' kiss."

"What's your name?"

"Caroline. What's yours?"

"Mitch."

She took my hand. "We go now," she said.

———

UP-HOLLOW THEY CALLED IT. There was water and grass with a mountainside of gray chestnuts for firewood, fifty years dead from the blight. There were deer runs and ducks nested in the reeds on the far side of the pond. Fish were for pulling or netting in the stream that coursed through the hollow and you didn't need a license. The road was packed dirt and where a cart or wagon could bog down, the soft spot was filled with head-sized rocks.

It was lush with planted things, bearing fruit heavily though seeded with the abandon of the agriculturally-ignorant. It was a place time had overlooked.

The three stores we passed bore the earmarks of a civilization far off, express stickers on the sides of barrels and cartons in the unloaded wagon, a small, limp mailsack... a window dressed with a rack of shotguns and rifles. The people outside looked our way with only passing curiosity, never thinking a newcomer could be here by design or desire.

The up-trail was serpentine and noisy with the sounds of wild life in the trees. A mile off a pack of hounds blared a welcome at the sound of our cart and came rushing to meet it. All of them grinned a dog grin at her and let their bristles up when they caught my smell on her. But they didn't try for me. I said, "Shut up," softly to the red one in the lead and we knew each other quick. His tail didn't wag or drop. But he looked and knew. I wasn't a patsy.

Then the cabin was there in the clearing with the six men standing on the porch watching. The old man in the wheelchair sat calmly, the cigar in his mouth drifting off lazy smoke. One of the men came down, flicked the ash off the stogie, then put it back in his mouth again.

Caroline said, "My papa. The other ones are my brothers."

The quiet came on again. "What's your last name, sugar?"

"Hart."

"Mine's Valler. In case you have to introduce me. What's wrong with the old man?"

"He got backbone shot by a Grady. That was ten years ago."

"What happened to Grady?"

"They ain't no more Gradys," she said.

The cart pulled up to the cabin, the mule nosing the rail familiarly. I jumped down, reached up for Caroline's arm and even though she pulled away, took it anyhow. She sprang off beside me and if I hadn't held her, would have gone ahead.

But not this time. I made sure of that. I walked up by myself and looked at the old guy in the wheelchair. I said, "My name is Mitch Valler, Mr. Hart." I didn't hold out my hand.

He nodded. "How come you here, man?"

Behind me Caroline said, "He come from the air, Pap. On a white sheet."

That struck the old man funny and he smiled. "You come outa the air?"

"That's right. From a lobster pot."

"From a lobster pot, Papa?" Caroline said. "Is there such?"

The smile stayed on. "There's such, girl." The smile changed. "But not upstairs. Not in the sky." He paused, then said, "You told my gal that?"

Caroline answered for me. "I seen him. It was for real, Papa. He came down from the sky."

"But not from a lobster pot, son," Old Man Hart said.

Now I smiled. "We call it that. *Lobster Pot* was her name, a C-47 by WW2 out of 13th AF. You catch, Papa?"

"I catch, son."

I let my shoulders relax. "Then get off my back."

"You nervous, son."

"No."

"I wasn't asking. I was telling."

"Still no, Papa."

"We don't like outsiders, son."

"Tough."

"We can make it that way."

This time I gave him my biggest smile. All the teeth. I looked up at the porch, at him, then at Caroline. "You ain't got enough men to even try, Pap," I said.

The bomb went off slow and easy. When it hit the old man all the way, the smile faded, but what he was waiting for didn't come soon enough. The first step on the porch steps took too long like somebody was saying *"You* do it first..." and when it did come the lad who took it hadn't really got the meaning of what I'd said.

He came down and edged up to me slowly, trying hard to be sure.

This had to be the tough one, so I said, "You slob. You stinking, miserable, inhospitable slob."

All the eyes in his own world were on him, so he came in swinging.

I knocked him cold with one shot. My guts were all gone and churning and now I couldn't be still anymore. I said, "I kissed the kid a shooting kiss too. I did it twice and I'll do it again and if you want to start shooting, then go ahead."

Down in the dirt the big guy rolled up in a ball and groaned. The old man said, "We don't want to shoot, son. Not yet. We ain't got claim yet. She's spoke for by Billy Bussy and he'll be over soon enough. A few days and he'll be over." He rubbed his chin against his chest to wipe off the cigar spit. "If he didn't, then we would. But we won't have to. Billy Bussy'll shoot you."

"Meanwhile I'll stick around, Papa."

"Meanwhile you gotta, son." He turned his head and looked at Caroline. "Get the boy fixed up, Carrie. Give him a runnin' room where he has a chance to git from."

"I'll stay outside," I said.

"The bugs'll get you," he told me.

"So I'll take the runnin' room, Papa," I grinned.

At supper I was guested at the far end of the table. I had taken off the coveralls and my slacks and black sport shirt looked almost formal for the occasion. Conversation was built on silence, on under-brow glances and grimaces that had their beginning in suspicion and hatreds.

Caroline came in with a tray loaded with foods peculiar to the country, smoking an aroma rare and exotic. She put the tray down, then served food in gluttonous portions to the old man and her brothers.

When it came my turn, their faces fell in a screwy disbelief. I got the tenderloin. What was best went on my plate. I looked at her, threw a kiss and said, "Thanks, sugar."

Old Man Hart made a noise eating. "There's a saying..." he started.

I nodded. "The condemned man, and so on..."

"That's the one I was thinking of," he said.

Two words I gave him. They weren't "Good night."

Down next to the old man at the end, Big George managed to chew in spite of the bump on his jaw and tried to kill me with his eyes.

I said, "Mr. Hart..."

"Yes, son?"

"What's with these lumps you raised? Seems like you've been around."

He answered noncommittally, "Environment, son. Or maybe what a man likes to do. Me, I got a taste for reading and knowin' things. The boys here'll have none of it."

Evidently he caught my glance toward the kitchen. "Some of it rubbed off me onto Carrie, but she's as wild as the rest too."

"But you like to see a good shooting," I said.

"Not so much a shootin' as a good killin'."

"Why me?"

Big George had enough listening. "Ye outsiders need killin'," he said. "Ye gonna git it too. Ye dig holes and scare folks hereabouts with them things and take their land so don't ye complain none about gettin' dead."

He had something else to say, but Caroline came in again and stacked the old man's plate so he could eat by just bending his head...and that ended the talking.

The boys all finished eating and went out to the porch where they lined up and smoked. In three hip pockets the butt-ends of single-action Colts lay at an angle.

The old man wiped his mouth against his shoulders before looking at me.

"It's the girl I care about, son," he told me. "Jest don't do my girl wrong. Y'hear? It's just an 'in case.' Billy Bussy'll kill you anyway, so it's just an 'in case.'" His eyes went real watery, then he turned his head and bellowed, "Carrie!"

She came out, barely glancing my way, then rolled the old man out of the room. I got up, walked outside, across the porch, then went down the steps. All six of them converged behind me. I swiveled fast with the .45 in my fist and said, "If any one of you got the guts of a snake, you'll draw and shoot. Go ahead. There's six of you. One's got to get me, but the rest are going to get their stomachs opened up."

Nobody moved. I let them see the hammer of the rod thumbed all the way back, then shoved it under my belt so it nestled against my navel. "You're a bunch a gutless pigs," I said. "Don't try for my back because I'll get at least one."

To make it real showy, I turned and started walking away. At ten feet I turned, dropped and shot the hat off Big George's head and the hand that was on the gun came back in front trembling a little and the expression on the faces of the rest was worth the dust I had to spit out of my mouth.

The rest of the way I didn't have to worry. I went down the road toward the stores and though they followed, it was out of range. It was a good three miles, but the walking was pleasant and the evening cool and comfortable. For a condemned man the freedom was great and I wondered how far I could go on the road.

When I turned the bend, I was smiling. Then I stopped.

Everybody was there. It wasn't Saturday night, but everybody was there.

A great telegraph system. Something like Chinese, I guessed. Nobody could figure out how, but it worked.

I turned in on the board sidewalks and let all the faces look at me. Sixty, I estimated. That would make the entire population. Sixty and most were interbred. Sixty toothy grins. Some maybe not so toothy.

At the far end of the road a wagon was drawn up and

two men and a boy sat there with rifles crooked across their arms. The road didn't go very far at all.

It could have been rough then if it weren't for Caroline. She came in on the cart, nosed the mule onto the rail and jumped out. She came straight for me and stood there tall and blonde and different from all the rest with her mouth set and said, "What you aim to do?"

"Nothing, honey." I reached for her hand, but instead of taking it, just touched it. She had to live here. Not me.

She said, "They heard how you come to be here. The Cahill boy saw you. They figger for another trick. You in bad trouble, man."

"So will you be if you stick too close to me."

"Townfolk won't bother me none."

I reached out and touched her again. "No, but I will."

Things happened in her eyes again and she sucked her breath in deep. This was a real dame, I thought. One of the few. Her smile was big and moist-looking when it came, her tongue making a nervous flick across her lips.

"I'm gonna hate for Billy Bussy to have to kill you, Mitch."

I grinned and shook my head. "He won't."

She grinned back and nodded. "Yes he will."

Across the street an old man giggled. It was high and nervous and out of proportion to the situation. It wasn't good to be stationary. I took her arm and started down the walk.

The hostility in their faces was ridiculous. Softly, I said, "Honey, why they so riled up?"

She looked at me queerly. "They love their land, Mitch. For a long time they've been here and they don't want it stole."

"I don't get it. Who's stealing it?"

She shook her head and said nothing. We kept on walking.

The post office was one corner of a store that bore a faded "DRY GOODS" sign on the window. Behind the counter on the wall were rows of boxes, each meticulously marked with spit-wet indelible pencil. Only two had letters; a few of the others held scrawled and folded notes, a roll of yarn. In one, in the lower left-hand corner, was a gun.

"Howdy, son."

I looked around and nodded at the old man who came from the back of the room. Then I grinned and pointed to the gun. "Whose mail is that?"

"Reckon you'll find out soon enough, son." He lifted the hinged counter-top and squeezed inside.

"It's not with the B's, Pop. Isn't that where it belongs?"

"Shouldn't make fun of Billy Bussy, son."

"I can't help it. He sounds like somebody out of Treasure Island."

"He'll be in for that gun soon. By now he heard."

"If he keeps his ears open, he'll hear even more."

"Billy's been to war, son. He even killed a few herebouts." He looked at me carefully. "You ever killed anybody, son?"

"Why you asking?"

"Kind of like you maybe."

I nodded, but I wasn't grinning anymore. "I've killed. I didn't like it any. Somebody forced it on me. Sometimes it was the one who forced it who got killed. If I have to, I'll do it again. But I don't figure on ever having to do it again. It makes me sick...you know why?"

"Don't get so wound-up, son. You're yelling."

I took a deep, slow breath. "Because I'm good at killing, Pop."

Something inside me makes me an expert and I hate it. I'm like a damn snake when it comes to killing and I can do it fast and quiet and get out and only a long time later do I feel the hate at myself building up." I leaned over the counter with my hands all balled-up and said, "If I find anybody who makes me want to do those things again, I'll tear him apart."

"No call to get wound-up son."

I stared at him and stood up. "Sure, Pop, sure."

"What was it you wanted?"

"There a phone in this town?"

"No phone. T'aint decent anyway. You want to say something to a body you..."

"How do you get out of here?"

He fingered the counter uneasily and shrugged. "Used to be a road, but..."

"Pop," I said.

"Son?"

"The mail comes in. It goes out. How?"

"Chigger Bolidy takes it out by mule. Been doin' it ten years now. Same mule."

"Pop... they don't give post-office franchises to go every other week. This is the government."

"...Goes over the mountain. Doesn't mean much 'cause there's never mail anyhow. Sometimes gov'ment stuff, sometimes a real letter. Gov'ment don't care much 'cause there ain't no other way. They got to go along. You know the gov'ment."

"Yeah," I said. "I know." I straightened up and tried again. "How does anybody get out at all?"

"To where, son? Who wants to go?"

He was starting to grate on me. "Anybody with sense."

"If you know what's outside, why go back? Hear tell there's nothing but trouble and taxes."

"Plus central heating, taxis, hotels..." I stopped, looked at him and grinned real big. "Pop, can you make a sucker out of me! A regular Groucho Marx, you are. Okay, I'll go along for the ride. I'll be the straight man. Now look...you have a handful of shops down the street out there. I saw some nice new guns, some modern hardware, household staples in pretty city-printed boxes and bags...well, hell, goodies I can pick up in any city. It all has to come in, Pop. Not by mule. By truck maybe. At the worst, by cart. But it comes in. How? We played our little game. Now how do things come in and go out?"

"Why so, son?"

"Because I want to leave."

"Why?"

I wiped my hand across my face. "Because I have an accident report to fill out for the Civil Aeronautics people. I have an insurance policy to collect on. I have some people to let know I am alive before they start collecting survivor's pay. Because the sky will be black with..."

This time I stopped cold and ran it down inside my head a bit. Then I said, "So how do those things come in, Pop?"

"Like you mentioned, son."

"What?"

"By cart. Billy Bussy brings 'em in. He got his own ways. But the only one who could ever do it is Billy Bussy."

"And Billy Bussy's going to shoot me."

He agreed. "So it shouldn't be no use trying to leave."

"The news passed fast, Pop."

Once more he nodded.

"Billy Bussy'll take me?"

"You're almost dead as of now, son. Billy likes to do it slow. He's real mean, he is."

"I can hardly wait."

"That's good, son, because he'll be in this afternoon. He's heard."

"And what will he do?"

The old man looked sad. "He'll get his gun. He'll hurt you first, then you'll get shot up."

"I will?"

"You will."

I looked up at the sign over his head that read, "U.S. Post Office" and under it in smaller letters, hand printed, "Oliver Cooper, Postmaster." I asked. "No law...?"

"County seat's in Pawley. Deputy comes sometimes when there's need, but never before."

For some reason I grinned again. "Isn't there need now?"

"Sure," he nodded, "but there ain't that much time." He tightened his face and there was pity in his eyes. "Besides," he added, "the deputy is scared headless of Billy. You see, Billy killed his last boss."

"Oh." I frowned and said, "Why didn't somebody do something about it. You just don't shoot people."

"He didn't shoot him, Billy didn't. They was wrestling friendly-like, sort of showing off in front of Caroline Hart and Billy broke his neck sort of."

"I told you I was like a snake, Pop. Cold blood all through. Billy won't kill me."

"Oh, it's not just Billy."

I stared at him. "I had a feeling it was more than that."

The old man waved a thumb toward the street. "Almost anybody out there'd be more than glad to do it, son."

"Why? What the hell's wrong with this place?"

He shrugged and came out from behind the counter. "People like you. What you come for?"

I grabbed his arm and squeezed it until he winced. "I bailed out of a C-47 at five thousand feet. I never would have been over this section at all if a weather front hadn't moved in." I let his arm go and watched while he rubbed it. "I could have picked one side of that damned mountain or the other and this time I sure goofed!"

"You knew what you were doing, son."

"What?"

"It was one way of getting in."

"I want to get out."

"You'll have to ask Billy Bussy. It's his road."

I breathed in deeply. "Sure, Pop, sure. See you around."

She was waiting for me outside, standing with her back to the sun without knowing it was playing tricks with her hair. In silhouette she was a lithe thing, and with the breeze pressing her dress tight against her you knew that there was nothing dainty or soft about her. Her thighs would be smooth, taut flesh, firm and supple with youth, hardened by hill-running.

When I touched her arm, she tightened and flicked a glance toward the group down the street. "Scared?"

"No, but after Billy kills you he'll beat me. Bad."

"Then your tough brothers can work him over," I said.

"They scared, man. Besides, they don't want you around. They guess I need to be beat. I kissed you back, man."

"Everybody know that?"

She nodded. "The Cahill boy saw it."

I had to laugh at her. "But we were under the sheet, remember?"

"It figured though," she said.

I stopped and looked at her a long time, drinking in the yellow of her hair that framed her face and the wet fullness of her mouth. There was a deep softness in her eyes, but they were unreadable. I said, "That's right, honey. It figured. There could have been no other answer."

She said, "What're you thinkin'?"

I shook my head. "I don't know. It has you in it, but I don't know." Before she could answer, I grabbed her arm and swung into a walk. We crossed the wheel-gouged street to the shady side and in the dusty face of the store windows I could count the hostile eyes behind us that counted each step we took.

A dirty little kid ran out from between the buildings, one arm pumping while the other held up his pants. He was laughing back over his shoulder at the pair chasing him and never saw us. The others did and kept straight on out into the street. He slammed head on into me, staggered back with his breath whooshing out of him and sat down.

I reached down and yanked him up. "Get hurt?"

His pants were halfway down his legs and he wasn't even trying to get them back up. He just stood there with his eyes big and round.

Caroline said, "That's the Cahill boy."

I let him go and half hissed between my teeth, *"Take me to your leader!"*

Nothing in the world ever jumped and ran so fast with half-hung pants as he did then.

"What'd you say to him, man?"

I squeezed her arm. "Science fiction joke, kitten. Never mind. Look ...Do you know where I can find Chigger Bolidy?"

She squinted at me curiously. "Down by the old barn where he keeps his mule, maybe."

"Come on."

"Mitch, man..." She paused, frowning. "You might make trouble for him. You strictly trouble, man and Chigger...he's had plenty."

I said, "Don't be silly. I won't hurt him. Come on."

Up close you could see that at one time the barn had been red. One half the door was gone and the huge hand-wrought hinges had been wrenched loose by too many chinning contests. The air was tangy with the smell of manure and dried hay, and inside heavy hooves shuffled impatiently on the dirt floor.

We found him propped up against the back of the place asleep, his hat down over his face. He was small and dried out like an old pea, his hands rein-calloused and brown from the sun. I shoved his hat back with my toe and nudged him and when his eyes worked open they were hangover-red and watery.

He knew who I was. He got that tight, scared look and struggled to his feet, his back pressed against the wall.

"Caroline Hart..." his voice had a wheeze to it, "what you... think you doin', girl!"

"Easy, Chigger. Relax."

He swallowed again. "What you want with me? You know what's goin' to happen to you?"

I nodded. "Yeah. Everybody's told me. I'm hep. Now you tell me something."

His face pulled so tight he had to talk between his teeth. "I ain't telling you nothin'! You dirty killin'..." He stopped suddenly. "What you want, mister?"

"You go over that mountain to the other side," I said. "I want to go along with you."

His teeth were chipped and worn close to the gums. They were brown with tobacco stain but he was real glad to let me see every one he had left inside his smile. "You goin' to stay here and get what's comin', mister."

"That could be a long time," I said.

"So."

"The mail franchise. You *have* to go out."

The smile stretched wider. "I don't have to do nothin'."

"The government..."

"You know what they can do," he finished. He shook his head before I could say it. "Nobody here writes hardly. If they do, nobody answers hardly. Post Office won't miss my trip none. Not till after you're dead."

The whole thing started to scratch at me. "Old man, you had to leave a trail someplace."

He came away from the wall, still grinning, but sure of himself now. "I did? Find it, son. Go look for it. I go over the same trail twice it's something. Can't even find it myself half the time." He stopped and looked me up and down. "Don't figger you could find it if I painted it white." He craned his neck toward the mountain. *"She'd* kill you, she would. Ain't scarcely nobody who can get over her. Sure you won't."

"You'd be real happy to see me dead, wouldn't you, Pop?"

"Real happy."

"Why?"

The smile faded. "Murdering, stealing sons, all of you..." He stopped there, then shuffled off into the barn.

"Mitch…"

I stared at the empty entrance of the building. "Wise guy," I said half to myself. "He knew there was another angle but didn't want to hear me ask it."

"Mitch…"

I swung around. "Okay, sugar, maybe you'll know the answer. Since I'm almost already dead it won't make much difference anyway. Chigger goes out by mule. So he's got his own trail. But how come he don't follow Billy Bussy's road out? The guy uses a cart and that's a trail nobody can hide —not even an Indian. How come?"

Her eyes showed the pity she felt. "Nobody has nothing much hereabouts. You have a farming patch, you keep it. You have a store, you keep that. What you got, you pass on. Nothing else to leave to kin 'cept what you got. Try to take it away and you got killin' takin'. Chigger...he's got his mule and his trail. Billy got his cart and his road. Take it away and you got a killin' takin'."

"Damn!"

"Mitch…"

"Aw, shut up." I turned and looked back at the row of buildings that lay dirty in the sun. "Is that all those slobs think of, what they got? Is this their whole damn world?"

Her hand touched my arm. "Ain't much, what they got, but everybody respects everybody else's. Chigger wouldn't go on Billy's trail."

"And if he did?" I turned and watched her. Very gently she bit on her lip.

"He'd never come back down off'n the mountain."

"And if Billy took Chigger's trail?"

Something happened in her eyes. She shrugged, not answering.

From the street back of us somebody shouted her name. We both looked and saw Big George standing there, his hands tight on his hips.

"I got to go. Pap and the boys are in."

"For the killin'?"

She sucked her breath in hard. "Maybe."

"Billy's due in soon?"

This time she looked at the sun first, then turned back to me and nodded. "Two more hours."

I glanced toward the buildings and she caught it.

"Pap and the boys like to get comfortable," she said.

"And you?"

Softly, she touched my hand.

I grinned, reached out and pulled her in close. Her body was warm and alive, pressing against me hard, searching to touch me all over. Her breathing was a quick sob—and then her mouth exploded into mine. For one brief second there was nobody in the world but us—then I pushed her away and looked into her eyes and saw what they said.

She ran then.

I said, "Hell, you can only get killed once."

From the doorway of the barn Chigger Bolidy grinned at me. "Once is enough, mister."

———

FROM THE RISE behind the buildings where the pines stood thick and tall I could see the mountain. From here she looked tall and soft, like the enveloping arms of some great mother.

Enveloping hell! Those same arms could smother you just as fast!

Height and distance were deceptive and you had the feeling that you were in the center of some natural coliseum. I grinned at the simile because in a way it was. This was the floor of an amphitheater and behind me were the cages of killers waiting for the right time to put on the show.

The sun had gone down far enough to put half the bowl

in shadows, but across the way all was gold and fiery-looking.

Pretty, I thought. Real nice. It was a beautiful spot to die in.

I felt the motion behind me before I heard it. I turned around easily, as though still watching the rim of the mountain, then paused a few seconds. It came again and this time I jumped so fast the thing in the bushes didn't have time to scream before I had a hand across its mouth.

I took it back to the clearing and laughed at the great big eyeballs that quivered almost as much as its skin.

I said, "What's your first name?"

It took a long time coming out. "Trumble."

"Trumble Cahill," I said, and dropped the kid who had seen me come down out of the blue.

"You... gonna kill me?"

I didn't say anything.

He looked up at the sky. "You ain't agonna..." then the full horror of it struck him, "... take me...up there!"

I could have had some fun, but I took the curse off it by laughing and there's one thing a kid knows for real and that's a laugh. When you mean it, he knows it and this one knew it.

He let go his hands, his shoulders dropped and those big eyes went back to normal. A quick smile jerked at the corner of this mouth.

"I seen you when you come."

"I know."

"How'd you do that?" He squirmed and drew back, another thought coming to his mouth. "You a man, ain'cha?"

"That's right."

He relaxed, then asked, "So how'd you do that?"

It took a while, but I got it across. I painted a big picture of the blue and the men who used it. He remembered the few times he had seen the growling birds glide past his part of the earth, and from the few magazines he had seen he recalled the puzzling machines that were so foreign to his mind.

But boys are boys and their imaginations can conjure up anything. It could have been no better had I come from the moon. There were lights in his eyes when I finished and I knew here I had a friend. He was a little one, but a friend.

When I finished, he was quiet a long while, then sadness touched him as it had Caroline and he said, "If it's like you said, it's real nice. It must be awful never to see them things no more."

"I'll see them again."

He stayed silent. Watching, saying nothing.

When he was ready again I asked, "What's the matter with Chigger?"

The Cahill kid wet his lips and plucked at the grass. "Men burned him out. Did him almost like the others."

"What men?"

"Like you."

"Trumble...all men are alike."

"You ain't. You like the others."

"How come?"

He picked at the grass again. "They had no-hole clothes. Big shoes. They had lots of *things*, too."

The way he said "things" was puzzling. "What things?"

"You know. Just *things*. They point one at you and you get killed."

I didn't get it. "Guns?"

"Not guns. *Things*. They made *that* noise and you got killed."

I leaned back against the tree. "You sure nobody around here has television?"

"What?"

"Just a thought. Skip it." I tried again. "About these men. How'd they get in here?"

His face went into a lopsided grin and he looked up at the mountainside. "See up there where the chunk is out?"

I followed his finger and nodded at the cleft in the almost smooth ridge.

"'Twas old Heller Beansy's Crotch, that's what. Tumble-ground set her up, Pap told me, way back 'fore Granny's time. Then tumble-ground closed her up after them men come through."

"What's this tumble-ground bit?"

"You kiddin'? Ground, she jump up and tumbles all round."

Earthquake.

"Boy. . .you should hear! Like a million guns all together. Shook old Heller Beansy right down the hill, it did. Can't nobody get through the crotch now."

"And all the men who came through first with the *things?*"

"Got killed in the tumble-ground where they chased Old Beansy. They ain't no more left of them, that's for sure."

I looked up at the niche in the rim of the bowl and tried to measure the distance. Twelve miles maybe. Could be fifteen. The dark side of the mountain was closer, at least no more than five miles.

I went out at 5,500 heading south. The *Lobster Pot* was trimmed back for a glide that should have dropped her in no more than a few miles from where I hit. But damn it, you can never figure out a C-47! They always gave it the old college try. She could be anyplace from here to Jax but if the law of aerodynamics and chance worked for a change, that wreck had to be inside the bowl!

I said, "Trumble...you remember when you saw me?"

His head bobbed hard.

"About that time did you hear any big noises down there?" I waved my hand to the southern ridge of mountains. "Or see any fires?"

He followed the sweep of my hand, studied it, then shook his head. "Not we."

"So not you. Who saw something?"

And the kid said, grinning, "Macbruder. He was up by the crotch when he sees this big thing and hears a awful noise and comes runnin' down. Figures it's a tumble-ground and gets out, but because he saw that thing he's scared to tell. Only me he told."

Maybe I was lucky, I thought. Maybe it was still there, intact. The ship didn't burn and if it hit on top of the trees, there might still be a chance I could get to the radio. If the main set was out I still had the Hallicrafters. The old S-38A receiver was there and the newer RD-56F transmitter and I could bring in the army with that if I had to.

Right then I remembered the cargo had some kid's hobby gear in it—and I felt good.

I said, "Look, Trumble... You think you could get this kid."

"Macbruder?"

"Yeah. Can you get him to show you where he saw this business?"

"Sure, I can get him. Why?"

"Never mind why."

His eyes got wise then. "Won't do you no good," he said.

"No?"

He looked up at the waning sun. "Billy Bussy'll be in town 'bout now. He'll be looking for you."

"Find out anyway, okay?"

"Sure. Won't do you no good though." His tongue wet his mouth down again, leaving a cleaned oval in his face. "Carrie...she liked you pretty good, huh?"

"Could be."

He bobbed his head. "Kind of liked you myself," he said.

"And this Bussy character?"

"Mean. Real mean. Too bad he's goin' to kill you."

"Really think he will?"

"He *got* to. Everybody's waitin' for him to. He will, too. He don't, then he ain't no head man nohow never again."

I got up and dusted off my pants. He jumped up with me, all excited. "You going down and let Billy kill you now?"

I laughed and gave him a fake chop in the jowls. "Not yet, sunshine. We'll have to let Billy wait awhile."

"But Billy'll..."

"He won't do anything. Now you get back there and tell him I'm going to take him apart in little pieces. You got that?"

He stared at me like I was brand new to this world. Then those lights came back in his eyes and he said softly, believingly, "Sure, I'll tell him all right. I'll sure tell him."

I hoped I was up to what the kid thought.

When we got to Chigger Bolidy's he was leaving the yard on his mule. I took him by the arm and he put the animal back in the stall and locked the gate.

I said, "You didn't always run mail, Chigger."

When he didn't answer, I squeezed a little and he said, "I hill-farmed."

"How long ago?"

"Before they came in."

"What'd you grow?"

"I had apples." He was scared almost voiceless now. "Didn't want no silver. They didn't have to burn me out!"

"Who, Chigger?"

"From the other side. Like 'em all. I know 'em on the other side, always killin' and stealing! I got the mail. I see..."

"Why'd they burn you, Chigger?"

"Burned me out, they did. Blew up my whole place. Damn them! I didn't want no silver! Damn..."

"How many?"

"Ten! They come in, ten all. Damn 'em! Ten all and they go one by one to the hill farms and I'm the only one alive 'ceptin' the Harts and iff'n they weren't so many they'd be dead too! Tooken land and killed. *Them and their things!*" He spit the last words out.

I had two hands on him, dragging him so high his feet barely touched the floor. "Who else died, Chigger? Say their names."

He breathed in short gasps. "Brother Melse. Cooper. All the Belcheys."

"And their places?"

"Land all blowed up. Nothing but rocks. Can't grow nothing now. All rocks. Did it with their things. Want every-body's land, they did. Took it. Took all the sayings."

Under my hands he was coming apart. I put him down and he sunk to his haunches, squatting there and drooling on the floor. I walked out into the dusk and looked down the street.

This could be my dying night, I thought. I grinned, felt the safe bulge of the .45 under my belt and walked toward the lights. It wasn't far, but it gave me a chance to remember how people were. You could fight without wanting to fight, but it was hard to kill without wanting to kill. It took time to work up to that point. Oh, it was easy to do, all right, but it took time to do it. Some place Billy Bussy was working up to it and when he was ready, he'd try it.

But first he had to be ready. Some place he'd be going through his mental war dance and putting on his hypothetical paint. But it would keep.

I winked at the stars that were showing and they winked back. Then I walked down past the stores and maybe even past the place where the medicine dance was going on. I grunted a laugh and kept on.

When I got to where the wagon was that had "HART" burned on its transom with a hot iron, I turned, opened the door and stepped inside.

I was wrong about passing the place where the medicine dance was going on. I hadn't passed it. It was here. They were all there, the Hart clan with the boys standing around the wheelchair and Caroline beside them. But they weren't talking. They were listening to the biggest guy I ever saw with the nastiest face that ever happened to anybody.

They all looked at me and the big one grinned. Then George moved and I had the .45 out and the grin on the big one's face stopped and I said, "So you're Billy Bussy."

He looked at me the hard way and if I had anything other than that .45 he would have jumped and even then he was counting off the odds of a misfire, a jam or an off-target shot.

Old Man Hart rolled the chair forward a foot. "You thinking to shoot somebody, son?"

I didn't look at him. I didn't watch any of them but the big one in the middle. I said, "I could shoot six, Pappy."

"We're many, son. One would get you sure."

"That's right, Pappy. But don't forget that you'd go first. Right through the old beano you'd catch one. I'd get at least four confirmed and two probables before I went down. This big slob here would get it right in the beginning too." I stopped, then added, "Now what?"

"That's up to you, son."

"Yeah," I said, "I guess it is," I watched Billy's face when I said, "Come here, Caroline."

I saw her move, saw her body go tight and saw the furtive glance she threw at her father.

The old boy said, "She won't do you no good as a hostage, son. You can't get away."

The routine was getting stale. I was getting damn sick and tired of the treatment. I let them see my mouth twist into a screwy grin and I said, "You've overlooked something, Pap."

He waited before he answered. "I did? I don't think so."

I let him wait just so long and I said, "Maybe I didn't come here accidentally, Pap. Maybe I wanted in. Maybe I wanted to take care of something real bad."

Some place in the room somebody sucked their breath in hard. So they wouldn't take chances I turned the .45 a little bit sidewise so they could all see the hammer lying back, ready to start the first one on the long road to nowhere.

I said, "Come here, Caroline," and she came over, never looking back. I reached behind me and opened the door, then touched her so she went out through it.

Bill Bussy just stood there. His face was hard, immobile. Above the week-old stubble of a beard his eyes were tiny slitted things, but they weren't quite expressionless. They were lying in wait, satisfied to take whatever time was necessary. There was a laugh in them too because no matter where he went he was always the biggest the strongest and the best. And now he was laughing at me, looking down across the room from his six-and-a-half feet—but not looking down too much because the .45 made me as big as he was.

Then he spoke. He sounded a little unreal because his voice wasn't as big as he was. He said, "I'm going to kill you, man."

I nodded. "Later I'll let you try. First I got business."

I started to back out the door but I couldn't make it without getting a hook in. I said, "Billy. . .you're bigger and stronger, but I'm something you're not."

His reedy voice was startling in the quiet. "What's that?"

I grinned real nasty-like. "You're going to have to find that out for yourself."

When I left, I closed the door, turned around and walked to where she waited. It was dark now, but I knew she was smiling.

"They'll come after you," she said.

"Uh-uh. Not with the light at their backs and me with a .45. There's no back door to that store anyway. No, sugar, they'll wait some. But meantime we walk away nice and slow so everybody can see us and the word can go around that the fly boy's no patsy."

"Where are we going?"

"Post Office."

"Closed."

"The light's on."

"I know, but Mr. Cooper, he's gone. He never stays after dark."

"You have many Coopers here?"

"Only Mr. Cooper. The others are all dead now."

She didn't have to speak an answer. She dropped my hand and stood there in the dark, rigid. I said, "Caroline...would you believe me if I told you I had nothing to do at all with the things that happened?"

"Back there you told Pap..."

"I was feeling for things. I never knew this whole damn valley existed until I blew an engine over it. You understand that?"

Again, she didn't have to answer. Her hand slipped back into mine, and she was close again. "Mitch," she whispered, "don't fool me. Please don't fool me."

I found her mouth in the dark. "I'll never fool you, kitten."

———

THE CABIN WAS in a lonely place. It was too big for one man and showed it with many doors that led to long unused rooms and furniture used to many people.

He sat there rocking gently before a small hearth fire, the table beside him set with supper scarcely eaten.

Caroline said, "Mr. Cooper..."

"Come in, Carrie."

"I have a friend."

"Bring him in, Carrie. I've been expecting him."

He turned when I came in, smiled tiredly and nodded. "I thought you might be dead by now."

"Dying takes time, Pop. Billy get his mail?"

"He got it. First thing. He see you?"

"He saw me."

"Then how come you still alive, son?"

"I saw him first. Easy. Just like that. Didn't you kind of expect it to be that way?"

"Let's say I ain't exactly surprised none."

We all stared at the fire, watching it flicker and spark. When he was ready he said, "You didn't come to say hello."

"No, I came for information." When he didn't answer, I went on, "What's a *saying?*"

He swung around slowly, his face strained. "I was thinking you'd be asking something like that sooner or later."

"So?"

"Why'd you ask?"

"Because the government might be pretty stupid and usually is, but they have a line they won't cross. They won't hire a postmaster who can't read."

He looked up at me, saying nothing.

I said, "Caroline...who can read around here?"

She stepped forward. "He can."

"Who else?"

"Pap and Billy Bussy and Big George and, 'fore his eyes went, Mr. Dukes could." She stopped, then said, "I can read."

"That's all?"

"Nobody else."

I walked around in front of him and leaned against the fieldstone pillars of the fireplace. "What's *a saying*, Mr. Cooper?"

The fire coughed sparks almost to his feet but he never moved. When he was ready, he said, "Can't you guess?"

I nodded. "Sure. I think I even heard the expression once from a crew chief I had back when I was flying P-51s."

He glanced up, his hand rubbing his chin. "I guess there's no harm in my tellin' you. Seems like you sorta know already." He nodded thoughtfully.

"All the way, Pop."

"A *saying's* a...when you have land like...well..."

"You mean a deed?"

"Sort of. You write a person a chunk of property, you give it on paper and it's his."

"And you're the recorder," I said. "You hold the paper because you can read."

He reached to the table for his pipe, loaded and lit it, and in the smoke of the drawing said, "That's right, son."

I tried hard to play it as slowly as he had. "And how often do you record these...*sayings?*"

He sucked on the pipe, letting the smoke curl over his head. "Well...people 'round here been trusting me a long while now. A long while."

"When did you record the last...deed...with the county, Mr. Cooper? How long ago?"

"Couple years ago. My own property, matter of fact."

"One more question. How long you been postmaster?"

"Eight years, son. Long time. Why did you ask?"

"Because I'm burned up at everybody wanting me dead. Besides that, there's no TV in this little hamlet and I'm no jerk who believes in men from Mars. I'm thinking. I got here by accident, but it looks like I got to think my way out. Well, by damn, this laddie doesn't figure to get his neck twisted by this Bussy boy and I don't like getting shot up by the Harts. I'm sick of all these crazy hillbillies glaring at me like I was Typhoid Terry!"

I had to stop and take a breath. My mouth was tight and when I looked over at Caroline, she was holding the back of the chair, watching me with guarded eyes. I turned back to the old boy.

"What did you do before you were postmaster?"

"I thought you asked your last question?"

"I'm thinking again."

"I was a farmer."

"Of what?"

"Corn. Pumpkins."

"How'd you get it to market?"

"I didn't. We traded here in the valley."

This time I grinned at him. "Who made you postmaster?"

"Government man came through the Crotch in war time to get the boys. Only one he got was Billy Bussy. He done it then. Made my brother Donan postmaster. When Donan got—when he died I wrote a letter. They made me postmaster."

"And official recorder."

He leaned forward and stirred up the fire again. "And everything. Like Donan. Government needed somebody."

"Tell me," I said, "the Crotch was open from before the war until—until there was a tumble-ground."

His face showed that he had caught the meaning of that. "Go on, son."

"How long ago did it happen?"

He kicked at the fire. "Few years back."

Before I could answer, Caroline drifted into the light of the fire and said, "It was nine years ago, Mr. Cooper. It was before you were postmaster."

Then I said, "Now I'm going to ask you the big one. Answer me straight and I'll damn well know it if you lie. Look at me, Cooper!" His head came up until he was meeting my eyes. "Who killed Melch and the Belcheys and your family? Who, Cooper? What happened to them!"

"Damn you and your kind!" He was up in my hands trying to claw at me and I had to shove him down in the chair. "You know what happened. You killed them!"

"Why, Cooper, why?"

He sat there, his face contorted with rage.

I said quietly. "You don't really know, do you. You've been thinking on it a long time, but you don't really know." I let a few seconds go by. "Think on it some more, Mr. Cooper. I'll be back. Meantime, you think on it."

From outside came a long thin wail. Another one joined it, deeper in tone. The others joined it then, yapping and howling and coming closer all the while.

Caroline said, "He got the dogs back, man. They only minutes away."

I joined her at the door, looked back and said, "Remember, think on it," then slammed the door shut and pushed Caroline ahead of me into the darkness.

The dogs were all downhill, quartering the field to pick up our scent.

The scallion patches had them foxed and the two

streams would stop them for a little while, but sooner or later they would find the perimeter of the false trails and close in on the true ones.

I took her hand and started running. Ahead the moon was blossoming over the mountain and the baleful light of it scoured a course through the fields. We followed the glow, running easily, and every once in a while I could hear her laugh. When we reached the trees, we stopped.

Below us the lights went on in the old man's cabin.

Caroline said, "They'll be coming up here."

"You want them to?"

"No. But they will. What can stop them?"

"Watch hard, honey. It won't be often that you get an answer to something like this, not when we're mixing getting killed and fun at the same time."

I pushed her away and took the matches from my pocket. You could see the flame from miles away, but before you could do anything about it, it was too late. The wind was at my back, blowing cross-field, and with half a dozen matches I had the entire damn field screaming in flames toward the cabin and down there the last sounds you could hear were the hate yells coming in over the hounds and one of the lasting ones was the reedy voice of Billy Bussy.

At our feet the flames toyed with the pine needles, barely enough to make her hair a shining gold. She was too pretty not to describe. She was something you wanted to tell everybody about. She stood there, tall and straight, always with that laugh trying hard not to show on her mouth. She was big in the shoulders and she breasted the downslope wind from the mountain with her legs spread wide under her dress, the taut lines of her thighs softening into the sweep of her hips. The wind in her hair was a caress that stirred it around her face; golden yellow, a rich, natural golden yellow. For a moment you could see the wet fullness of her mouth, eyes that had a touch of Hawaiian mischief, eyes that could love or kill, eyes not quite tamed yet.

I said, "They'll be expecting us to run. They'll search the flanks."

"And us, Mitch."

"Not *us*, sugar. Me. They're expecting me to run."

I swooped her up in my arms, kissed her face and her eyes, then lowered her gently to the soft pine needles.

Down where the fire raced you could see the tiny figures trying desperately to hold it back. If you listened hard, you could hear the dogs and almost sense their disappointment.

There was none of the burning in front of us any longer. The wind had whipped it all downhill and the only light came from the full risen moon. I stood watching the frantic commotion in front of the cabin, wondering what crazy streak of fate ever dropped me into the middle of such a situation.

The whole world is my oyster, I thought. I knew it intimately, every country, every city, every swamp.

Now I'm crowded again. The last time was in Stalag 4, but that was in '44. It happened again in Korea. Now I'm home and they're still crowding me. They're pushing hard to kill me. There's a home base, but it's sure getting hard to get to. It was like Ring-a-levio if you know what that means.

I let the mad eke out slowly, took a deep breath and watched the little people below me. I hardly heard the sounds behind me because they were so foreign to what I was watching.

When I turned around, Caroline was lying there, the only white thing in the moonlight, and white. There had never been anything more beautiful before. In the lights and shadows of that pale glow she was a Valkyrie, blonde, and ever so blonde. Big. The soft rises of her ever so big and so noticeable.

I stood over her, feeling the things crawl along my skin that you feel when you see a sight like that, a tightness that makes your voice sound strange and makes it hard to swallow.

"You're lovely, girl," I said.

She seemed to caress my name. "Mitch..."

My legs crossed under me and I sat down beside her. "Not yet, kitten." I let my hand pass over her, my fingertips barely touching. "It would be wonderful, but, for you, wonderful isn't enough."

"I never had a man, Mitch."

"I know."

"I want you, man."

"No. Not when we'd have to be watching the skyline for...them. Or be listening for dogs." I paused and found her hand.

She lay there quietly, her eyes studying my face. "That isn't the reason."

My hand tightened around hers and a small laugh got away from me. "I want it to be right, Sugar. I think from that first minute under the chute I knew that I wanted you. Not for one night and not because time could be running out fast for me."

"Tell it to me then."

"Billy's really going to have to fight for you, kitten," I said. "If he blows his chance, I'm taking you out of this place."

I kissed her, feeling the hunger that made her quiver and pushed her away gently while there was still time.

Above, the sky was ablaze with stars. I watched them awhile, then closed my eyes.

————

A STRANGE SORT of music brought me out of the blackness of sleep. There was a gentle warmth, a tangy freshness in the air, and, from what seemed far off, the chuckle of voices.

I squinted against the long reaches of sunlight that washed across my face and sat up. It was the time of morning when the whole mountain was alive with sound and color, smelling fresh with dew after a nighttime of rest.

When I heard the voices again, I swung around and saw Caroline, her hair wet and skin-tight against shoulders showing pink from an icy creek bath. The other one was Trumble Cahill and he had two loops of smoked sausage hung around his neck and a bag of biscuits in his hand.

He waved and said in a light tone, "You sure sleep late, mister."

I looked at my watch. It was 5:10.

Caroline slipped a sausage loose and tossed it to me, a grin making her face impish. "You fell asleep fast last night."

"I had a big day."

"I tried to wake you up."

After I bit into the sausage, I faked a swipe at her chin. I picked up a biscuit, bit into each and grunted with satisfaction. For some it might have been one hell of a breakfast, but right then nothing ever tasted better to me.

When I had the second biscuit I said, "How'd you find us?"

He grinned all the way across his face. "Saw the fire last night. Everybody had to fight it 'fore it reached the buildings and didn't think you'd be hanging around.

"Didn't guess you could go far at night. Guess you'd be hungry this morning, though. Swiped the sausage. Ma made the biscuits. Thunk she I was takin' off for fishin'. Gimme 'em."

Minutes later, Trumble said, "Saw Macbruder last night."

"And—"

"Told me where it is, he did. He's scared to go up there, but not me."

My breath went out in a long sigh. "It didn't burn?"

"No fire. He said it's all busted up, but there weren't no fire."

"How long will it take to get there?"

His face screwed up and he bit his lip. He glanced up at the sun. "Go straight there in three hours maybe. Only we can't go straight. They'll be coming up searching, so we got to take the rocks around."

"So how long!"

"Come sundown we be there."

———

We had been taking a roundabout route up the mountain side for three hours, my watch told me. We stayed in the trees, keeping them between us and the plateaus below. When we could, we took to stone ridges where we left no tracks. Twice we followed streams to their sources in the face of the slope before we cut back to the grass.

When the wind was right, you could hear the shrill yips of the dogs, and every so often the crack of a gunshot would roll across the hills. We weren't in any danger yet. The hunt had just begun, and as long as we could keep from being seen, it would take its natural course.

Neither Caroline nor the Cahill kid seemed too concerned yet, figuring the shooting to be somebody knocking down a squirrel. I had told them nothing of my purposes, nor did they ask them. It couldn't have been blind faith, I thought. More likely they were too sure of the outcome. Nobody was willing to give me any reasonable chance at all.

We broke out into a clearing around noon. It was too squared off to be a natural formation and when I looked around I saw the charred remains of a building. In a half dozen places on the ten-acre spread the ground had been torn up through the scant topsoil exposing the jagged teeth of a shale formation.

Caroline said, "Brother Melse had the place."

I nodded toward the wreckage. "He die there?"

"No. Not there. They just found him dead one day."

Trumble had crowded over close to me, not liking it here at all. "Them things done it, that's what. Them men with their things."

I turned him around. "*What* things?"

He licked his mouth nervously. "They point 'em at you and they go *zip-zip-zip-zip* and you got dead. That's what they are!"

"Do you know what he means, Caroline?"

"No, but they sure had them. Everybody says."

"And Brother Melse. It left a hole in him too?"

Trumble shook his head and pointed to a ridge a quarter of a mile away. "No holes, man. He got his head broke instead. Like to tooken him right off that rim rock it did."

"He couldn't have fallen?"

"Nope. Landed too far out. He got *thinged* off it."

"The rest of the Coopers. The Belcheys. How did they die?"

"The Coopers were flung off their wagon in Silverman's ravine. Flung mule and all off the road," Caroline said.

"Where?"

Before she could answer, Trumble said, "We going to

pass that place. You'll see. Somebody tooken the wheels off, but the rest of the wagon's still down there."

I said, "Okay, let's go," and followed him off. We went by two of the torn patches and when I paused to scratch up the dirt with my toe, the kid came back and watched me. I said, "How'd they do this?"

"Powder blowed it somehow. Done it out of pure meanness 'cause they wouldn't sell. Burned the shack. Killed everybody."

I grunted and waved them off. It would take some pretty fancy handling of explosives just to blow the topsoil off the ground. Not impossible, but pretty fancy. At the other end of the field I stopped again and looked back. We were a lot higher now and the patch stood out clearly. Something about the layout bothered me and I stood there until I saw what it was.

The gouges blown into the ground weren't the result of any haphazard operation. They followed a rise that crossed the clearing and from any angle I could see where second-growth brush all but closed what could have once been a wide pathway.

By the time we reached the road, I was soaked wet with sweat and all three of us took a breather. The kid found a spring that gushed finger-thick from the sheer rock and it put us back on our feet again.

It was easier then, following the road. The surface was powdered rock and dirt worn smooth from years of use. The steel bands of wagon wheels had etched furrows in the softer sections and scarred the saplings on either side.

The road swung then, curving around an outcropping, then suddenly angled upward sharply. For a thousand feet we stayed at that twenty-degree climb, then we burst out into the open with sheer rock face on one side and a drop-off on the other. The wagon tracks blended into a single pair that patiently followed the dangerously narrow road until it disappeared again into the brush.

Nobody had to point out the accident site. You could see the wagon bed, bottom up, impaled on the rocks at the bottom of the precipice.

"Caroline, nobody would cross this point if somebody were coming the other way, would they?"

"No. I know what you mean. Nobody could run them off because there's not that much room."

"Did you see the tracks?"

She pointed to the kid and he bobbed his head. "I seen 'em. They just stopped like and went over the edge. Telling you...they got *thinged off* too."

"Suppose a man was waiting there?"

"Old mule they had wouldn't move for no man," Caroline said. "Fact is, nobody'd get in front of Blue but Bud Cooper without getting teethed." She shook her hair around her shoulders. "No, weren't a soul on that road."

"That could be too," I told her.

At the mid-point you could still see where the wagon had torn the leading edge off the lip. You could still follow the groove with your eyes until it ended at the wreckage. I turned and studied the wall at our backs. It went up a hundred feet or so then leveled off out of sight.

It didn't take long to find it. The vertical fault in the rock wall was a foot wide and not much more than four feet in. It was almost directly in line with the spot where the wagon went over and I didn't wonder about it anymore. I reached in, rubbed my hand over the stone interior, working through surface dirt and grit to the stone itself. When I pulled my arm out, I showed it to Caroline. There was more on it than grit and natural dirt. My skin was carbon-black.

Her brow pulled together, puzzled. "What is it?"

"Booby trap."

She didn't get it.

I said, "Somebody laid a charge of powder in there and exploded it from up above. That mule who wouldn't move for any man did a quick leap when the blast hit him. A loud bang in the ear and over he leaped, cart, baggage and all."

Her face went cold then. "They were killed deliberate-like."

"Let's call it murder, kitten." I brushed at the grime on my arm.

"Where does this road go to?"

"Forks up ahead. Takes off one way to some of the hill farms. Other fork goes to Billy Bussy's."

———

THERE DIDN'T SEEM to be anything special about Billy Bussy's place. There were two buildings, one a house and the other obviously a barn. But at least they were painted. There was nothing ramshackle about either and, by comparison, every other place I had seen was a shack.

I left the two of them by the road and hustled across the yard to the house.

It looked better up close. There was a generator in the back with a portable windmill all together in what was supposed to be a woodbin. The house was locked tight and the shades drawn, but from the discard piles carelessly laid up, I could see Billy had more modern conveniences than anyone else in the valley.

The barn was locked too, an oversized hasp and padlock quiet signs that the place was more than a stable. Caroline came over, the kid trailing behind.

I tapped Trumble's shoulder, "You ever follow Billy's road out?"

His negative was a quick jerk.

"Why not?"

"Billy Bussy...he got..." He stopped and squinted at Caroline and she nodded understandingly.

"Billy fixed it so you'd get blowed up good if you try to cross his land. Folks hereabouts don't like trespassers."

"Even your neighbors!"

"Nobody. That's why Billy fixed it. He's pretty clever at booby-trapping."

"Trumble." I waved my thumb at the barn. "You know what's inside?"

"Not me. Seen his cart and the mule once, but that's all."

"Big wagon?"

"Small wagon."

"Big loads?"

"Never loaded high. Just what folks want down below."

"How many carts has he got?"

"Just one."

I pointed to the tracks leading away from the building to the hidden pass in the mountains. "He changes his wheels to go to town, sugar. Those tracks going thataway were made by automobile tires. Clever boy, this Billy."

"Why?"

"I don't know, honey. Not yet."

There was little else left to look at. I went back to the front of the house, stepped up on the porch and tried to peer in the window. I couldn't see past the shade so stepped back and was coming down the single step when I saw the topographical map stuck in a handy place under the eaves.

I pulled it out, unfolded it all the way and saw the entire valley and mountain ridge laid out in detail. There were areas circled, some blocked out, while marginal notes ran down both sides of the sheet. On the reverse side a rubber stamp had imprinted NEWHOPE EXPLORATION CO.

My watch said 1:10. I folded the map, stuck it in my pocket and said, "We better roll if we're going to make it."

Trumble said, "We ain't going, mister."

I looked up fast, and saw Billy Bussy coming across the yard.

The shotgun in his hands was almost toylike. He walked light, and you knew he was a fast one and you could almost read what went on in his head.

He was still a hundred feet off when I stepped off the porch with the .45 in my fist and I said, "One step more friend, just one, that's all, and you're dead."

He started to take it, so I shot one ear right off his head.

It shouldn't have hurt that fast, but he choked out a yell, grabbed at what was left and the shotgun fell at his feet.

Trumble whispered, "Glory be!"

You really had to be close up to see what he was like. Black and scowling, with blood smeared across one side of his face dripping through his beard. His whole face was pulled into a grimace that made tiny slits where his eyes were. His muscles were bunched into knotty mounds and I knew damn well that if I didn't get the bull on him fast I'd never get it at all.

I gave him the smile with all the teeth showing and let

him look down the hole in the .45, then I said, "You don't get tough by getting big, you pig. I told you the first time that you had an item to remember. I'm something you're not."

His answer was the same as before. The crazy rage left his face and was replaced by a crafty smirk. "What?"

I tossed the .45 away. "I'm meaner," I said.

For one second he just stood there, then his hand came away from the remains of his ear and a kill-crazy lust hit his eyes like somebody pushed a button. With a silly, high-pitched bellow he did the wrong thing and ducked for the shotgun without going for me and while he was bent over I kicked every tooth out of his face and rocked him back on his neck.

He tried to scream when I put both feet in his mouth and what came out made all red bubbles. It didn't stop him. He rolled away, dazed, but with his arms sweeping out. He grabbed me then, tight around the hips, but it was what I wanted. My two hands dug into him and I squeezed harder than I had ever squeezed anything. I squeezed and twisted at the same time and the high shriek that tore out of the thing he had for a mouth reached a crescendo, stopped abruptly and Billy Bussy was totally unconscious from the kind of pain he had never even imagined before.

I stood up, booted him again for fun and said, "After that he's going to be a real soprano."

Trumble's breathing was almost a wheeze and when I looked at Caroline her hands were tight against her face. I pulled them down and she trembled hard against me. "Is he dead?"

"Nah. He'll maybe wish he was, though."

"You didn't have to do...that to him."

"No? I got news for you, sugar. I had to. I don't like the idea of getting killed...and since I'm not fond of murder either I learned that it's not a bad idea to put in people's minds what will happen if they play it hard. The next time that bastard even touches me I'll kill him sure. They get oversize big like that, then all of a sudden they get tough. Well, damn it, this one can look in the mirror or hum a tune, then he'll remember what tough is really like."

Before she could answer the kid turned away abruptly,

listening. He ran to the road, sighted down it, then came tearing back. "Your Pap and the boys, Carrie! They comin'!"

I said, "How far?"

"Ten minutes they be here!"

"Mitch..." Her face was white and drawn. "You go."

"Not without you. Damn it, after they see..."

"No. It was only him..." she looked at Billy stretched out on the grass, "... who would beat on me. He won't now."

"Listen..."

"I'll stay, Mitch. The boys'll follow faster'n you can git, 'less I steer them off. Clemson, he'll smell you out. You go, Mitch."

I said, "You can tell 'em from me that if you get touched that what happened to Billy boy will be nothing."

We left then, me and the kid, running like crazy across the grass and dirt to the trees, then reaching the road, going up it to the notch where Trumble stopped for the first breather.

———

BEHIND US THERE was no sound of the chase as yet. Billy was going to need taking care of for a while and after one look at him none of them were going to be too anxious to start up a blind alley. With Caroline playing it hill-smart, she could set the whole pack off on a phony trail without any trouble.

I winked at Trumble and he blinked back at me. "How much longer, son?"

He glanced at the sun and shrugged. "We'll hit the Crotch. Dunno if'n we'll get there all the way tonight."

"Okay, let's not fight it then. The morning's time enough."

The sun was behind the mountain again when we reached the Crotch. Or what was left of it. The slanting rays of deep red turned it into a jigsaw puzzle of light and shadow, but distinguishable enough for somebody who had seen it before to know what had happened.

I said, "This is the tumble-ground place?"

His nod was vigorous. "Kilt old Heller, wiped out his place. Kilt them others and their things too."

"You remember it?"

"No. Only hear tell. I was a mite then. Tooken plenty of looks around here, though. Tooken plenty."

"Never saw anything?"

He shivered and said no. "Saw bones," he added. "Saw bones only once. Me and Macbruder run like hell then. When we come back, they was gone. All et. Something scratched them up and et' 'em."

"Like what?"

"Pigs." He shivered again at the thought. "Plenty pigs around here. They eat anything. Crunch the bones even."

I started off through the split rocks and the ground that had been heaved up. I followed the pattern of light that was still left, poking into some of the depressions that showed shock wave formations. When I finished, I walked back to the kid and we skirted the entire Crotch to the tree line and found a small hollow that looked like a good place to stop for the night.

The kid started raking in pine needles with his feet and so did I. He had his bed pile formed and stopped to look at me because I was staring at a spot I had cleared. He looked down and almost choked on his breath. When he got it out again, it came spasmodically and he yelled, *"It's from the things! They were in the things!"* His finger was a rigid pointer.

I reached down and picked up the battery. *"Things* my foot," I said. "They're batteries from a Geiger counter." I looked around and nodded thoughtfully. "Somebody else has camped here before us. Maybe the same people who blew the Crotch to hell and back to close off an entry and make a good excuse for murder."

The Cahill kid just stared. His mouth was dry and his tongue didn't help any. "You ain't scairt none?"

"Not none," I told him.

———

I patted the tail of the *Lobster Pot* and kissed her gently on her busted fuselage. She had come down easy into the trees and hadn't scattered much. Most of the cargo was still alive, tumbled out into the wet mossy ground and it was going to be a sad animal who came on those big Maine jobs with unpegged claws.

The first time he saw one, the kid almost threw a fit, but when I explained what a Maine lobster was, he calmed down and almost believed me. But it took a fire, and one roasted the hard way before he got the point.

By noon I had broken through the wreck to the mid-section where the radio was and had it dragged out on the ground. Both receiver and transmitter were intact, nicely bundled in their wrappers without a scratch on them.

But it was a fumble. When I went back for the battery from the plane, all I found was a smashed, smelly compartment fuming gently from acid-eaten metal.

Sometimes you don't even have dirty words to fit the occasion. I just stood there and kicked at the radio cases, trying hard to keep from booting them all the way across the mountain.

The kid said, "It ain't no good?"

"No good."

Above us the sky went purple. In the trees the night things sang their songs and from a long way off a howl rose and fell. Life that had been dormant during the bright hours suddenly took form in noise and soft *swooshes* that glided by.

Trumble Cahill said, "Billy Bussy had one down the store."

For a minute it didn't sink in, then, "What?"

"Seen him spark it once. Was lookin' in the window we was. Sparked it hard and we lit out."

I sat up slowly. "You know what I'm talking about?"

"Yup. Same thing. Thunk it over hard."

"He's got one...in a store?"

The kid grinned. "Same place you was where the Harts met Billy. Used to be a meetin' place only nobody ever met. Harts trade off stuff there. Billy keeps his stuff back there too."

"Yeah, it's beginning to figure."

His eyes questioned me.

"Forget it."

"Can't forget it. Keep thinkin' what you did to Billy. Things're different since you came."

"What do you mean?"

"Dunno. Everything's different. Like things'll change."

I grinned at him. "Optimist. But, by damn, that's all you have. It's about time something different happened around here." I looked down into the valley. "If there's a storage battery down there I can be sure. I know what the scoop is already, but then I can be sure and we can cream the bastards who have pulled all this crap. Maybe..."

"Mister?"

I stopped and breathed in hard.

"I don't even know what you're talking about," he said.

Very slowly, I let it ooze out, all the tight feeling in my chest. I inched off the box and lay out on the ground beside it. "I'll spell it out later in small letters, Trumble. Right now let's cork off. Tomorrow we go to town. I mean really go to town."

For a long time after the kid's light snoring told me he was asleep, I lay awake. It was getting clear now. All this business about "tumble-ground" and "things" and outsiders killing everyone could sound like something from the supernatural to the ignorant hill folks—but then they hadn't seen what I'd seen. I knew damn well no earthquake ever planted a man-made booby trap. And I knew that that tumble-ground earthquake wasn't even a natural quake, much less a supernatural phenomenon. And those "things" weren't out of Buck Rogers either. They were something anyone who went to the outside once in a while—like say Billy Bussy—could buy just about any place.

No, it wasn't really that much of a puzzle when you got to see all the pieces. Someone had started his own earthquake. Why? Easy. It was either to destroy something or hide something. I bet on the second choice. But what was it that was worth so much to hide? I was still wondering when another thought took hold of my mind. All I knew wasn't going to do me any good, unless I found out the most important thing there was to know about this valley—how to get out of it alive. I was still thinking about that little matter when I conked off.

We roasted two more of the Maine cargo for breakfast before we started off downhill. I had the radios in a Jerry rig built from the spare chute harness on my back. The kid picked the way from long knowledge of the mountainside, staying close to water, but well out of sight of anyone who could be following the old trail.

Any party coming up behind us would be shortstopped by the wreckage of the plane and all the goodies that were there for the taking, so neither of us was worried about the rear.

Occasionally Trumble looked at me and grinned, his face splitting into a grimy smile. He was a funny little kid, a real wood's colt. But he was relaxed and happy and whatever I wanted to do was all right with him.

The snapping of a stick a little too close made his grin fade. He sat rigid, like a bird, listening hard. A funny little whistle came from the trees and he whistled back and nodded happily to me. When I looked over my shoulder, the other kid came out of the brush, skirted us until he was well-protected behind Trumble and rolled his eyes at me so that the white showed all the way around the irises.

My little buddy said, "He's Macbruder."

"Hi."

His head moved, but nothing came out of his mouth. He had to stare awhile, swallow, then with a tremendous effort, "People gonna hang you."

"Me, Macbruder?"

This time his eyes rolled from Trumble to me. "Both." He swallowed again. "Billy come to town. He all cut, he is. Old Man Hart, him mean mad. Boys even worse. Billy, he beat on all the boys up by his place. Him real mad at 'em for something. They 'low how they going to hang you both."

"Wait..." I hunched forward and scowled at him. "They're hanging who?"

His eyes rolled again. "Both you. Trumble, they gonna hang...*you!*"

I stood up and shrugged into the backpack. "In a pig's whozis they're going to hang anybody. Who says this?"

Trumble's face twisted into a grin. "Mister here did it to 'im. Mister here give it to him good."

"To Billy!"

"Sure," Trumble said. "Now let's go. Mister's ready."

I said, "Macbruder...how did you find us?"

He looked uphill. "Said you gonna look fer what's...up there. No place to go after that 'cept down this way."

"Okay," I said.

"But Billy..."

"He won't hang anybody. Come on."

———

DUSK WAS heavy in the air when we reached the outskirts of the single street that was the town. The sun paint was still on one side of the mountain, diminishing rapidly into the deep blue that was almost night.

Along the street the wagons and carts were nose-to-tail, the animals standing patiently in their harnesses. Lights showed in nearly all the buildings this time. The Dry Goods and Post Office was dark, the store marked with the weather-beaten feed sign was empty, and the single blank space on the other side was the one Trumble mentioned as the old meeting place.

Down at the end a couple dozen kids milled around the hitch rail outside the hardware store. You could hear the rumble of voices from inside, some one single monotone leading them into impassioned yells, and whenever it happened the kids would all gather to one side, quiet and frightened.

When it was dark enough, I edged across to the other side, circled the buildings and came up behind the one I wanted. I let down my pack and shoved the harness at Trumble. "I'm going in there, kid. You stay here and don't show yourself, understand?"

"Yeah, but suppose..."

"Be still and it'll be all right." I tried the window and it slid up easily. When I went to climb in, the .45 came out of my waistband and fell to the ground. I threw the map down with it and called over quietly, "Hang on to this stuff too."

He picked them up, shuffled back to the pack and I slipped into the room. The darkness was thick, too thick to see in, so I felt my way along. My hand hit a box that rattled to the floor and spilled out its contents. I raked some of it over, felt the heads of stick matches and flicked one alive with my thumbnail.

For one moment the room flared yellow and I could see it all, the household items, the tightly nailed and steel strap bound boxes against the wall...and the two storage batteries. I blew out the match, hefted one of the batteries and eased back to the window. I balanced it on the sill while I climbed out, lifted it down and turned around.

The whole top of my head seemed to fly off then. There was that single wooden sound, an incredible flash of pain that raked across the inside of my skull and all my parts seemed to suddenly rot off and fall away. I knew when the ground hit my face, but that was all.

––––––––

DAYLIGHT POURED in a window high over my head and I tried to look at my watch. But I wasn't about to see it. There must have been fifty feet of quarter-inch hemp wound around me, strapping my hands tight to my sides, my legs together with the ends knotted together between my shoes.

A whole night. I had been unconscious a whole night. I tried to move and stopped with a quick intake of breath. My body was one giant bundle of pain and when I squeezed my face together I could feel the pull of dried blood that caked it. Somebody had really worked me over.

Outside, a door banged open and indistinct voices spoke across the room. Heavy feet walked across the floor, then another door slammed open behind me. The mangled face of Billy Bussy leered down at me and before he could kick me in the head, Big George Hart nudged him to quit and pointed outside. "He be kilt in here, it ain't no good. You do it like we said."

His split lips tried hard to laugh. "Sure," he said. Then he looked at me. "We're hanging you. Not later. Right now. You're going to be a good sight to see, hanging from a tree."

He reached down, grabbed a handful of rope and dragged me out into the other room and dumped me at the feet of the Harts. The old man smiled at me from his chair and shook his head in sympathy. "Too bad, son. Jest got to be, though, you know how it is."

I didn't bother to answer him.

"Before you die, you can satisfy an old man's curiosity." He sat back and sucked on his teeth. "How come you here? You told Caroline about the *Lobster Pot.* 'Twas a good story, son, but why you really here?"

I said, "I already told you. I *wanted to* come here."

"Why, son?"

I forced a grin and stayed quiet.

Old Man Hart leaned out in his chair. "I'd say it was an accident. Like you told Carrie. You die now, we tell folks you dies in the accident. We know about what's up there on the mountain side. All we do is put you back inside it, light a little fire and who can say different?"

He smiled sadly again and sat back. I said, "I could be with the New Hope Exploration outfit. I could've come looking to see how the others *really* died."

One of the boys cursed softly and the old man silenced him with a wave. "You talkin' big now, boy. Way over your head."

"I am?" I looked around and saw the tight faces above me, like a television scene of an operation from the patient's eyes. I said, "You're a bunch of amateurs at murder, you slobs. With me you're only feeling the beginning of the heat. There'll be more coming in."

"You're not saying much, son." The interest in his eyes was a deadly interest. "You got more to say?"

"Yeah. I'll give it to you all the way and you can start sweating. What I know others will know and one day you'll be swinging yourself. You left an easy trail to follow, but the picture is even easier to see. Right after the war the New Hope Company came in looking for uranium and found it."

I looked at the old man first. "You were the smart one. You knew what they were up to because you could read. You kept up with the events. You and Billy were the only ones who had any appreciation at all for the outside. You knew what money could buy and you wanted it all."

Billy's face was black with malice. I said to him, "You

pulled some nice stunts with explosives. You caved in the Crotch, you blasted the Coopers off the road with a gimmick..."

Old Man Hart grunted and cursed the suddenly-astonished Billy. Then he relaxed and smiled again. "You smart boy."

"I've been told," I said. "I even know how Melse got it." I looked at Billy again. "This big guy here picked him up and threw him off that ledge. Just like that."

From what happened to Billy's face, I knew that I was right. He bared his broken mouth and bent down to grab me when Hart cursed him again. He stopped, his eyes wild.

"Someplace," I said, "the Belcheys are waiting to be uncovered. I wonder what it was they found out?"

"Go on, son."

"And the suckers are the ones in the valley. The ones you kept closed off all these years. Ignorant slobs, they couldn't read, they had no desire to go outside this section and they listened to everything you set up. Billy would haul in supplies, but separately he'd haul in mining equipment. You're getting all ready for the big project, aren't you?"

"You're saying it."

Softly, I went on, "Somehow you faked it so the original uranium prospectors got negative reports through. But that wouldn't have been hard. Then you and your bunch here killed them off in one beautiful landslide. You convinced the people here it was an earthquake, so it wasn't hard to get it put down as an accident on the report that went in to the New Hope Company. The bodies were buried under tons of rubble that nobody was about to disturb. To be on the safe side, you've waited until you were positive there would be no delayed-action investigation. And all this time you were making ready for the day when you could really start digging."

The old man's face was an impassive mask. For a moment he listened to the sounds from outside, the frantic sounds that precede a lynching.

I said, "It's great, the way you worked them up out there. The story about the *things* was a good one. A strange-looking box that made clicking noises could be turned into a pretty weird weapon, especially when a lot of bodies were around to see. They're so worked up at outsiders they're ready to kill the first new face they see, especially when it's been told that the new one is like 'the others.'"

From the wheelchair he gave me a smile that was almost benevolent. "That's a good story, son, but jest who'd ever believe it?"

The answer came quietly from the back of the room. "Guess I'd believe it, Paw."

They all swung around, went to move, then stopped short. Lovely, wild Caroline stood there with a shotgun in her hands and nobody had to be told that she'd use it as fast as she'd blink an eye.

"Carrie..."

"Jest stay still, Paw. Killin' you won't hurt me none. Better remind the boys to be quiet. Billy too."

"Your move, Pop," I grinned.

His eyes narrowed slightly and he nodded again. He looked toward Caroline and said, "He didn't tell it true, girl."

"I believe him, Paw. I love that man."

Her father shook his head gently. "He's one of the others, Carrie."

"He ain't."

"He brung in a *thing*. That's why he came. Like the others."

She looked straight at me, and said, "Don't believe it."

Very casually the old man rolled himself around in the chair, his hands well in sight. I craned my neck around and saw him attaching connectors to the battery. He turned, smiled at me and picked up the Hallicrafters receiver, and with only me to see what he was doing, switched it on, flipped it to CW and turned it to the short-wave selector. With the first faint hum he found a station, held the volume down until he turned around, then ran the volume up and shouted, "Here's what he brung down from the hills. He brung a *thing* like the others!"

The noisy clicking of the high-speed radio transmission filled the room like a dozen Geiger counters working all at once and when he shut it off I could see the horror in Caroline's face tighten into absolute disgust at herself and me too.

Then she sobbed once, dropped the shotgun and ran from the room.

"You made your point, old man," I said. "What now?"

"You're getting throwed to the dogs, son. We're going out there and open a barrel of corn likker for the folks, then coming back for you when things look ready."

He nodded to Big George and was wheeled out the door. The lock clicked shut and I tried to swallow but there wasn't even any saliva left.

From some place I heard the whispered call. I twisted hard to look back. The kid was there, shaking with nervous excitement.

"Trumble! Come here, damn it. Get me out of these ropes!"

Staying crouched down, he angled over to me.

"What happened to you, boy?"

"Last night...we seen Billy and the Harts come up. We had to run like hell, mister. Billy, he hit you. Got you good. Old Man Hart, he said he guessed you'd come to here for something."

"Kid, untie these ropes, will you?"

Without answering he whipped out a clasp knife, felt its honed edge then drew it down my side. The ropes came apart like thread and so did I, lying there like a suddenly bloated balloon. It wasn't until the circulation was normal that I started to ache again.

But pain could be cured. Not hanging. I followed the kid out the back way, let him help me over the window and through the trash to the trees and the mule he had ready. Somehow I got on and collapsed over his neck.

———

When I woke up again, I was in a hay pile on a floor heavy with animal smell and Trumble was holding water to my mouth.

I felt better then. The pain in my skull had dulled and I could move without being helped.

Dusk was coming on fast outside. I said to the kid, "Can you get to Cooper?"

"Guess so." He squinched around a bit. "What you want I should do?"

"Just bring him back here. Can do?"

"Sure. Take an hour. We ain't far off." He slid out of the hay and ducked out the door.

He wasn't gone quite an hour. He let me know he was coming with a piping whistle, stepped in the barn and waved in the old boy. I said, "Evening, Mr. Cooper."

At first he couldn't locate me, then his face turned in my direction. "You raising hell, youngster."

"Isn't it about time somebody did?"

"What you mean?"

I spelled it out for him nice and easy, giving him all the little details. I knew I got through to him and when I finished I asked him the final question. "The *sayings* we talked about. Who's been picking up land options?"

"Hart. He been gettin' 'em one way or another fer years. Ever since them men were here. Got 'em with whiskey, got 'em with guns. Folks, they don't care none. Half never owned the places anyway. Jest squatted. Hart, he took over."

"Okay, thanks."

"What should I do, son?"

"You take care of this kid here. Make sure nothing happens to him. I'll do the rest."

Cooper shook his head. "You can't do much. Harts all out looking for you. Them and Billy. They'll catch you."

"Not this time. They had their chance. I'm not looking any more. I'm moving. I've been through a rat-race like this before and the tricks are all still up here." I tapped my head and grinned at him. "You do what I told you."

Trumble edged forward. "You goin' out alone?"

"Soon's I get a gun."

"Heck, mister..." He walked forward, reached under the hay and came out with my .45 and the map. "Kept 'em like you said." He pulled the box of shells from his shirt and laid them in my lap.

"I'll be damned," I said. "What an orderly! Got a light?"

The kid didn't, but Cooper pulled out some stick matches and we stretched out the map. It didn't take long to spot the positions I asked for and mark out the directions I needed. When it was done I put the map away, checked the load in the gun and walked to the door with Cooper and the kid.

"I'll be away for a while, but I'll be back, Trumble. I'm coming back and take you over the mountains with me. It won't be a long time to wait. You just be patient. Okay?"

For a moment I thought he'd cry, then his face grew serious and he nodded. "You sure 'nuff coming back?"

"Promise. Now you stay with Mr. Cooper here."

"All right. But you come back, hear?"

I winked at him, put him down and slipped his hand into Cooper's. They walked away and at the treeline Trumble looked back, waved and was gone into the night.

———

By MORNING I stood on the crest of the slope that overlooked the Hart place, watching carefully to make sure she was alone.

I had traveled fast to get here, bypassing the rest of the clan an hour earlier. The old man and his wheelchair governed their speed and it was unlikely any of them would go ahead.

She came out of the cabin below me, threw a bucket of water into the yard and went back inside. When she was out of sight, I walked in easily, not bothering the dogs or the chickens scratching around the house.

I opened the door, stepped in and said, "Hi, kitten."

Little muscles twitched in her back. She turned slowly, expressionless, big and blonde and beautiful, but with a deadness in her eyes that didn't belong there. Her breathing was shallow, controlled, her breasts straining against her blouse with the tension inside her. "Get out," she said.

"Not until I tell you something."

"No need."

"Your old man tricked you. The thing he had wasn't a... a *thing*, a Geiger counter. It was a short-wave radio. He put it on high-speed code and it sounded the same."

"I heard," she said stiffly.

"He told you wrong, Caroline."

"You sayin' Pap's a liar?"

"Uh-huh. Pap's a liar. A murderer, a thief and a liar." She didn't answer me so I went on. "I'm getting out of here, kitten."

She shook her head and the yellow of her hair shimmered in the light. "Nobody can get out."

I held up the map. "It's not so hard."

After a moment she said, "Then why don't you go?"

"Because I want to take you with me, kitten. I wouldn't be a damn bit good by myself."

It seemed that a sheen went over her eyes. "I'm spoke for by Billy."

"Nuts. That bastard wanted you for insurance. He wanted to marry into the family to solidify his position in the deal. The old man held all the property."

"You lie."

"I want you, kid."

"You want me to show you the way out, is all."

"I want you, kid. Here or anyplace else. Coming?"

She smiled a tiny smile and I thought she was coming into my arms. Her hands went out long enough to feint me off guard, then she spun, grabbed a shotgun from beside the closet, wheeled and fired and I thought my hand had been torn off. I smashed the gun out of her hand before she could fire the other barrel and knocked her on her tail.

There was still feeling in my hand so it was still on. I looked at it, opened the fingers and the scrap that was the remainder of the map fell out. The charge had ripped the rest of it out and blew the pieces all over the room. I'd have a sore hand from the concussion, but that was all.

Caroline came up into a sitting position, her hand touching her face. There were tears streaming down her cheeks, but she wasn't crying. I said, "Okay, honey, let it be." I kicked at the paper at my feet. "I guess now it's the way you like it."

I reached down, snatched her to her feet. She didn't get a chance to stop me before I kissed her quickly. I shoved her away, ran to the door and looked out.

The Hart clan had heard the shot and had scattered. The first section was coming in fast with Big George and

Billy leading the pack. I said, "So long, kitten," and took off for the hills with the house screening my maneuver.

Inside Caroline was screaming for them to hurry...hurry...

———

THE THREE BOGIES overhead wheeled in the updrafts, then spiraled down for a closer look. They came low enough so I could see the quick movement of their heads and the anticipation in their eyes. This was their death watch and they were ready to ply their trade.

There was quiet in the gully again. Now that I was on the other side of them they'd have to plan a new approach. From where I lay I could retreat across the mountainside and if I played it smart I wouldn't get where they could flank me. But they could afford to wait. Sooner or later sleep would catch me and that would be the end. The best I could do was play for that one chance in a million and maybe make a few good dead Harts out of bad live Harts.

I picked my way slowly around the ridge, flat against the ground. Twice I saw movement at the bottom of the hill, but it could have been deliberate carelessness to draw my fire.

After a half-hour, the wind came about slowly and I picked up traces of a whisper from my left before it stopped. I crawled toward it, waited, bellied down and inched some more. It took thirty minutes to go fifty feet. Then all I did was lie there and wait until the head poked around the rock. The butt end of the .45 smashed down and the head rammed the ground and never moved. I knew by the feel of it that this one was for the birds upstairs. I didn't even bother to see which one I got.

I found another spot that seemed to be good cover and sat waiting. The sun toured the sky and started to glow red with approaching sunset. It made the whole valley a beautiful place, alive with color, a place seemingly distant from death.

With Caroline it could have been nice. With Caroline anything could have been nice. Very softly I said, "Caroline..."

And she said, "Mitch..."

I flipped onto my stomach with the .45 out, pointing right at her head. She stood there, screened in the bushes, her face flushed and tear streaked, the blouse and skirt torn and grimy. But this time her hands were held out to me, pleadingly.

"I had to come, Mitch."

My hand waved her to silence, made her go flat on her face. I crawled up to her. "This could be a sweet trick, kitten."

The tears told me it wasn't. "Please, Mitch." She wiped her hand across her eyes. "When Pap chased you, he...he left it there. The *thing*. I turned the knobs. Pretty soon...music came out. Pap...was lying to me. It was like you said."

I patted her face gently. "I know, kid. Too bad it's so late."

"No. It ain't late. I know how we can get away."

"And you're ready to go?"

She nodded. "I'll go anyplace with you, Mitch."

I kissed her, tasting the tears and the love she was asking for, all of a sudden alive again and happy. "Which way?"

"Billy Bussy's road. We run like hell when it gets dark. The boys know the way, but they won't want to get too close."

"When it gets dark," I said.

The sun still had a long way to go. Down below, there was no movement. No sound. They were playing it cute and waiting. I rolled over close to her, feeling the warmth of her body through my clothes. Her hand found mine and brought it to her mouth and we stayed like that for long minutes. Then she looked up and her face was close, her mouth full, and lushly-red, wet, and wanting hard to be kissed. Her body was a trembling thing screaming silently and when I touched her lips, she twitched against me spasmodically.

The sun swung through its oval and death stayed only yards away, but we hardly knew it at all.

———

This NIGHT WAS different from the others. There was a stillness that hadn't existed before as if the whole valley wanted to hear the hunt and the kill. The moon scoured the ground with a pale light, the shadows throwing mimic trails and obscuring the real one.

Caroline stayed in front, trotting steadily, never seeming to stray from the animal path she followed. No other sound seemed to reach us, but there was no doubt that they were back there. She knew it too and turned off the trail to another one that led against the summit. It would be longer this way, she said, but she didn't want to tip off our destination. Otherwise they'd be there waiting.

From our new position we were able to see them as they passed the turnoff. Billy Bussy, the four boys, and on Big George's back like a leech was Old Man Hart. While we still had a lead, we ran because they wouldn't stay on that false trail long.

It was 12:10 when we intersected the road. We stopped, sprawled out on the wet ground, breathing harshly from the climb. I said, "How far?"

Caroline shook her head. "I...can't tell. Never been past here. We follow the road... that's all."

"Okay. We'll sit here an hour and rest up. We're going to need it. I haven't got enough left to go ten feet."

She sat up suddenly. "Better have, Mitch."

"Why?"

"Listen." She cocked her head. "I hear them coming. They found out and took the short way!"

We got up shakily and began to run again. It was a dream kind of a run, getting nowhere, having to force your way through the air. Our feet were too heavy, the road too steep and too long. For a second I thought that we should have fought it out back in the hills, then I put the thought away and plodded ahead.

———

TIME LOST its meaning and its sense of importance. Time was just something that swam around you. Time was something Old Man Hart's voice swam in and yelled, "Mitch, damn you. You stop, hear? You stop and maybe we'll let you go. I know who you got there!"

Caroline looked back tiredly and shook her head. "He don't want fer me to git killed. That'll make folks think. He don't want 'em to think."

I had nothing left to answer with, so I nodded.

"Mitch, damn you!"

We rounded a bend in the trees and came on a widening-out point. But it made the sweetest little trap you saw because on each side of the bulge was a twenty-foot high rock face and stretched across the road was a multi-strand barb-wire fence with a gate set right in the middle of it.

I said, "Hold it, kitten," and stopped her before she touched it. It only took about five seconds to find the wire and just as long to detach it. "Booby trap, sugar. He's got this place rigged to go off the minute anybody touches the gate. Ten-to-one the Belcheys got it here trying to get out of the valley."

When I shoved the gate open, I waved her through. Then with the gate swung halfway in I re-attached the gimmick.

There was no sound from the trail. They were waiting to see what would happen. They were waiting for the big boom.

The moon flooded the bottleneck now, showing every detail of it clearly. I walked out of its glow to the road and yelled, "All right, you stinking killers, come and get it! Come and get it!" Then I emptied the .45 at the sky.

It happened like I knew it would, when Billy Bussy yelled his weasel yell and came tearing around the corner knowing the rod was empty, ready to nail me or force me through the gate. The others were right behind him and when they saw the open gate all they could do was think that something went wrong with the trap and the chase was still going.

They came on, every one of them, swearing, yelling their crazy rage, and nobody at all heard the old man who was the only one who could read through the picture. I did. I heard him yell. "NO...NO...IT'S A TRAP! BILLY...GEORGE...BY DAMN..."

Then they pushed the gate open the rest of the way in

their mad rush to get to us and the sky was split apart, and for the span of a full breath the valley below lay painted in the bright red and yellow of the blast.

We came away from the rocks that sheltered us and I looked at the girl I loved so much. I felt her face and there were no tears, no remorse. I kissed her gently and she kissed me back.

We stepped out on the road that we knew would take us out, then started up it hand in hand.

Together We Kill

Together We Kill

I AVOIDED the street for six months; I kept the hell away from it all that time. Yet, I knew as sure as the grass grows green that the first time I set foot on it she'd be there. It wouldn't be something that she'd plan or I'd plan, no, nothing so simple as that. It would be that evil little fate that's followed me ever since the day I was born who would do it. Laughing, always laughing at me. A mean snicker I could hear, and my insides would go all in a knot again because there was nothing I could do about it.

Any other time I wanted to go west from Broadway I'd take some other street, but never this one. It was one block long, but only a little way off the corner was the theater and her picture outside. Several pictures. That, and a long line of people demanding tickets for "Fair Is the Wind" and the chance to see the beauty that was Claire.

Every day she was there in magazines, newspapers, on billboards, beautiful and blonde with the loveliness of youth and maturity combined, exotically appealing and so alive with that radiance that comes only from the soul. And everybody wanted her. Hollywood screamed for her and Broadway wouldn't let her go. There was never a moment when she wasn't surrounded by men who fought for her smiles and who would give anything they owned for just the chance to touch her.

Claire was beauty. Claire was love. She was everything all women want to be and all men want.

But to me Claire was a memory. You see, I had Claire.

But that was seven years ago in a different world, and this was Broadway and there she was in front of me. If I hurried I knew I could catch her before she turned and went into the street-level bistro, the one with the big wooden rooster hanging over the door.

But I didn't hurry, because even the sign of the rooster was part of the joke fate was playing. The Rooster was the place we promised to meet seven years ago. Now it was noon, and the Rooster was only a few doors from Claire's theater and she was going there for lunch with never a thought of that last moment in France or of me. So I didn't hurry at all. I watched her go in and kept going past the theater.

Now that I saw her, at last, I could forget her and all she'd done to me. I could go up to see Gus Kimball who had his office up the block and tell him to skip the whole deal. It was off, finished, kaput.

Four months ago he'd called me in and said, "Joe, we're putting that tunnel through in Bolivia. The engineer who's to tie the job together has to be tops. That guy is you. It's big money, and a chance to make a name for yourself, even a better one than you have now. How about it?"

That was a silly question. Does a bee want honey? I got one of those grins on my face that wouldn't wipe off because the world was in my lap. "You bought yourself an engineer, Gus."

He grinned back and poured a pair of shot glasses full. "We'll drink to it then. Frankly, Joe, I was worried for fear you wouldn't take it. It's a lonely place to be and you'll be there for a few years. In some respects it isn't *the* dream job."

"Nuts," I said. "For me it's beautiful."

"Fine, then there's only one other detail to iron out. You know the company policy. It may sound extreme, but we found that it works. All our company officers are required to take their wives on the job."

My grin was hard to hold. I threw the drink down fast.

"Not that I'm worried," he added. "Guys like you aren't

without women...not from what I've heard about you. Aren't you engaged?"

"I was. Several times."

"Lucky you," he chuckled. "I wish I was thirty and on the brawny side again. Well, you have four months to get things settled. Stop in then and we'll go over the details and arrange for transportation of your personal effects. A woman needs a lot of pretty things down there to keep her morale up."

I said something I don't remember and we shook hands. That was four months ago. Helen and Jean and Gloria and Francis ago. All beautiful, all ready to share a life with me that couldn't be shared because Claire had been there before them and would always be there before anybody else. That was what my personal fate did to me—let me climb for the top on a ladder that was one big fat rung short.

But there was always the memory of having had her. I could reach back through the seasons to that time when St. Marie was nothing but a huddled mass of hills and houses on the ground below me, and when the moonlight filtered past the canopy of my parachute to sketch a fuzzy round shadow on the meadows...

———

It was a bad night for the jump. It left you a dangling target for anybody who happened to look up, but it had to be that way. The bridge had to go. The push was due in the morning; a whole army was coming through the slot that had been opened up the day before. But the push wasn't a secret any longer and the Krauts were moving up an army that could plug the hole. It depended on me, one guy with a sackful of high explosives strapped to his back, and a bridge over a river that ran through St. Marie.

When the bridge went, the Krauts went.

There was only the faintest whisper of sound when I hit the grass. I rolled with the fall and snagged the bottom shrouds to spill the air out of my chute, snatching up the lines and the nylon so the white blob wouldn't be there to give me away. I was tearing the sod away to bury it when the voice said, "No...m'sieu, not there!"

I went flat on my face, the .45 in my hand ready to spit when I saw her, a white face speaking to me from the folds of a cape. "You damn near died, girl," I told her. My hand and my voice shook together.

"I die every night, m'sieu. Come with me, please. If I saw you, then perhaps others saw you, too. Quickly."

She took my arm and led me away from the field to a footpath, then to a low stone house built into the side of the hill. I went in behind her and stood with my back to the door while she covered the windows and touched a match to the candle on the table. When she turned around she saw the gun in my hand still pointing at her stomach.

"I am not of...*them!*" She spit the word out.

"Maybe not, kid. It's just that I've seen all kinds of traps and I'm not taking any chances." I grinned at her because I was jumpy and didn't want her to know that I was scared, too.

She tossed off the cape. Maybe that's when I fell in love with her. It happened too fast, and all of a sudden I felt slippery inside and wanted to come apart at the seams. I thought a lot of things all at once, but most of all I thought what suckers war made of us, how it could make a man's mind forget what his body never stops remembering.

She was beautiful even then. Twenty maybe, soft and beautiful, with eyes that burned holes in your soul. Hell, you don't describe that kind of beauty. You have to think it or imagine it. Her body was the fulfillment of a dream, every movement more than a subtle invitation...a complete giving if you were *the* man. For anyone else it would be torture. I slid the gun back in the shoulder holster and stood there. She smiled and the room went bright.

"It is the bridge you want, is it not?"

I didn't answer her. She sat down quickly, her fingers drumming the table.

"We have known this would come. So have *they.*" She spit it out again. "You will not be able to do it according to your plans, m'sieu. Only this afternoon they have brought in many men to guard the place. They are all over because the bridge is their only weak link. You see, they know."

"We found that out," I said.

"And your plans?"

I laughed. "To do it anyway." I started climbing out of my jump suit, stripping down until I was in ragged breeches and the torn shirt of a farmer. I tucked the gun in my belt and the explosives in a sack over my shoulder.

"You will be shot if you are caught, of course."

"Of course."

Her laugh was deep and throaty, a laugh of devilish amusement. "You Americans have too much of the...bravery. Sometimes you forget that one need not be so...direct. There are other ways of doing things and not getting shot."

I looked at her carefully, alive to the woman, yet alert to every sound that came through the night. From the village I could hear the rumble of trucks going over the pavement. "Who are you, girl?"

"In the underground I have a code number. Always, since I was a little girl, I have played under the bridge and along the banks of the river. When the people of the village moved I was directed to stay. You see...for long we knew that this time would come, and since I was the only one who was familiar with every spot that would be of importance about the bridge, the job was assigned to me. I am to...guide you, shall I say?"

"No, let's not say it. The thing's too pat."

"There is not time to argue. Certainly your intelligence knows how heavily the bridge has been guarded."

"They know it."

"Then how can I convince you that you must trust me?"

"You can't," I said. "It's still too pat. We never communicated with the French underground on this movement."

Her fingers stopped tapping the table. "I said we expected this. The railway is the only one on which troops can be moved. All the roads are out of service."

I said, "Sorry, kid," but I made it easy by backing it up with a smile.

"I see." Her eyes bored into mine, searching for the answer. "And what will you do with me?"

"Tie you up so you can get loose after a while. Like I said, there are too many traps for me to step in one blind."

A smile played with the corners of her mouth. It stayed a while then danced into her eyes. "I should curse you in the name of France for being so stupid. But too, I should curse myself and the others for being so cautious as not to leave any proof of my identity behind."

I had a coil of rope wound around my waist and I started to shake it loose. "In the name of France and the others you'll do better if you let me alone. I told you that I wasn't taking chances. The Krauts come across with nice prizes for dragging in a saboteur or two."

"And why couldn't I have turned you in before?"

I held the rope in my hand and fiddled with it. "Because I'm a man and you're a woman, chicken. A beautiful woman, but still a woman."

Her hand had a gun in it and it was aimed right at my head. My fingers jerked the rope tight and my mouth felt dry. "If I had wanted to I could have killed you before. Or I could have drawn a prize as you seem to think." She laid the gun on the table with the butt toward me. "Do you still think I shouldn't be trusted?"

The stiffness left my fingers and I wound the rope back around my waist. "Someday I'll smarten up," I said. When she saw that I wasn't going to touch the gun she put it back in the folds of her skirt. I glanced at her sharply. "You know what will happen if they catch you with that thing?"

"Yes. First I will kill several of them, then myself."

She meant it, every word of it. I finished tucking the ends of the rope in, then straightened up. "Okay, what gives? Tell me two things: if you knew how important the bridge was, why didn't the underground do something about it? When you tell me that tell me how we're going to go about it."

"The thing you carry in your pack is the thing we lacked. We have no explosive. Nor is it a job for one person."

"Why?"

"You'll see. As for the plans, they were arranged long ago. I told you that was why I was left behind."

"Go on."

"The war came close to us, m'sieu..."

"My name is Joe."

"And mine is Claire. As I said, the war came close. Rather than risk destruction the populace moved to the hills beyond."

"Not even token resistance?"

Her voice had a sharp edge. "It was hardly necessary. It happens that here we had the radio transmitters and the printing plants that was the lifeblood of the underground. We could not afford to have it captured."

"Sorry," I said. "You're brave."

Her eyes got gray and cloudy. "No braver than you, Joe. You expected to die when you came here, did you not?"

I shrugged my shoulders. "I figured it would happen sometime."

"It may not be necessary. You have made arrangements to be picked up?" I nodded a yes. "Then we shall hope for the best. However, it is agreed that I will lead you there?"

I was doing everything I shouldn't do. I was taking a chance on an unknown quantity in violation of all my training. How many lives depended on my judgment—thousands? All because a woman was beautiful, with a deep, rich voice and eyes that burned holes into my soul. I was fully briefed to do my job, yet here I was letting a woman change plans that had been made by experts.

And I knew I was right, I knew it damn well! I looked at my watch, and said, "Let's go."

The bridge is part of history now, but not that night. That's pure screaming torture that has etched itself into my memory with an acid so strong it will never leave. I could forget it, if within an hour I hadn't found myself loving her and having it returned.

But it happened and I can't forget it, see? She was mine. She was beautiful and soft, and she was mine before the moon was at its peak...

———

THAT NIGHT the air and the ground were alive with death. We heard the sharp metallic noises it made and felt the force of it waiting to thunder into reality. It was there in light and shadows, and we walked through it safely. Claire took my hand and I responded to the slightest pressure of her touch, letting her show me the path until we had the sounds behind us and the sound of the river coming our way.

We still had two hours to wait, timing ourselves so the job could be completed with precious minutes left over for me to reach the field where the plane would come down.

We didn't speak of our plans. Somehow we both knew what was to be done, and whatever she had to do I didn't want to know about.

That was where we found life, there right in the middle of death. We forgot about it and talked of the things that were and would still be when it was over, lying on our backs facing the stars. I was counting them when a shadow of golden hair moved across my vision and I tasted the warmth of her mouth and the sweetness of her breath. She said, "We love each other, Joe."

My answer was in my arms and in the present. I had to come across a continent to find her. I was hers until the hands on my watch marked the time to end the life we had found.

After she was mine she took me to the banks of the river, leading the way through the weeds. She was calm, but I didn't dare speak. Along the causeway and on the bridge itself I could see the file of the sentries back and forth. They shouted instructions and commands, following any object that moved with the white beam of the searchlights. Then there would be the short snarl of the machine guns and the questions asked afterward. Nothing moved and lived.

"Notice, Joe..." I turned my head to her. "The river flows under the bridge, but here starts a little offshoot of the river that winds through the rushes. The bottom is clay, and if you walk softly without splashing and keep in the shadow of the tall grass, you can get under the bridge. From above this looks like part of the bank and they will not be watching. Their lights are trained on the river itself and the road along the bank. Only in this one section of the river is the footing solid enough to follow. None of them are under the bridge because no man can stand long in the ooze of the silt without sinking under."

I nodded, picking out the way with my eyes, glad that the moon was directly above, so that I'd leave no trailing shadow. "I may not be able to be quiet."

Her voice was very soft. "They will not hear you, Joe."

"Why?" My chest felt tight.

"Because I am beautiful. Because I am the only woman in the village and they are men, Joe. Kiss me once more."

I kissed her. I tried to crush the life out of her so nothing would take her away from me, but she was too strong and pulled back with a sad smile. "Always I will love you, Joe," she said.

There were only seconds left now. "No matter where I am I'll be loving you, Claire. Remember this, the present doesn't last long. When it's over I'll be looking for you, if we can live through it. It might take a while to find you because even in peace there are problems. I can't give you much, but it will be more than you ever had before. If I can't get to you, try to come to me. Right off Broadway there's a tiny bistro. A red rooster hangs outside the door and we'll meet there. No matter where I am, I'll come back on this day, the ninth of each month, looking for you."

"I'll remember, Joe." Then she was gone. A white shadow that simply disappeared. I shifted the sack of explosives and stepped into the stream.

A cat couldn't have been more silent. I left nothing to reveal my passage through the brush. Not even a splash or the snapping of a twig. Sure, I made it. No trouble at all because she was right all along the line. It was a snap getting under the bridge and it left me feeling good because there was nothing to it. The boys back in HQ better get their medals ready, I kept thinking.

———

IT MADE NICE THINKING, until I got a good look at the underside of the structure, then I felt like a jerk. There was a keystone there that would pull the whole works down, but getting up to it meant a scramble and a lot of noise. Swell.

Just one lousy sound and I'd be dead. You know what I felt like. Not too far south a thousand guys could figure on dying because the job was too big for me. Maybe one of those guys was somebody *you* knew. Then you know how I felt.

Twenty feet above me the muted noises of soldiers on guard sounded like the drone of bees, never loud enough to muffle foreign sounds. I couldn't wait any longer. I shook my rope out and stood ready to throw it over the projecting beam above. One lousy sound and I'd die. Nice.

It didn't come. Like everything else I froze because the only other sound in the night was a deep, rich voice lifted in song. Somebody barked an order and the lights came around. Two of them. They pointed down river and merged on the banks where she stood so lovely and white and naked.

Somebody choked out a whistle.

She dived into the water, flashed to the surface and shook her hair back from her face, then swam to the shore again, framed in the lights that never left her, laughing and waving toward the bridge.

Sound? Who could have heard me? There was so much sound that I whistled while I tied the explosive into place and set off the long fuse. They screamed from the rail, whistled and shouted to that vision so tantalizingly close to them, yet so far out of reach. Hell, I even laughed too.

Yeah, I laughed. I finished the job and got away.

I made the field where the plane picked me up, but the laugh was a frozen grimace of hate and fury because I'll never forget the light picking up the officers throwing their clothes on the banks and diving in after her. She swam away, her arms flashing in the light, laughing over her shoulder, letting them draw closer and closer so every eye on the bridge was focused on the wanton sight, their eager shouts and cheers drowning out the noise of my escape and the sputtering of the fuse and even the sound of the light plane taking off again from the field.

And from the air I could see the bright fingers of the light trained on the banks of the river now, and I said, "Oh, God! Oh, God!" and I thought I could hear their laughter even up there. Then when the flash came there was nothing. No noise. Just that one intense glare and I went on into the night. Later, I wondered if she gave all that for me or for her country. I tried to joke about it. It wasn't funny. Not even to myself.

———

I saw her again. Sure, so did you. Beauty didn't die that easily. The present went and the future came after it. The world settled back and enjoyed the beauty that had been hidden by the war, and you saw a star come out of France that was a bright light of fame and fortune that glittered from the stage.

Those soldiers on the bridge weren't the only ones she drove mad. Whenever you saw her picture you saw someone staring at it with that funny look on his face. Everybody wanted her and she had everything she wanted. What was it I was going to take her away from—the poverty that was Europe? That was another laugh.

The price of a necklace she wore at a premiere was more than I could save in five years. It was a real big laugh, a regular howl, because I could go through a succession of Helens and Jeans and Frans and it was Claire who kept them out. Claire, the memory.

So she wound up in New York, the hit of the year's biggest play. And she ate at the bistro with the sign of the rooster over the door, but that was only because it was noon and time for lunch and it was only a few doors away from the theater...

I started past the door for my appointment with Gus Kimball and then I got curious. Hell, I thought, why be a dope? Any guy likes to shake hands with fame, and maybe she'd remember me if she thought hard enough. I wouldn't prod her with unpleasant memories. That's what the psychiatrists would say. Go in and face your problem, and then you'll have nerve enough to walk up the street again without going all shaky inside.

I opened the door and stepped in. Henri hadn't seen me for years, but his memory was good. He said, "Why, good afternoon, Joe! It is good to have you back. A table, yes?"

"No, Henri, not right now." I was looking across the room. "I just came in to speak to somebody a moment."

My feet pulled me through the tables. She was by herself off in a corner and didn't see me until I was in front of her. "Hello, kid," I said.

"Joe." Just like that, "Joe." That's all she said.

I pulled a cigarette out and stuck a light to it. Funny, but my hand didn't shake. I blew the smoke toward the ceiling and grinned at her. "Imagine us crossing again. Didn't think you'd remember me. I saw you turn in here and had to come in to be sure. You look good."

"Do I?" I damned Henri for not having more lights in the place. I couldn't see her face very well.

"Yeah. You did all right for yourself, too. I see your name in the papers every day. How do you like our country?"

"I like it, Joe."

She hadn't moved. Now that I was in the dark a while, after the brightness of the street, I began to see the vague outline of her face. The fires started inside of me and I couldn't let them do it to me again. Not anymore.

"Well, I got an appointment, kid. Maybe one day I'll look you up if you're not too busy. I have to go now."

People were looking over at us, and I thought I saw her teeth bite her lips. Maybe she was thinking back to those searchlights.

She stood up quickly, scooping her handbag under her arm. What the hell, I didn't blame her a bit. Nobody famous wants to be hamstrung by something from a forgotten past.

"It is I who has to go, Joe," she said. Then she was gone.

Henri stood at my elbow. "You were to have lunch with the lady?"

"No, Henri. I was just saying hello."

"A strange woman, Joe. Always she comes in once a month and sits here. Always the same day, the ninth of each month. It is that she has a pact, perhaps?"

The fires wouldn't go out. The cigarette fell from my fingers and scattered sparks on the floor. The tight knot inside me jerked even tighter and something was going on in my head, fighting and screaming to free itself. Something that didn't sound like my voice said. "And today, Henri...?"

"Is the ninth, Joe."

I ran. I pushed everything aside and I ran, and if I went fast enough I could catch her before she disappeared again, and I could tell Gus that the job was fine and I'd be there with bells on. Wedding bells.

I caught her.

The Girl Behind The Hedge

The Girl Behind The Hedge

THE STOCKY MAN handed his coat and hat to the attendant and went through the foyer to the main lounge of the club. He stood in the doorway for a scant second, but in that time his eyes had seen all that was to be seen; the chess game beside the windows, the foursome at cards and the lone man at the rear of the room sipping a drink.

He crossed between the tables, nodding briefly to the card players, and went directly to the back of the room. The other man looked up from his drink with a smile. "Afternoon, Inspector. Sit down. Drink?"

"Hello, Dunc. Same as you're drinking."

Almost languidly, the fellow made a motion with his hand. The waiter nodded and left. The Inspector settled himself in his chair with a sigh. He was a big man, heavy without being given to fat. Only his high shoes proclaimed him for what he was. When he looked at Chester Duncan he grimaced inwardly, envying him his poise and manner, yet not willing to trade him for anything.

Here, he thought smugly, *is a man who should have everything yet has nothing. True, he has money and position, but the finest of all things, a family life, was denied him.* And with a brood of five in all stages of growth at home, the Inspector felt that he had achieved his purpose in life.

The drink came and the Inspector took his, sipping it gratefully. When he put it down he said, "I came to thank you for that, er...tip. You know, that was the first time I've ever played the market."

"Glad to do it," Duncan said. His hands played with the glass, rolling it around in his palms. His eyebrows shot up suddenly, as though he was amused at something. "I suppose you heard all the ugly rumors."

A flush reddened the Inspector's face. "In an offhand way, yes. Some of them were downright ugly." He sipped his drink again and tapped a cigarette on the side table.

"You know," he said, "if Walter Harrison's death hadn't been so definitely a suicide, you might be standing an investigation right now."

Duncan smiled slowly. "Come now, Inspector. The market didn't budge until after his death, you know."

"True enough. But rumor has it that you engineered it in some manner." He paused long enough to study Duncan's face. "Tell me, did you?"

"Why should I incriminate myself?"

"It's over and done with. Harrison leaped to his death from the window of a hotel room. The door was locked and there was no possible way anyone could have gotten in that room to give him a push. No, we're quite satisfied that it was suicide, and everybody that ever came in contact with Harrison agrees that he did the world a favor when he died. However, there's still some speculation about you having a hand in things."

"Tell me, Inspector, do you really think I had the courage or the brains to oppose a man like Harrison, and force him to kill himself?"

The Inspector frowned, then nodded. "As a matter of fact, yes. You *did* profit by his death."

"So did *you,*" Duncan laughed.

"Ummmm."

"Though it's nothing to be ashamed about," Duncan added. "When Harrison died the financial world naturally expected that the stocks he financed were no good and tried to unload. It so happened that I was one of the few who knew they were good as gold and bought while I could. And, of course, I passed the word on to my friends. Somebody had might as well profit by the death of a...a rat."

Through the haze of the smoke Inspector Early saw his face tighten around the mouth. He scowled again, leaning forward in his chair. "Duncan, we've been friends quite a while. I'm just cop enough to be curious and I'm thinking that our late Walter Harrison was cursing you just before he died."

Duncan twirled his glass around. "I've no doubt of it," he said. His eyes met the Inspector's. "Would you really like to hear about it?"

"Not if it means your confessing to murder. If that has to happen I'd much rather you spoke directly to the D.A."

"Oh, it's nothing like that at all. No, not a bit, Inspector. No matter how hard they tried, they couldn't do a thing that would impair either my honor or reputation. You see, Walter Harrison went to his death through his own greediness."

The Inspector settled back in his chair. The waiter came with drinks to replace the empties and the two men toasted each other silently.

"Some of this you probably know already, Inspector," Duncan said.

———

NEVERTHELESS, I'll start at the beginning and tell you everything that happened. Walter Harrison and I met in law school. We were both young and not too studious. We had one thing in common and only one. Both of us were the products of wealthy parents who tried their best to spoil their children. Since we were the only ones who could afford certain—er—pleasures, we naturally gravitated to each other, though when I think back, even at that time, there was little true friendship involved.

It so happened that I had a flair for my studies whereas Walter didn't give a damn. At examination time, I had to carry him. It seemed like a big joke at the time, but actually I was doing all the work while he was having his fling around town. Nor was I the only one he imposed upon in such a way. Many students, impressed with having his friendship, gladly took over his papers. Walter could charm the devil himself if he had to.

And quite often he had to. Many's the time he's talked his way out of spending a weekend in jail for some minor offense —and I've even seen him twist the dean around his little finger, so to speak. Oh, but I remained his loyal friend. I shared everything I had with him, including my women, and even thought it amusing when I went out on a date and met him, only to have him take my girl home.

In the last year of school the crash came. It meant little to me because my father had seen it coming and got out with his fortune increased. Walter's father tried to stick it out and went under. He was one of the ones who killed himself that day.

Walter was quite stricken, of course. He was in a blue funk and got stinking drunk. We had quite a talk and he was for quitting school at once, but I talked him into accepting the money from me and graduating. Come to think of it, he never did pay me back that money. However, it really doesn't matter.

After we left school I went into business with my father and took over the firm when he died. It was that same month that Walter showed up. He stopped in for a visit and wound up with a position, though at no time did he deceive me as to the real intent of his visit. He got what he came after and in a way it was a good thing for me. Walter was a shrewd businessman.

His rise in the financial world was slightly less than meteoric. He was much too astute to remain in anyone's employ for long, and with the Street talking about Harrison, the Boy Wonder of Wall Street, in every other breath, it was inevitable that he open up his own office. In a sense, we became competitors after that, but always friends.

Pardon me, Inspector, let's say that I was his friend, he never was mine. His ruthlessness was appalling at times, but even then he managed to charm his victims into accepting their lot with a smile. I for one know that he managed the market to make himself a cool million on a deal that left me gasping. More than once he almost cut the bottom out of my business, yet he was always in with a grin and a big hello the next day as if it had been only a tennis match he had won.

If you've followed his rise then you're familiar with the social side of his life. Walter cut quite a swath for himself. Twice, he was almost killed by irate husbands, and if he had been, no jury on earth would have convicted his murderer. There was the time a young girl killed herself rather than let her parents know that she had been having an affair with Walter and had been trapped. He was very generous about it. He offered her money to travel, her choice of doctors and anything she wanted...except his name for her child. No, he wasn't ready to give his name away then. That came a few weeks later.

I was engaged to be married at the time. Adrianne was a girl I had loved from the moment I saw her and there aren't words enough to tell how happy I was when she said she'd marry me. We spent most of our waking hours poring over plans for the future. We even selected a site for our house out on the Island and began construction. We were timing the wedding to coincide with the completion of the house and if ever I was a man living in a dream world, it was then. My happiness was complete, as was Adrianne's, or so I thought. Fortune seemed to favor me with more than one smile at the time. For some reason my own career took a sudden spurt and whatever I touched turned to gold, and in no time the Street had taken to following me rather than Walter Harrison. Without realizing it, I turned several deals that had him on his knees, though I doubt if many ever realized it. Walter would never give up the amazing front he affected."

———

AT THIS POINT Duncan paused to study his glass, his eyes narrowing. Inspector Early remained motionless, waiting for him to go on.

———

WALTER CAME to see me [Duncan said]. It was a day I shall never forget. I had a dinner engagement with Adrianne and invited him along. Now I know that what he did was done out of sheer spite, nothing else. At first I believed that it was my fault, or hers, never giving Walter a thought...

Forgive me if I pass over the details lightly, Inspector. They aren't very pleasant to recall. I had to sit there and watch Adrianne captivated by this charming rat to the point where I was merely a decoration in the chair opposite her. I had to see him join us day after day, night after night, then hear the rumors that they were seeing each other without me, then discover for myself that she was in love with him.

Yes, it was quite an experience. I had the idea of killing them both, then killing myself. When I saw that that could never solve the problem I gave it up.

Adrianne came to me one night. She sat and told me how much she hated to hurt me, but she had fallen in love with Walter Harrison and wanted to marry him. What else was there to do? Naturally, I acted the part of a good loser and called off the engagement. They didn't wait long. A week later they were married and I was the laughing stock of the Street.

Perhaps time might have cured everything if things didn't turn out the way they did. It wasn't very long afterwards that I learned of a break in their marriage. Word came that Adrianne had changed and I knew for a fact that Walter was far from being true to her.

You see, now I realized the truth. Walter never loved her. He never loved anybody but himself. He married Adrianne because he wanted to hurt me more than anything else in the world. He hated me because I had something he lacked...happiness. It was something he searched after desperately himself and always found just out of reach.

In December of that year Adrianne took sick. She wasted away for a month and died. In the final moments she called for me, asking me to forgive her; this much I learned from a servant of hers. Walter, by the way, was enjoying himself at a party when she died. He came home for the funeral and took off immediately for a sojourn in Florida with some attractive showgirl.

God, how I hated that man! I used to dream of killing him! Do you know, if ever my mind drifted from the work I was doing I always pictured myself standing over his corpse with a knife in my hand, laughing my head off.

Every so often I would get word of Walter's various escapades, and they seemed to follow a definite pattern. I made it my business to learn more about him and before long I realized that Walter was almost frenzied in his search to find a woman he could really love. Since he was a fabulously wealthy man, he was always suspicious of a woman wanting him more than his wealth, and this very suspicion always was the thing that drove a woman away from him.

It may seem strange to you, but regardless of my attitude I saw him quite regularly. And equally strange, he never realized that I hated him so. He realized, of course, that he was far from popular in any quarter, but he never suspected me of anything else save a stupid idea of friendship. But having learned my lesson the hard way, he never got the chance to impose upon me again, though he never really had need to.

It was a curious thing, the solution I saw to my problem. It had been there all the time, I was aware of it being there, yet using the circumstance never occurred to me until the day I was sitting on my veranda reading a memo from my office manager. The note stated that Walter had pulled another coup in the market and had the Street rocking on its heels. It was one of those times when any variation in Wall Street reflected the economy of the country, and what he did was undermine the entire economic structure of the United States. It was with the greatest effort that we got back to normal without toppling, but in doing so a lot of places had to close up. Walter Harrison, however, had doubled the wealth he could never hope to spend anyway.

As I said, I was sitting there reading the note when I saw her behind the window in the house across the way. The sun was streaming in, reflecting the gold in her hair, making a picture of beauty so exquisite as to be unbelievable. A servant came and brought her a tray, and as she sat down to lunch I lost sight of her behind the hedges and the thought came to me of how simple it would all be.

I met Walter for lunch the next day. He was quite exuberant over his latest adventure, treating it like a joke.

I said, "Say, you've never been out to my place on the Island, have you?"

He laughed, and I noticed a little guilt in his eyes. "To tell the truth," he said, "I would have dropped in if you hadn't built the place for Adrianne. After all..."

"Don't be ridiculous, Walter. What's done is done. Look, until things get back to normal, how about staying with me a few days. You need a rest after your little deal."

"Fine, Duncan, fine! Anytime you say."

"All right, I'll pick you up tonight."

We had quite a ride out, stopping at a few places for drinks and hashing over the old days at school. At any other time I might have laughed, but all those reminiscences had taken on an unpleasant air. When we reached the house I had a few friends in to meet the fabulous Walter Harrison, left him accepting their plaudits and went to bed.

We had breakfast on the veranda. Walter ate with relish, breathing deeply of the sea air with animal-like pleasure. At exactly nine o'clock the sunlight flashed off the windows of the house behind mine as the servant threw them open to the morning breeze.

Then she was there. I waved and she waved back. Walter's head turned to look and I heard his breath catch in his throat. She was lovely, her hair a golden cascade that tumbled around her shoulders. Her blouse was a radiant white that enhanced the swell of her breasts, a gleaming contrast to the smooth tanned flesh of her shoulders.

Walter looked like a man in a dream. "Lord, she's lovely!" he said. "Who is she, Dunc?"

I sipped my coffee. "A neighbor," I said lightly.

"Do you... do you think I can get to meet her?"

"Perhaps. She's quite young and just a little bit shy and it would be better to have her see me with you a few times before introductions are in order."

He sounded hoarse. His face had taken on an avid, hungry look. "Anything you say, but I have to meet her." He turned around with a grin. "By golly, I'll stay here until I do, too!"

We laughed over that and went back to our cigarettes,

but every so often I caught him glancing back toward the hedge with that desperate expression creasing his face.

Being familiar with her schedule, I knew that we wouldn't see her again that day, but Walter knew nothing of this. He tried to keep away from the subject, yet it persisted in coming back. Finally he said, "Incidentally, just who is she?"

"Her name is Evelyn Vaughn. Comes from quite a well-to-do-family."

"She here alone?"

"No, besides the servants she has a nurse and a doctor in attendance. She hasn't been quite well."

"Hell, she looks the picture of health."

"Oh, she is now," I agreed. I walked over and turned on the television and we watched the fights. For the sixth time a call came in for Walter, but his reply was the same. He wasn't going back to New York. I felt the anticipation in his voice, knowing why he was staying, and had to concentrate on the screen to keep from smiling.

Evelyn was there the next day and the next. Walter had taken to waving when I did and when she waved back his face seemed to light up until it looked almost boyish. The sun had tanned him nicely and he pranced around like a colt, especially when she could see him. He pestered me with questions and received evasive answers. Somehow he got the idea that his importance warranted a visit from the house across the way. When I told him that to Evelyn neither wealth nor position meant a thing he looked at me sharply to see if I was telling the truth. To have become what he was he had to be a good reader of faces and he knew that it *was* the truth beyond the shadow of a doubt.

So I sat there day after day watching Walter Harrison fall helplessly in love with a woman he hadn't met yet. He fell in love with the way she waved until each movement of her hand seemed to be for him alone. He fell in love with the luxuriant beauty of her body, letting his eyes follow her as she walked to the water from the house, aching to be close to her. She would turn sometimes and see us watching, and wave.

At night he would stand by the window not hearing what

I said because he was watching her windows, hoping for just one glimpse of her, and often I would hear him repeating her name slowly, letting it roll off his tongue like a precious thing.

It couldn't go on that way. I knew it and he knew it. She had just come up from the beach and the water glistened on her skin. She laughed at something the woman said who was with her and shook her head back so that her hair flowed down her back.

Walter shouted and waved and she laughed again, waving back. The wind brought her voice to him and Walter stood there, his breath hot in my face. "Look here, Duncan, I'm going over and meet her. I can't stand this waiting. Good Lord, what does a guy have to go through to meet a woman?"

"You've never had any trouble before, have you?"

"Never like this!" he said. "Usually they're dropping at my feet. I haven't changed, have I? There's nothing repulsive about me, is there?"

I wanted to tell him the truth, but I laughed instead. "You're the same as ever. It wouldn't surprise me if she was dying to meet you, too. I can tell you this...she's never been outside as much as since you've been here."

His eyes lit up boyishly. "Really, Dunc. Do you think so?"

"I think so. I can assure you of this, too. If she does seem to like you it's certainly for yourself alone."

As crudely as the barb was placed, it went home. Walter never so much as glanced at me. He was lost in thought for a long time, then: "I'm going over there now, Duncan. I'm crazy about that girl. By God, I'll marry her if it's the last thing I do."

"Don't spoil it, Walter. Tomorrow, I promise you, I'll go over with you."

His eagerness was pathetic. I don't think he slept a wink that night. Long before breakfast he was waiting for me on the veranda. We ate in silence, each minute an eternity for him. He turned repeatedly to look over the hedge and I caught a flash of worry when she didn't appear.

Tight little lines had appeared at the corner of his eyes

and he said, "Where is she, Dunc? She should be there by now, shouldn't she?"

"I don't know," I said. "It does seem strange. Just a moment." I rang the bell on the table and my housekeeper came to the door. "Have you seen the Vaughns, Martha?" I asked her.

She nodded sagely. "Oh, yes, sir. They left very early this morning to go back to the city."

Walter turned to me. "Hell!"

"Well, she'll be back," I assured him.

"Damn it, Dunc, that isn't the point!" He stood up and threw his napkin on the seat. "Can't you realize that I'm in love with the girl? I can't wait for her to get back!"

His face flushed with frustration. There was no anger, only the crazy hunger for the woman. I held back my smile. It happened. It happened the way I planned for it to happen. Walter Harrison had fallen so deeply in love, so truly in love that he couldn't control himself. I might have felt sorry for him at that moment if I hadn't asked him, "Walter, as I told you, I know very little about her. Supposing she is already married."

He answered my question with a nasty grimace. "Then she'll get a divorce if I have to break the guy in pieces. I'll break anything that stands in my way, Duncan. I'm going to have her if it's the last thing I do!"

He stalked off to his room. Later I heard the car roar down the road. I let myself laugh then.

I went back to New York and was there a week when my contacts told me of Walter's fruitless search. He used every means at his disposal, but he couldn't locate the girl. I gave him seven days, exactly seven days. You see, that seventh day was the anniversary of the date I introduced him to Adrianne. I'll never forget it. Wherever Walter is now, neither will he.

When I called him I was amazed at the change in his voice. He sounded weak and lost. We exchanged the usual formalities; then I said, "Walter, have you found Evelyn yet?"

He took a long time to answer. "No, she's disappeared completely."

"Oh, I wouldn't say that," I said.

He didn't get it at first. It was almost too much to hope for. "You...mean you know where she is?"

"Exactly."

"Where? Please, Dunc...where is she?" In a split second he became a vital being again. He was bursting with life and energy, demanding that I tell him.

I laughed and told him to let me get a word in and I would. The silence was ominous then. "She's not very far from here, Walter, in a small hotel right off Fifth Avenue." I gave him the address and had hardly finished when I heard his phone slam against the desk. He was in such a hurry he hadn't bothered to hang up...

Duncan stopped and drained his glass, then stared at it remorsefully. The Inspector coughed lightly to attract his attention, his curiosity prompting him to speak. "He found her?" he asked eagerly.

"Oh yes, he found her. He burst right in over all protests, expecting to sweep her off her feet."

This time the Inspector fidgeted nervously. "Well, go on."

Duncan motioned for the waiter and lifted a fresh glass in a toast. The Inspector did the same. Duncan smiled gently. "When she saw him she laughed and waved. Walter Harrison died an hour later...from a window in the same hotel."

It was too much for the Inspector. He leaned forward in his chair, his forehead knotted in a frown. "But what happened? Who was she? Damn it, Duncan..."

Duncan took a deep breath, then gulped the drink down.

"Evelyn Vaughn was a hopeless imbecile," he said.

"She had the beauty of a goddess and the mentality of a two-year-old. They kept her well tended and dressed so she wouldn't be an object of curiosity. But the only habit she ever learned was to wave bye-bye..."

The Pickpocket

The Pickpocket

WILLIE CAME into the bar smiling. He couldn't understand why he did it, but he did it anyway. Ever since the day he had married Sally and had stopped in for a bottle of beer to bring home for his wedding supper, he had come in smiling. Sally, he thought, three years with Sally, and now there was little Bill and a brother or maybe a sister on the way.

The bartender waved, and Willie said, "Hello, Barney." A beer came up and he pushed a quarter out, looking at himself in the big mirror behind the wall. He wasn't very big, and he was far from good looking. Just an ordinary guy, a little on the small side. He was respectable now. A real law-abiding citizen. Meeting Sally had done that.

He remembered the day three winters ago when he'd tried to lift a wallet from a guy's pocket. Hunger and cold had made his hand shake and the guy had collared him. He was almost glad to be run into the station house where it was warm. But the guy must have known that, too, and refused to press any charges. So he got kicked out in the cold again. That was where Sally had found him.

He remembered the taxi, and Sally and the driver half-carrying him into her tiny apartment. The smell of the hot soup did more to revive him than anything else. She didn't ask any questions, but he told her nevertheless. He was a pickpocket. A skinny little mug who had lived by his hands ever since he was a kid. She'd told him, right away, that it didn't matter.

He had eaten her food and slept on her couch for a week before he got smart. Then he did something he had never done before in his life. He got a job. It wasn't much at first, just sweeping up in a loft where they made radio parts. Slowly he found out he had hands that could do better things than push a broom. The boss found it out, too, when he discovered Willie assembling sections in half the time that it took a skilled mechanic to do it. They gave the broom to someone else.

Only then did he ask Sally to marry him. She gave up her job at the department store and they settled down to a regular married life. The funny part was that he liked it.

The cops never gave up, though. As regularly as clockwork they came around. A real friendly visit, understand? But they came around. The first of the month Detective Coggins would walk in right after supper, talk a while, looking at him with those cynical, cold blue eyes, then leave. That part worried Willie—not for himself, but for little Bill. It wouldn't be long now before he'd be in school, and the other kids...they'd take it out on him. Your old man was a crook...a pickpocket...yeah, then why do the coppers come around all the time? Willie drained his beer quickly. Sally was waiting supper for him.

He had almost reached the door when he heard the shots. The black sedan shot past as he stepped outside and for one awful instant he saw a face. Black eyebrows... the sneer...the scar on the cheek. The face of a guy he had known three years ago. And the guy had seen him, too. In his mind, Willie ran. He ran faster than he had ever run in his life—but his legs didn't run. They carried him homeward as the self-respecting should walk, but his mind ran.

Three years wasn't so long after all.

As soon as he came in Sally knew something was wrong. She said, "What happened?" Willie couldn't answer. "Your job..." she said hesitantly. Willie shook his head.

It was the hurt look that made his lips move. "Somebody got shot up the street," he told her. "I don't know who it was, but I know who did it."

"Did anyone else..."

"No, just me. I think I was the only one."

He could tell Sally was almost afraid to ask the next question. Finally, she said: "Did they see you?"

"Yes. He knows me."

"Oh, Willie!" Her voice was muffled with despair. They stood in silence, not knowing what to say, not daring to say anything. But both had the same thoughts. Run. Get out of town. Somebody was dead and it wouldn't hurt to kill a couple more to cover the first.

Sally said: "... The cops. Should we..."

"I don't dare. They wouldn't believe me. My word wouldn't be any good anyway."

It came then, the sharp rap on the door. Willie leaped to his feet and ran, reaching for the key in the lock. He was a second too late. The door was tried and pushed open. The guy that came in was big. He filled the door from jamb to jamb with the bulk of his body. He grabbed Willie by the shirt and held him tight in his huge hands.

"Hello, shrimp," he said.

Willie punched him. It was as hard as he could hit, but it didn't do a bit of good. The guy snarled: "Cut it out before I break your skinny neck!" Behind him he closed the door softly. Sally stood with the back of her hand to her mouth, tense, motionless.

With a rough shove the big guy sent Willie staggering into the table, his thick lips curling into a tight sneer. "Didn't expect somebody so soon, did you, Willie? Too bad you're not smart. Marty doesn't waste any time. Not with dopes that see too much. You know, Marty's a lucky guy. The only one that spots the shooting turns out to be a punk he can put the finger on right away. Anybody else would be down at headquarters picking out his picture right now."

His hand went inside his coat and came out with a .45 automatic. "I always said Marty was lucky."

The big guy didn't level the gun. He just swung it until it covered Willie's stomach. Sally drew in her breath to scream quickly, just once, before she died.

But before the scream came Willie gave a little laugh and said: "You won't shoot me with that gun, Buster."

Time stood still. Willie laughed again. "I slipped out the magazine when you grabbed me." The big guy cursed. His finger curled under the butt and felt the empty space there. Willie was very calm now. "And I don't think you've got a shell in the chamber, either."

The big guy took one step, reaching for Willie, a vicious curse on his lips; then the sugar bowl left Sally's hand and took him on the forehead. He went down.

Willie didn't hesitate this time. He picked up the phone and called the station house. He asked for Detective Coggins. In three minutes the cop with the cold blue eyes was there, listening to Willie's story. The big guy went out with cuffs on. Willie said: "Coggins..."

"Yes?"

"When the trial comes up...you can count on me to testify. They won't scare me off."

The detective smiled, and for the first time the ice left those cold blue eyes. "I know you will, Willie." He paused. "And Willie...about those visits of mine...I'd like to come up and see you. I think we could be good friends. But I'd like to have you ask me first."

A grin covered Willie's face. "Sure! Come up...anytime at all! Let's say next Saturday night. Bring the missus!"

The detective waved and left. As he closed the door Willie could imagine the chant of young voices. They were saying:

"Yeah...and you better not get funny with Bill because his pop is friends with that cop. Sure, they're all the time playing cards and..."

Willie laughed. "Sometimes," he said, "I'm almost glad that I had some experience. Finally came in handy!"

I'll Die Tomorrow

I'll Die Tomorrow

THE FRIENDLY-LOOKING gentleman in the neat charcoal gray suit was a killer. But like any good predator, his disguise was excellent. To all appearances, he was a moderately successful businessman with offices, perhaps, high in a Manhattan building, where the street fumes and noises didn't reach.

Offhand, you would guess his age in the late forties, and if asked to describe him, could do little more than say he was, well, average. No, there was nothing suspicious in his walk or talk or behavior and if you had any reason to trust anyone it would be this gentleman. Why, he even looked happy.

And with all of that, his disguise *was* perfect, simply because it was not an artificial disguise at all. It was real. He did have an office, although not in Manhattan, and he was happy. Rudolph Less was a man well satisfied with life, especially when he was working, and now he was on a job again.

Upstairs was a man he was going to kill and the going price on his demise was to be 10,000 lovely dollars that would go toward supporting his single secret pastime in his converted summer house on the Island. He smiled at the thought, feeling a tiny, vicarious thrill touch his parts. Women, he thought, could be taught…or even forced…to do such wonderful things.

Yes, life was fine. Only the select few knew of his true

nature and of his niche in life. Through these few, others could come by his services—and many had.

How many now? Was it 46 times? Or 48? Sometimes it was difficult to recall. Once he had kept track, but as in all other businesses, tabulating inventory became boring. Now it was better simply to look ahead.

It was a good business and of all those engaged in it, he was the best. No doubt of it. (He smiled at the doorman who smiled back, but the smile was only a gesture.) He was thinking of the many times he had read the accounts in the papers of his work. Always, the police were puzzled, or another was taken in custody. He chuckled when he thought of the three who had already died in the chair mistakenly. Wouldn't *that* shake up the administration if it ever came out! But they were only punks and the error of their death was really a boon to society, doing earlier what would have happened later anyway.

Things like that only added to his business reputation, though. It had paid off, really it had. He thought again of Theresa of the dark flesh and darker hair who had loved those things he had done to her. She really had. She had done things to him that in his frenzy of wild emotion he couldn't even recall. He could only remember the terrible pleasure of the experience. Well, he could get Theresa again now.

That's what being the best meant. They hired him because he never failed. For a brief second his face clouded as if he were angry with himself, then he shook his head dismissing the thought because it couldn't be.

It was too bad, he thought, that he hadn't checked further, but experience wasn't on his side then. He had cleared out too soon. He wasn't absolutely certain. He smiled again, tentatively. But they had paid him, so everything must have gone all right.

He couldn't help but think about it and try to recall the details merely to satisfy his desire for perfection. It had been his first contract, and a simple one. A kid called Buddy ...he couldn't remember his last name, but he had a dime-size hole through his right ear that was supposed to be from a stray .45 bullet during the war. Buddy had hijacked seventeen grand from the paymaster to the Jersey City group and rather than remain a laughingstock to their pseudo-dignity, Buddy had to go, but with no apparent connection to the group, of course.

It hadn't been difficult. Buddy was a talkative guy so he simply engaged him in conversation, walked him close to the water, enjoyed the final moment of conversation by telling Buddy who he was and what he was about to do and while Buddy stood dumfounded, with his mouth open and a light from the opposite shore visible through the hole in his ear, he chest-shot him and watched the body smash back into the water.

If only they had found the remains he could be satisfied. However, the river was running fast, it *had* been blowing up a storm, and the ocean was close by. Buddy (what *was* his last name?) never showed up, not even to reclaim the bundle of money he had left behind in his room. At the thought Rudolph Less breathed deeply and smiled, satisfied that his record was perfect. Yes, a good record. Big Tim Sheely of Detroit and the western Senator and Marco Leppert who was a Mafia courier were on that list. He chuckled again. How the Mafia had searched for him! They killed four men thinking they had the right one each time and he was never even suspected. After their last failure it was the Mafia itself who gave him the job of axman to rid the organization of their own killers who blundered.

That job got him Joan, he remembered. Such a woman, such a hungry, hungry woman. She was so big all over. So big, so big. Everything so big. Yes, he would have Joan again too. Perhaps even Theresa and Joan together. Who knew what he could do then. It might be bad for his constitution, but he was in good health yet, he thought wryly. There were still some things to be experienced that he could stand.

He had no need to look at the wall directory before going into the elevator. He was part of the crowd now, seen, yet unnoticed. He coughed gently from the smoke of the cigar in the mouth of the man next to him but said nothing. Instead, he thought suddenly, *I'd like to kill him!*

Like Lew Smith who stood right in front of him in the back of the darkened theater and never felt the ice pick slide into his heart. He simply collapsed and they carried him out thinking that he had fainted, and no one saw Rudolph leave at all. Lew smelled of cigar smoke too. And Lew had bought him Francie who would make him sit back and watch while she did the damnedest dance he ever did see until his eyes were bugging out and he could hardly breathe and when by the time she let him get his hands on her he had lost almost all his senses and had to be slapped back to normal. But Francie had smiled then and loved what he had done to her although she pouted a while over his bite marks.

He was breathing too heavily, and down the neck of the woman in front of him. She almost turned around, when he caught himself and forced his breath to come easier.

It was because he was getting close to his business arrangement again. It was like that lately. He tasted the fruits of success before the actual planting. But the conclusion was foregone anyway. Success was not problematical any longer. It was a certainty. That was why he could ask for so much to do so little.

Sometimes he wondered about those who lingered a few moments. What did they think? Who was he? What had they done to him that he should snuff out their lives? Oh, there were those who knew. He remembered that two even seemed relieved. For years they had lived in fear of this day and now it had come. There was no more fear for them. Actuality had arrived as a medium-sized man with a friendly smile and it was over very quickly without much pain at all because he was an expert at his work. He was quite sure that one man even whispered a quiet "Thank you" before he died.

Well, that was one thing about his method. There was no flight involved, no loud histrionics. They didn't know him, there was nothing fearful about his appearance and if anything registered at all, generally it was surprise.

Someday, maybe, he thought he might like to change his method. If he could get his assignment in the proper place he would like to try a few experiments. Like extensions of the things he had done with Lulu who had some savage blood and liked to be beaten in certain ways. Pain peculiarly inflicted with her fullest cooperation was her delight and she had taught him things his mind had begun to dwell on lately. He shrugged off the thought impatiently and looked up at the indicator over the operator's head. The car had stopped and the doors opened.

Sixteen.

He remembered *his* number 16.

She was a showgirl named Cindy Valentine who knew too much about the operations of another group through an already dead boyfriend. The District Attorney had her secretly marked for investigation, but money, being able to buy anything, bought the tip and now Cindy was being canceled out.

Cindy Valentine, number 16, had been somewhat of a pleasure. In fact, it had been Cindy who had showed him the ultimate use to which he could put the many dollars he had accumulated. So far he merely rented an office from which he sold, and profitably, trinkets and novelties via pages of certain magazines. One employee really did all the work but it gave him a sense of wellbeing, a place in society. Daily, he commuted from his house. It wasn't much, but it was secluded. There was nothing he couldn't do there at his pleasure and he was so situated that there were no prying eyes at all. To the world outside, he lived a simple and secluded life. Sort of a friendly recluse, he thought.

Yes, Cindy had brought new meaning into his life. He had called ahead and said he was a jeweler who was instructed to let Miss Valentine have a single pick from his collection. She had been overjoyed at the thought and although she tried to cajole the name of his sponsor from him, he said he was sworn not to tell. Hers was a secret admirer. No doubt she had had many. She believed everything he told her. She squealed with delight when she admitted him to her apartment, seeing the flat sample case under his arm.

At first she didn't notice the flush in his face. She was too excited, then, in the living room, she saw his consternation and smiled. The filmy nylon negligee was all Cindy had on. Her smile grew impish and she had said, "Since you're going to give me something, I'm going to give you something." Then she let the negligee fall to the floor and when she was done he was a shaken but strangely elated man. She said, "Now you give me something," and looked at the case on the table. Well, he gave her something, all right. Very quickly and there was hardly any blood and he picked up his case and went out. They all called it a passion kill and in a way it had been.

Cindy certainly had introduced something new to his life. Now, rather than merely having the satisfaction of a job well done, he had an end result that was far greater than anything he had ever dreamed of. The satisfaction he would get tonight would be far greater than the satisfaction of job perfection he used to consider enough. Perfection was quite a word. It gnawed at him like a little mouse. If only he could have been sure of that first one. Buddy, the one with the hole in his ear.

Well, the one upstairs would merely add to his list of accomplishments. This was a curious one. Different insofar as he never had time to study the man. He would be alone in his office counting the weekly take, a secret office he used solely for bookkeeping and accounting purposes. He rented it under an assumed name and made a deliberate point to go there disguised. His operation was illegal and deftly concealed. Only after long and arduous investigation did Rudolph Less's client discover his whereabouts. Since his connection with the dead man would be obvious, it was necessary for his client to have an airtight alibi at the time of the kill, making Rudolph's talents necessary.

Ordinarily he wouldn't have gone for the second part of the arrangement, but lately he was beginning to enjoy new facets of an old thrill. The client said he could keep whatever money he found there in addition to his regular pay. Thousands extra! Enough to buy...well, if that man was right about that one down in Cuba he could bring her here at once. Complete muscular control, he had said. Think of it! He swallowed hard and dimmed the mental picture. Not yet. Later he could sit in his room savoring the anticipation when the job was done, but first the job.

He got out at 20 with two others but before the doors shut a giddy young girl ran up and grabbed his sleeve and said too loudly, "Mr. Brisson? Are you Mr. Brisson...they just called from downstairs and said..."

"I'm not Mr. Brisson," he smiled. Inwardly he swore, something he hadn't done in years. He saw the elevator boy grinning at the girl's stammer of embarrassment before the doors closed. An incident like that could cause that boy to remember his face. But nevertheless, he'd never be back again, never see the boy again, and if he described anyone at all, or did the girl, it would be the average man of the street.

The girl walked off, her buttocks in violent motion. Ordinarily he would feel a warm glow at such a sight, but the momentary pleasure of another sort ahead that could be completely consummated overrode such a simple delight of watching a girl from behind.

Yet the sight introduced a new thought, something that had been on his mind for months now, something that touched him whenever he saw a young and pretty girl on the street. So far he had bought his pleasures. Oh, they had been expensive, but worth every bit of it. But the thrills and sensations they provided finally reached a limit. Repetition turned original wonders into almost commonplace boredom and it was getting more difficult all the time to find something *really* different.

There *was* one thing. Supposing, and it shouldn't be difficult, that he could lure some unsuspecting girl...on the promise of a job, perhaps...or really, if one was honest about it, by actual force...that would take a car, maybe drugs; there would be untold risks but that would only add to the delicacy...yes, it was something to think about. Maybe after the one from Cuba. He would like to experience one with complete muscular control first.

Annoyed at himself he stopped and adjusted his coat, although there was no one in the corridor to see him. He held the leather folio more securely under his arm, feeling in it the flat contours of the Browning and the extended length of the silencer he had gotten from that odd man in Germany. Silencers were fine. Why didn't they fight wars with silencers? It shouldn't be expensive and think of how quietly and efficiently the war could be fought. Ah, the advantage of the bow and arrow. Too bad it was such a clumsy weapon.

He stopped at the door marked *STAR DISTRIBUTING*, smiled to himself and fitted the key he had been given into the lock. It opened easily and he stepped inside. As the diagram showed, he was in a small anteroom, and facing him was the lighted square of a frosted glass door. That had no lock. Rudolph Less smiled again.

He heard someone cough and nodded to himself. Feet shuffled and a chair scraped back. He heard a phone picked up and dialed and held his position. He could not enter while the phone was on. There was no need for someone else giving an alarm. The way it was, if done right, the body wouldn't be found until it started to stink and that would be several days. No, he could wait a minute.

Inside, his assignment said, "You got everything ready for tonight...yeah...yeah ...okay, I'll call you. I'm going to make up the payroll now. Sure...sure...so long." The phone clicked and the man coughed again.

Rudolph said softly, "Now," and opened the door.

He smiled at his assignment.

His assignment looked startled, then frowned uncompre-hendingly at the Browning with the silencer pointing at his chest. He was a big man, thick through the chest and neck, his hair gray at the sides. He was well dressed and from first glance Rudolph wouldn't have taken him for someone in the rackets. But appearances were deceiving, weren't they? Who would take *him* for an *eliminator?* Now that was a good word.

The man said, "What do you want?"

Rudolph's eyes took him in quickly. He was big, all right. Most likely it would take more than one shot. Two quick body hits to stop him if he tried to move, then a head shot to complete the job. One thing about a silencer, you could hear the bullets hit too. Not so much in the stomach, of course, but if they went through a rib or in the skull...

"What I want is your money," Rudolph said. It sounded peculiar to him. Shoddy, somehow. "Where is it?"

"In the safe, that's where, and if you expect..."

"If I don't get it I'll kill you anyway," Rudolph told him.

There was no mistaking the tone of his voice. The big

guy nodded, was about to say something and stopped. He walked across the room to the safe and dragged out a small, obviously heavy, steel box. Rudolph saw the combination lock on it and waved the gun to the desk. He surely couldn't carry the box out of here. "Open it," he said.

The guy sat down and began spinning the dial. Outside there was a burst of laughter and a key rattled the lock. The door opened and two girls laughed again. A male voice joined theirs.

Rudolph's heart jumped, but then quieted. He had been in situations like this before. He put the gun into the folio, keeping his hand on it and casually sat down. The door to the office opened and a girl said, "Mr. Riley, your friend Mr. Brisson is here. Do you want..." She glanced around the door and saw Rudolph. "Oh," she giggled, "I'm sorry. I didn't know you had company. I thought this man was Mr. Brisson before."

"That's all right," Mr. Riley told her. "I'll be out shortly."

The girl giggled again and closed the door. Outside several more people came in and typewriters began to rattle. Two men were discussing a sales meeting.

Rudolph could feel the dryness of his skin, but still he could smell sweat. Sweat? Or was it fear? Someplace something had gone wrong. This was supposed to be an empty office. Just one man. Damn! Why didn't he do the job the way he had done all the others. That's what happens when you leave the details up to somebody else. Damn it all to hell! But you wouldn't know that was what Rudolph Less was thinking because he was smiling in a very friendly fashion.

The big man said softly, "You're in trouble, friend," and as he said it opened the lid of the box. The money was there as it was supposed to be. Packets of hundreds and Riley was dumping it out on the desk. He looked across the room at his smiling visitor. "You can't get out very well and pretty soon somebody will be coming in here. If you do get out you won't be a hard one to identify. Those girls out there are all artists and could sketch you to perfection. Show it to the papers and you'd be turned in in no time."

"That is problematical," Rudolph said.

"You picked a lousy time for a stickup, mister."

Rudolph smiled again. "Yes, I did." The smile didn't last long because Riley was smiling too.

He said, "Buddy, if I could get the jump on you, you'd be in a mess."

"Oh?" His teeth flashed and he lifted the Browning out of the folio.

"You had a key to this place, you came on a day when the payroll was being made up and you came armed. A planned stickup. I kill you..." he shrugged..."one day in court is all. Self-defense."

"That could hardly happen," Rudolph said. For some reason he felt edgy. Events weren't at all like they should be. His assignment, a better word than victim, was being too aggressive. What had to be done had to be done quickly and his mind raced over the possibilities. Several were available to him. He would take the money, of course. He would tell them outside that Mr. Riley would be busy all day and not to disturb him. He'd hate to leave his house, especially his paraphernalia he had so carefully assembled, but he lived there under a fictitious name and he could do it over again, perhaps this time with certain innovations he desired. Suntan, hair dye, whiskers in any number of combinations could alter his appearance sufficiently. No it wouldn't be an insurmountable problem at all.

He was so engrossed in his thoughts, that although his eyes were on Riley, the big man's voice came to him as a steady drone.

"...it took so long to find you. You're mighty clever, I guess you know. Proof for a court of law would be impossible to obtain. And me, I don't want to stick my neck out. I'm not going to kill somebody who needs killing bad then pay for it myself. I'm a little on the smart side too.

"But contacts I made. Finally the right guy put me through. In returning a big favor I did him he put me in touch with you. We made the arrangements together, you and I. Clever, eh?"

The big guy smiled and sucked in his breath. He was too big, Rudolph thought. Maybe even two chest hits wouldn't do it. He carried five in the Browning so what he'd have to do was give him four in the chest quickly and then hold the last one for the coup. Nobody could take four. The smashing impact in the lungs even prevents a yell and the only sound would be the body falling. However, the noise outside would cover that up.

Somehow the droning voice made sense. His mind, charged now to frenzied activity, raced back over the words, picked them up and went over them again. There was something here now that shouldn't be at all. Something terrible if he heard right. The smile seemed frozen on his face now and for the first time his eyes made a little rat's movement around the room.

"I hired you to kill me," Riley said. "I never knew who you were or where you were and I finally figured out the only way to have you in front of me so you could die where I can see it happen without any heat coming my way at all."

Rudolph's voice was strained. "You can't!"

"I have, pal, I have. But first let me tell you thanks. I have a nice straight business going for me and there won't be any heat. In fact, I'll be a hero. How about that?"

He felt cold. He had never felt so cold as now. There was no spit in his mouth and his insides were rolling. Had he eaten earlier he was sure he would have vomited at that moment. For some reason he could hear the voices of Cindy and Lulu and Francie and Joan and all those others and far away mocking him with a Cuban accent the untasted one he hungered after, and somewhere from a deep invisible fog came the scared bleatings of the ones he would have had by cajolery or by force if necessary.

Would have had! Not at all! Not at all, Mr. Riley. "You forgot something, Mr. Riley," Rudolph said, bringing the Browning into line with his chest. "I have the gun."

"And I have one in this box under my hand, friend. A big fat .45 automatic for which I have a license."

Rudolph nodded sagely. "The moment you move your hand toward it I'll shoot you," he said softly.

"Fair enough," Riley said.

Rudolph was on his feet. What was the matter with this man? Was he mad! Then his hand moved and Rudolph pulled the trigger. The Browning jumped once...twice...three times...four...he could see the shots hitting his chest right in the heart area. Go down, damn you, go down! He had to go down. The big guy had the .45 out of the box when Rudolph Less pulled the trigger on the last shot and saw it rip into his arm, but it was the wrong arm. The other one had the .45. And he was grinning, damn him!

He looked at the blood pumping from his arm. "This makes it all the better," he said, then laughed again and ripped open his shirt.

With mouth agape, Rudolph saw the overlapping plates of the bulletproof vest. Riley brought the gun up and pointed it at his head.

Rudolph was old looking now, sallow, his cheeks sunken in fear. His invincibility shattered for no reason, no reason at all. All those wonderful pleasures gone, gone, because this big fool in front of him had tricked him. Where had he made his mistake? It had to be somewhere. Where then?

He said, "Why?" His voice was weak, faltering.

Riley lifted a hand to his ear and felt for the piece of cosmetic wax that fitted so cleverly. Then he squeezed the trigger of the .45.

In the awful blast of the gun that Rudolph could still hear while his skull was shattering into tiny bits his last remembrance was that the round hole in the nose of his final lover, the terrible .45, was exactly the same size as the one in the big guy's ear and that Riley's first name had to be Buddy.

Everybody's Watching Me

Everybody's Watching Me

I HANDED the guy the note and shivered a little bit because the guy was as big as they come, and even though he had a belly you couldn't get your arms around, you wouldn't want to be the one who figured you could sink your fist in it. The belly was as hard as the rest of him, but not quite as hard as his face.

Then I knew how hard the back of his hand was because he smashed it across my jaw and I could taste the blood where my teeth bit into my cheek.

Maybe the guy holding my arm knew I couldn't talk because he said, "A guy give him a fin to bring it, boss. He said that."

"Who, kid?"

I spit the blood out easy so it dribbled down my chin instead of going on the floor. "Gee, Mr. Renzo . . ."

His hand made a dull, soggy crack on my skin. The buzz got louder in my ears and there was a jagged, pounding pain in my skull.

"Maybe you didn't hear me the first time, kid. I said who."

The hand let go my arm and I slumped to the floor. I didn't want to, but I had to. There were no legs under me any more. My eyes were open, conscious of only the movement of ponderous things that got closer. Things that moved quickly and seemed to dent my side without causing any feeling at all.

That other voice said, "He's out, boss. He ain't saying a thing."

"I'll make him talk."

"Won't help none. So a guy gives him a fin to bring the note. He's not going into a song and dance with it. To the kid a fin's a lot of dough. He watches the fin, not the guy."

"You're getting too damn bright," Renzo said.

"That's what you pay me for being, boss."

"Then act bright. You think a guy hands a note like this to some kid? Any kid at all? You think a kid's gonna bull in here to deliver it when he can chuck it down a drain and take off with the fin?"

"So the kid's got morals."

"So the kid knows the guy or the guy knows him. He ain't letting no kid get away with his fin." The feet moved away from me, propped themselves against the dark blur of the desk. "You read this thing?" Renzo asked.

"No."

"Listen then. 'Cooley is dead. Now my fine fat louse, I'm going to spill your guts all over your own floor.'" Renzo's voice droned to a stop. He sucked hard on the cigar and said, "It's signed, *Vetter.*"

You could hear the unspoken words in the silence. That hush that comes when the name was mentioned and the other's half-whispered "Son of a bitch, they were buddies, boss?"

"Who cares? If that crumb shows his face around here, I'll break his lousy back. Vetter, Vetter, Vetter. Everyplace you go that crumb's name you hear."

"Boss, look. You don't want to tangle with that guy. He's killed plenty of guys. He's . . ."

"He's different from me? You think he's a hard guy?"

"You ask around, boss. They'll tell you. That guy don't give a damn for nobody. He'll kill you for looking at him."

"Maybe in his own back yard he will. Not here, Johnny, not here. This is my city and my back yard. Here things go my way and Vetter'll get what Cooley got." He sucked on the cigar again and I began to smell the smoke. "Guys what pull a fastie on me get killed. Now Cooley don't work on my tables for no more smart plays. Pretty soon the cops can take Vetter off their list because he won't be around no more either."

"You going to take him, boss?" Johnny said.

"What do you think?"

"Anything you say, boss. I'll pass the word around. Somebody'll know what he looks like and'll finger him." He paused, then, "What about the kid?"

"He's our finger, Johnny."

"Him?"

"You ain't so bright as I thought. You should get your ears to the ground more. You should hear things about Vetter. He pays off for favors. The errand was worth a fin, but he's gonna look in to make sure the letter got here. Then he spots the kid for his busted up face. First time he makes contact we got him. You know what, Johnnie? To Vetter I'm going to do things slow. When they find him the cops get all excited but they don't do nothing. They're glad to see Vetter dead. But other places the word gets around, see? Anybody can bump Vetter gets to be pretty big and nobody pulls any more smart ones. You understand, Johnny?"

"Sure, boss. I get it. You're going to do it yourself?"

"Just me, kid, just me. Like Helen says, I got a passion to do something myself and I just got to do it. Vetter's for me. He better be plenty big, plenty fast and ready to start shooting the second we meet up."

It was like when Pop used to say he'd do something and we knew he'd do it sure. You look at him with your face showing the awe a kid gets when he knows fear and respect at the same time and that's how Johnny must have been looking at Renzo. I knew it because it was in his voice when he said, "You'll do it, boss. You'll own this town, lock, stock and gun butt yet."

"I own it now, Johnny. Never forget it. Now wake that kid up."

This time I had feeling and it hurt. The hand that slapped the full vision back to my eyes started the blood running in my mouth again and I could feel my lungs choking on a sob.

"What was he like, kid?" The hand came down again and this time Renzo took a step forward. His fingers grabbed my coat and jerked me to the floor.

"You got asked a question. What was he like?"

"He was . . . big," I said. The damn slob choked me again and I wanted to break something over his head.

"How big?"

"Like you. Bigger'n six. Heavy."

Renzo's mouth twisted into a sneer and he grinned at me. "More. What was his face like?"

"I don't know. It was dark. I couldn't see him good."

He threw me. Right across the room he threw me and my back smashed the wall and twisted and I could feel the tears rolling down my face from the pain.

"You don't lie to Renzo, kid. If you was older and bigger I'd break you up into little pieces until you talked. It ain't worth a fin. Now you start telling me what I want to hear and maybe I'll slip you something."

"I . . . I don't know. Honest, I . . . if I saw him again it'd be different." The pain caught me again and I had to gag back my voice.

"You'd know him again?"

"Yes."

Johnny said, "What's your name, kid?"

"Joe. . .Boyle."

"Where do you live?" It was Renzo this time.

"Gidney Street," I told him. "Number three."

"You work?"

"Gordon's. I . . . push."

"What'd he say?" Renzo's voice had a nasty tone to it.

"Gordon's a junkie," Johnny said for me. "Has a place on River Street. The kid pushes a cart for him collecting metal scraps."

"Check on it," Renzo said, "then stick with him. You know what to do."

"He won't get away, boss. He'll be around whenever we want him. You think Vetter will do what you say?"

"Don't things always happen like I say? Now get him out of here. Go over him again so he'll know we mean what we say. That was a lousy fin he worked for."

After things hurt so much they begin to stop hurting completely. I could feel the way I went through the air, knew my foot hit the railing and could taste the cinders that ground in my mouth. I lay there like I was passing out, waiting for the pain to come swelling back, making sounds I didn't want to make. My stomach wanted to break loose but couldn't find the strength and I just lay there cursing guys like Renzo who could do anything they wanted and get away with it.

Then the darkness came, went away briefly and came back again. When it lost itself in the dawn of agony there were hands brushing the dirt from my face and the smell of flowers from the softness that was a woman who held me and said, "You poor kid, you poor kid."

My eyes opened and looked at her. It was like something you dream about because she was the kind of woman you always stare at, knowing you can't have. She was beautiful, with yellow hair that tumbled down her neck like a torch that lit up her whole body. Her name was Helen Troy and I wanted to say, "Hello, Helen," but couldn't get the words out of my mouth.

Know her? Sure, everybody knew her. She was Renzo's feature attraction at his Hideaway Club. But I never thought I'd live to have my head in her lap.

There were feet coming up the path that turned into one of the men from the stop at the gate and Helen said, "Give me a hand, Finney. Something happened to the kid."

The guy she called Finney stood there with his hands on his hips shaking his head. "Something'll happen to you if you don't leave him be. The boss gives orders."

She tightened up all over, her fingers biting into my shoulder. It hurt but I didn't care a bit. "Renzo? The pig!" She spat it out with a hiss. She turned her head slowly and looked at me. "Did he do this, kid?"

I nodded. It was all I could do.

"Finney," she said, "go get my car. I'm taking the kid to a doctor."

"Helen, I'm telling you . . ."

"Suppose I told the cops . . . no, not the cops, the feds in this town that you have holes in your arms?"

I thought Finney was going to smack her. He reached down with his hand back but he stopped. When a dame looks at you that way you don't do anything except what she tells you to.

"I'll get the car," he said.

She got me on my feet and I had to lean on her to stay there. She was just as big as I was. Stronger at the moment. Faces as bad off as mine weren't new to her, so she smiled and I tried to smile back and we started off down the path.

We said it was a fight and the doctor did what he had to do. He laid on the tape and told me to rest a week then come back. I saw my face in his mirror, shuddered and turned away. No matter what I did I hurt all over and when I thought of Renzo all I could think of was that I hoped somebody would kill him. I hoped they'd kill him while I watched and I hoped it would take a long, long time for him to die.

Helen got me out to the car, closed the door after me and slid in behind the wheel. I told her where I lived and she drove up to the house. The garbage cans had been spilled all over the sidewalk and it stank.

She looked at me curiously. "Here?"

"That's right," I told her. "Thanks for everything."

Then she saw the sign on the door. It read, "rooms."
"Your family live here too?"

"I don't have a family. It's a rooming house."

For a second I saw her teeth, white and even, as she pulled her mouth tight. "I can't leave you here. Somebody has to look after you."

"Lady, if . . ."

"Ease off, kid. What did you say your name was?"

"Joe."

"Okay, Joe. Let me do things my way. I'm not much good for anything but every once in awhile I come in handy for something decent."

"Gee, lady . . ."

"Helen."

"Well, you're the nicest person I've ever known."

I said she was beautiful. She had the beauty of the flashiest tramp you could find. That kind of beauty. She was like the dames in the big shows who are always tall and sleepy looking and who you'd always look at but wouldn't marry or take home to your folks. That's the kind of beauty she had. But for a long couple of seconds she seemed to grow a new kind of beauty that was entirely different and she smiled at me.

"Joe . . ." and her voice was warm and husky, "that's the nicest thing said in the nicest way I've heard in a very long time."

My mouth still hurt too much to smile back so I did it with my eyes. Then something happened to her face. It got all strange and curious, a little bit puzzled and she leaned forward and I could smell the flowers again as that impossible something happened when she barely touched her mouth to mine before drawing back with that searching movement of her eyes.

"You're a funny kid, Joe."

She shoved the car in to gear and let it roll away from the curb. I tried to sit upright, my hand on the door latch. "Look, I got to get out."

"I can't leave you here."

"Then where . . ."

"You're going back to my place. Damn it, Renzo did this to you and I feel partly responsible."

"That's all right. You only work for him."

"It doesn't matter. You can't stay there."

"You're going to get in trouble, Helen."

She turned and flashed me a smile. "I'm always in trouble."

"Not with him."

"I can handle that guy."

She must have felt the shudder that went through me.

"You'd be surprised how I can handle that fat slob," she said. Then added in an undertone I wasn't supposed to hear, "Sometimes."

It was a place that belonged to her like flowers belong in a rock garden. It was the top floor of an apartment hotel where the wheels all stayed in the best part of town with a private lawn twelve stories up where you could look out over the city and watch the lights wink back at you.

She made me take all my clothes off and while I soaked in a warm bath full of suds she scrounged up a decent suit that was a size too big, but still the cleanest thing I had worn in a long while. I put it on and came out in the living room feeling good and sat down in the big chair while she brought in tea.

Helen of Troy, I thought. So this is what she looked like. Somebody it would take a million bucks and a million years to get close to . . . and here I was with nothing in no time at all.

"Feel better, Joe?"

"A little."

"Want to talk? You don't have to if you don't want to."

"There's not much to say. He worked me over."

"How old are you, Joe?"

I didn't want to go too high. "Twenty-one," I said.

There it was again, that same curious expression. I was glad of the bandages across my face so she couldn't be sure if I was lying or not.

I said, "How old are you?" and grinned at her.

"Almost thirty, Joe. That's pretty old, isn't it?"

"Not so old."

She sipped at the tea in her hand. "How did you happen to cross Renzo?"

It hurt to think about it. "Tonight," I said, "it had just gotten dark. A guy asked me if I'd run a message to somebody for five bucks and I said I would. It was for Mr. Renzo and he told me to take it to the Hideaway Club. At first the guy at the gate wouldn't let me in, then he called down that other one, Johnny. He took me in, all right."

"Yes?"

"Renzo started giving it to me."

"Remember what the message said?"

Remember? I'd never forget it. I'd hope from now until I died that the guy who wrote it did everything he said he'd do.

"Somebody called Vetter said he'd kill Renzo," I told her.

Her smile was distant, hard. "He'll have to be a pretty tough guy," she said. What she said next was almost under her breath and she was staring into the night when she said it. "A guy like that I could go for."

"What?"

"Nothing, Joe." The hardness left her smile until she was a soft thing. "What else happened?"

Inside my chest my heart beat so fast it felt like it was going to smash my ribs loose. "I . . . heard them say . . . I would have to finger the man for them."

"You?"

I nodded, my hand feeling the soreness across my jaw.

She stood up slowly, the way a cat would. She was all mad and tense but you couldn't tell unless you saw her eyes. They were the same eyes that made the Finney guy jump. "Vetter," she said. "I've heard the name before."

"The note said something about a guy named Cooley who's dead."

I was watching her back and I saw the shock of the name make the muscles across her shoulders dance in the light. The tightness went down her body until she stood there stiff-legged, the flowing curves of her chest the only things that moved at all.

"Vetter," she said. "He was Cooley's friend."

"You knew Cooley?"

Her shoulders relaxed and she picked a cigarette out of a box and lit it. She turned around, smiling, the beauty I had seen in the car there again.

"Yes," Helen said softly, "I knew Cooley."

"Gee."

She wasn't talking to me anymore. She was speaking to somebody who wasn't there and each word stabbed her deeper until her eyes were wet. "I knew Cooley very well. He was . . . nice. He was a big man, broad in the shoulders with hands that could squeeze a woman . . ." She paused and took a slow pull on the cigarette. "His voice could make you laugh or cry. Sometimes both. He was an engineer with a quick mind. He figured how he could make money from Renzo's tables and did it. He even laughed at Renzo and told him crooked wheels could be taken by anybody who knew how."

The tears started in the corners of her eyes but didn't fall. They stayed there, held back by pride maybe.

"We met one night. I had never met anyone like him before. It was wonderful, but we were never meant for each other. It was one of those things. Cooley was engaged to a girl in town, a very prominent girl."

The smoke of the cigarette in her hand swirled up and blurred her face.

"But I loved him," she said. With a sudden flick of her fingers she snapped the butt on the rug and ground it out with her shoe. "I hope he kills him! I hope he kills him!"

Her eyes drew a line up the floor until they were on mine. They were clear again, steady, curious for another moment, then steady again. I said, "You don't . . . like Renzo very much?"

"How well do you know people, Joe?"

I didn't say anything.

"You know them too, don't you? You don't live in the nice section of town. You know the dirt and how people are underneath. In a way you're lucky. You know it now, not when you're too old. Look at me, Joe. You've seen women like me before? I'm not much good. I look like a million but I'm not worth a cent. A lot of names fit me and they belong. I didn't get that way because I wanted to. He did it, Renzo. I was doing fine until I met him.

"Sure, some young kids might think I'm on top, but they never get to peek behind the curtain. They never see what I'm forced into and the kind of people I have to know because others don't want to know me. If they do they don't want anybody to know about it."

"Don't say those things, Helen."

"Kid, in ten years I've met two decent people. Cooley was the first."

She grinned and the hate left her face. "You're the other one. You don't give a hang what I'm like, do you?"

"I never met anybody like you before."

"Tell me more." Her grin got bigger.

"Well, you're beautiful. I mean real beautiful. And nice. You sure are built . . ."

"Good enough," she said and let the laugh come out. It

was a deep, happy laugh and sounded just right for her. "Finish your tea."

I had almost forgotten about it. I drained it down, the heat of it biting into the cuts along my cheek. "Helen . . . I ought to go home. If Mr. Renzo finds out about this, he's going to burn up."

"He won't touch me, Joe."

I let out a grunt.

"You either. There's a bed in there. Crawl into it. You've had enough talk for the night."

I woke up before she did. My back hurt too much to sleep and the blood pounded in my head too hard to keep it on the pillow. The clock beside the bed said it was seven-twenty and I kicked off the covers and dragged my clothes on.

The telephone was in the living room and I took it off the cradle quietly. When I dialed the number I waited, said hello as softly as I could and asked for Nick.

He came on in a minute with a coarse, "Yeah?"

"This is Joe, Nick."

"Hey, where are you, boy? I been scrounging all over the dump for you. Gordon'll kick your tail if you don't get down here. Two other guys didn't show. . ."

"Shut up and listen. I'm in a spot."

"You ain't kidding. Gordon said . . ."

"Not that, jerk. You see anybody around the house this morning?"

I could almost hear him think. Finally he said, "Car parked across the street. Think there was a guy in it." Then, "Yeah, yeah, wait up. Somebody was giving the old lady some lip this morning. Guess I was still half asleep. Heard your name mentioned."

"Brother!"

"What's up, pal?"

"I can't tell you now. You tell Gordon I'm sick or something, okay?"

"Nuts. I'll tell him you're in the clink. He's tired of that sick business. You ain't been there long enough to get sick yet."

"Tell him what you please. Just tell him. I'll call you

tonight." I slipped the phone back and turned around. I hadn't been as quiet as I thought I'd been. Helen was standing there in the doorway of her bedroom, a lovely golden girl, a bright morning flower wrapped in a black stem like a bud ready to pop.

"What is it, Joe?"

There wasn't any use hiding things from her. "Somebody's watching the house. They were looking for me this morning."

"Scared, Joe?"

"Darn right I'm scared! I don't want to get laid out in some swamp with my neck broken. That guy Renzo is nuts. He'll do anything when he gets mad."

"I know," Helen said quietly. Her hand made an unconscious movement across her mouth. "Come on, let's get some breakfast."

We found out who Vetter was that morning. At least Helen found out. She didn't cut corners or make sly inquiries. She did an impossible thing and drove me into town, parked the car and took a cab to a big brownstone building that didn't look a bit different from any other building like it in the country. Across the door it said "precinct no. 4" and the cop at the desk said the captain would be more than pleased to see us.

The captain was more than pleased, all right. It started his day off right when she came in and he almost offered me a cigar. The nameplate said his name was Gerot and if I had to pick a cop out to talk to, I'd pick him. He was in his late thirties with a build like a wrestler and I'd hate to be in the guy's shoes who tried to bribe him.

It took him a minute to settle down. A gorgeous blonde in a dark green gabardine suit blossoming with curves didn't walk in every day. And when he did settle down, it was to look at me and say, "What can I do for you?" but looking like he already knew what happened.

Helen surprised him. "I'd like to know something about a man," she said. "His name is Vetter."

The scowl started in the middle of his forehead and spread to his hairline.

"Why?"

She surprised him again. "Because he promised to kill Mark Renzo."

You could watch his face change, see it grow intense, sharpen, notice the beginning of a caustic smile twitch at his lips. "Lady, do you know what you're talking about?"

"I think so."

"You think?"

"Look at me," she said. Captain Gerot's eyes met hers, narrowed and stayed that way. "What do you see, Captain?"

"Somebody who's been around. You know all the answers, don't you?"

"All of them, Captain. The questions, too."

I was forgotten. I was something that didn't matter and I was happy about it.

Helen said, "What do you think about Renzo, Captain?"

"He stinks. He operates outside city limits where the police have no jurisdiction and he has the county police sewed up. I think he has some of my men sewed up too. I can't be sure but I wish I were. He's got a record in two states, he's clean here. I'd like to pin a few jobs on that guy. There's no evidence, yet he pulled them. I know this. . .if I start investigating I'm going to have some wheels on my neck."

Helen nodded. "I could add more. It really doesn't matter. You know what happened to Jack Cooley?"

Gerot's face looked mean. "I know I've had the papers and the state attorney climb me for it."

"I don't mean that."

The captain dropped his face in his hands resignedly, wiped his eyes and looked up again. "His car was found with bullet holes in it. The quantity of blood in the car indicated that nobody could have spilled that much and kept on living. We never found the body."

"You know why he died?"

"Who knows? I can guess from what I heard. He crossed Renzo, some said. I even picked up some info that said he was in the narcotics racket. He had plenty of cash and no place to show where it came from."

"Even so, Captain, if it was murder, and Renzo's behind it, you'd like it to be paid for."

The light blue of Gerot's eyes softened dangerously. "One way or another . . . if you must know."

"It could happen. Who is Vetter?"

He leaned back in his chair and folded his hands behind his neck. "I could show you reams of copy written about this guy. I could show you transcripts of statements we've taken down and copies that the police in other cities have sent out. I could show you all that but I can't pull out a picture and I can't drop in a print number on the guy. The people who got to know him and who finally saw him, all seem to be dead."

My voice didn't sound right. "Dead?"

Gerot's hands came down and flattened on the desk. "The guy's a killer. He's wanted every place I could think of. Word has it that he's the one who bumped Tony Briggs in Chicago. When Birdie Cullen was going to sing to the grand jury, somebody was paid fifty thousand to cool him off and Vetter collected from the syndicate. Vetter was paid another ten to knock off the guy who paid him the first time so somebody could move into his spot."

"So far he's only a name, Captain?"

"Not quite. We have a few details on him but we can't give them out. That much you understand, of course."

"Of course. But I'm still interested."

"He's tough. He seems to know things and do things nobody else would touch. He's a professional gunman in the worst sense of the word and he'll sell that gun as long as the price is right."

Helen crossed her legs with a motion that brought her whole body into play. "Supposing, Captain, that this Vetter was a friend of Jack Cooley? Supposing he got mad at the thought of his friend being killed and wanted to do something about it?"

Gerot said, "Go on."

"What would you do, Captain?"

The smile went up one side of his face. "Most likely nothing." He sat back again. "Nothing at all . . . until it happened."

"Two birds with one stone, Captain? Let Vetter get Renzo . . . and you get Vetter?"

"The papers would like that," he mused.

"No doubt." Helen seemed to uncoil from the chair. I stood up too and that's when I found out just how shrewd the captain was. He didn't bother to look at Helen at all. His blue eyes were all on me and being very, very sleepy.

"Where do you come in, kid?" he asked me.

Helen said it for me. "Vetter gave him a warning note to hand to Renzo."

Gerot smiled silently and you could see that he had the whole picture in his mind. He had our faces, he knew who she was and all about her, he was thinking of me and wanted to know all about me. He would. He was that kind of cop. You could tell.

We stood on the steps of the building and the cops coming in gave her the kind of look every man on the street gave her. Appreciative. It made me feel good just to be with her. I said, "He's a smart cop."

"They're all smart. Some are just smarter than others." A look of impatience crossed her face. "He said something . . ."

"Reams of copy?" I suggested.

I was easy for her to smile at. She didn't have to look up or down. Just a turn of her head. "Bright boy."

She took my hand and this time I led the way. I took her to the street I knew. It was off the main drag and the people on it had a look in their eyes you don't see uptown. It was a place where the dames walked at night and followed you into bars if they thought you had an extra buck to pass out.

They're little joints, most of them. They don't have neon lights and padded stools, but when a guy talks he says something and doesn't play games. There's excitement there and always that feeling that something is going to happen.

One of those places was called The Clipper and the boys from the *News* made it their hangout. Cagey boys with the big think under their hats. Fast boys with a buck and always ready to pay off on something hot. Guys who took you like you were and didn't ask too many questions.

My kind of people.

Bucky Edwards was at his usual stool getting a little bit potted because it was his day off. I got the big stare and the exaggerated wink when he saw the blonde which meant I'd finally made good about dragging one in with me. I didn't feel like bragging, though. I brought Helen over, went to introduce her, but Bucky said, "Hi, Helen. Never thought I'd see you out in the daylight," before I could pass on her name.

"Okay, so you caught a show at the Hideaway," I said. "We have something to ask you."

"Come on, Joe. Let the lady ask me alone."

"Lay off. We want to know about Vetter."

The long eyebrows settled down low. He looked at me, then Helen, then back at me again. "You're making big sounds, boy."

I didn't want anyone else in on it. I leaned forward and said, "He's in town, Bucky. He's after Renzo."

He let out a long whistle. "Who else knows about it?"

"Gerot. Renzo. Us."

"There's going to be trouble, sure."

Helen said, "Only for Renzo."

Bucky's head made a slow negative. "You don't know. The rackets boys'll flip their lids at this. If Vetter moves in here there's going to be some mighty big trouble."

My face started working under the bandages. "Renzo's top dog, isn't he?"

Bucky's tongue made a swipe at his lips. "One of 'em. There's a few more. They're not going to like Renzo pulling in trouble like Vetter." For the first time Bucky seemed to really look at us hard. "Vetter is poison. He'll cut into every-thing and they'll pay off. Sure as shooting, if he sticks around they'll be piling the cabbage in his lap."

"Then everybody'll be after Vetter," I said.

Bucky's face furrowed in a frown. "Uh-uh. I wasn't thinking that." He polished off his drink and set the empty on the bar. "If Vetter's here after Renzo they'll do better nailing Renzo's hide to the wall. Maybe they can stop it before it starts."

It was trouble, all right. The kind I wasn't feeling too bad about.

Bucky stared into his empty glass and said, "They'll bury Renzo or he'll come out of it bigger than ever."

The bartender came down and filled his glass again. I shook my head when he wanted to know what we'd have. "Good story," Bucky said, "if it happens." Then he threw the drink down and Bucky was all finished. His eyes got frosty and he sat there grinning at himself in the mirror with his mind saying things to itself. I knew him too well to say anything else so I nudged Helen and we walked out.

Some days go fast and this was one of them. She was nice to be with and nice to talk to. I wasn't important enough to hide anything from so for one day she opened her life up and fed me pieces of it. She seemed to grow younger as the day wore on and when we reached her apartment the sun was gilding her hair with golden reddish streaks and I was gone, all gone. For one day I was king and there wasn't any trouble. The laughter poured out of us and people stopped to look and laugh back. It was a day to remember when all the days are done with and you're on your last.

I was tired, dead tired. I didn't try to refuse when she told me to come up and I didn't want to. She let me open the door for her and I followed her inside. She had almost started for the kitchen to cook up the bacon and eggs we had talked about when she stopped by the arch leading to the living room.

The voice from the chair said, "Come on in, sugar pie. You too, kid."

And there was Johnny, a nasty smile on his mouth, leering at us.

"How did you get in here?"

He laughed at her. "I do tricks with locks, remember?" His head moved with a short jerk. "Get in here!" There was a flat, nasal tone in his voice.

I moved in beside Helen. My hands kept opening and closing at my side and my breath was coming a little fast in my throat.

"You like kids now, Helen?"

"Shut up, you louse," she said.

His lips peeled back showing his teeth. "The mother type. Old fashioned type, you know." He leered again like it was funny. My chest started to hurt from the breathing. "Too big for a bottle, so . . ."

I grabbed the lamp and let it fly and if the cord hadn't caught in the wall it would have taken his head off. I was all set to go into him but all he had to do to stop me was bring his hand up. The rod was one of those Banker's Specials that were deadly as hell at close range and Johnny looked too much like he wanted to use it for me to move.

He said, "The boss don't like your little arrangement, Helen. It didn't take him long to catch on. Come over here, kid."

I took a half step.

"Closer.

"Now listen carefully, kid. You go home, see. Go home and do what you feel like doing, but stay home and away from this place. You do that and you'll pick up a few bucks from Mr. Renzo. Now after you had it so nice here, you might not want to go home, so just in case you don't, I'm going to show you what's going to happen to you."

I heard Helen's breath suck in with a harsh gasp and my own sounded the same way. You could see what Johnny was setting himself to do and he was letting me know all about it and there wasn't a thing I could do. The gun was pointing right at my belly even while he jammed his elbows into the arms of the chair to get the leverage for the kick that was going to maim me for the rest of my life. His shoe was hard and pointed, a deadly weight that swung like a gentle pendulum.

I saw it coming and thought there might be a chance even yet but I didn't have to take it. From the side of the room Helen said, "Don't move, Johnny. I've got a gun in my hand."

And she had.

The ugly grimace on Johnny's face turned into a snarl when he knew how stupid he'd been in taking his eyes off her to enjoy what he was doing to me.

"Make him drop it, Helen."

"You heard the kid, Johnny."

Johnny dropped the gun. It lay there on the floor and I hooked it with my toe. I picked it up, punched the shells out of the chambers and tossed them under the sofa. The gun followed them.

"Come here, Helen," I said.

I felt her come up behind me and reached around for the .25 automatic in her hand. For a second Johnny's face turned pale and when it did I grinned at him.

Then I threw the .25 under the sofa too.

They look funny when you do things like that. Their little brains don't get it right away and it stuns them or something. I let him get right in the middle of that surprised look before I slammed my fist into his face and felt his teeth rip loose under my knuckles.

Helen went down on her knees for the gun and I yelled for her to let it alone, then Johnny was on me. He thought he was on me. I had his

arm over my shoulder, laid him into a hip roll and tumbled him easy.

I walked up. I took my time. He started to get up and I chopped down on his neck and watched his head bob. I got him twice more in the same place and Johnny simply fell back. His eyes were seeing, his brain thinking and feeling but he couldn't move. While he lay there, I chopped twice again and Johnny's face became blotched and swollen while his eyes screamed in agony.

I put him in a cab downstairs. I told the driver he was drunk and fell and gave him a ten spot from Johnny's own wallet with instructions to take him out to the Hideaway and deliver same to Mr. Renzo. The driver was very sympathetic and took him away.

Then I went back for Helen. She was sitting on the couch waiting for me, the strangeness back in her eyes. She said, "When he finished with you, he would have started on me."

"I know."

"Joe, you did pretty good for a kid."

"I was brought up tough."

"I've seen Johnny take some pretty big guys. He's awfully strong."

"You know what I do for a living, Helen? I push a junk cart, loaded with iron. There's competition and pretty soon you learn things. Those iron loaders are strong guys too. If they can tumble you, they lift your pay."

"You had a gun, Joe," she reminded me.

And her eyes mellowed into a strange softness that sent chills right through me. They were eyes that called me closer and I couldn't say no to them. I stood there looking at her, wondering what she saw under the bandages.

"Renzo's going after us for that," I said.

"That's right, Joe."

"We'll have to get out of here. You, anyway."

"Later we'll think about it."

"Now, damn it."

Her face seemed to laugh at me. A curious laugh. A strange laugh. A bewildered laugh. There was a sparkling dance to her eyes she kept half veiled and her mouth parted just a little bit. Her tongue touched the tip of her teeth, withdrew and she said, "Now is for something else, Joe. Now is for a woman going back a long time who sees somebody she could have loved then."

I looked at her and held my breath. She was so completely beautiful I ached and I didn't want to make a fool of myself. Not yet.

"Now is for you to kiss me, Joe," she said.

I tasted her.

I waited until midnight before I left. I looked in her room and saw her bathed in moonlight, her features softly relaxed into the faintest trace of a smile, a soft, golden halo around her head.

They should take your picture like you are now, Helen. It wouldn't need a retoucher and there would never be a man who saw it who would forget it. You're beautiful, baby. You're lovely as a woman could ever be and you don't know it. You've had it so rough you can't think of anything else and thinking of it puts the lines in your face and that chiseled granite in your eyes. But you've been around and so have I. There have been dozens of dames I've thought things about but not things like I'm thinking now. You don't care what or who a guy is; you just give him part of yourself as a favor and ask for nothing back.

Sorry, Helen, you have to take something back. Or at least keep what you have. For you I'll let Renzo push me around. For you I'll let him make me finger a guy. Maybe at the end I'll have a chance to make a break. Maybe not. At least it's for you and you'll know that

much. If I stay around, Renzo'll squeeze you and do it so hard you'll
never be the same. I'll leave, beautiful. I'm not much. You're not much
either. It was a wonderful day.

I lay the note by the lamp on the night table where she couldn't miss it. I leaned over and blew a kiss into her hair, then turned and got out of there.

Nobody had to tell me to be careful. I made sure nobody saw me leave the building and double-checked on it when I got to the corner. The trip over the back fences wasn't easy, but it was quiet and dark and if anybody so much as breathed near me I would have heard it. Then when I stood in the shadows of the store at the intersection I was glad I had made the trip the hard way. Buried between the parked cars along the curb was a police cruiser. There were no markings. Just a trunk aerial and the red glow of a cigarette behind the wheel.

Captain Gerot wasn't taking any chances. It made me feel a little better. Upstairs there Helen could go on sleeping and always be sure of waking up. I waited a few minutes longer then drifted back into the shadows toward the rooming house.

That's where they were waiting for me. I knew it a long time before I got there because I had seen them wait for other guys before. Things like that you don't miss when you live around the factories and near the waterfronts. Things like that you watch and remember so that when it happens to you, it's no surprise and you figure things out beforehand.

They saw me and as long as I kept on going in the right direction they didn't say anything. I knew they were where I couldn't see them and even if I made a break for it, it wouldn't do me any good at all.

You get a funny feeling after a while. Like a rabbit walking between rows of guns wondering which one is going to go off. Hoping that if it does you don't get to see it or feel it. Your stomach seems to get all loose inside you and your heart makes too much noise against your ribs. You try not to, but you sweat and the little muscles in your hands and thighs start to jump and twitch and all the while there's no sound at all, just a deep, startling silence with a voice that's there just the same. A statue, laughing with its mouth open. No sound, but you can hear the voice. You keep walking, and the breathing keeps time with your footsteps, sometimes trying to get ahead of them. You find yourself chewing on your lips because you already know the horrible impact of a fist against your flesh and the uncontrollable spasms that come after a pointed shoe bites into the muscle and bone of your side.

So much so that when you're almost there and a hand grabs your arm you don't do anything except look at the face above it and wait until it says, "Where you been, kid?"

I felt the hand tighten with a gentle pressure, pulling me in close. "Lay off me, I'm minding my own . . ."

"I said something, sonny."

"So I was out. What's it to you?"

His expression said he didn't give a hang at all. "Somebody wants to know. Feel like taking a little ride?"

"You asking?"

"I'm telling." The hand tightened again. "The car's over there, bud. Let's go get in it, huh?"

For a second I wondered if I could take him or not and I knew I couldn't. He was too big and too relaxed. He'd known trouble all his life, from little guys to big guys and he didn't fool easily. You can tell after you've seen a lot of them. They knew that some day they'd wind up holding their hands over a bullet hole or screaming through the bars of a cell, but until then they were trouble and too big to buck.

I got in the car and sat next to the guy in the back seat. I kept my mouth shut and my eyes open and when we started to head the wrong way, I looked at the guy next to me. "Where we going?"

He grinned on one side of his face and looked out the window again.

"Come on, come on, quit messing around! Where we going?"

"Shut up."

"Nuts, brother. If I'm getting knocked off I'm doing a lot of yelling first, starting right now. Where . . ."

"Shut up. You ain't getting knocked off." He rolled the window down, flipped the dead cigar butt out and cranked it back up again. He said it too easily not to mean it and the jumps in my hands quieted down a little.

No, they weren't going to bump me. Not with all the trouble they went to in finding me. You don't put a couple dozen men on a mug like me if all you wanted was a simple kill. One hopped up punk would do that for a week's supply of snow . . .

We went back through town, turned west into the suburbs and kept right on going to where the suburbs turned into estates and when we came to the right one the car turned into a surfaced driveway that wound past a dozen flashy heaps parked bumper to bumper and stopped in front of the fieldstone mansion.

The guy beside me got out first. He jerked his head at me and stayed at my back when I got out too. The driver grinned, but it was the kind of face a dog makes when he sees you with a chunk of meat in your fist.

A flunky met us at the door. He didn't look comfortable in his monkey suit and his face had scar tissue it took a lot of leather-covered punches to produce. He waved us in, shut the door and led the way down the hall to a room cloudy with smoke, rumbling with the voices of a dozen men.

When we came in the rumble stopped and I could feel the eyes crawl over me. The guy who drove the car looked across the room at the one in the tux, said, "Here he is, boss," and gave me a gentle push into the middle of the room.

"Hi, kid." He finished pouring out of the decanter, stopped it and picked up his glass. He wasn't an inch bigger than me, but he had the walk of a cat and the eyes of something dead. He got up close to me, faked a smile and held out the glass. "In case the boys had you worried."

"I'm not worried."

He shrugged and sipped the top off the drink himself. "Sit down, kid. You're among friends here." He looked over my shoulder. "Haul a chair up, Rocco."

All over the room the others settled down and shifted into position. A chair seat hit the back of my legs and I sat. When I looked around everybody was sitting, which was the way the little guy wanted it. He didn't like to have to look up to anybody.

He made it real casual. He introduced the boys when they didn't have to be introduced because they were always in the papers and the kind of guys people point out when they go by in their cars. You heard their names mentioned even in the junk business and among the punks in the streets. These were the big boys. Top dogs. Fat fingers. Big rings. The little guy was biggest of all. He was Phil Carboy and he ran the West Side the way he wanted it run.

When everything quieted down just right, Carboy leaned on the back of a chair and said, "In case you're wondering why you're here, kid, I'm going to tell you."

"I got my own ideas," I said.

"Fine. That's just fine. Let's check your ideas with mine, okay? Now we hear a lot of things around here. Things like that note you delivered to Renzo and who gave it to you and what Renzo did to you." He finished his drink and smiled. "Like what you did to Johnny, too. That's all straight now, isn't it?"

"So far."

"Swell. Tell you what I want now. I want to give you a job. How'd you like to make a cool hundred a week, kid?"

"Peanuts."

Somebody grunted. Carboy smiled again, a little thinner. "The kid's in the know," he said. "That's what I like. Okay, kid. We'll make it five hundred per for a month. If it don't run a month you get it anyway. That's better than having Renzo slap you around, right?"

"Anything's better than that." My voice started getting chalky.

Carboy held out his hand and said, "Rocco . . ." Another hand slid a sheaf of bills into his. He counted it out, reached two thousand and tossed it into my lap. "Yours, kid."

"For what?"

His lips were a narrow gash between his cheekbones. "For a guy named Vetter. The guy who gave you a note. Describe him."

"Tall," I said. "Big shoulders. I didn't see his face. Deep voice that sounded tough. He had on a trench coat and a hat."

"That's not enough."

"A funny way of standing," I told him. "I saw Sling Herman when I was a kid before the cops got him. He stood like that. Always ready to go for something in his pocket the cops said."

"You saw more than that, kid."

The room was too quiet now. They were all hanging on, waiting for the word. They were sitting there without smoking, beady little eyes waiting for the finger to swing until it stopped and I was the one who could stop it.

My throat squeezed out the words. I went back into the night to remember a guy and drag up the little things that would bring him into the light. I said, "I'd know him again. He was a guy to be scared of. When he talks you get a cold feeling and you know what he's like." My tongue ran over my lips and I lifted my eyes up to Carboy. "I wouldn't want to mess with a guy like that. Nobody's ever going to be tougher."

"You'll know him again. You're sure?"

"I'm sure." I looked around the room at the faces. Any one of them a guy who could say a word and have me dead the next day. "He's tougher than any of you."

Carboy grinned and let his tiny white teeth show through. "Nobody's that tough, kid."

"He'll kill me," I said. "Maybe you too. I don't like this."

"You don't have to like it. You just do it. In a way you're lucky. I'm paying you cash. If I wanted I could just tell you and you'd do it. You know that?"

I nodded.

"Tonight starts it. From now on you'll have somebody close by, see? In one pocket you'll carry a white handker-chief. If you gotta blow, use it. In the other one there'll be a red wiper. When you see him blow into that."

"That's all?"

"Just duck about then, kid," Phil Carboy said softly, "and maybe you'll get to spend that two grand. Try to use it for run-out money and you won't get past the bus station." He stared into his glass, looked up at Rocco expectantly and held it out for a refill. "Kid, let me tell you something. I'm an old hand in this racket. I can tell what a guy or a dame is

like from a block away. You've been around. I can tell that.
I'm giving you a break because you're the type who knows
the score and will play on the right side. I don't have to warn
you about anything, do I?"

"No. I got the pitch."

"Any questions?"

"Just one," I said. "Renzo wants me to finger Vetter too.
He isn't putting out any two grand for it. He just wants it,
see? Suppose he catches up with me? What then?"

Carboy shouldn't've hesitated. He shouldn't have let that
momentary look come into his eyes because it told me everything I wanted to know. Renzo was higher than the whole
pack of them and they got the jumps just thinking about it.
All by himself he held a fifty-one percent interest and they
were moving slowly when they bucked him. The little guy
threw down the fresh drink with a quick motion of his hand
and brought the smile back again. *In that second he had done a
lot of thinking and spilled the answer straight out.* "We'll take care
of Mark Renzo," he said. "Rocco, you and Lou take the kid
home."

So I went out to the car and we drove back to the slums
again. In the rear the reflections from the headlights of
another car showed and the killers in it would be waiting for
me to show the red handkerchief Carboy had handed me. I
didn't know them and unless I was on the ball every minute
I'd never get to know them. But they'd always be there,
shadows that had no substance until the red showed, then
the ground would get sticky with an even brighter red and
maybe some of it would be mine.

They let me out two blocks away. The other car didn't
show at all and I didn't look for it. My feet made hollow
sounds on the sidewalk, going faster and faster until I was
running up the steps of the house and when I was inside I
slammed the door and leaned against it, trying hard to stop
the pain in my chest.

Three-fifteen, the clock said. It ticked monotonously in
the stillness, trailing me upstairs to my room. I eased inside,
shut the door and locked it, standing there in the darkness
until my eyes could see things. Outside a truck clashed its

gears as it pulled up the hill and off in the distance a horn sounded.

I listened to them; familiar sounds, my face tightening as a not-so-familiar sound echoed behind them. It was a soft thing, a whisper that came at regular intervals in a choked-up way. Then I knew it was a sob coming from the other room and I went back to the hall and knocked on Nick's door.

His feet hit the floor, stayed there and I could hear his breathing coming hard. "It's Joe—open up."

I heard the wheeze his breath made as he let it out. The bedsprings creaked, he fell once getting to the door and the bolt snapped back. I looked at the purple blotches on his face and the open cuts over his eyes and grabbed him before he fell again. "Nick! What happened to you?"

"I'm . . . okay." He steadied himself on me and I led him back to the bed. "You got. . .some friends, pal."

"Cut it out. What happened? Who ran you through? Damn it, who did it?"

Nick managed to show a smile. It wasn't much and it hurt, but he made it. "You . . . in pretty big trouble, Joe."

"Pretty big."

"I didn't say nothing. They were here. . .asking questions. They didn't . . . believe what I told them, I guess. They sure laced me."

"The miserable slobs! You recognized them?"

His smile got sort of twisted and he nodded his head. "Sure, Joe. . .I know 'em. The fat one sat in . . . the car while they did it." His mouth clamped together hard. "It hurt. . . brother, it hurt!"

"Look," I said. "We're . . .''

"Nothing doing. I got enough. I don't want no more. Maybe they figured it's enough. That Renzo feller . . . he got hard boys around. See what they did, Joe? One. . .used a gun on me. You shoulda stood with Gordon, Joe. What the hell got into you to mess with them guys?"

"It wasn't me, Nick. Something came up. We can square it. I'll nail that fat slob if it's the last thing I do."

"It'll be the last thing. They gimme a message for you,

pal. You're to stick around, see? You get seen with any other big boys in this town . . . and that's all. You know?"

"I know. Renzo told me that himself. He didn't have to go through you."

"Joe . . ."

"Yeah?"

"He said for you to take a good look . . . at me. I'm an example. A little one. He says to do what he told you."

"He knows what he can do."

"Joe . . . for me. Lay off, huh? I don't feel so good. Now I can't work for a while."

I patted his arm, fished a hundred buck bill out of my pocket and squeezed it into his hand. "Don't worry about it," I told him.

He looked at the bill unbelievingly, then at me.

"Dough can't pay for . . . this, Joe. Kind of . . . stay away from me . . . for awhile anyway, okay?" He smiled again, lamely this time. "Thanks for the C anyway. We been pretty good buddies, huh?"

"Sure, Nick."

"Later we'll be again. Lemme knock off now. You take it easy." His hands came up to his face and covered it. I could hear the sobs starting again and cursed the whole damn system up and down and Renzo in particular. I swore at the filth men like to wade in and the things they do to other men. When I was done I got up off the bed and walked to the door.

Behind me Nick said, "Joey . . ."

"Right here."

"Something's crazy in this town. Stories are going around . . . there's gonna be a lot of trouble. Everybody is after. . .you. You'll . . . be careful?"

"Sure." I opened the door, shut it softly and went back to my room. I stripped off my clothes and lay down in the bed, my mind turning over fast until I had it straightened out, then I closed my eyes and fell asleep.

My landlady waited until a quarter to twelve before she gave it the business on my door. She didn't do it like she usually did it. No jarring smashes against the panels, just a light tapping that grew louder until I said, "Yeah?"

"Mrs. Stacey, Joe. You think you should get up? A man is downstairs to see you."

"What kind of a man?"

This time the knob twisted slowly and the door opened a crack. Her voice was a harsh whisper that sounded nervous. "He's got on old clothes and a city water truck is parked outside. He didn't come to look at my water."

I grinned at that one. "I'll be right down," I said. I splashed water over my face, shaved it close and worked the adhesive off the bridge of my nose. It was swollen on one side, the blue running down to my mouth. One eye was smudged with purple.

Before I pulled on my jacket I stuffed the wad of dough into the lining through the tear in the sleeve, then I took a look in Nick's room. There were traces of blood on his pillow and the place was pretty upset, but Nick had managed to get out somehow for a day's work.

The guy in the chair sitting by the window was short and wiry looking. There was dirt under his fingernails and a stubble on his chin. He had a couple of small wrenches in a leather holster on his belt that bulged his coat out but the stuff was pure camouflage. There was a gun further back and I saw the same thing Mrs. Stacey saw. The guy was pure copper with badges for eyes.

He looked at me, nodded and said, "Joe Boyle?"

"Suppose I said no?" I sat down opposite him with a grin that said I knew all about it and though I knew he got it nothing registered at all.

"Captain Gerot tells me you'll cooperate. That true?"

There was a laugh in his eyes, an attitude of being deliberately polite when he didn't have to be. "Why?" I asked him. "Everybody seems to think I'm pretty hot stuff all of a sudden."

"You are, junior, you are. You're the only guy who can put his

finger on a million dollar baby that we want bad. So you'll cooperate."

"Like a good citizen?" I made it sound the same as he did. "How much rides on Vetter and how much do I get?"

The sarcasm in his eyes turned to a nasty sneer.

"Thousands ride, junior . . . and you don't get any. You just cooperate. Too many cops have worked too damn long on Vetter to let a crummy kid cut into the cake. *Now I'll tell you why you'll cooperate. There's a dame, see? Helen Troy. There's ways of slapping that tomato with a fat conviction for various reasons and unless you want to see her slapped, you'll cooperate. Catch now?"*

I called him something that fitted him right down to his shoes. He didn't lose a bit of that grin at all. "Catch something else," he said. "Get smart and I'll make your other playmates look like school kids. I like tough guys. I have fun working 'em over because that's what they understand. What there is to know I know. Take last night for instance. The boys paid you off for a finger job. Mark Renzo pays but in his own way. Now I'm setting up a deal. Hell, you don't have to take it . . . you can do what you please. Three people are dickering for what you know. I'm the only one who can hit where it really hurts.

"Think it over, Joey boy. Think hard but do it fast. I'll be waiting for a call from you and wherever you are, I'll know about it. I get impatient sometimes, so let's hear from you soon. Maybe if you take too long I'll prod you a little bit." He got up, stretched and wiped his eyes like he was tired. "Just ask for Detective Sergeant Gonzales," he said. "That's me."

The cop patted the tools on his belt and stood by the door. I said, "It's stinking to be a little man, isn't it? You got to keep making up for it."

There was pure hate in his eyes for an answer. He gave me a long look that a snake would give a rabbit when he isn't too hungry yet. A look that said wait a little while, feller. Wait until I'm real hungry.

I watched the truck pull away, then sat there at the window looking at the street. I had to wait almost an hour before I spotted the first, then picked up the second one ten minutes later. If there were more I didn't see them. I went back to the kitchen and took a look through the curtains at the blank behinds of the warehouses across the alley. Mrs. Stacey didn't say anything. She sat there with her coffee, making clicking noises with her false teeth.

I said, "Somebody washed the windows upstairs in the wholesale house."

"A man. Early this morning."

"They haven't been washed since I've been here."

"Not for two years."

I turned around and she was looking at me as if something had scared her to death. *"How much are they paying you?"* I said.

She couldn't keep that greedy look out of her face even with all the phony indignation she tried to put on. Her mouth opened to say something when the phone rang and gave her the chance to cover up. She came back a few seconds later and said, "It's for you. Some man."

Then she stood there by the door where she always stood whenever somebody was on the phone. I said, "Joe Boyle speaking," and that was all. I let the other one speak his few words and when he was done I hung up.

I felt it starting to burn me. A nasty feeling that makes you want to slam something. Nobody asked me. . .they just told and I was supposed to jump. I was the low man on the totem pole, a lousy kid who happened to fit into things . . . just the right size to get pushed around.

Vetter, I kept saying to myself. They were all scared to death of Vetter. The guy had something they couldn't touch. He was tough. He was smart. He was moving in for a kill and if ever one was needed it was needed now. They were all after him and no matter how many people who didn't belong there stood in the way their bullets would go right through them to reach Vetter. Yeah, they wanted him bad. So bad they'd kill each other to make sure he died too.

Well, the whole pack of 'em knew what they could do.

I pulled my jacket on and got outside. I went up the corner, grabbed a downtown bus and sat there without bothering to look around. At Third and Main I hopped off, ducked into a cafeteria and had a combination lunch. I let Mrs. Stacey get her calls in, gave them time to keep me well under cover, then flagged down a roving

cab and gave the driver Helen's address. On the way over I looked out the back window for the second time and the light blue Chevy was still in place, two cars behind and trailing steadily. In a way it didn't bother me if the boys inside were smart enough to check the black Caddie that rode behind it again.

I tapped the cabbie a block away, told him to let me out on the corner and paid him off. There wasn't a parking place along the street so the laddies in the cars were either going to cruise or double park, but it would keep them moving around so I could see what they were like anyway.

When I punched the bell I had to wait a full minute before the lobby door clicked open. I went up the stairs, jolted the apartment door a few times and walked right into those beautiful eyes that were even prettier than the last time because they were worried first, then relieved when they saw me. She grabbed my arm and gave me that quick grin then pulled me inside and stood with her back to the door.

"Joe, Joe, you little jughead," she laughed. "You had me scared silly. Don't do anything like that again."

"Had to, Helen. I wasn't going to come back but I had to do that too."

Maybe it was the way I said it that made her frown. "You're a funny kid."

"Don't say that."

Something changed in her eyes. "No. Maybe I shouldn't, should I?" She looked at me hard, her eyes soft, but piercing. "I feel funny when I look at you. I don't know why. Sometimes I've thought it was because I had a brother who was always in trouble. Always getting hurt. I used to worry about him too."

"What happened to him?"

"He was killed on the Anzio beachhead."

"Sorry."

She shook her head. "He didn't join the army because he was patriotic. He and another kid held up a joint. The owner was shot. He was dead by the time they found out who did it."

"You've been running all your life too, haven't you?"

The eyes dropped a second. "You could put it that way."

"What ties you here?"

"Guess."

"If you had the dough you'd beat it? Some place where nobody knew you?"

She laughed, a short jerky laugh. It was answer enough. I reached in the jacket, got out the pack of bills and flipped off a couple for myself. I shoved the rest in her hand before she knew what it was. "Get going. Don't even bother to pack. Just move out of here and keep moving."

Her eyes were big and wide with an incredulous sort of wonder, then slightly misty when they came back to mine and she shook her head a little bit and said, "Joe . . . why? Why?

"It would sound silly if I said it."

"Say it."

"When I'm all grown up I'll tell you maybe."

"Now."

I could feel the ache starting in me and my tongue didn't want to move, but I said, "Sometimes even a kid can feel pretty hard about a woman. Sad, isn't it?"

Helen said, "Joe," softly and had my face in her hands and her mouth was a hot torch that played against mine with a crazy kind of fierceness and it was all I could do to keep from grabbing her instead of pushing her away. My hands squeezed her hard, then I yanked the door open and got out of there. Behind me there was a sob and I heard my name said again, softly.

I ran the rest of the way down with my face all screwed up tight.

The blue Chevy was down the street on the other side. It seemed to be empty and I didn't bother to poke around it. All I wanted was for whoever followed me to follow me away from there. So I gave it the full treatment. I made it look great. To them I must have seemed pretty jumpy and on the way to see somebody important. It took a full hour to reach The Clipper that way and the only important one around was Bucky Edwards and he wasn't drunk this time.

He nodded, said, "Beer?" and when I shook my head, called down the bar for a tall orange. "Figured you'd be in sooner or later."

"Yeah?"

That wise old face wrinkled a little. "How does it feel to be live bait, kiddo?"

"You got big ears, grandma."

"I get around." He toasted his beer against my orange, put it down and said, "You're in pretty big trouble, Joe. Maybe you don't know it."

"I know it."

"You don't know how big. You haven't been here that long. Those boys put on the big squeeze."

It was my turn to squint. His face was set as if he smelled something he didn't like and there was ice in his eyes. "How much do you know, Bucky?"

His shoulders made a quick shrug. "Phil Carboy didn't post the depot and the bus station for nothing. He's got cars cruising the highways too. Making sure, isn't he?"

He looked at me and I nodded.

"Renzo is kicking loose too. He's pulling the strings tight. The guys on his payroll are getting nervous but they can't do a thing. No, sir, not a thing. Like a war. Everybody's just waiting." The set mouth flashed me a quick grin. "You're the key, boy. *If there was a way out I'd tell you to take it.*"

"Suppose I went to the cops?"

"Gerot?" Bucky shook his head. "You'd get help as long as he could keep you in a cell. People'd like to see him dead too. He's got an awfully bad habit of being honest. Ask him to show you his scars someday. It wouldn't be so bad if he was just honest, but he's smart and mean as hell too."

I drank half the orange and set il down in the wet circle on the bar. "Funny how things work out. All because of Vetter. And he's here because of Jack Cooley."

"I was wondering when you were gonna get around to it, kid," Bucky said.

"What?"

He didn't look at me. "Who *are* you working for?"

I waited a pretty long time before he turned his head around. I let him look at my face another long time before I said anything. Then: "I was pushing a junk cart, friend. I was doing okay, too. I wasn't working for trouble. Now I'm getting pretty curious. In my own way I'm not so stupid, but now I want to find out the score. One way or another I'm finding out. So they paid me off but they aren't figuring on me spending much of that cabbage. After it's over I get chopped down and it starts all over again, whatever it is. That's what I'm finding out. Why I'm bait for whatever it is. Who do I see, Bucky? You're in the know. Where do I go to find out?"

"Cooley could have told you," he said quietly.

"Nuts. He's dead."

"Maybe he can still tell you."

My fingers were tight around the glass now. "The business about Cooley getting it because of the deal on Renzo's tables is out?"

"Might be."

"Talk straight unless you're scared silly of those punks too. Don't give me any puzzles if you know something."

Bucky's eyebrows went up, then down slowly over the grin in his eyes. "Talk may be cheap, son," he said, "but life comes pretty expensively." He nodded sagely and said, "I met Cooley in lotsa places. Places he shouldn't have been. He was a man looking around. He could have found something."

"Like why we have gangs in this formerly peaceful city of ours. Why we have paid-for politicians and clambakes with some big faces showing. They're not eating clams . . . they're talking."

"These places where you kept seeing Cooley . . ."

"River joints. Maybe he liked fish."

You could tell when Bucky was done talking. I went down to Main, found a show I hadn't seen and went in. There were a lot of things I wanted to think about.

At eleven-fifteen the feature wound up and I started back outside. In the glass reflection of the lobby door I saw somebody behind me but I didn't look back. There could have been one more in the crowd that was around the entrance outside. Maybe two. Nobody seemed to pay any attention to me and I didn't care if they did or not.

I waited for a Main Street bus, took it down about a half mile, got off at the darkened supermarket and started up the road. You get the creeps in places like that. It was an area where some optimist had started a factory and ran it until the swamp crept in. When the footings gave and the walls cracked, they moved out, and now the black skeletons of the buildings were all that were left, with gaping holes for eyes and a mouth that seemed to breathe out a fetid swamp odor. But there were still people there. The dozen or so company houses that were propped against the invading swamp showed dull yellow lights, and the garbage smell of unwanted humanity fought the swamp odor. You could hear them, too, knowing that they watched you from the shadows of their porches. You could feel them stirring in their jungle shacks and catch the pungency of the alcohol they brewed out of anything they could find.

There was a low moan of a train from the south side and its single eye picked out the trestle across the bay and followed it. The freight lumbered up, slowed for the curve that ran through the swamps and I heard the bindle stiffs yelling as they hopped off, looking for the single hard topped road that took them to their quarters for the night.

The circus sign was on the board fence. In the darkness it was nothing but a bleached white square, but when I lit a cigarette I could see the faint orange impressions that used to be supposedly wild animals. The match went out and I lit another, got the smoke fired up and stood there a minute in the dark.

The voice was low. A soft, quiet voice more inaudible than a whisper. "One is back at the corner. There's another a hundred feet down."

"I know," I said.

"You got nerve."

"Let's not kid me. I got your message. Sorry I had to cut it short, but a pair of paid-for ears were listening in."

"Sorry Renzo gave you a hard time."

"So am I. The others did better by me."

Somebody coughed down the road and I flattened against the boards away from the white sign. It came again, farther away this time and I felt better. I said, "What gives?"

"You had a cop at your place this morning."

"I spotted him."

"There's a regular parade behind you." *A pause, then,* "What did you tell them?"

I dragged in on the smoke, watched it curl. "I told them he was big

Tough. I didn't see his face too well. What did you expect me to tell them?"

I had a feeling like he smiled.

"They aren't happy," he said.

I grinned too. "Vetter. They hate the name. It scares them." I pulled on the butt again. "It scares me too when I think of it too much."

"You don't have anything to worry about."

"Thanks."

"Keep playing it smart. You know what they're after?"

I nodded, even though he couldn't see me. "Cooley comes into it someplace. It was something he knew."

"Smart lad. I knew you were a smart lad the first time I saw you. Yes, it was Cooley."

"Who was he?" I asked.

Nothing for a moment. I could hear him breathing and his feet moved but that was all. The red light on the tail of the caboose winked at me and I knew it would have to be short.

"An adventurer, son. A romantic adventurer who went where the hunting was profitable and the odds long. He liked long odds. He found how they were slipping narcotics in through a new door and tapped them for a sweet haul. They say four million. It was a paid-for shipment and he got away with it. Now the boys have to make good."

The caboose was almost past now. He said, "I'll call you if I want you."

I flipped the butt away, watching it bounce sparks across the dirt. I went on a little bit farther where I could watch the fires from the jungles and when I had enough of it I started back.

At the tree the guy who had been waiting there said, "You weren't thinking of hopping that freight, were you kid?"

I didn't jump like I was supposed to. I said, "When I want to leave, I'll leave."

"Be sure to tell Mr. Carboy first, huh?"

"I'll tell him," I said.

He stayed there, not following me. I passed the buildings again, then felt better when I saw the single street light on the corner of Main. There was nobody there that I could see, but that didn't count. He was around someplace.

I had to wait ten minutes for a bus. It seemed longer than it was.

I stayed drenched in the yellow light and thought of the voice behind the fence and what it had to say. When the bus pulled up I got on, stayed there until I reached the lights again and got off. By that time a lot of things were making sense, falling into a recognizable pattern. I walked down the street to an all-night drug store, had a drink at the counter then went back to the phone booth.

I dialed the police number and asked for Gonzales, Sergeant Gonzales. There was a series of clicks as the call was switched and the cop said, "Gonzales speaking."

"This is Joe, copper. Remember me?"

"Don't get too fresh, sonny," he said. His voice had a knife in it.

"Phil Carboy paid me some big money to finger Vetter. He's got men tailing me."

His pencil kept up a steady tapping against the side of the phone. Finally he said, "I was wondering when you'd call in. You were real lucky, Joe. For a while I thought I was going to have to persuade you a little to cooperate. You were real lucky. Keep me posted."

I heard the click in my ear as he hung up and I spat out the things into the dead phone I felt like telling him to his face. Then I fished out another coin, dropped it in and dialed the same number. This time I asked for Captain Gerot. The guy at the switchboard said he had left about six but that he could probably be reached at his club. He gave me the number and I checked it through. The attendant who answered said he had left about an hour ago but would probably call back to see if there were any messages for him and were there? I told him to get the number so I could put the call through myself and hung up.

It took me a little longer to find Bucky Edwards. He had stewed in his own juices too long and he was almost all gone. I said, "Bucky, I need something bad. I want Jack Cooley's last address. You remember that much?"

He hummed a little bit. "Rooming house. Between Wells and Capitol. It's all white, Joe. Only white house."

"Thanks, Bucky."

"You in trouble, Joe?"

"Not yet."

"You will be. Now you will be."

That was all. He put the phone back so easily I didn't hear it go. Damn, I thought, he knows the score but he won't talk. He's got all the scoop and he clams up.

I had another drink at the counter, picked up a deck of smokes and stood outside while I lit one. The street was quieting down. Both curbs were lined with parked heaps, dead things that rested until morning when they'd be whipped alive again.

Not all of them though. I was sure of that. I thought I caught a movement across the street in a doorway. It was hard to tell. I turned north and walked fast until I reached Benson Road, then cut down it to the used car lot.

Now was when they'd have a hard time. Now was when they were playing games in my back yard and if they didn't know every inch of the way somebody was going to get hurt. They weren't kids, these guys. They had played the game themselves and they'd know all the angles. Almost all, anyway. They'd know when I tried to get out of the noose and as soon as they did, they'd quit playing and start working. They wouldn't break their necks sticking to a trail when they could bottle me up.

All I had to do was keep them from knowing for a while.

I crossed the lot, cutting through the parked cars, picked up the alley going back of the houses and stuck to the hedgerows until I was well down it. By that time I had a lead. If I looked back I'd spoil it so I didn't look back. I picked up another block at the fork in the alley, standing deliberately under the lone light at the end, not hurrying, so they could see me. I made it seem as though I were trying to pick out one of the houses in the darkness, and when I made up my mind, went through the gate in the fence.

After that I hurried. I picked up the short-cuts, made the street and crossed it between lights. I reached Main again, grabbed a cruising cab in the middle of the block, had him haul me across town to the docks and got out. It took fifteen minutes longer to reach the white house Bucky told me about. I grinned to myself and wondered if the boys were still watching the place they thought I went into. Maybe it would be a little while before they figured the thing out.

It would be time enough.

The guy who answered the door was all wrapped up in a bathrobe, his hair stringing down his face. He squinted at me, reluctant to be polite, but not naturally tough enough to be anything else but. He said, "If you're looking for a room you'll have to come around in the morning. I'm sorry."

I showed him a bill with two numbers on it.

"Well . . ."

"I don't want a room."

He looked at the bill again, then a quick flash of terror crossed his face. His eyes rounded open, looked at me hard, then dissolved into curiosity. "Come . . . in."

The door closed and he stepped around me into a small sitting room and snapped on a shaded desk lamp. His eyes went back down to the bill. I handed it over and watched it disappear into the bathrobe. "Yes?"

"Jack Cooley."

The words did something to his face. It showed terror again, but not as much as before.

"I really don't . . ."

"Forget the act. I'm not working for anybody in town. I was a friend of his."

This time he scowled, not believing me.

I said, "Maybe I don't look it, but I was."

"So? What is it you want?" He licked his lips, seemed to tune his ears for some sound from upstairs. "Everybody's been here. Police, newspapers. Those . . . men from town. They all want something."

"Did Jack leave anything behind?"

"Sure. Clothes, letters, the usual junk. The police have all that."

"Did you get to see any of it?"

"Well . . . the letters were from dames. Nothing important."

I nodded, fished around for a question a second before I found one. "How about his habits?"

The guy shrugged. "He paid on time. Usually came in late and slept late. No dames in his room."

"That's all?"

He was getting edgy. "What else is there? I didn't go out with the guy. So now I know he spent plenty of nights in Renzo's joint. I hear talk. You want to know what kind of butts he smoked? Hobbies, maybe? Hell, what is there to tell? He goes out at night. Sometimes he goes fishing. Sometimes . . ."

"Where?" I interrupted.

"Where what?"

"Fishing."

"On one of his boats. He borrowed my stuff. He was fishing the day before he got bumped. Sometimes he'd slip me a ticket and I'd get away from the old lady."

"How do the boats operate?"

He shrugged again, pursing his mouth. "They go down the bay to the tip of the inlet, gas up, pick up beer at Gulley's and go about ten miles out. Coming back they stop at Gulley's for more beer and for the guys to dump the fish they don't want. Gulley sells it in town. Everybody is usually drunk and happy." He gave me another thoughtful look. "You writing a book about your friend?" he said sarcastically.

"Could be. Could be. I hate to see him dead."

"If you ask me, he never should've fooled around Renzo. You better go home and save your money from now on, sonny."

"I'll take your advice," I said, "and be a handyman around a rooming house."

He gave me a dull stare as I stood up and didn't bother to go to the door with me. He still had his hand in his pocket wrapped around the bill I gave him.

The street was empty and dark enough to keep me wrapped in a blanket of shadows. I stayed close to the houses, stopping now and then to listen. When I was sure I was by myself I felt better and followed the water smell of the bay.

At River Road a single-pump gas station showed lights and the guy inside sat with his feet propped up on the desk. He opened one eye when I walked in, gave me the change I wanted for the phone, then went back to sleep again. I dialed the number of Gerot's club, got the attendant and told him what I wanted. He gave me another number and I punched it out on the dial. Two persons answered before a voice said, "Gerot speaking."

"Hello, Captain. This is Joe. I was . . ."

"I remember," he said.

"I called Sergeant Gonzales tonight. Phil Carboy paid me off to finger Vetter. Now I got two parties pushing me."

"Three. Don't forget us."

"I'm not forgetting."

"I hear those parties are excited. Where are you?"

I didn't think he'd bother to trace the call, so I said, "Some joint in town."

His voice sounded light this time. "About Vetter. Tell me."

"Nothing to tell."

"You had a call this morning." I felt the chills starting to run up my back. They had a tap on my line already. "The voice wasn't familiar and it said some peculiar things."

"I know. I didn't get it. I thought it was part of Renzo's outfit getting wise. They beat up a buddy of mine so I'd know what a real beat-up guy looks like. It was all double talk to me."

He was thinking it over. When he was ready he said, "Maybe so, kid. You hear about that dame you were with?"

I could hardly get the words out of my mouth. "Helen? No . . . What?"

"Somebody shot at her. Twice."

"Did . . ."

"Not this time. She was able to walk away from it this time."

"Who was it? Who shot at her?"

"That, little chum, is something we'd like to know too. She was waiting for a train out of town. The next time maybe we'll have better luck. There'll be a next time, in case you're interested."

"Yeah, I'm interested . . . and thanks. You know where she is now?"

"No, but we're looking around. *I hope we can find her first.*"

I put the phone back and tried to get the dry taste out of

my mouth. When I thought I could talk again I dialed Helen's apartment, hung on while the phone rang endlessly, then held the receiver fork down until I got my coin back. I had to get Renzo's club number from the book and the gravelly voice that answered rasped that the feature attraction hadn't put in an appearance that night and for something's sake to cut off the chatter and wait until tomorrow because the club was closed.

So I stood there and said things to myself until I was all balled up into a knot. I could see the parade of faces I hated drifting past my mind and all I could think of was how bad I wanted to smash every one of them as they came by. Helen had tried to run for it. She didn't get far. Now where could she be? Where does a beautiful blonde go who is trying to hide? Who would take her in if they knew the score?

I could feel the sweat starting on my neck, soaking the back of my shirt. All of a sudden I felt washed out and wrung dry. Gone. All the way gone. Like there wasn't anything left of me any more except a big hate for a whole damn city, the mugs who ran it and the people who were afraid of the mugs. And it wasn't just one city either. There would be more of them scattered all over the states. For the people, by the people, Lincoln had said. Yeah. Great.

I turned around and walked out. I didn't even bother to look back and if they were there, let them come. I walked for a half hour, found a cab parked at a corner with the driver sacking it behind the wheel and woke him up. I gave him the boarding house address and climbed in the back.

He let me off at the corner, collected his dough and turned around.

Then I heard that voice again and I froze the butt halfway to my mouth and squashed the matches in the palm of my hand.

It said, "Go ahead and light it."

I breathed that first drag out with the words, "You nuts? They're all around this place."

"I know. Now be still and listen. The dame knows the score. They tried for her . . ."

We heard the feet at the same time. They were light as a cat, fast. Then he came out of the darkness and all I could see was the glint of the knife in his hand and the yell that was in my throat choked off when his fingers bit into my flesh. I had time to see that same hardened face that had looked into mine not so long ago, catch an expressionless grin from the hard boy, then the other shadows opened and the side of a palm smashed down against his neck. He pitched forward with his head at a queer, stiff angle, his mouth wrenched open and I knew it was only a reflex that kept it that way because the hard boy was dead. You could hear the knife chatter across the sidewalk and the sound of the body hitting, a sound that really wasn't much yet was a thunderous crash that split the night wide open.

The shadows the hand had reached out from seemed to open and close again, and for a short second I was alone. Just a short second. I heard the whisper that was said too loud. The snick of a gun somewhere, then I closed in against the building and ran for it.

At the third house I faded into the alley and listened. Back there I could hear them talking, then a car started up down the street. I cut around behind the houses, found the fences and stuck with them until I was at my place, then snaked into the cellar door.

When I got upstairs I slipped into the hall and reached for the phone. I asked for the police and got them. All I said was that somebody was being killed and gave the address. Then I grinned at the darkness, hung up without giving my name and went upstairs to my room. From way across town a siren wailed a lonely note, coming closer little by little. It was a pleasant sound at that. It would give my friend from the shadows plenty of warning too. He was quite a guy. Strong. Whoever owned the dead man was going to walk easy with Vetter after this.

I walked into my room, closed the door and was reaching for the bolt when the chair moved in the corner. Then she said, "Hello, Joe." and the air in my lungs hissed out slowly between my teeth.

I said, "Helen." I don't know which of us moved. I like to think it was her. But suddenly she was there in my arms with her face buried in my shoulder, stifled sobs pouring out of her body while I tried to tell her that it was all right. Her body was pressed against me, a fire that seemed to dance as she trembled, fighting to stay close.

"Helen, Helen, take it easy. Nothing will hurt you now. You're okay." I lifted her head away and smoothed back her hair. "Listen, you're all right here."

Her mouth was too close. Her eyes too wet and my mind was thinking things that didn't belong there. My arms closed tighter and I found her mouth, warm and soft, a salty sweetness that clung desperately and talked to me soundlessly. But it stopped the trembling and when she pulled away she smiled and said my name softly.

"How'd you get here, Helen?"

Her smile tightened. "I was brought up in a place like this a long time ago. There are always ways. I found one."

"I heard what happened. Who was it?"

She tightened under my hands. "I don't know. I was waiting for a train when it happened. I just ran after that. When I got out on the street, it happened again."

"No cops?"

She shook her head. "Too fast. I kept running."

"They know it was you?"

"I was recognized in the station. Two men there had caught my show and said hello. You know how. They could have said something."

I could feel my eyes starting to squint. "Don't be so damn calm about it."

The tight smile twisted up at the corner. It was like she was reading my mind. She seemed to soften a moment and I felt her fingers brush my face. "I told you I wasn't like other girls, Joe. Not like the kind of girl you should know. Let's say it's all something I've seen before. After a bit you get used to it."

"Helen . . ."

"I'm sorry, Joe."

I shook my head slowly. "No . . . I'm the one who's sorry. People like you should never get like that. Not you."

"Thanks." She looked at me, something strange in her eyes that I could see even in the half light of the room. And this time it happened slowly, the way it should be. The fire was close again, and real this time, very real. Fire that could have burned deeply if the siren hadn't closed in and stopped outside.

I pushed her away and went to the window. The bearers of the flashlights traced paths up the sidewalk. The two cops were cursing the cranks in the neighborhood until one stopped, grunted something and picked up a sliver of steel that lay by the curb. But there was nothing else. Then they got back in the cruiser and drove off.

Helen said, "What was it?"

"There was a dead man out there. Tomorrow there'll be some fun."

"Joe!"

"Don't worry about it. At least we know how we stand. It was one of their boys. He made a pass at me on the street and got taken."

"You do it?"

I shook my head. "Not me. A guy. A real big guy with hands that can kill."

"Vetter." She said it breathlessly.

I shrugged.

Her voice was a whisper. "I hope he kills them all. Every one." Her hand touched my arm. "Somebody tried to kill Renzo earlier. They got one of his boys." Her teeth bit into her lip. "There were two of them so it wasn't Vetter. You know what that means?"

I nodded. "War. They want Renzo dead to get Vetter out of town. They don't want him around or he'll move into their racket sure."

"He already has." I looked at her sharply and she nodded. "I saw one of the boys in the band. Renzo's special car was hijacked as it was leaving the city. Renzo claimed they got nothing but he's pretty upset. I heard other things too. The whole town's tight."

"Where do you come in, Helen?"

"What?" Her voice seemed taut.

"You. Let's say you and Cooley. What string are you pulling?" Her hand left my arm and hung down at her side. If I'd slapped her she would have had the same expression on her face. I said, "I'm sorry. I didn't mean it like that. You liked Jack Cooley, didn't you?"

"Yes." She said it quietly.

"You told me what he was like once. What was he really like?"

The hurt flashed in her face again. "Like them," she said. "Gay, charming, but like them. He wanted the same things. He just went after them differently, that's all."

"The guy I saw tonight said you know things."

Her breath caught a little bit. "I didn't know before, Joe."

"Tell me."

"When I packed to leave . . . then I found out. Jack. . .left certain things with me. One was an envelope. There were cancelled checks in it for thousands of dollars made out to Renzo. The one who wrote the checks is a racketeer in New York. There was a note pad too with dates and amounts that Renzo paid Cooley."

"Blackmail."

"I think so. What was more important was what was in the box he left with me. *Heroin.*"

I swung around slowly. "Where is it?"

"Down a sewer. I've seen what the stuff can do to a person."

"Much of it?"

"Maybe a quarter pound."

"We could have had him," I said. "We could have had him and you dumped the stuff!"

Her hand touched me again. "No . . . there wasn't that much of it. Don't you see, it's bigger than that. What Jack had was only a sample. Some place there's more of it, much more."

"Yeah," I said. I was beginning to see things now. They were starting to straighten themselves out and it made a pattern. The only trouble was that the pattern was so simple it didn't begin to look real.

"Tomorrow we start," I said. "We work by night. Roll into the sack and get some sleep. If I can keep the landlady out of here we'll be okay. You sure nobody saw you come in?"

"Nobody saw me."

"Good. Then they'll only be looking for me."

"Where will you sleep?"

I grinned at her. "In the chair."

I heard the bed creak as she eased back on it, then I slid into the chair. After a long time she said, "Who are you, Joe?"

I grunted something and closed my eyes. I wished I knew myself sometimes.

I woke up just past noon. Helen was still asleep, restlessly tossing in some dream. The sheet had slipped down to her waist, and every time she moved, her body rippled with sinuous grace. I stood looking at her for a long time, my eyes devouring her, every muscle in my body wanting her. There were other things to do, and I cursed those other things and set out to do them.

When I knew the landlady was gone I made a trip downstairs to her ice box and lifted enough for a quick meal. I had to wake Helen up to eat, then sat back with an old magazine to let the rest of the day pass by. At seven we made the first move. It was a nice simple little thing that put the whole neighborhood in an uproar for a half hour but gave us a chance to get out without being spotted.

All I did was call the fire department and tell them there was a gas leak in one of the tenements. They did the rest. Besides holding everybody back from the area they evacuated a whole row of houses, including us and while they were trying to run down the false alarm we grabbed a cab and got out.

Helen asked, "Where to?"

"A place called Gulley's. It's a stop for the fishing boats. You know it?"

"I know it." She leaned back against the cushions. "It's a tough place to be. Jack took me out there a couple of times."

"He did? Why?"

"Oh, we ate, then he met some friends of his. We were there when the place was raided. Gulley was selling liquor after closing hours. Good thing Jack had a friend on the force."

"Who was that?"

"Some detective with a Mexican name."

"Gonzales," I said.

She looked at me. "That's right." She frowned. "I didn't like him."

That was a new angle. One that didn't fit in. Jack with a friend on the force. I handed Helen a cigarette, lit it and sat back with mine.

It took a good hour to reach the place and at first glance it didn't seem worth the ride. From the highway the road weaved out onto a sand spit and in the shadows you could see the parked cars and occasionally couples in them. Here and there along the road the lights of the car picked up the glint of beer cans and empty bottles. I gave the cabbie an extra five and told him to wait and when we went down the gravel path, he pulled it under the trees and switched off his lights. Gulley's was a huge shack built on the sand with a porch extending out over the water. There wasn't a speck of paint on the weather-racked framework and over the whole place the smell of fish hung like a blanket. It looked like a creep joint until you turned the corner and got a peek at the nice modern dock setup he had and the new addition on the side that probably made the place the yacht club's slumming section. If it didn't have anything else it had atmosphere. We were right on the tip of the peninsula that jutted out from the mainland and like the sign said, it was the last chance for the boats to fill up with the bottled stuff before heading out to deep water.

I told Helen to stick in the shadows of the hedge row that ran around the place while I took a look around, and though she didn't like it, she melted back into the brush. I could see a couple of figures on the porch, but they were talking too low for me to hear what was going on. Behind the bar that ran across the main room inside, a flat-faced guy leaned over reading the paper with his ears pinned inside a headset. Twice he reached back, frowning and fiddled with a radio under the counter. When the phone rang he scowled again, slipped off the headset and said, "Gulley speaking. Yeah. Okay. So long."

When he went back to his paper I crouched down under the rows of windows and eased around the side. The sand was a thick carpet that silenced all noise and the gentle lapping of the water against the docks covered any other racket I could make. I was glad to have it that way too. There were guys spotted around the place that you couldn't see until you looked hard and they were just lounging. Two were by the building and the other two at the foot of the docks, edgy birds who lit occasional cigarettes and shifted around as they smoked them. One of them said something and a pair of them swung around to watch the twin beams of a car coming up the highway. I looked too, saw them turn in a long arc then cut straight for the shack.

One of the boys started walking my way, his feet squeaking in the dry sand. I dropped back around the corner of the building, watched while he pulled a bottle out from under the brush, then started back the way I had come.

The car door slammed. A pair of voices mixed in an argument and another one cut them off. When I heard it I could feel my lips peel back and I knew that if I had a knife in my fist and Mark Renzo passed by me in the dark, whatever he had for supper would spill all over the ground. There was another voice swearing at something. Johnny. Nice, gentle Johnny who was going to cripple me for life.

I wasn't worrying about Helen because she wouldn't be sticking her neck out. I was hoping hard that my cabbie wasn't reading any paper by his dome light and when I heard the boys reach the porch and go in, I let my breath out hardly realizing that my chest hurt from holding it in so long.

You could hear their hellos from inside, muffled sounds that were barely audible. I had maybe a minute to do what I had to do and didn't waste any time doing it. I scuttled back under the window that was at one end of the bar, had time to see Gulley shaking hands with Renzo over by the door, watched him close and lock it and while they were still far enough away not to notice the movement, slid the window up an inch and flattened against the wall.

They did what I expected they'd do. I heard Gulley invite them to the bar for a drink and set out the glasses. Renzo said, "Good stuff."

"Only the best. You know that."

Johnny said, "Sure. You treat your best customers right."

Bottle and glasses clinked again for another round. Then the headset that was under the bar started clicking. I took a quick look, watched Gulley pick it up, slap one earpiece against his head and jot something down on a pad.

Renzo said, "She getting in without trouble?"

Gulley set the headset down and leaned across the bar. He looked soft, but he'd been around a long time and not even Renzo was playing any games with him. "Look," he said, "you got your end of the racket. Keep out of mine. You know?"

"Getting tough, Gulley?"

I could almost hear Gulley smile. "Yeah. Yeah, in case you want to know. You damn well better blow off to them city lads, not me."

"Ease off," Renzo told him. He didn't sound rough any more. "Heard a load was due in tonight."

"You hear too damn much."

"It didn't come easy. I put out a bundle for the information. You know why?" Gulley didn't say anything. Renzo said, "I'll tell you why. I need that stuff. You know why?"

"Tough. Too bad. You know. What you want is already paid for and is being delivered. You ought to get your head out of your whoosis."

"Gulley. . ." Johnny said really quiet. "We ain't kidding. We need that stuff. The big boys are getting jumpy. They think we pulled a fast one. They don't like it. They don't like it so bad maybe they'll send a crew down here to straighten everything out and you may get straightened too."

Inside Gulley's feet were nervous on the floorboards. He passed in front of me once, his hands busy wiping glasses. "You guys are nuts. Carboy paid for this load. So I should stand in the middle?"

"Maybe it's better than standing in front of us," Johnny said.

"You got rocks. Phil's out of the local stuff now. He's got a pretty big outfit."

"Just peanuts, Gulley, just peanuts."

"Not any more. He's moving in since you dumped the big deal."

Gulley's feet stopped moving. His voice had a whisper in it. "So you were big once. Now I see you sliding. The big boys are going for bargains and they don't like who can't deliver, especially when it's been paid for. That was one big load. It was special. So you dumped it. Phil's smart enough to pick it up from there and now he may be top dog. I'm not in the middle. Not without an answer to Phil and he'll need a good one."

"Vetter's in town, Gulley!" Renzo almost spat the words out. "You know how he is? He ain't a gang you bust up. He's got a nasty habit of killing people. Like always, he's moving in. So we pay you for the stuff and deliver what we lost. We make it look good and you tell Phil it was Vetter. He'll believe that."

I could hear Gulley breathing hard. "Jerks, you guys," he said. There was a hiss in his words. "I should string it on Vetter. Man, you're plain nuts. I seen that guy operate before. Who the hell you think edged into that Frisco deal? Who got Morgan in El Paso while he was packing a half million in cash and another half in powder? So a chowder-head hauls him in to cream some local fish and the guy walks away with the town. *Who the hell is that guy?"*

Johnny's laugh was bitter. Sharp. Gulley had said it all and it was like a knife sticking in and being twisted. "I'd like to meet him. Seems like he was a buddy of Jack Cooley. You remember Jack Cooley, Gulley? You were in on that. Cooley got off with your kick too. Maybe Vetter would like to know about that."

"Shut up."

"Not yet. We got business to talk about."

Gulley seemed out of breath. "Business be damned. I ain't tangling with Vetter."

"Scared?"

"Damn right, and so are you. So's everybody else."

"Okay," Johnny said. "So for one guy or a couple he's trouble. In a big town he can make his play and move fast. Thing is with enough guys in a burg like this he can get nailed."

"And how many guys get nailed with him? He's no dope. Who you trying to smoke?"

"Nuts, who cares who gets nailed as long as it ain't your own bunch? You think Phil Carboy'll go easy if he thinks Vetter jacked a load out from under him? Like you told us,

Phil's an up and coming guy. He's growing. He figures on being the top kick around here and let Vetter give him the business and he goes all out to get the guy. So two birds are killed. Vetter and Carboy. Even if Carboy gets him, his load's gone. He's small peanuts again."

"Where does that get me?" Gulley asked.

"I was coming to that. You make yours. The percentage goes up ten. Good?"

Gulley must have been thinking greedy. He started moving again, his feet coming closer. He said, "Big talk. Where's the cabbage?"

"I got it on me," Renzo said.

"You know what Phil was paying for the junk?"

"The word said two million."

"It's gonna cost to take care of the boys on the boat."

"Not so much." Renzo's laugh had no humor in it. "They talk and either Carboy'll finish 'em or Vetter will. They stay shut up for free."

"How much for me?" Gulley asked.

"One hundred thousand for swinging the deal, plus the extra percentage. You think it's worth it?"

"I'll go it," Gulley said.

Nobody spoke for a second, then Gulley said, "I'll phone the boat to pull into the slipside docks. They can unload there. The stuff is packed in beer cans. It won't make a big package so look around for it. They'll probably shove it under one of the benches."

"Who gets the dough?"

"You row out to the last boat mooring. The thing is red with a white stripe around it. Unscrew the top and drop it in."

"Same as the way we used to work it?"

"Right. The boys on the boat won't like going in the harbor and they'll be plenty careful, so don't stick around to lift the dough and the stuff too. That 'breed on the ship got a lockerful of chatter guns he likes to hand out to his crew."

"It'll get played straight."

"I'm just telling you."

Renzo said, "What do you tell Phil?"

"You kidding? I don't say nothing. All I know is I lose

contact with the boat. Next the word goes that Vetter is mixed up in it. I don't say nothing." He paused for a few seconds, his breath whistling in his throat, then, "But don't forget something . . . You take Carboy for a sucker and maybe even Vetter. Lay off me. I keep myself covered. Anything happens to me and the next day the cops get a letter naming names. Don't ever forget that."

Renzo must have wanted to say something. He didn't. Instead he rasped, "Go get the cash for this guy."

Somebody said, "Sure, boss," and walked across the room. I heard the lock snick open, then the door.

"This better work," Renzo said. He fiddled with his glass a while. "I'd sure like to know what that punk did with the other stuff."

"He ain't gonna sell it, that's for sure," Johnny told him. "You think maybe Cooley and Vetter were in business together?"

"I'm thinking maybe Cooley was in business with a lot of people. That lousy blonde. When I get her she'll talk plenty. I should've kept my damn eyes open."

"I tried to tell you, boss."

"Shut up," Renzo said. "You just see that she gets found."

I didn't wait to hear any more. I got down in the darkness and headed back to the path. Overhead the sky was starting to lighten as the moon came up, a red circle that did funny things to the night and started the long fingers of shadows drifting out from the scraggly brush. The trees seemed to be ponderous things that reached down with sharp claws, feeling around in the breeze for something to grab. I found the place where I had left Helen, found a couple of pebbles and tossed them back into the brush. I heard her gasp.

She came forward silently, said, "Joe?" in a hushed tone.

"Yeah. *Let's get out of here.*"

"What happened?"

"Later. I'll start back to the cab to make sure it's clear. If you don't hear anything, follow me. Got it?"

". . . Yes." She was hesitant and I couldn't blame her. I got off the gravel path into the sand, took it easy and tried to search out the shadows. I reached the clearing, stood there until I was sure the place was empty then hopped over to the cab.

I had to shake the driver awake and he came out of it stupidly. "Look, keep your lights off going back until you're on the highway, then keep 'em on low. There's enough moon to see by."

"Hey . . . I don't want trouble."

"You'll get it unless you do what I tell you."

"Well . . . okay."

"A dame's coming out in a minute. Soon as she comes start it up and try to keep it quiet."

I didn't have long to wait. I heard her feet on the gravel, walking fast but not hurrying. Then I heard something else that froze me a second. A long, low whistle of appreciation like the kind any blonde'll get from the pool hall boys. I hopped in the cab, held the door open. "Let's go feller," I said.

As soon as the engine ticked over Helen started to run. I yanked her inside as the car started moving and kept down under the windows. She said, "Somebody . . ."

"I heard it."

"I didn't see who it was."

"Maybe it'll pass. Enough cars came out here to park."

Her hand was tight in mine, the nails biting into my palm. She was half-turned on the seat, her dress pulled back over the glossy knees of her nylons, her breasts pressed against my arm. She stayed that way until we reached the highway then little by little eased up until she was sitting back against the cushions. I tapped my forefinger against my lips then pointed to the driver. Helen nodded, smiled, then squeezed my hand again. This time it was different. The squeeze went with the smile.

I paid off the driver at the edge of town. He got more than the meter said, a lot more. It was big enough to keep a man's mouth shut long enough to get him in trouble when he opened it too late. When he was out of sight we walked until we found another cab, told the driver to get us to a small hotel someplace. He gave the usual leer and blonde inspection, muttered the name of a joint and pulled away from the curb.

It was the kind of place where they don't ask questions and don't believe what you write in the register anyway. I signed *Mr. and Mrs. Valiscivitch*, paid the bill in advance for a week and when the clerk read the name I got a screwy look because the name was too screwballed to be anything but real to him. Maybe he figured his clientele was changing. When we got to the room I said, "You park here for a few days."

"Are you going to tell me anything?"

"Should I?"

"You're strange, Joe. A very strange boy."

"Stop calling me a boy."

Her face got all beautiful again and when she smiled there was a real grin in it. She stood there with her hands on her hips and her feet apart like she was going into some part of her routine and I could feel my body starting to burn at the sight of her. She could do things with herself by just breathing and she did them, the smile and her eyes getting deeper all the time. She saw what was happening to me and said, "You're not such a boy after all." She held out her hand and I took it, pulling her in close. "The first time you were a boy. All bloody, dirt ground into your face. When Renzo tore you apart I could have killed him. Nobody should do that to another one, especially a boy. But then there was Johnny and you seemed to grow up. I'll never forget what you did to him."

"He would have hurt you."

"You're even older now. Or should I say matured? I think you finished growing up last night, Joe, last night . . . with me. I saw you grow up, and I only hope I haven't hurt you in the process. I never was much good for anybody. That's why I left home, I guess. Everyone I was near seemed to get hurt. Even me."

"You're better than they are, Helen. The breaks were against you, that's all."

"Joe . . . do you know you're the first one who did anything nice for me without wanting . . . something?"

"Helen . . ."

"No, don't say anything. Just take a good look at me. See everything that I am? It shows. I know it shows. I was a lot of things that weren't nice. I'm the kind men want but who won't introduce to their families. I'm a beautiful piece of dirt, Joe." Her eyes were wet. I wanted to brush away the wetness but she wouldn't let my hands go. "You see what I'm telling you? You're young . . . don't brush up against me too close. You'll get dirty and you'll get hurt."

She tried to hide the sob in her throat but couldn't. It came up anyway and I made her let my hands go and when she did I wrapped them around her and held her tight against me. "Helen," I said. "Helen . . ."

She looked at me, grinned weakly. "We must make a funny pair," she said. "Run for it, Joe. Don't stay around any longer."

When I didn't answer right away her eyes looked at mine. I could see her starting to frown a little bit and the curious bewilderment crept across her face. Her mouth was red and moist, poised as if she were going to ask a question, but had forgotten what it was she wanted to say. I let her look and look and look and when she shook her head in a minute gesture of puzzlement I said, "Helen . . . I've rubbed against you. No dirt came off. Maybe it's because I'm no better than you think you are."

"Joe . . ."

"It never happened to me before, kid. When it happens I sure pick a good one for it to happen with." I ran my fingers through her hair. It was nice looking at her like that. Not down, not up, but right into her eyes. "I don't have any family to introduce you to, but if I had I would. Yellow head, don't worry about me getting hurt."

Her eyes were wide now as if she had the answer. She wasn't believing what she saw.

"I love you, Helen. It's not the way a boy would love anybody. It's a peculiar kind of thing I never want to change."

"Joe . . ."

"But it's yours now. You have to decide. Look at me, kid. Then say it."

Those lovely wide eyes grew misty again and the smile

came back slowly. It was a warm, radiant smile that told me more than her words. "It can happen to us, can't it? Perhaps it's happened before to somebody else, but it can happen to *us*, can't it? Joe . . . It seems so . . . I can't describe it. There's something . . ."

"Say it out."

"I love you, Joe. Maybe it's better that I should love a little boy. Twenty . . . twenty-one you said? Oh, please, please don't let it be wrong, please . . ." She pressed herself to me with a deep-throated sob and clung there. My fingers rubbed her neck, ran across the width of her shoulders then I pushed her away. I was grinning a little bit now.

"In eighty years it won't make much difference," I said. Then what else I had to say her mouth cut off like a burning torch that tried to seek out the answer and when it was over it didn't seem important enough to mention anyway.

I pushed her away gently, "Now, listen, there isn't much time. I want you to stay here. Don't go out at all and if you want anything, have it sent up. When I come back, I'll knock once. Just once. Keep that door locked and stay out of sight. You got that?"

"Yes, but. . ."

"Don't worry about me. I won't be long. Just remember to make sure it's me and nobody else." I grinned at her. "You aren't getting away from me anymore, blondie. Now it's us for keeps, together."

"All right, Joe."

I nudged her chin with my fist, held her face up and kissed it. That curious look was back and she was trying to think of something again. I grinned, winked at her and got out before she could keep me. I even grinned at the clerk downstairs, but he didn't grin back. He probably thought anybody who'd leave a blonde like that alone was nuts or married and he wasn't used to it.

But it sure felt good. You know how. You feel so good you want to tear something apart or laugh and it may be a little crazy, but that's all part of it. That's how I was feeling until I remembered the other things and knew what I had to do.

I found a gin mill down the street and changed a buck

into a handful of coins. Three of them got my party and I said, "Mr. Carboy?"

"That's right. Who is this?"

"Joe Boyle."

Carboy told somebody to be quiet then, "What do you want, kid?"

I got the pitch as soon as I caught the tone in his voice. "Your boys haven't got me, if that's what you're thinking," I told him.

"Yeah?"

"I didn't take a powder. I was trying to get something done. For once figure somebody else got brains too."

"You weren't supposed to do any thinking, kid."

"Well, if I don't, you lose a boatload of merchandise, friend."

"What?" It was a whisper that barely came through.

"Renzo's ticking you off. He and Gulley are pulling a switch. Your stuff gets delivered to him."

"Knock it off, kid. What do you know?"

"I know the boat's coming into the slipside docks with the load and Renzo will be picking it up. You hold the bag, brother."

"Joe," he said. "You know what happens if you're queering me."

"I know."

"Where'd you pick it up?"

"Let's say I sat in on Renzo's conference with Gulley."

"Okay, boy. I'll stick with it. You better be right. Hold on." He turned away from the phone and shouted muffled orders at someone. There were more muffled shouts in the background then he got back on the line again. "Just one thing more. What about Vetter?"

"Not yet, Mr. Carboy. Not yet."

"You get some of my boys to stick with you. I don't like my plans interfered with. Where are you?"

"In a place called Patty's. A gin mill."

"I know it. Stay there ten minutes. I'll shoot a couple guys down. You got that handkerchief yet?"

"Still in my pocket."

"Good. Keep your eyes open."

He slapped the phone back and left me there. I checked

the clock on the wall, went to the bar and had an orange, then when the ten minutes were up, drifted outside. I was half a block away when a car door slapped shut and I heard the steady tread of footsteps across the street.

Now it was set. Now the big blow. The show ought to be good when it happened and I wanted to see it happen. There was a cab stand at the end of the block and I hopped in the one on the end. He nodded when I gave him the address, looked at the bill in my hand and took off. In back of us the lights of another car prowled through the night, but always looking our way.

You smelt the place before you reached it. On one side the darkened store fronts were like sleeping drunks, little ones and big ones in a jumbled mass, but all smelling the same. There was the fish smell and on top that of wood the salt spray had started to rot. The bay stretched out endlessly on the other side, a few boats here and there marked with running lights, the rest just vague silhouettes against the sky. In the distance the moon turned the train trestle into a giant spidery hand. The white sign, "slipside," pointed on the dock area and I told the driver to turn up the street and keep right on going. He picked the bill from my fingers, slowed around the turn, then picked it up when I hopped out. In a few seconds the other car came by, made the turn and lost itself further up the street. When it was gone I stepped out of the shadows and crossed over. Maybe thirty seconds later the car came tearing back up the street again and I ducked back into a doorway. Phil Carboy was going to be pretty sore at those boys of his.

I stood still when I reached the corner again and listened. It was too quiet. You could hear the things that scurried around on the dock. The things were even bold enough to cross the street and one was dragging something in its mouth. Another, a curious elongated creature whose fur shone silvery in the street light pounced on it and the two fought and squealed until the raider had what it went after.

It happens even with rats, I thought. Who learns from who? Do the rats watch the men or the men watch the rats?

Another one of them ran into the gutter. It was going to cross, then stood on its hind legs in an attitude of attention, its face pointing toward the dock. I never saw it move, but it disappeared, then I heard what it had heard, carefully muffled sounds, then a curse.

It came too quick to say it had a starting point. First the quick stab of orange and the sharp thunder of the gun, then the others following and the screams of the slugs whining off across the water. They didn't try to be quiet now. There was a startled shout, a hoarse scream and the yell of somebody who was hit.

Somebody put out the street light and the darkness was a blanket that slid in. I could hear them running across the street, then the moon reached down before sliding behind a cloud again and I saw them, a dozen or so closing in on the dock from both sides.

Out on the water an engine barked into life, was gunned and a boat wheeled away down the channel. The car that had been cruising around suddenly dimmed its lights, turned off the street and stopped. I was right there with no place to duck into and feet started running my way. I couldn't go back and there was trouble ahead. The only other thing was to make a break for it across the street and hope nobody spotted me.

I'd pushed it too far. I was being a dope again. One of them yelled and started behind me at a long angle. I didn't stop at the rail. I went over the side into the water, kicked away from the concrete abutment and hoped I'd come up under the pier. I almost made it. I was a foot away from the piling but it wasn't enough. When I looked back the guy was there at the rail with a gun bucking in his hand and the bullets were walking up the water toward me. He must have still had half a load left and only a foot to go when another shot blasted out over my head and the guy grabbed at his face with a scream and fell back to the street. The guy up above said, "Get the son . . ." and the last word had a whistle to it as something caught him in the belly. He was all doubled up when he hit the water and his tombstone was a tiny trail of bubbles that broke the surface a few seconds before stopping altogether.

I pulled myself further under the dock. From where I was I could hear the voices and now they had quieted down.

Out on the street somebody yelled to stand back and before the words were out cut loose with a sharp blast of an automatic rifle. It gave the bunch on the street time to close in and those on the dock scurried back farther.

Right over my head the planks were warped away and when a voice said, "I found it," I could pick Johnny's voice out of the racket.

"Where?"

"Back ten feet on the pole. Better hop to it before they get wise and cut the wires."

Johnny moved fast and I tried to move with him. By the time I reached the next piling I could hear him dialing the phone. He talked fast, but kept his voice down. *"Renzo? Yeah, they bottled us. Somebody pulled the cork out of the deal. Yeah. The hell with that, you call the cops. Let them break it up.* Sure, sure. Move it. We can make it to one of the boats. They got Tommy and Balco. Two of the others were hit but not bad. Yeah, it's Carboy all right. He ain't here himself, but they're his guys. Yeah, I got the stuff. Shake it."

His feet pounded on the planking overhead and I could hear his voice without making out what he said. The next minute the blasting picked up and I knew they were trying for a standoff. Whatever they had for cover up there must have been pretty good because the guys on the street were swearing at it and yelling for somebody to spread out and get them from the sides. The only trouble was that there was no protection on the street and if the moon came out again they'd be nice easy targets.

It was the moan of the siren that stopped it. First one, then another joined in and I heard them running for their cars. A man screamed and yelled for them to take it easy. Something rattled over my head and when I looked up, a frame of black marred the flooring. Something was rolled to the edge, then crammed over. Another followed it. Men. Dead. They bobbed for a minute, then sank slowly. Somebody said, "Damn, I hate to do that. He was okay."

"Shut up and get out there." It was Johnny.

The voice said, "Yeah, come on, you," then they went over the side. I stayed back of the piling and watched them swim for the boats. The sirens were coming closer now. One had a lead as if it knew the way and the others didn't. Johnny didn't come down. I grinned to myself, reached for a cross-brace and swung up on it. From there it was easy to make the trapdoor.

And there was Johnny by the end of the pier squatting down behind a packing case that seemed to be built around some machinery, squatting with that tenseness of a guy about to run. He had a box in his arms about two feet square and when I said, "Hello, chum," he stood up so fast he dropped it, but he would have had to do that anyway the way he was reaching for his rod.

He almost had it when I belted him across the nose. I got him with another sharp hook and heard the breath hiss out of him. It spun him around until the packing case caught him and when I was coming in he let me have it with his foot. I skidded sidewise, took the toe of his shoe on my hip then had his arm in a lock that brought a scream tearing out of his throat. He was going for the rod again when the arm broke and in a crazy surge of pain he jerked loose, tripped me, and got the gun out with his good hand. I rolled into his feet as it coughed over my head, grabbed his wrist and turned it into his neck and he pulled the trigger for the last time in trying to get his hand loose. There was just one last, brief, horrified expression in his eyes as he looked at me, then they filmed over to start rotting away.

The siren that was screaming turned the corner with its wail dying out. Brakes squealed against the pavement and the car stopped, the red light on its hood snapping shut. The door opened opposite the driver, stayed open as if the one inside was listening. Then a guy crawled out, a little guy with a big gun in his hand. He said, "Johnny?"

Then he ran. Silently, like an Indian, I almost had Johnny's gun back in my hand when he reached me.

"You," Sergeant Gonzales said. He saw the package there, twisted his mouth into a smile and let me see the hole in the end of his gun. I still made one last try for Johnny's gun when the blast went off. I half expected the sickening smash of a bullet, but none came. When I looked up, Gonzales was still there. Something on the packing crate had hooked his coat and held him up.

I couldn't see into the shadows where the voice came from. But it was a familiar voice. It said, "You ought to be more careful son."

The gun the voice held slithered back into the leather.

"Thirty seconds. No more. You might even do the job right and beat it in his car. He was in on it. The cop . . . he was working with Cooley. Then Cooley ran out on him too so he played along with Renzo. Better move, kid."

The other sirens were almost there. I said, "Watch yourself. And thanks."

"Sure, kid. I hate crooked cops worse than crooks."

I ran for the car, hopped in and pulled the door shut. Behind me something splashed and a two foot square package floated on the water a moment, then turned over and sunk out of sight. I left the lights off, turned down the first street I reached and headed across town. At the main drag I pulled up, wiped the wheel and gearshift free of prints and got out.

There was dawn showing in the sky. It would be another hour yet before it was morning. I walked until I reached the junkyard in back of Gordon's office, found the wreck of a car that still had cushions in it, climbed in and went to sleep.

Morning, afternoon, then evening. I slept through the first two. The last one was harder. I sat there thinking things, keeping out of sight. My clothes were dry now, but the cigarettes had a lousy taste. There was a twinge in my stomach and my mouth was dry. I gave it another hour before I moved, then went back over the fence and down the street to a dirty little diner that everybody avoided except the boys who rode the rods into town. I knocked off a plate of bacon and eggs, paid for it with some of the change I had left, picked up a pack of butts and started out. That was when I saw the paper on the table.

It made quite a story. Gang war flares on waterfront, and under it a subhead that said, *Cop, Hoodlum, Slain in Gun Duel.* It was a masterpiece of writing that said nothing, intimated much and brought out the fact that though the place was bullet sprayed and though evidence of other wounded was found, there were no bodies to account for what had happened. One sentence mentioned the fact that Johnny was connected with Mark Renzo. The press hinted at police inefficiency. There was the usual statement from Captain Gerot.

The thing stunk. Even the press was afraid to talk out. How long would it take to find out Gonzales didn't die by a shot from Johnny's gun? Not very long. And Johnny. . .a cute little twist like that would usually get a big splash. There wasn't even any curiosity shown about Johnny. I let out a short laugh and threw the paper back again.

They were like rats, all right. They just went the rats one better. They dragged their bodies away with them so there wouldn't be any ties. Nice. Now find the doctor who patched them up. Find what they were after on the docks. Maybe they figured to heist ten tons or so of machinery. Yeah, try and find it.

No, they wouldn't say anything. Maybe they'd have to hit it a little harder when the big one broke. When the boys came in who paid a few million out for a package that was never delivered. Maybe when the big trouble came and the blood ran again somebody would crawl back out of his hole long enough to put it into print. Or it could be that Bucky Edwards was right. Life was too precious a thing to sell cheaply.

I thought about it, remembering everything he had told me. When I had it all back in my head again I turned toward the place where I knew Bucky would be and walked faster. Halfway there it started to drizzle. I turned up the collar of my coat.

It was a soft rain, one of those things that comes down at the end of a summer, making its own music like a dull concert you think will have no end. It drove people indoors until even the cabs didn't bother to cruise. The cars that went by had their windows steamed into opaque squares, the drivers peering through the hand-wiped panes.

I jumped a streetcar when one came along, took it downtown and got off again. And I was back with the people I knew and the places made for them. Bucky was on his usual stool and I wondered if it was a little too late. He had that all gone look in his face and his fingers were caressing a tall amber-colored glass.

When I sat down next to him his eyes moved, giving me a glassy stare. It was like the cars on the street, they were cloudy with mist, then a hand seemed to reach out and rub them clear. They weren't glass any more. I could see the white in his fingers as they tightened around the glass and he said, "You did it fancy, kiddo. Get out of here."

"Scared, Bucky?"

His eyes went past me to the door, then came back again. "Yes. You said it right. I'm scared. Get out. I don't want to be around when they find you."

"For a guy who's crocked most of the time you seem to know a lot about what happens."

"I think a lot. I figure it out. There's only one answer."

"If you know it why don't you write it?"

"Living's not much fun any more, but what there is of it, I like. Beat it, kid."

This time I grinned at him, a big fat grin and told the bartender to get me an orange. Large. He shoved it down, picked up my dime and went back to his paper.

I said, "Let's hear about it, Bucky." I could feel my mouth changing the grin into something else. "I don't like to be a target either. I want to know the score."

Bucky's tongue made a pass over dry lips. He seemed to look back inside himself to something he had been a long time ago, dredging the memory up. He found himself in the mirror behind the back bar, twisted his mouth at it and looked back at me again.

"This used to be a good town."

"Not that," I said.

He didn't hear me. "Now anybody who knows anything is scared to death. To death, I said. Let them talk and that's what they get. Death. From one side or another. It was bad enough when Renzo took over, worse when Carboy came in. It's not over yet." His shoulders made an involuntary shudder and he pulled the drink halfway down the glass. "Friend Gulley had an accident this afternoon. He was leaving town and was run off the road. He's dead."

I whistled softly. "Who?"

For the first time a trace of humor put lines at the corner of his lips. "It wasn't Renzo. It wasn't Phil Carboy. They were all accounted for. The tire marks are very interesting. It looks like the guy wanted to stop friend Gulley for a chat but

Gulley hit the ditch. You could call it a real accident without lying." He finished the rest of the drink, put it down and said, "The boys are scared stiff." He looked at me closely then. "Vetter," he said.

"He's getting close."

Bucky didn't hear me. "I'm getting to like the guy. He does what should have been done a long time ago. By himself he does it. They know who killed Gonzales. One of Phil's boys saw it happen before he ran for it. There's a guy with a broken neck who was found out on the highway and they know who did that and how." He swirled the ice around in his glass. "He's taking good care of you, kiddo."

I didn't say anything.

"There's just one little catch to it, Joe. One little catch."

"What?"

"That boy who saw Gonzales get it saw something else. He saw you and Johnny tangle over the package. He figures you got it. Everybody knows and now they want you. It can't happen twice. Renzo wants it and Carboy wants it. You know who gets it?"

I shook my head.

"You get it. In the belly or in the head. Even the cops want you that bad. Captain Gerot even thinks that way. You better get out of here, Joe. Keep away from me. There's something about you that spooks me. Something in the way your eyes look. Something about your face. I wish I could see into that mind of yours. I always thought I knew people, but I don't know you at all. You spook me. You should see your own eyes. I've seen eyes like yours before but I can't remember where. They're familiar as hell, but I can't place them. They don't belong in a kid's face at all. Go on, Joe, beat it. The boys are all over town. They got orders to do just one thing. Find you. When they do I don't want you sitting next to me."

"When do you write the big story, Bucky?"

"You tell me."

My teeth were tight together with the smile moving around them. "It won't be long."

"No. . .maybe just a short obit. They're tracking you fast. That hotel was no cover at all. Do it smarter the next time."

The ice seemed to pour down all over me. It went down over my shoulders, ate through my skin until it was in the blood that pounded through my body. I grabbed his arm and damn near jerked him off the stool. "What about the hotel?"

All he did was shrug. Bucky was gone again.

I cursed silently, ran back into the rain again and down the block to the cab stand.

The clerk said he was sorry, he didn't know anything about room 612. The night man had taken a week off. I grabbed the key from his hand and pounded up the stairs. All I could feel was that mad frenzy of hate swelling in me and I kept saying her name over and over to myself. I threw the door open, stood there breathing fast while I called myself a dozen different kinds of fool.

She wasn't there. It was empty.

A note lay beside the telephone. All it said was, *"Bring it where you brought the first one."*

I laid the note down again and stared out the window into the night. There was sweat on the backs of my hands. Bucky had called it. They thought I had the package and they were forcing a trade. Then Mark Renzo would kill us both. He thought.

I brought the laugh up from way down in my throat. It didn't sound much like me at all. I looked at my hands and watched them open and close into fists. There were callouses across the palms, huge things that came from Gordon's junk carts. A year and a half of it, I thought. Eighteen months of pushing loads of scrap iron for pennies then all of a sudden I was part of a multi-million dollar operation. The critical part of it. I was the enigma. Me, Joey the junk pusher. Not even Vetter now. Just me. Vetter would come after me.

For a while I stared at the street. That tiny piece of luck that chased me caught up again and I saw the car stop and the men jump out. One was Phil Carboy's right hand man. In a way it was funny. Renzo was always a step ahead of the challenger, but Phil was coming up fast. He'd caught on too and was ready to pull the same deal. He didn't know it had already been pulled.

But that was all right too.

I reached for the pen on the desk, lifted a sheet of cheap stationery out of the drawer and scrawled across it, *"Joe . . . be back in a few hours. Stay here with the package until I return. I'll have the car ready."* I signed it, *Helen,* put it by the phone and picked up the receiver.

The clerk said, "Yes?"

I said, "In a minute some men will come in looking for the blonde and me. You think the room is empty, but let them come up. You haven't seen me at all yet. Understand?"

"Say . . ."

"Mister, if you want to walk out of here tonight you'll do what you're told. You're liable to get killed otherwise. Understand that?"

I hung up and let him think about it. I'd seen his type before and I wasn't worried a bit. I got out, locked the door and started up the stairs to the roof. It didn't take me longer than five minutes to reach the street and when I turned the corner the light was back on in the room I had just left. I gave it another five minutes and the tall guy came out again, spoke to the driver of the car and the fellow reached in and shut off the engine. It had worked. The light in the window went out. The vigil had started and the boys could afford to be pretty patient. They thought.

The rain was a steady thing coming down just a little bit harder than it had. It was cool and fresh with the slightest nip in it. I walked, putting the pieces together in my head. I did it slowly, replacing the fury that had been there, deliberately wiping out the gnawing worry that tried to grow. I reached the deserted square of the park and picked out a bench under a tree and sat there letting the rain drip down around me. When I looked at my hands they were shaking.

I was thinking wrong. I should have been thinking about fat, ugly faces; ratfaces with deep voices and whining faces. I should have been thinking about the splashes of orange a rod makes when it cuts a man down and blood on the street. Cops who want the big payoff. Thinking of a town where even the press was cut off and the big boys came from the city to pick up the stuff that started more people on the long slide down to the grave.

Those were the things I should have thought of.

All I could think of was Helen. Lovely Helen who had

been all things to many men and hated it. Beautiful Helen who didn't want me to be hurt, who was afraid the dirt would rub off. Helen who found love for the first time . . . and me. The beauty in her face when I told her. Beauty that waited to be kicked and wasn't because I loved her too much and didn't give a damn what she had been. She was different now. Maybe I was too. She didn't know it, but she was the good one, not me. She was the child that needed taking care of, not me. Now she was hours away from being dead and so was I. The thing they wanted, the thing that could buy her life I saw floating in the water beside the dock. It was like having a yacht with no fuel aboard.

The police? No, not them. They'd want me. They'd think it was a phony. That wasn't the answer. Not Phil Carboy either. He was after the same thing Renzo was.

I started to laugh, it was so damn, pathetically funny. I had it all in my hand and couldn't turn it around. What the devil does a guy have to do? How many times does he have to kill himself? The answer. It was right there but wouldn't come through. It wasn't the same answer I had started with, but a better one.

So I said it all out to myself. Out loud, with words. I started with the night I brought the note to Renzo, the one that promised him Vetter would cut his guts out. I even described their faces to myself when Vetter's name was mentioned. One name, that's all it took, and you could see the fear creep in because Vetter was deadly and unknown. He was the shadow that stood there, the one they couldn't trust, the one they all knew in the society that stayed outside the law. He was a high-priced killer who never missed and always got more than he was paid to take. So deadly they'd give anything to keep him out of town, even to doing the job he was there for. So deadly they could throw me or anybody else to the wolves just to finger him. So damn deadly they put an army on him, yet so deadly he could move behind their lines without any trouble at all.

Vetter.

I cursed the name. I said Helen's. Vetter wasn't important any more.

The rain lashed at my face as I looked up into it. The

things I knew fell into place and I knew what the answer was. I remembered something I didn't know was there, a sign on the docks by the fishing fleet that said "season lockers."

Jack Cooley had been smart by playing it simple. He even left me the ransom.

I got up, walked to the corner and waited until a cab came by. I flagged him down, got it and gave the address of the white house where Cooley had lived.

The same guy answered the door. He took the bill from my hand and nodded me in. I said, "Did he leave any old clothes behind at all?"

"Some fishing stuff downstairs. It's behind the coal bin. You want that?"

"I want that," I said.

He got up and I followed him. He switched on the cellar light, took me downstairs and across the littered pile of refuse a cellar can collect. When he pointed to the old set of dungarees on the nail in the wall, I went over and felt through the pockets. The key was in the jacket. I said thanks and went back upstairs. The taxi was still waiting. He flipped his butt away when I got in, threw the heap into gear and headed toward the smell of the water.

I had to climb the fence to get on the pier. There wasn't much to it. The lockers were tall steel affairs, each with somebody's name scrawled across it in chalk. The number that matched the key didn't say Cooley, but it didn't matter any more either. I opened it up and saw the cardboard box that had been jammed in there so hard it had snapped one of the rods in the corner. Just to be sure I pulled one end open, tore through the other box inside and tasted the white powder.

Heroin.

They never expected Cooley to do it so simply. He had found a way to grab their load and stashed it without any trouble at all. Friend Jack was good at that sort of thing. Real clever. Walked away with a couple million bucks' worth of stuff and never lived to convert it. He wasn't quite smart enough. Not quite as smart as Carboy, Gerot, Renzo . . . or even a kid who pushed a junk cart. Smart enough to grab the load, but not smart enough to keep on living.

I closed the locker and went back over the fence with the box in my arms. The cabbie found me a phone in a gin mill and waited while I made my calls. The first one got me Gerot's home number. The second got me Captain Gerot himself, a very annoyed Gerot who had been pulled out of bed.

I said, "Captain, this is Joe Boyle and if you trace this call you're going to scramble the whole deal."

So the captain played it smart. "Go ahead," was all he told me.

"You can have them all. Every one on a platter. You know what I'm talking about?"

"I know."

"You want it that way?"

"I want you, Joe. Just you."

"I'll give you that chance. First you have to take the rest. There won't be any doubt this time. They won't be big enough to crawl out of it. There isn't enough money to buy them out either. You'll have every one of them cold."

"I'll still want you."

I laughed at him. "I said you'll get your chance. All you have to do is play it my way. You don't mind that, do you?"

"Not if I get you, Joe."

I laughed again. "You'll need a dozen men. Ones you can trust. Ones who can shoot straight and aren't afraid of what might come later."

"I can get them."

"Have them stand by. It won't be long. I'll call again."

I hung up, stared at the phone a second, then went back outside. The cabbie was working his way through another cigarette. I said, "I need a fast car. Where do I get one?"

"How fast for how much?"

"The limit."

"I got a friend with a souped-up Ford. Nothing can touch it. It'll cost you."

I showed him the thing in my hand. His eyes narrowed at the edges. "Maybe it won't cost you at that," he said. He looked at me the same way Helen had, then waved me in.

We made a stop at an out of the way rooming house. I kicked my clothes off and climbed into some fresh stuff, then tossed everything else into a bag and woke up the landlady of the place. I told her to mail it to the post office address on the label and gave her a few bucks for her trouble. She promised me she would, took the bag into her room and I went outside. I felt better in the suit. I patted it down to make sure everything was set. The cabbie shot me a half smile when he saw me and held the door open.

I got the Ford and it didn't cost me a thing unless I piled it up. The guy grinned when he handed me the keys and made a familiar gesture with his hand. I grinned back. I gave the cabbie his fare with a little extra and got in the Ford with my box. It was almost over.

A mile outside Mark Renzo's roadhouse I stopped at a gas station and while the attendant filled me up all around, I used his phone. I got Renzo on the first try and said, "This is Joe, fat boy."

His breath in the phone came louder than the words. "Where are you?"

"Never mind. I'll be there. Let me talk to Helen."

I heard him call and then there was Helen. Her voice was tired and all the hope was gone from it. She said, "Joe . . ."

It was enough. I'd know her voice any time. I said, "Honey . . . don't worry about it. You'll be okay."

She started to say something else, but Renzo must have grabbed the phone from her. "You got the stuff kid?"

"I got it."

"Let's go, sonny. You know what happens if you don't."

"I know," I said. "You better do something first. I want to see the place of yours empty in a hurry. I don't feel like being stopped going in. Tell them to drive out and keep on going. I'll deliver the stuff to you, that's all."

"Sure, kid, sure. You'll see the boys leave."

"I'll be watching," I said.

Joke.

I made the other call then. It went back to my hotel room and I did it smart. I heard the phone ring when the clerk hit the room number, heard the phone get picked up and said as though I were in one big hurry, *"Look, Helen, I'm hopping the stuff out to Renzo's. He's waiting for it. As soon as he pays off we'll blow. See you later."*

When I slapped the phone back I laughed again then got Gerot again. This time he was waiting. I said, "Captain. . .they'll all be at Renzo's place. There'll be plenty of fun for everybody. You'll even find a fortune in heroin."

"You're the one I want, Joe."

"Not even Vetter?"

"No, he comes next. First you." This time he hung up on me. So I laughed again as the joke got funnier and made my last call.

The next voice was the one I had come to know so well. I said, "Joe Boyle. I'm heading for Renzo's. Cooley had cached the stuff in a locker and I need it for a trade. I have a light blue Ford and need a quick way out. The trouble is going to start."

"There's a side entrance," the voice said. "They don't use it any more. If you're careful you can come in that way and if you stay careful you can make it to the big town without getting spotted."

"I heard about Gulley," I said.

"Saddening. He was a wealthy man."

"You'll be here?"

"Give me five minutes," the voice told me. "I'll be at the side entrance. I'll make sure nobody stops you."

"There'll be police. They won't be asking questions."

"Let me take care of that."

"Everybody wants Vetter," I said.

"Naturally. Do you think they'll find him?"

I grinned. "I doubt it."

The other voice chuckled as it hung up.

I saw them come out from where I stood in the bushes. They got into cars, eight of them and drove down the drive slowly. They turned back toward town and I waited until their lights were a mile away before I went up the steps of the club.

At that hour it was an eerie place, a dimly lit ghost house showing the signs of people that had been there earlier. I stood inside the door, stopped and listened. Up the stairs I

heard a cough. It was like that first night, only this time I
didn't have somebody dragging me. I could remember the
stairs and the long, narrow corridor at the top, and the oak-
panelled door at the end of it. Even the thin line of light
that came from under the door. I snuggled the box under my
arm and walked in.

Renzo was smiling from his chair behind the desk. It was
a funny kind of smile like I was a sucker. Helen was huddled
on the floor in a corner holding a hand to the side of her
cheek. Her dress had been shredded down to the waist, and
tendrils of tattered cloth clung to the high swell of her
breasts, followed the smooth flow of her body. Her other
hand tried desperately to hide her nakedness from Renzo's
leer. She was trembling, and the terror in her eyes was an
ungodly thing.

And Renzo grinned. Big, fat Renzo. Renzo the louse
whose eyes were now on the package under my arm, with
the grin turning to a slow sneer. Renzo the killer who found
a lot of ways to get away with murder and was looking at
me as if he were seeing me for the first time.

He said, "You got your going away clothes on, kid."

"Yeah."

"You won't be needing them." He made the sneer bigger,
but I wasn't watching him. I was watching Helen, seeing the
incredible thing that crossed her face.

"I'm different, Helen?"

She couldn't speak. All she could do was nod.

"I told you I wasn't such a kid. I just look that way.
Twenty. . . twenty-one you thought?" I laughed and it had a
funny sound. Renzo stopped sneering. "I got ten years on
that, honey. Don't worry about being in love with a kid."

Renzo started to get up then. Slowly, a ponderous
monster with hands spread apart to kill something. "You two
did it. You damn near ruined me. You know what happens
now?" He licked his lips and the muscles rolled under his
shirt.

My face was changing shape and I nodded. Renzo never
noticed. Helen saw it. I said, "A lot happens now, fat boy." I
dropped the package on the floor and kicked it to one side.
Renzo moved out from behind the desk. He wasn't thinking

any more. He was just seeing me and thinking of his empire that had almost toppled. The package could set it up again. I said, "Listen, you can hear it happen."

Then he stopped to think. He turned his head and you could hear the whine of engines and the shots coming clear across the night through the rain. There was a frenzy about the way it was happening, the frenzy and madness that goes into a *banzai* charge and above it the moan of sirens that seemed to go ignored.

It was happening to Renzo too, the kill hate in his eyes, the saliva that made wet paths from the corners of his tight mouth. His whole body heaved and when his head turned back to me again, the eyes were bright with the lust of murder.

I said, "Come here, Helen," and she came to me. I took the envelope out of my pocket and gave it to her, and then I took off my jacket, slipping it over her shoulders. She pulled it closed over her breasts, the terror in her eyes fading. "Go out the side . . . the old road. The car is waiting there. You'll see a tall guy beside it, a big guy all around and if you happen to see his face, forget it. Tell him this. Tell him I said to give the report to the Chief. Tell him to wait until I contact him for the next assignment then start the car and wait for me. I'll be in a hurry. You got that?"

"Yes, Joe." The disbelief was still in her eyes.

Renzo moved slowly, the purpose plain in his face. His hands were out and he circled between me and the door. There was something fiendish about his face.

The sirens and the shooting were getting closer.

He said, "Vetter won't get you out of this, kid. I'm going to kill you and it'll be the best thing I ever did. Then the dame. The blonde. Weber told me he saw a blonde at Gulley's and I knew who did this to me. The both of you are going to die, kid. There ain't no Vetter here now."

I let him have a long look at me. I grinned. I said, "Remember what that note said? It said Vetter was going to spill your guts all over the floor. You remember that, Renzo?"

"Yeah," he said. "Now tell me you got a gun, kid. Tell

me that and I'll tell you you're a liar. I can smell a rod a mile away. You had it, kid. There ain't no Vetter here now."

Maybe it was the way I let myself go. I could feel the loosening in my shoulders and my face was a picture only Renzo could see. "You killed too many men, Renzo, one too many. The ones you peddle the dope to die slowly, the ones who take it away die quick. It's still a lot of men. You killed them, Renzo, a whole lot of them. You know what happens to killers in this country? It's a funny law, but it works. Sometimes to get what it wants, it works in peculiar fashion. But it works.

"Remember the note. Remember hard what it said." I grinned and what was in it stopped him five feet away. What was in it made him frown, then his eyes opened wide, almost too wide and he had the expression Helen had the first time.

I said to her, "Don't wait, Helen," and heard the door open and close. Renzo was backing away, his feet shuffling on the carpet.

Two minutes at the most.

"I'm Vetter," I said. "Didn't you know? Couldn't you tell? Me. . . Vetter. The one everybody wonders about, even the cops. Vetter the puzzle. Vetter the one who's there but isn't there." The air was cold against my teeth. "Remember the note, Renzo. No, you can't smell a gun because I haven't got one. But look at my hand. You're big and strong . . . you're a killer, but look at my hand and find out who the specialist really is and you'll know that there was no lie in that note."

Renzo tried to scream, stumbled and fell. I laughed again and moved in on him. He was reaching for something in the desk drawer, knowing all the time that he wasn't going to make it and the knife in my hand made a nasty little snick and he screamed again so high it almost blended with the sirens.

Maybe one minute left, but it would be enough and the puzzle would always be there and the name when mentioned would start another ball rolling and the country would be a little cleaner and the report when the Chief read it would mean one more done with . . . done differently, but done.

Tomorrow I Die

Tomorrow I Die

THE NOON TRAIN had pulled into Clarksdale at the hottest part of the day, an hour late. Twice a day that cross-country special stopped there for a thirty-minute layover giving the reporters a chance to photo and interview the celebs making the trip. The station even went so far as to set up a real deal for anybody who felt like stretching his legs. Local food and souvenirs.

Trouble was, the heat. The passengers preferred the air conditioning to the shimmering blasts of sunlight that waited outside. So only three of us got off.

One was met by a fat woman in a new Buick. The other guy and me headed straight across the street for the same thing...a fat draught beer.

Both of us half ran across the intersection, made the door at the same time and helped the other one in. Then the cold hit you. So cold it hurt, but it was wonderful.

At the bar the Sheriff smiled and asked, "Too hot for you gentlemen?"

When the beer came, I let it all go down, tasting every swallow.

My train buddy took longer and when I asked him to have one on me he shook his head sadly, "Thanks, but no go. The wife can't stand my breath." He threw a quarter on the bar and left.

"A shame, the way women run men," the Sheriff said.

"Awful. That guy isn't finished growing up."

"Well, that ain't always the case."

Before I could answer a low, rich voice laughed, "You better say that, Dad."

The tan brought out the gray in her eyes. The sun had made her blonde and riding too much had made her belly flat. The swell of her thighs showed right through the skirt and melted into lush curves that the blouse couldn't hide.

"My daughter Carol," the Sheriff said. "You look familiar, son."

"Rich Thurber," I grinned.

The dish frowned at me, then her face made up into a smile. "Certainly. Hollywood, post-war. One of the young up and comings. I remember you."

"Thanks," I said.

"What happened?"

I waved over my shoulder toward Hollywood. "The land of the gas pipe. All the good ones came home and replaced us. In simple, we had one thing in common. No talent."

The Sheriff fingered his hat back. Under it the hair was full and white. "Why do I know you? I never go to the movies, son."

Carol gave her pop an annoyed glance. "You didn't have to. He used to be on all the magazine covers." She smiled back at me. "You just don't quite look like yourself."

I put the beer down. "Sugar, let me remind you painfully. The war ended ten years ago. I'm not the same boy anymore."

The laugh came out of her like music. She threw back her head and let it dance out lightly. "I was fifteen then. You were one of my many heroes." She saw my face then and stopped the laugh. She looked at me through a woman's eyes and said, "I mean for real. You came out of the war and all that. I had a small girl's crush on you."

"I like big girls," I said.

"Uh-uh." She lifted those eyes toward the top of my head. "That hat. Who'd ever wear a hat like that?"

"Our Mayor," her father answered.

"Except the Mayor," she answered.

I reached up and took the kady off. "I always wanted

one. My old man wore one and I thought he looked like a million. So I got one." I put it back on, tapped it in place with a grin and finished my beer.

I ordered a refill, downed it and had another. The bartender pushed it across pretty fast. He seemed a little too anxious and kept watching the clock. I had one more and it was the pay-off one.

My stomach went into those warning motions and while there was still plenty of time to be casual about it, I walked off to the can in the back and tried to be quiet. I should have known better, but it was my own fault. The bartender came in and said, "Two minutes till train time, feller."

"...hell with it."

"Okay..."

I was long past caring when the train left. I heard the whistle and the wheels and by the time I could face myself in the mirror again it was quiet outside with only the noise of the wind in the eaves. I went to the basin, doused my face with cold water and called myself some names.

Stupid. I was stupid. I wasn't drunk. Not on four quick beers. I'd just made myself sick as a slob on heat and thirst. I stayed there cooling down from the exertion, wondering why the bartender hadn't given me at least a second call when the door opened again and he walked in.

Or at least partly in. He was all shook up.

"Gotta come out, stranger. You gotta." His bottom lip quivered and under his pants his thighs were giving his bones a massage.

"What?"

"You...gotta. There's a man here..."

The man didn't wait to be introduced. He shoved the bartender against the door jamb and slid in so I could see him but all that I bothered watching was the rod in his fist. It was big and black with the gray noses of the slugs showing in the cylinder and the hammer cocked back to start them moving. There was another one in his belt at a ready angle and from the expression on his face he was looking for an excuse to shoot somebody.

He was crazy. Crazy as a loon. And he was a killer.

"You don' wanna come out here, mister?" His voice was too high.

I nodded quickly. "I'm coming. Right now."

He stepped back and let me go past with the bartender crowding my heels.

Whatever happened to make him go off I didn't see. There was just a grunt, then a sharp curse from the hood. The sound the gun made as it cracked against the bartender's skull had a nasty splitting note to it. He went down against my back, almost tumbled me, then his face hit the floor with a meaty smack. When I looked back, the gun pointed at my eyes and nudged me ahead. I kept right on going. Straight.

Since I left, the bar had filled up. At one of the tables two men sat quietly waiting, saying nothing, doing nothing. There was one more at the door with a shotgun in his hands and he kept watching out the window.

The Sheriff was at the other table. He had a welt over his eye and was just starting to wake up. Carol had a cloth pressed to his head and her lip between her teeth, trying hard to keep back the sobs.

I heard the gun boy say, "He was in the John, Mr. Auger."

Auger was the small fat one. He smiled and said, "Good boy, Jason."

"Please don't call me Jason, Mr. Auger." Something went wrong with the high voice. It had a warble to it and I wondered if the gun guy was asking or telling.

The fat one smiled even bigger and nodded solemnly. "I'm sorry, Trigger. I won't forget again."

"That's all right, Mr. Auger."

Then the fat one stared hard at me, his smile fading back into his cheeks again. "Who are you?"

"Just passing through, buddy. That's all."

Behind me gun-happy said, "Watch me make him talk, Mr. Auger," and I tightened up, hoping I'd pull away in the right direction when it came.

Before I had to Auger said, "He's telling the truth, Trigger. You can tell by his accent. He's no native." He looked back at me again. "You have a car outside?"

"No. I came in on the special."

"Why didn't you go out on it then?"

"I got sick and missed it."

"Uh-huh."

Someplace a clock ticked loudly and you could hear the ice settling in the cooler. Twice, somebody passed by the place on the sidewalk, but neither came in nor bothered to look in.

By rough estimation we stayed that way five minutes. The Sheriff opened his eyes and they were dull and hurt-looking. He moaned softly and put a hand to the lump that was turning a deep blue color.

Carol said, "Can I wet this rag again?"

Auger beamed paternally. "Certainly, my dear. But just wet the rag, nothing else." The smile turned to the one behind me. "If she takes out a gun...or anything dangerous, then shoot her—Trigger."

"Sure, Mr. Auger."

I heard the guy turn and take two steps. Carol went across the room with him behind her and I knew he was hoping for any excuse to put one in her back. There was a fever in the eyes of the Sheriff as he watched his daughter walk in front of that gun and all the hate in the world was in the set of his face.

All the hate, that is, except mine. I knew I was getting set to go when the small muscles in my shoulders began to jump. I was almost ready and close to where I couldn't stop if it came and it wasn't time. It wasn't the time! My gut was sucked in so far that my pants fell away loose and I had to swallow before I could talk. I had to get off it, damn it, I had to get off.

I said, "As long as you're doing favors...can I sit down, mister?"

Auger showed me his slow smile. "You are nervous?"

"Very nervous."

"That's good. It's good to be nervous. It keeps you from making mistakes."

He didn't know how right he was. He didn't know how big the mistake could have been. Someplace in back a faucet ran, then stopped. Carol came back with the wet cloth in her hand and laid it on her father's head. Auger pointed to their table. "You can sit with them. Just sit. I think you understand?"

"I couldn't miss, mister."

When I moved my feet, the feeling went away. My shoulders got still and I could feel my gut taking up the slack in my pants again. It was too close. I looked at Carol and for the first time in a long while felt scared down deep. Not so it showed. Just so I knew it.

Carol looked up at me and smiled when I reached the table. Two people in trouble together, her eyes said. Two people mixed up in a crazy impossible nightmare together.

The Sheriff's eyes were closed, but his hand on the table was clenching and unclenching. His chest moved deeply, but too slow, as if he were controlling it to keep back a sob. Carol reached out and covered his hand patting it gently, cradling his head against her cheek.

It was very quiet.

You know how it is when you feel somebody looking hard at your back? You get crawly all over like it's too cold and at the same time there's a funny burn that grows inside your chest cavity. The hairs on the back of your arms stand up and you don't know whether to look around fast or slow.

The voice was so deep a bass it almost growled. It said, "Turn around, you."

So I turned slow and looked at the dark one next to Auger. His face showed a hard anger and I knew that this was the bad one. This was the one who ran things when the chips were down. Trigger was only a killer, but this one was a murderer.

"I know this guy, Auger," he said.

Auger only smiled.

"Why should I know you, guy?"

My shrug was to work the jumps out of my shoulders again. I felt it starting but this time it wasn't so bad. "I was a movie actor," I told him.

"In what ones?"

I named three. I was lucky to remember the titles.

The guy's face was getting nasty edges to it. "I don't remember them. What's your name?"

Before I could answer him Auger said, "Thurber. Richard Thurber." He glanced at the dark guy with just a shade too much cunning. "You should leave these details to me, Allen."

The anger on Allen's face disappeared. He almost smiled, almost let his teeth match the look in his eyes, then he stopped and I knew if he had smiled all the way somebody would have died.

"Sorry, Mr. Auger. I just don't like to meet people I know. Not on a job, anyway. If I know them, then they know me. Oke?"

"A good thought, Allen. But actually, what difference would it have made?"

Carol didn't look up. She was crying inside and not for herself. She was crying for the old man against her cheek because we were all going to die and nobody could stop it. You could stop some things, but you couldn't stop this.

Auger's chair scraped as he swung around in it. The guy at the door pulled back a little and spoke over his shoulder. "Here comes Bernie, Mr. Auger."

"Whom does he have, Leo?"

"Short guy. Guy's got a gun on him. They're talking."

"No trouble?" Auger asked.

"Nothing so far. It's just like fishing. He's being suckered right in."

"Anything of Carmen?"

"Can't see him, Mr. Auger."

Auger leaned back in his chair. "Be nice when they come in, Leo."

Leo was big and he had teeth missing, three knuckles wide, but he still liked to grin. It was mostly all fun with a fat tongue in the middle. "I'll be real sweet to him, Mr. Auger," he said.

Then he stepped back and faced the bar like he was a customer as the two men came in the door. It was all very neat. The boy he called Bernie came in first, paused fast so the other bumped into him, and as Leo slid the gun out of the holster from behind, Bernie poked one into his middle section from in front.

The guy didn't know what was going on. Carol let out a

stifled, "George!" the same time Leo belted him behind the ear with his own gun and as George was heading face into the sawdust, he got the idea.

George was a deputy.

Auger swung forward in the chair and peered at him. "Carry him over by the other, Bernie. He'll be all right. Did it come off as we planned?"

Bernie hefted the deputy and grunted, "Sure. He was eating in the back room alone."

"Find their car?"

"Around the corner." He threw the deputy into a chair. "This one didn't have the keys on him."

"We got the keys," Auger said, and nodded toward the Sheriff.

On the wall the clock whirred and a bent hammer tapped a muffled gong. Three times. For a brief instant every eye checked a watch and at the door Leo said, "I see Carmen, Mr. Auger. He's alone."

Allen's bass voice said something dirty.

"You're sure, Leo?"

"Positive, Mr. Auger. He's coming slow. No trouble. He's just alone."

Auger's fat little face showed its paternal smile again. He swung around the way fat men do and looked at us. At first I thought it was me he was going to speak to. Then I saw Carol flinch and go white around the mouth.

"The Mayor, Miss LaFont. Every day at exactly the same time he goes to his office to take care of his private practice. Every day. Without fail." There was something too pregnant in the pause that followed. He said, "Well?" and though his smile was still there, his eyes had a wetness of murder in them.

I was surprised at the calm in her voice. "He's out of town. He left Friday night to attend the State Bar Convention and is on this morning's program so he won't be home until tonight."

Trigger said, "You want me to make sure for you, Mr. Auger?"

"No, Trigger. She's telling the truth. People just can't make up a lie that fast and that sound." He stood up and the

other two did the same. Allen was almost a foot taller so it
seemed funny to hear Auger give the orders.

I said, "Any chance finding out what the hell's
going on?"

"I was wondering when you'd ask," Auger laughed.
"We're robbing the bank. Simple? You'll be the hostages. If
followed, somebody is killed and thrown out the door. The
chase will stop then. That is, if there will be a chase. We'll go
in the Sheriff's car with lights, sirens and radio. However, we
expect no chase."

"Then?"

"Then you'll all be shot. Very simple."

"That could urge a guy like me into making a break for
it anytime."

His smile broadened. "No, it couldn't really. Everybody
wants to hang right on to life. It's the most precious item.
The minute you start to fuss—dead. It's all very simple."

"It's after three o'clock," I suggested.

"I know. The Sheriff will be our passport in. Two million
dollars awaits. Pleasant thought?"

"From your angle. You'll get picked up," I said.

"Did they get the Brink's boys yet?"

"Nobody got shot on that job. It's different when somebody gets shot."

"So? You're familiar with criminology?"

"I read mystery books."

He smiled at my joke. He let everybody smile at my joke.
Then he looked at his watch and the tension was back with
all its implications when he said, "Go look at the bartender,
Trigger."

The killer went back past the bar and skirted its edge.
He bent out of sight for a second, then straightened. "Guy's
dead, Mr. Auger."

"We'll lock the place up. You have the keys, Trigger?"

"I have them."

"Very well," Auger said. "Let us go then."

On the floor the deputy was coming up into a sitting
position and he drooled. He knew what was happening and
it was too big for him.

Even Trigger's eyes were pointed at the corners like he

was trying too hard to seem normal and beside Auger, the tall one called Allen was suppressing something that wasn't quite a grin.

I said, "I want my hat."

The tension turned to surprised silence. Trigger's gun came up and his head cocked like a parrot's. Auger asked, "What?"

"My hat. I don't leave without my lid."

"Should I shoot him, Mr. Auger?"

My shoulders started in again. I could feel it beginning but this time I sat on it quickly enough and it went away.

"The fruitcake shoots me," I said, "and outside they pile in on you. Like somebody once said, 'the jig's up.' You know?"

I think Auger smiled for real this time. He said, "Let him go get his hat, Trigger." The fine line of his teeth showed under his lip. "Just go with him to be sure that's all he gets."

"Sure, Mr. Auger."

So I got up and walked back to the men's room. I went in with Trigger holding the door open and came out with my hat. When I was back beside Carol, I slapped the kady on, tapped the crown and said, "Okay, kids, put on the show."

I didn't quite expect the reaction I got. Allen's face was a dull mask and the other guy just stared at Auger. Our little fat friend looked like a pickpocket who got his pocket picked and for an instant a little shake ran right down his pudgy frame.

"Imagine that," he said. His eyes glinted at me. "You have nerve, our misnomered friend."

"You got took, Auger," Allen said softly.

"No...not took...just taken temporarily. His Honour is a shrewdy."

I started to squint when I got the picture. It came all at once and was so damn funny I almost started laughing right then.

Auger shook his head. "Don't laugh. It isn't appreciated. I've been fooled before and it's one thing I don't appreciate." His face flattened back into that smile again. "Though I do appreciate the humor of *his* situation, Allen. His Honor, whom we never saw up close, was to be identified as the only one in town who would forego a Stetson for a straw hat. He was also to be identified as a non-native. Whether he wanted to be or not, he was caught...and he wants to die with his hat on, so to speak."

Allen's voice held a stubborn tone. "The dame, Auger. She was lying."

His head bobbed. "Something our informants over-looked. They're in love. Lovers can think clearly when the loved one is in trouble."

"He's a movie actor, Auger?"

The smile went all the way to a laugh. "No...but so close a look-alike he can capitalize on it when he wants to."

This time I played it all the way. I said, "Do you blame me? So I was figuring. Maybe I could've had an out if you counted on survivors."

"Very smart. It's too bad you have to die."

"It is?"

I could see the back of his tongue now. "It is," he said. "Now let's go."

"Me?"

"That's right. You and the Sheriff. Our in and our out." He stopped a moment, smiled gently, then said, "Need I remind you that anyone sounding off will be shot? We're playing for big stakes. You can take your choice. Sheriff... I'll warn you that one peep from you and your daughter will be killed. Understood?"

I saw the Sheriff nod and his face showed each line deeper than ever.

Carol's face didn't seem so tan anymore. I grinned at her real big, almost as if the whole thing were funny and what-ever she saw in that grin brought the tan back to her face and her eyes were gray again. She gave me a twisted little smile and one eyebrow had the slightest cock to it like she was trying to figure out the gimmick that should never have been there at all.

She looked and wondered, and our eyes were saying hello all over again. I tried to stop looking at her but couldn't make it and inside me a tight, hot little fire started to burn.

I wasn't grinning anymore. I was watching her, trying to

say a soundless, "No...!" to both of us that something stifled before it could come out.

At the door Auger said, "Get the Sheriff's car, Carmen. Allen...are you ready to load the other?"

"I'm ready."

Carmen walked back to the deputy, his hand in one pocket palming a gun. He eased the deputy from his chair with, "Up, laddie boy. Let's make like an official."

Without a word, the deputy started toward the door. I thought he was going to be sick. Allen followed them out and the rest of us waited.

Nobody had tried to come in as yet. Nobody had even passed the place as yet. It was going to be an easy grab. A mark. A first-class creampuff.

The cars pulled in to the curb, a dark blue Olds sedan behind the black Ford with the whiplash aerial and blinker-siren combo. The Sheriff drove while I rode beside him. Auger and the killer stayed in the back seat. The deputy was unconscious on the floor again. All the others were behind us in the Olds and there was no way out. No way at all. It was all going nice and easy.

And that's the way it happened at the bank, too.

They robbed it at 3:22 with no complications at all because the Sheriff saw the only possible hitch in the deal and took the lead almost willingly. The guard opened the doors for him and seemed more hurt than mad when a gun covered him.

Auger walked us to the manager's cage and indicated us with his gun. "This is a holdup. Touch the alarm and you and these hostages die. Others outside will die too and since you are fully covered by insurance, don't try to be a hero."

The manager was almost cordial. "No... I won't."

It didn't need any more than that. They even did the work themselves. The cashier and two clerks brought it out stacked and packed while the killer's mouth worked wetly, hoping for a mistake. Auger's head bobbed like a satisfied customer and clucked at the killer to be patient. The mother-hen noises were a promise of better pickings later and his hands relaxed around the butt of the gun.

Quietly I asked, "What's the angle, Sheriff?"

Just as quietly he answered, "She's engaged to the Mayor. He'll get us out."

––––––

THE VASTNESS of the desert disappeared into the darkness closing in behind us, while ahead the last groping fingers of sunlight poked over the range of mountains to probe the gullies and ravines of the foothills with splashes of dull reds and oranges.

Beside me the Sheriff's face was as tight as his hands on the wheel, his eyes bloodshot and tired. His breath was harsh in nostrils dilated taut and I knew just what he was feeling. Right in the back of my head was a cold spot where the bullet would land if we moved too fast or too wrong. Behind us sat Auger and his gun boy and even over the sound of the engine I could hear the lazy fingering and cocking of the triggers on the two rods.

It was worse for the Sheriff. In the blue Olds behind us his daughter was on the end of another rod and whether she lived or died depended on what he did. Me too, in a way. Back there was the dough, a deputy and a daughter. Back there was a lot of reasons for playing it their way.

The Sheriff had inched up on the wheel until the bottom of it was in his belly. Without turning, he said, "Either we stop and get the dirt and bugs off this windshield or you better let me turn the lights on."

Auger's voice was totally calm. Completely without emotion. "You'll do neither."

"We'll wind up in a hole someplace then."

"I don't think so," Auger told him. "You have a reputation for knowing every inch of road to the border."

"Not the holes, mister."

He slowed for a turn, braked to ease over the sandy potholes, then downshifted to get through the rubble of a rockslide. I saw the Olds jouncing in the ruts and almost run up our trunk. The Sheriff hit the go-pedal to get away from the sedan and his face got tighter than ever.

"You better let me put them dims on, mister."

For a second I thought Auger was going to agree when

the radio suddenly kicked up a carrier-wave hum and a woman's high voice mouthed a call signal.

Auger said, "Turn it up!"

The gesture was automatic. The Sheriff's hand touched the knob and the voice came in, faint but clear. "The Marshal's call," he said before he was asked.

"Shut up!"

"...using two cars, carrying Sheriff LaFont and several others. Sighted going west on ninety-two. High Section Six, can you report? Over."

Another hum was overlaid on the first, but there was no voice.

Auger's calm was still there. "Who is High Section Six?"

"Forestry Service. They send on another frequency. We can't pick them up."

"Mr. Auger..."

"Yes, Trigger?"

"We in trouble?"

Instead of answering, he spoke to the Sheriff. "You tell him," he said. The calm in his voice had turned deadly. I felt my shoulders hunching again.

I could see the Sheriff's teeth through his grimace. "No. Not yet. It'll be a while before they figure this road."

The hum went into a series of clicks, then, "...all sections report moving lights. Do not radio. Repeat, do not radio. Telephone all reports. Out."

"Neat," I said.

"Not for you," Auger told me.

I think I was reaching for a wise answer. I had it in my mouth when I stopped, just barely glancing at the Sheriff. The Ford was moving too fast and the car had a peculiar set to it. There was a trace of swoosh in the tail section and I knew the wheels were on the edge of a drift. The road ahead was barely outlined and seemed to have the slightest curve to it.

Right away I knew what he was playing for. He was setting up a dust storm behind us hoping the Olds would cut on its lights and maybe be spotted from one of those towers. He was doing it nice, but he did it wrong.

From back there came the raucous blast of a horn, a

screaming of tires scraping rock and the smashing, tinny racket of a car going end over end.

The Sheriff didn't try to hit the brakes because two guns were right against our necks. He eased to a stop, horsed into reverse and backed through the dust. There was no way of seeing anything, and at the same time we heard the yells as the rear end of the Ford plowed into metal and glass and with a sickening jolt the Olds rolled once more.

Just once, then it toppled off the road into the ravine and you could have counted three before you heard it hit the bottom.

The horror of what had happened swept into the Sheriff's face and while he was starting to shrivel up and die inside, Carol's voice, sobbing quietly, carried through the settling dust.

Just as quickly, Allen was framed in the door with a gun in his fist pointing at me and his face twisted into a mad snarl. "You damn fool..."

"Put that gun down, Allen."

The big guy turned his snarl to Auger without moving the gun. "Carmen and Leo were in there. They were getting the money out!" His hand tightened on the rod. "Let's get that dough up here."

Auger moved slowly. He got out, then waved the Sheriff and me out and let Trigger stand behind us with the two guns at full cock. I could tell that Trigger was wearing his hoping smile. The big one.

Out of the side of my mouth I told the Sheriff, "She's okay. Just don't move, that's all."

He knew what I meant and nodded, never taking his eyes from Carol. She sat by the side of the road, dazed and crying but obviously unhurt. The deputy had a cut across his nose and was holding his ankle, his face twisting in pain.

Allen said, "What about the dough?"

There were just a few final snatches of light. Just enough to make out forms and vague shapes. The Sheriff moved to the edge of the ravine and peered over it. He shook his head. "Nobody gets down there until there's light. Even then you got to go in from the cut up yonder."

Allen and Auger looked at each other quickly. I knew

damn well what they were thinking because I would have thought about it myself. The pie was going to be cut in bigger slices now. The grin I tried to hold back picked up my lip because when you start that stuff it keeps going on and on. The pie looks best whole. Carol saw the grin and her sobbing stopped. It probably was too dark for her to see it, but I made like a kiss and blew it her way. She did something with her mouth too, but I couldn't be quite sure just what.

It was Trigger who finally asked the question. "What are we going to do now, Mr. Auger?"

"You'll see, Jason."

Behind me I could feel the gun goon go cold, ice cold. "You said you wouldn't call me that anymore, Mr. Auger."

The fat man nodded solemnly. "I'm sorry, Trigger. I forgot." Then his face showed that he had all the answers and he pointed his finger at me. "You can start clearing away all bits of metal and glass you can find on the road. You and the girl both. Watch them, Trigger."

"Sure, Mr. Auger."

I didn't wait to be prodded. I walked to Carol, helped her up and wiped the dirt off her face. "You okay?"

She nodded briefly. "Shaken up a little, that's all. George twisted his ankle, but I don't think it's broken."

"You were lucky."

"I guess so. The three of us were thrown clear when the car rolled. I... I think both the others were dead...before the car went over."

"Don't think about it. Let's get this road cleared."

I had to pull a handful of brush from the shoulder of the road to make a couple of sweeps. It took a while, but we got up what glass and odd bits that were around. When there wasn't anything left on top to show there was an accident I took Carol's hand and walked back to the car.

"That's done. Now what?"

Auger smiled. "You seem awfully unconcerned for a man who will be dead shortly."

"I don't count on dying."

"You have to, Mr. Mayor. You just have to."

"That wasn't what I asked."

From the darkness Allen half whispered, "Stop talking to him. Damn...let's roll."

Trigger said, "We going, Mr. Auger?"

Carol's hand was squeezing mine hard. Auger turned to the Sheriff, his face a pale oval in the dark. "This house you mentioned?"

The Sheriff waved toward the southwest. "Fourteen-fifteen miles maybe. Feller works a claim there."

"Completely alone?"

"Don't get to see folks for months."

"You know what happens if you lead us into any trap?" The Sheriff didn't answer. Auger said, "First your daughter gets it. Then you. Then the others. We're far enough off to be able to make our way without help now."

The Sheriff nodded. "There's no trap."

Allen came in closer, the gun in his hand held too tensely. "I don't like it. We ought to go after it now. Right now."

"And get ourselves killed, Allen? Don't be silly. It's too much to be clumsy about. We'll do it the smart way." He paused a moment, looking us over in that arrogant way he had. "Sheriff, you drive. Your daughter can sit between you and the Mayor. I want the deputy on the floor in the back with the rest of us."

"We ought to dump the crip, Auger. That's a big load."

"Buzzards, Allen. They have them in this country. Why tip our hand? This time we'll take it slowly, won't we, Sheriff?"

"Without lights we got to."

"And no mistakes."

I saw the Sheriff glance at Carol. "Don't reckon so," he said.

——————

THE OLD MAN was big and angular, with arthritis. He had pale eyes that you knew had killed a dozen times and the type of face you wouldn't have messed with even ten years ago. There was a leanness of age and of work in his hips and shoulders but over it all was the mantle of desert philosophy.

His time had come and he knew it.

He opened the door and in that single second he saw all of us there and knew what had happened. He saw the despair in the Sheriff's face and the anxiety in Carol's. He saw the abject fear of the deputy and the total lack of humanity in Auger. There was a touch of pity when he looked on Trigger and cold hatred for Allen.

I was last. He stared at me longest, the corner of his mouth twitching with a strange quirk, then he flipped the door wide and let us all come in. He smiled when Allen patted him down, and smiled again when Trigger jacked the shells out of the rifle on the wall. The smile even stayed there when they pulled the ancient .44s out of the gun belt and punched them out of the Colt.

Then he looked past the gunman and said, "Evenin' Sheriff...Miss Carol...George."

He saved the faintest of smiles for me and barely nodded. Yet he knew. *He knew damn well!*

Auger pulled a chair out with a wave to Allen and the gun boy. He sat down with a sigh and mopped his face with a clean folded handkerchief. "Old man...you seem to have gotten the picture here very rapidly."

The old boy nodded again.

"You know what happened?"

"I have a radio."

"Phone?"

"No telephone."

"Perhaps you expect visitors. A neighbor. Someone from the Forestry Service?"

"Nobody. Not until two weeks from now. Then Tillson comes with my trailer hitch for the Jeep. Then he can bury us all."

"Very perceptive. You're not afraid?"

"No."

"That's too bad. It's better to be afraid. You can stay alive just that much longer sometimes."

"I'm no kid."

"But you might be enjoying the twilight years."

"I am."

"For only a while. A pity."

He shouldn't have looked at me. I felt the crazy itch across my shoulders and the sudden hunching in my shoulders. The old man looked at me and grinned and he was the only one who found out. His eyes saw the creases and curves on the outside and the dips and contortions on the inside. His eyes were little feelers tipped with needles and they were on me.

"You can never tell," he said, "never."

Auger frowned at his tone. "I can tell."

It was Allen who broke the long stillness that followed. He leaned on the battered hand-carved table, the gun beside his hand and his voice filled with controlled rage. "Maybe you can tell me what we're going to do next?"

For the first time I saw the deadliness in Auger's character. It wasn't something added; it was something lacking and even deadlier than murder. It was some barbaric callousness that nullified human life or feeling and fed on the lusting that led to death and destruction. With the first word Allen drew back slowly, recognizing something that wasn't there by sight nor sound, seeing something that only I saw too.

Or maybe the old man. He knew about those things.

"Yes, Allen," Auger said quietly, "I can tell you."

Something was about to happen then. I didn't want to see it spelled out so I broke into it. I wasn't welcome because I put out the flame but if a fire started I wanted it to be one I started myself. I said, "Sure, tell us. Give us a clue."

And Auger looked at me a long time, long enough so I began to wonder if he knew too. My shoulders felt funny again and for the first time I looked down and saw my fingers splayed.

His character had a fault in it. A crack where the juice could leak out easy. He licked his lips until they shone wet. "I'll enjoy telling you," he said. "I think it's funny. Tomorrow the girl and the Mayor go back for the money. If there's any hitch her father is shot along with the others."

"You're nuts!"

"Allen..."

"They'll take off."

"It's her father, Allen."

"Okay, so the guy takes off..."

"They're in love. Remember?"

"Listen..."

"No, you listen, Allen. Listen very carefully and you'll know why this operation is mine, carefully conceived, planned and executed." He looked at all of us while he spoke, a dramatist watching his audience for each reaction.

"We picked that one town for its amazing cash wealth. We took their loved citizens as hostages knowing their incredible affection for each other, knowing that life is put above wealth. We selected an escape route impossible to trace." He smiled at us gently. "And tomorrow, the Mayor and his girl recover our wealth. If they are interrupted...they think. If they don't think, the Sheriff is dead."

"So what do they think?"

"How to cover the situation. How to stay alive, bring the cash back here and keep her father alive."

I grinned at him. "You already said we were as good as dead."

Auger's smile had the devil's benevolence in it. "And I say it again. You just forget that there's always that one chance."

"We might get out?"

"That's right," Auger told me. "That you might win the game. Hopeless, but a game."

Allen said something filthy and wiped his mouth with the back of his hand. Trigger was there too, the idiot's grin in his jaws. He watched Allen and both triggers were cocked on his guns. They were held idly, but ready.

I didn't feel that shaking anymore. I was away ahead of them all and being careful so it wouldn't show on my face. I was thinking of how easy it was going to be to get away from there, how that one chance Auger thought was an impossibility was a fat reality after all and how fast and slick I was going to take it.

Then I saw Carol's face and though I knew she couldn't see what I was thinking she was wondering about it just the same.

There was one other angle. The big one. The one only

the old man got and his mouth was making faces at me because he knew for sure now. He was thinking what I was trying hard not to remember and I didn't want to look at him. His eyes went back too deep and penetrated too far into a guy's mind.

"Mr. Mayor..."

I grinned. "Yes, Mr. Auger?"

"Do you need any further explanation?"

"No."

"There is only one road. You'll be able to find the site?"

"I'll find it."

"The Sheriff will tell you how to get into the ravine."

"I know where it is," Carol said.

"Good," Auger beamed. "That makes it so much easier. And of course you realize the consequences of any nonsense, my dear?"

Carol simply nodded, not speaking.

"You'll bring the money up and come directly here. I'm going to estimate a time of twelve hours. If you have not appeared by then, your father, his deputy and this old man will be shot. That much is clear?"

We both nodded this time.

"If, then, there is any sign of any trickery...any at all, understand, they die and we figure another way out. Don't underestimate us. Don't think we won't do exactly as we say. That's clear?"

"Clear," I said.

"You take the road back in..." he checked his watch, "two hours. No lights. You travel slowly. Be sure not to raise a dust cloud or otherwise attract attention. You'll arrive at the site after daybreak and have ample time to do what is expected of you." He looked at Carol first then me. "Any questions?"

I nodded. "Yeah. What about the bodies in the car?"

"Forget them."

"The buzzards might be up early."

That got to him. Something twitched in his cheek. "If they have fallen out of the car, put them back. Buzzards hunt on sight."

"Yeah."

He got that twitch again. "You're being awfully solicitous about our safety."

"Certainly," I said, "I wouldn't want anything to happen to my friends."

I smiled. A real easy one. Only the old man knew what it meant.

"You'll take the Jeep. Our aged friend here will check you out on it."

"I don't need checking out."

"Good, good. I'm expecting a whole lot of you, Mr. Mayor."

There wasn't a sound in the entire room. Outside the wind blew gently and whispered across the eaves. Carol shuddered gently then was still.

———

"Here's where we turn off," she said. "The road only goes down a few hundred feet then we'll have to walk."

I stopped the Jeep without turning and looked at her. The sun had washed her face with the first red light of morning and in its glow she looked tired. Tired and sorry. She hadn't spoken since we left the cabin and there was a peculiar apathy in her voice.

"Or do we?" she asked suddenly.

For some reason she smiled wanly and there was a wetness in her eyes that threw back the sun.

Then she turned her head and her smile grew a little twisted. "I guess we don't. I...can't blame you."

"You're scrambled, kid," I said.

"Why should you?"

"Why?" I shoved the straw kady back on my head and pawed the dirt out of my eyes. "Let's say I could go through with this out of common decency. My love for my fellow man."

"That's a lot of love. We take the money back and all get killed. It would be more sensible if you let me take it back while you went on."

"You'd still get bumped."

"But they'd be caught. It's something." She dropped her eyes when they got too wet. "This is none of your affair."

"It could be, sugar. It sure could be."

"What?" Her voice was tight in her chest.

"You forgot the other angle. There's a perfect crime involved." I let my grin stretch out into a short laugh. "I could bump you, take the cabbage and let the boys kill the others. I could put your body in the car with the other two and it'll all look legit. I could stash the dough for a year then come back and pick it up when all is cooled down. The law gets the boys, blames the deal on them, they cook and that's that."

"Would you?"

"I gave it some thought."

Carol looked at the road where we had stopped. There was a puzzle written in the set of her face and I saw her shoulders tighten and her fingers go white around each other.

"Would you?" she asked again.

I nodded. "I would."

But I didn't move. I sat there lazy-like, still grinning, hoping nothing was showing, wondering if she had the normal intuitive quality a woman was supposed to have, trying to figure what I'd do if she had.

Her face came back to mine slowly. "But *will* you?"

"No," I said, "I'll go back with you."

"Why?" Her eyes weren't wet any longer. They were curious now.

"Does there have to be a reason?"

"There are too many reasons why you shouldn't go back. You can only die back there."

"Maybe the future holds nothing better anyway," I told her quietly. "Maybe I already died someplace else and once more won't make any difference anyway."

"But that isn't why."

"No," I admitted. "It's you. I'm doing it for you. Something stupid has hold of me and when I look at you, I start to go fuzzy. I know it's you and the Mayor all the way but right now I feel like being noble and I don't feel like talking about it. Just take it for what it's worth. I'm going back with you."

"What then?"

"We'll think about it when it happens."

"Rich..."

Up ahead there was a speck in the sky.

"Rich." She touched my arm lightly. "Rich..."

I caught myself quickly reaching out for her hand.

"Thanks," she said.

"Forget it. We'll make out all right."

I started the Jeep up, snatched it into gear and started straight down the road. Carol grabbed my sleeve and pulled. "We can't...Rich, we have to go back down the road! We can't go over the cliff side!"

When I pulled my arm free, I pointed into the sun. "Plane up there. They could be looking for us. We drag the police in now there'll be trouble." Down toward the south a haze was rising into the morning sky. "Dust cloud. They're coming this way."

"What will we do?"

"We get out of here. The dust is coming from more than one car and I don't think the police will like the set of our plans."

"You think they know where we are?"

"I doubt it. They're just starting to fan out." I edged closer to the sheer rise of rock on my left and rode the hard-pan, trying hard not to fly a dirt flag behind us.

Overhead, the plane came toward us, banked and headed back to the dust cloud. I tried to remember back through time and distance to where we turned off and when I thought I had it, stepped the Jeep up to beat the dust cloud to the intersection. I could be wrong, but I wasn't taking chances.

Carol licked the alkali from her lips and shouted, "What will we tell them, Rich?"

I had that one figured out too. "They don't know me, remember? So I picked you up. You were walking back the highway and I picked you up. You don't know where you came from or where the others are. Just give them that, no more."

"All right, Rich."

The plane spotted us first. It came down low, an old Army L-5 and I waved at the uniformed trooper in the rear seat. He looked at us hard, tapped the pilot and they both stared quickly before they pulled up and around for another pass. This time I gave them the okay sign and jerked my thumb at Carol.

That was all they needed. The L-5 pulled up, throttled back and started a glide ahead of us. It came down on the highway, stopped and I pulled up beside it. The trooper was out, his hand on the gun in his holster, taking big strides our way.

"You all right, Miss LaFont?"

"Yes, thanks."

"Who're you?"

I didn't have to answer. Carol did it for me. "He gave me a ride. I...got away from them and reached the highway."

"Glad to help," I said. "I heard the news."

"Where are they, Miss LaFont?"

Carol shook her head. The tears that went with it were real. "I don't know!" Her face went into her hands to muffle the sobbing.

I fanned myself with the straw kady. It was pretty dirty now. I said, "Lady told me she got away someplace in the hills. Must've walked ten miles across the brush fields before I picked her up. I can take you back and show you."

"Never mind. We can pick up her trail if she came across the brush. You can track a mouse in that sand."

Behind the plane the dust took shape, a brown plume like a cock's tail following the six cars driving abreast. They came up and disgorged the hunters, avid men with guns in their hands and identical expressions on their faces. They were all angry men. They were all intent and serious. They all had a touch of lust too. Blood lust.

The big guy in front ran to the Jeep and half lifted Carol out of the seat. "Honey, honey," he crooned to her, "you okay, baby?"

"I'm all right, Harold."

"You take it easy baby. I'll take care of you now. You just take it easy."

The trooper raised a finger to his hat brim. "Pardon me, Mr. Mayor, we better start backtracking Miss LaFont while her tracks are fresh. This feller here..." he nodded toward me, "picked her up about ten miles back coming across the brush."

"You can't miss it," I said. "There's a dead dog by the side of the road just where she came on."

The trooper gave me a funny look. "Dog? No dogs out here, feller. Must be a coyote. Where you from, boy?"

I didn't answer the question. I said, "A dog, officer. A black Scotty. Somebody probably tossed him from their car. He's got a collar on."

The trooper squinted his apology and nodded, then turned back to the Mayor. "Excuse me, sir, but do you want to stay with Miss LaFont or go with the posse?"

For the first time I had a good look at the big guy, and saw all the parts of him I didn't like. He was too big and too good-looking. He reeked of maleness and you could almost feel the destiny that rode his shoulders. He looked at the trooper quickly and you could see the momentary flash of lust and blood scent in his mouth and nostrils. Then something else followed just as briefly that I couldn't quite identify, but immediately hated.

He took Carol's hand in his and the other went around her waist. "Go ahead, officer. I'll be sure that Carol is all right then I'll follow you. Take my car along with you. We'll stay with the Jeep here."

"Yes, sir." The trooper saluted again, waved the pack of cars off the road and let the L-5 get back into the blue. It circled once, then paralleled the highway behind us. The rest piled back into the cars, the trooper in the first one, and went by with their wheels throwing up dust from the shoulder.

Ten miles, I thought. I should have made it further. If I was lucky, they'd look for the dog and keep right on going.

Maybe it was the way Carol looked at me. Maybe it was the drawn expression and the way her eyes seemed to slant up at the corners. The Mayor stopped his soft talk and his lips hardened into a tight line.

His voice was a soft hiss. "What is it, Carol?"

"Harold..."

"Tell me."

"We had to get rid of them. They would have spoiled it."

"We?" He watched me with a careful disdain for a moment, then: "Who are you, feller?"

"A victim, buster. Part of the *we* she mentioned."

"Go on."

It was better letting her tell it. I could watch his face then and make a play of getting out of the Jeep. When she got to the part about the money, that look came back on his face and stayed long enough for me to see the greed that was there.

When she finished, he forced the excitement from his face and pounded a fat fist into his palm. "Good heavens, Carol, you can't expect us to let you go through with a thing like that! You can't jeopardize your life by going back there!"

"What else can she do?" I put in.

"Do? I'll show you what we'll do! We'll go back to that cabin and shoot them out of there like they deserve. We'll kill every one of those thieving skunks..."

"And the Sheriff, and the deputy, and the old man," I said.

Carol's face was white. Chalk-white. "You can't, Harold."

His tongue made a pass across his lips. "We have to. There are some things that must be done."

"Like being governor?"

He knew the greed had shown then. He knew I saw what was in his mind, the AP and UPI headlines. *Mayor recovers stolen millions. Leads fight on thieves' den.* In subheads they'd tell about the three who died with the thieves in line of civic duty.

"You're talking out of turn, mister." His grimace had a snarl in it.

He started to burn when I turned on the grin. "I don't think so. My hide's wrapped up in this mess too. You figure a way to pull it off and get the kid's dad out whole? You have an angle to snake out all three maybe?"

"Somebody is bound to get hurt. I could be myself, too."

"Harold..."

"Yes, Carol?"

"You can't do it. I won't let you." She had trouble getting the words out. She was looking at this guy she had never seen before and what she saw shook her bad. "You said you loved me, Harold..."

"I do, sugar. You know I do." He paused and sucked in his breath. "But I'm still the Mayor, honey. We can't let a thing like this happen."

"It means my father's life."

"And yours if you go back."

Slowly, very slowly, Carol turned her face to me. She smiled gently and I winked her a kiss and told myself that I was a sucker, a real, prime, first-class sucker who went up the pipe for a broad when the odds you were bucking were rigged from the very start.

The Mayor said, "I'm sorry, Carol," and this time all the hardness was there in his voice. It spelled out what he was going to do and he didn't have to say anything more to make it clear. "You two can wait here for the posse. I'll go in after that money and they can meet me there." He paused and looked at her as he would a pawn he willingly lost to gain a better position. "And Carol... I'm sorry. Truly sorry."

"So am I," I said.

"What?"

I grinned again. All the teeth this time. Then I splashed him. He turned blood all over and his jaw hung at a crazy angle and even before the dust had settled the flies were drifting down on his face. My knuckles went puffy before I could rub them but it was worth it. I picked him up, dumped him in the back of the Jeep and nodded for Carol to get aboard.

Almost out of sight down the highway was the thin brown plume. There was still time if we hurried but we'd have to make it fast. I spun the Jeep around, geared it up and floorboarded it to the cut off. This time I wasn't bothered about being followed and could make better time along the curves and switchbacks of the trail.

Carol was shouting for me to slow down and I braked the Jeep to a crawl. "The next turn and we can go down the ravine. Don't pass it!"

"How long will it take?" I shouted back.

"A half hour to reach the car." She leaned closer, squinting into the wind. "Can we do it?"

My fingers were crossed when I said it. "I think so. It'll be close, but we might just do it."

"What about Harold?"

"We'll leave him here. He'll come around. That posse won't have too much trouble tailing us in this dirt and our boy here will put them on the cabin right off."

She reached out and laid her hand on mine. It was warm and soft with a little burning place in the middle of her palm. Her thumb ran back and forth across my wrist lightly and all of a sudden a whole minute was yanked out of eternity and given to us for our own.

"Rich...we don't have much time any more...do we?"

"We can hurry..."

"I mean...for us, Rich. There's only one answer if we go back."

"Perhaps. Why?"

Her smile was a beautiful thing. "I'm just finding out...certain things."

"I knew them right along," I said.

"Harold..."

"Greedy. Ambitious. Mean. He'll spoil anything to get what he wants."

"I thought he wanted me."

"He did for a while, kid. But just now he saw a little more he could have and he took his choice."

"Why are you so perceptive?"

My face felt tight and all I said was, "I've been around, kid."

"Rich..."

"What?"

She leaned toward me. I knew what she was going to say and I didn't let her. I could taste the dust through the wet of her mouth and feel the life and fire of her as she pressed against me. Everything inside me seemed to turn over suddenly. Then I pushed her away before it could get worse.

There were tears in her eyes, the path of one etching its

way down her cheek. She frowned through them, watching me closely, her hand squeezing mine even tighter.

"There's something about you, Rich..."

"Don't look at it."

"We're only going back to die, aren't we?"

"Not you, kitten."

For a second it was like it was with the old man. For an instant she saw that one thing, but before she could hold it long enough it passed and left only the trace of a puzzle, barely long enough to get a glimmer of understanding.

But somehow it was enough. There was that change in her eyes and the taut way she held herself. The shadow of bewilderment was obscured in a moment of reality.

"Why are you doing it, Rich?"

"You'll never know," I said.

She brushed back her hair with one hand and looked past me into the ravine. "And when it's over?"

"I'll be gone. One way or another."

"And then there'll be no more."

"That's right."

"Rich..."

"Don't say it, kitten. Look at it and squeeze it with your hand, but don't say it."

"I love you, Rich."

"I told you, don't say it. It's because of the trouble. It's now, that's all. Maybe it will be gone tomorrow."

"Maybe there'll be no tomorrow."

"It always comes," I said. "I hate it too, but tomorrow always comes."

In the back the Mayor moaned softly. I said, "Let's get to it," and spun the wheel of the Jeep.

The road went down a quarter of a mile before the rock-slide wiped it out. I used the tarp ropes to snag the Mayor to the seat backs and waved Carol out. Overhead the sun was tracing its arc through the sky too fast, too fast. By my watch we had only two hours more to go and if there was anything in the way we'd be too late.

Had I been alone I never would have made it, but Carol knew the path and could pick it up even when there was nothing to mark it. We skirted the stream in the belly of the gorge, climbed to the shoulder that was gouged and ripped by the roll of the dead Olds and tore open the metal corpse.

Both bodies were inside, huddled together like kids asleep in the same bed. But here there was a difference. Both of them wore their rods over their pajamas. They were better off the way they were. I took a quick look at Carol and there was nothing about her that was soft or afraid. She took the satchels I handed her, tossed them to the ground and helped me out of the wreck. I closed the door against the buzzards and waved her to go ahead, then picked up the bags and followed her.

The Mayor was awake when we got back. He was awake and mad but hurting too hard to set up a fuss. His eyes were little things that wanted to rip into me, and when they turned on Carol the hatred was there too. They saw the bags and the governorship going up in smoke at the same time and something like a sob caught in his throat.

Carol said, "So long, Harold."

He didn't answer. I untied his hands and feet, and while they were still numb, dragged him out of the Jeep. He lay there in the dirt looking up at me, watching the crazy smile I wore while I did all the things I did and I knew that he had found out too. Not a little bit like Carol...but like the old man. He knew too.

We had one hour left. One time around the clock before it was too late. I spun the heap in the dust, rode the gears up as high as I could in second and kept it there. Beside me Carol hung on to the seat back, one hand braced against the dash. Her hair was a blonde swirl in the wind and twice I heard her laugh over the howl of the engine.

There was only one straight in the road, one half-mile stretch that eased the pull on the shoulders and let the engine go into high.

I felt Carol's hand on my arm and looked over at her. There was a smile on her mouth and a lifetime in her eyes. "You're a great actor, Rich," she said. I sensed the words more than heard them.

This time I shook my head. "Hell, I'm no actor."

"You're a great one," she disagreed with another smile.

The laugh she heard was something that hadn't come

out of me in a long time. It was a laugh that said everything
was screwy funny because it never should have happened at
all. Everything was all balled up like a madman's dream. It
was giving a starving man a turkey dinner that was sure to
kill him the minute he ate it.

———

When we reached the end of the stretch, I was glad. There
in the distance was the cabin and the killers and I was glad.
There was where the big bang would be and it would all be
over. There would be a chance here and a chance there but
in the end it would all be the same. You die. You catch the
one you didn't expect and die.

Up ahead the dust sifted up from the hardpan and I
braked easily before I hit it. I pulled in close to the uprise of
rock and took out the bags.

Carol didn't get it. I winked and said, "Insurance.
They're playing hostage with us. They got what we want.
Friend Auger forgot we got what he wants too."

She didn't see where I went and I didn't want her to. I
opened the bag, took out handfuls at a time and laid the
sacks of money beside definite markers, noting the location
of each on the back of a hundred-dollar bill. It wasn't a
good job, but if anybody was in a big hurry, they were going
to have trouble rounding it all up. When I finished with one,
I took the other and did the same across the road. In each
bag I left a thousand bucks, neatly wrapped. Then I started
the Jeep up and drove back to the cabin. Someplace behind
us the Mayor was staggering to the highway to intercept the
posse. It wouldn't be long now before they found him and
followed our trail back.

There was very little time left at all.

The killer opened the door with his foot and pointed the
one gun at me. He wore a stupid smile on his face and he
had sucked on the unlit butt so long the paper was
completely wet and starting to unfurl at the end. He said,
"Here they are, Mr. Auger."

In the soft glow of the kerosene lamp the fat man looked
like a little Buddha. "Show them in, Trigger," he smiled.

The stiff fingers of the gun muzzles prodded us in. The door was kicked shut again and Trigger mumbled, "Hold still." His hands did a professional job of patting me down from my chest to my legs. He took a little longer with Carol and kept grinning all the while.

I was thinking how nice it would be to kill him right there.

The guns probed the small of our backs again and pushed us forward. Trigger sounded puzzled this time. "They ain't loaded, Mr. Auger. They didn't take no guns from Carmen or Leo."

"I really didn't expect them to. It was merely a precaution, Trigger."

And in the back where it was dark I heard the Sheriff curse a wild one softly and mutter, *"Why didn't she stay away...why!"*

"You had twelve minutes more, Rich." Auger smiled gently. "You almost didn't come back?"

I grinned to him.

The dark blob on the cot came to his feet slowly and Allen mouthed his murderer's smile. "He's been thinking."

"That right?"

I shrugged. "For a while, maybe. It all came to a dead end, so to speak."

"You're a brave man, Rich. There aren't many left like you. Do you know why?"

"Sure," I nodded, "they're all dead."

"Yes."

In back of us the killer kicked the door shut. Someplace I heard George, the deputy, sobbing as he breathed.

Auger asked, "You met anyone?"

"We met everyone."

For a second there was no sound, not even that of someone breathing. Allen took a step forward into the light.

"So?"

"They're turning over every rock. They'll be here, but not for a while yet."

Very slowly, Auger came to his feet. "You told them anything?"

"I sent them looking for a dead dog," I said. Then I

smiled back at the fat man and put my straw kady on and
tapped it in place. I shouldn't have been so damned wise.
Allen took a quick stride and rapped one across my jaw and
I went down on the floor with the kady rolling over beside
the chair the Sheriff was tied to.

He looked big, standing over me. He was bastard-mean
and big and the cold murder in him was leaking out every
pore. He was the methodical kind that looked at life and
death with the same expression of contempt and used either
to suit his own purpose. The gun came out of his pocket, the
hammer was thumbed back and he was smiling... smiling
hard, even bigger than Auger.

He stopped smiling when I kicked him across the shins
and lost the rod when my other foot caught him in the belly.
Trigger picked the gun up, laughed, and it wasn't at me.

Auger took the rod from Trigger and said, "All right.
Enough, Allen."

It took a while for him to talk. It took a time that never
seemed to end for him to tear his eyes away from Trigger
who still laughed, silently.

"Enough?" He sucked his breath in deep. "I'm going to
kill this boy."

"Not now."

"So later, Auger. Then I'm going to powder Jason here."

Everything got tight too fast. There was a chuckle in
Trigger's throat and Auger said, "Keep it down, laddies.
Way down. We have two million in front of us. When there's
shooting to be done, let's do it right."

Money was the magic word. They all looked at the cases
on the floor, and I didn't want them to look too long. I said,
"Yeah, think of the loot. Two million bucks which you won't
get without trouble."

Auger was the second one who got it. The old man
caught it first and his eyes did the talking when they looked
at me. They were funny eyes, eyes that had looked over guns,
eyes that had looked over corpses, eyes that had seen too
much and now they were watching me and laughing hard.
They were eyes that had lived too long and didn't care
anymore.

"Allen...open the bags."

He had to stoop down close to me and I was almost hoping he'd take another swipe my way. I could feel the tight feeling in my shoulders and down deep in the pit of my stomach unseen hands were tying me into a knot. They squeezed hard and the thing that coursed through me was like a voice saying to be quiet, be still, be patient, for soon it would be over. Soon it could all come out one way or another and then it would be over.

Allen's fingers fumbled open the catches, reached in and came out with an expression of disbelief across his face.

I said, "My hostage, Auger. My guarantee for a few minutes more of living."

His neck was livid with rage. It showed there and no place else. His voice was almost conversational. "A trade, perhaps?"

"Don't be silly."

"Of course not. You die anyway."

"But I got more minutes."

"Yes, you have that. Where is the money?"

I turned and looked outside. The sun was settling down into the west, the long fingers reaching out again to probe the hills and valleys that surrounded the cabin.

"Someplace there," I said. "You won't find it easily."

"Why, Mr. Mayor? Shall we squeeze the girl until you show us where you put it?"

"No." I laughed and pushed myself up, dusting the dirt off my pants. "I said all I wanted was minutes. I'm stalling."

Allen had started to breath normally again. His face had a flat look and his thumbs were hooked in his belt. "I want to kill this guy, Auger."

"Not yet. He hasn't explained yet."

I reached up to my shirt pocket and flipped out the hundred buck bill with the lines and writing on it. I spread it open, folded it lengthwise and sailed it across to Auger. "There it is, friend. Two million bucks. Out there in the brush. You want it, go find it."

"He'll show us," Allen said.

Auger had that paternal smile again. "No...we really don't need him, Allen. He's telling the truth, can't you see? He wants us to go look for it to give him time. Oh, we'll be able to find it, but that's part of the game, see...like a treasure hunt. Each find stimulates us to go find the rest before it gets dark and not to go back to see whether or not they've broken loose or not. It's a very cute...and daring plan, Allen."

"He's nuts."

Auger put the bill in his pocket. "No...but shrewd. Not shrewd enough, but shrewd." He looked at me, his tongue making a wet smear of his lips. He had the stuff in his hands now and he knew it and all he had to do was pull out his ace card.

"I won't even bother tying you, Mr. Mayor. Allen and I shall go and leave you in the care and keeping of Trigger here. A pleasant prospect? Trigger...would you like that?"

"I'd like that, Mr. Auger."

"We'll take the patrol car back to the site, pick up the money and come back for you, Trigger. I expect you'll be alone by then?"

"I'll be alone, Mr. Auger."

"Take your time, Trigger. Don't hurry. Let them think some. Let them see how well they didn't make out after all. You know what I mean, Trigger?"

"I won't hurry none, Mr. Auger."

Very deliberately, Allen pulled his hand back and cut one across my jaw. My head rocked and I was on the floor again with the taste of blood in my mouth. I said, "Thanks."

"No trouble," Allen said. He bent down, picked up the cases and walked out.

For the second time I got up off the floor and watched the fat man. He put the gun in his coat pocket and looked up at me. "In a way I'm sorry that I can't kill you myself," he said, "but I promised Trigger here the pleasure."

"You expect to get away with it?"

His nod was serious, even to me. "I expect to get away with it."

"Want to bet?" I said.

He smiled for the last time and walked out. The car started, pulled around from the back and Trigger closed the door with his elbow.

There was a peculiar expression in his eyes. Like hunger.

NOBODY NOTICED it until the sound of the car diminished into the distance, but there was a clock on the back wall. It was an old fashioned job and the works in it were worn thin. The walls were a sounding board and each *tick* was loud. There was something unnatural about the sound because it wasn't ticking us into the future, but bringing us closer to the end of the present.

Even Trigger noticed it and knew what we were thinking. He liked the idea. It made him king for a minute and gave him the power of life or death over his subjects. He watched the clock and us, his mouth working around the ruins of the cigarette.

The Sheriff sat there in his chair, roped tight, and I wondered what he had tried while we were gone to get him there. I wondered what happened to his deputy to make him cry like that.

Then I looked at Carol and wondered why it had to be like this at all. She seemed tired and even while I watched the tears welled up in her eyes.

"Carol..."

She looked up slowly.

Behind me Trigger said, "Why don'tcha go kiss her, Mac?"

"Yeah, thanks," I said. I crossed the room and held out my hand to her. All she did was touch it.

The end, I thought. Everything was all gone now. It was over. Climax, anticlimax.

I turned around and looked at Trigger. "You figure me for a screwball, don'tcha?" he asked me.

"That's right."

"I ain't dumb." He fiddled with the hammers on the guns. "You ain't the Mayor."

"No?" The clock sounded loud again. "Who am I?"

"You ain't the Mayor."

"I could have told you that."

"Nobody really asked, feller." His smile got real crooked then. "I got the play. Them guys..." he jerked his head toward the door, "they're too smart. They didn't get you quick like I did, Mac."

"No?"

"Un-uh. You're a cutie. You figure Allen and Auger, they go out there and get in a rumble about the money. You figure that, don't you? They rumble and somebody catches it. That it?"

I shook my head. "Not quite."

"That's good. You figure anything and you die real fast, feller. You and everybody else. Allen and Auger rumble and sure as hell I'll rumble everybody here. You'll get real rumbled, boy."

I said, "That's not what I figured."

You could hear the ropes creak as the Sheriff tightened his hands on the arm of the chair. His face was a hot white glow of hate, stiff with creases and marked by the slash of his eyes and mouth. "You fool," he said. "You young damn fool. You could've stayed off. You didn't have to bring her back here. Yourself either."

Very quietly Carol said, "He had to, Dad."

"Damn fool actor..."

"He's no actor," the old man laughed.

All of us looked at him and I shook my head. I tried to tell him no but he wouldn't have any part of it. He saw what was coming and wanted in.

"Pop..."

"You're no actor like he thinks, are you, son? You're no mayor and no actor at all." He paused and let the corner of his mouth wrinkle up. "Or maybe you're an awfully good one."

The metallic clicking of the gun hammers was too loud. I turned to where Trigger was standing stiff against the door. "What you figger, man?"

I looked at my watch. It was about time. They could all know now. I said, "There's a posse out there, Jason. I made them mad at us and about now they'll have backtracked us and they can't miss seeing your pals poking around for that dough. They won't ask questions. They'll shoot and that's all for you."

In the back of his eyes a dawn of reason came through.

"Not for me. The Jeep is outside. Not for me. Just for you."
His eyes swept the room and the reason left him. He was
hungry again. "For all of you."

The Sheriff was watching me avidly. There was something drawn about him I didn't like. "You're no actor, son?"

"That's right. No actor."

"Rich...?"

The old man didn't let me answer. "He's not what you
think he is, Carol."

"Rich..."

"I'm not Thurber, Carol." Her eyes were even more
puzzled now. "I look like him, that's all. I'm no movie actor.
Sometimes it helps to say so."

"Rich...I love you."

"Don't," the old man said simply.

"I'll always love you, Rich."

"Don't," the old man said again.

Across time and space there was just the two of us. Two
people looking and saying silent words nobody else in the
world could ever understand. There was love, and want, and
understanding in that one meeting and a sudden revelation
that was so shocking that her eyes could only widen imper-
ceptibly, then go wet with tears.

It was quiet then. The clock sounded loud and alone
until the killer at the door moved. He said, "You called me
Jason, mister."

"That's right, Jason."

"You're crazy, mister."

"Not me, Jason. Just you. Just you."

His mouth made a tight oval. "I don't care what happens
outside now, mister. You know?"

"It doesn't matter. It's over."

"Sure it's over. I can do it now. Like Mr. Auger said, you
gimme a reason now." He licked his mouth, wiping it dry on
his shoulder. "I can do it now like I want to and not wait for
them to come back."

Like an echo from a tunnel the old man's voice said,
"Why don't you warn the slob?"

And Jason smiled because he thought the old man was
talking to him.

"I warned him," he chuckled.

The clock ticked again, whirred a moment, then struck a quarter hour note on a muffled bell.

From outside, from someplace far off, came the flat continued cough of a Tommy gun. Another answered it and in agreement was the dull thunder of wide bore rifles and the sharp *splat* of small arms. It lasted through two minutes and I thought that even before we heard the guns the thing was over out there.

It was over in here too. All over. Everybody knew it, even Jason. Softly, almost so I didn't hear it, Carol said, "I love you, Rich..."

And I repeated it. "I love you, Carol."

I said it looking at the old man. He shook his head. "Don't..."

The killer looked at me with those crazy, fruity eyes and I knew we were right at the end. He was grinning real big with his face twisted like he was enjoying it and you could tell that he was all gone upstairs. All gone.

Carol was crying softly in the corner sitting there with her hands bunched in her lap, fear not even a part of her anymore. She had been afraid too long. There was nothing left except anticipation; dull, deadly anticipation. The killer looked at her, grinned and licked his lips. He didn't know whether to take her first or last...whichever would be better.

The Sheriff said nothing. There wasn't an expression on his face either. The ropes holding him down were too tight and his hands looked like white gloves. He was trying to hate the killer to death and it wasn't working.

His deputy was crying too. A dry cry like an idiot. With the empty holster on his belt he reminded me of a kid who had fallen down a well while playing cops and robbers.

Beside Carol the old man who had seen too much of life stood with his bony hands shoved under his belt and shook his head in pity at what was going on. He was neither afraid nor expectant. Death had passed him up too many times for him to be afraid of it when it came for certain. For some reason he was feeling sorry for the killer. There was abject pity in his face for the goon boy with the all-gone eyes and the two rods in his fists.

My straw hat was on the floor beside me and very slowly the killer snaked it back with his foot until he had it in front of him, then even slower still, stood on it.

There was something nasty and ominous in the act, in the sound of it. One old-fashioned straw kady mashed to nothing. Then the killer grinned at me and cocked the hammers on the two rods. I was to be the first.

I could tell that he didn't know why I was grinning too.

Outside was the Jeep and without too much trouble I could reach the border. It would be close, but I could still do it. If I stayed, the cops or papers would make me for sure and if they dusted for prints it would all come out in the wash.

Someday it was going to happen, but when it did it wouldn't be where Carol was. She could have her dream and I'd have mine and maybe she'd never find out.

Life, I thought.

The killer grinned again and brought the guns up and I knew that in the back the old man was waiting to see if he was right.

The grin got real wide, then stopped altogether and tried to see why I was grinning even bigger.

He didn't know why. He couldn't tell.

When I pulled the little .32 from the sleeve holster he knew, but by then it was too late and the Jeep and the border were outside and he was dying in a slow puddle of red on the floor.

The old man laughed because *he knew he had been right.*

I was a killer too!

Hot Cat

She's lying quietly out there on the bottom now—melted, fragmented pieces of metal scattered like dust across the sand, nameless, traceless, but evoking a memory that could make you sweat cold if you knew the truth about her.

Not too far away is another mass of metal, twisted and corroded by now, but still recognizable for what it was. Both masses had been born together and served together, then separated for 20 years to meet again in a fusion of terror that was, fortunately, almost totally unseen.

There was still one other memory...a sudden, bright-red, misty memory better forgotten.

Chapter One

I SAT THERE with the half-finished coffee in my hand, watching them service the battered old Mustang on the runway outside. There was nothing of interest there; I had seen it done too many times before. But the blonde reflected in the plate glass window of the bar *was* interesting, especially when she knew I was watching her and arranged herself so I could see her legs from the best angle.

Step one in the big play, I thought. She was chumming for me and next would come the hook. Cute, real cute, I looked like something out of the "Late Show" in an old AAF A-2 jacket with a leather helmet and goggles jammed into my pocket, and she was a dream in a fitted covert suit that made her hair look like a summer sunset.

The trouble was, I knew her, only she didn't know me. Three years ago, Lois Hays had interviewed me in a German hospital to find out why I was interested in making an air drop of ammo into Hungary from an old Ju-88. I could have told her it was for the loot, but my face was bandaged and still hurt from the shrapnel slice so I didn't bother. That time she had played the part in a nurse's outfit.

Dominick Lolla, who got me smuggled back to the States on a tramp steamer, knew her, too. He was an accredited *Circut* correspondent and didn't hold much with anybody doing legwork for Duncan Knight, whose "Washington Inside" column was dedicated to ripping apart our military policy.

I grinned at her reflection. *So what the hell, if you need leg-work done, get someone with pretty legs to do it.* Hers were beautifully rounded and shiny with nylon until the sheen stopped and there was a quick flash of tan before she pulled the hem of her skirt down.

And when you're looking at legs you don't see people, so when the big guy said, "Mr. Fallon?" it caught me by surprise.

He had an angular face, almost devoid of expression, but ready to be friendly if he had to. His suit was well cut, but not new, and fitted with some peculiar purpose in mind. The smaller man with him was on the mouse side, with an irritated squint to his eyes.

I stood up. "Cop?"

"Lieutenant Trusky, city police." He held out his hand. "It shows?" His voice sounded amused.

His hand was hard. "To some."

"This is Mr. Del Reed from the state's attorney's office."

The smaller guy nodded curtly and shifted his briefcase. "If you have a few minutes I'd like to talk to you," he said.

"What about?"

"You have a few minutes?" Trusky asked politely.

"Sure."

"Then let's find out."

Behind me the blonde uncrossed those legs again and watched us. Del Reed nodded toward the small restaurant section, across the room, and when Trusky moved up beside me I could feel the gun at his hip.

"How long did you know Tucker Stacy, Mr. Fallon?"

Del Reed didn't waste any time with pleasantries. "Since 'forty-two," I said. "We were in the Army together. Air Force cadets."

"You were in the same outfit together. Two hundred-fifty-second Fighter Squadron, I believe."

"If you know so damn much, why the questions?"

Reed's face tightened, but a wave from Lieutenant Trusky calmed him down. "All right, let's get to the point," he said. He pulled a folder from his briefcase, held it in his lap and fingered the contents. "You and Stacy were discharged together, shared a brief business venture..."

"Crop-dusting," I interrupted. "We went broke."

"...Corresponded a few times and except for a squadron reunion in nineteen fifty-four, apparently never had any further contact." His eyes left the folder and drifted up to meet mine.

"So what?" I said.

"So out of a clear blue sky he left you a half-million-dollar investment."

I put down my coffee and leaned on the table. The little man was getting to me.

"Is his family contesting his will?" I asked.

Reed's mouth twitched. "You know he has none."

"Is the state?"

"Well, no."

"Don't hesitate, Mr. Reed. You're off limits and you know it. Put it on the line or take a walk. You just don't impress me at all."

"Del is trying to...let's say, forestall action, Mr. Fallon," Trusky said quietly.

"The will hasn't even been probated yet," I reminded him. "I'm here because Tuck's lawyer wrote me. Now where does the state come in? So Tuck leaves his old buddy an airfield, the Capital K. I come down here to see what it's all about and the action starts before I even get there."

"Had you known about the will?" Reed said.

"No. But it doesn't surprise me."

"Why not?"

"Because we're two of a kind. Neither one of us had anybody else. In the Army we took pretty good care of each other, and if one of us had been knocked off the other would have gotten his gear."

"Who was your National Service Insurance made out to, Mr. Fallon?"

"An orphanage, Mr. Reed. So was Tuck's. If you read all those papers you should know that."

He ignored the remark. "Do you have a will?"

"What for? Outside of that Mustang, I don't have anything."

Trusky tapped the table with a forefinger. "Old fighter plane, isn't it?"

"You know it. You were there, weren't you?"

The cop smiled and shrugged. "Practical to own?"

"For my purposes," I told him.

Reed snapped the folder shut. "And what may those purposes be?"

I pointed toward his lap. "What do the papers say, buddy?"

"That you worked for a motion picture company. I can't see where owning an airplane..."

"You don't see much at all. Were you elected or appointed?"

"Appointed, but..."

"Then somebody's pretty damn stupid."

"Listen!"

"Aw, shut up." I looked at Trusky and he was trying not to grin. I said, "I've worked with Demeret Pictures off and on for ten years. When they go on location, I fly the daily takes back to the lab for developing, then hustle them up to the location for screening the next day. But that's beside the point. Let's get to the business you're trying to involve me in."

Trusky said, "If you inherit the Capital K, what do you intend doing with it?"

"Run it...sell it...how the hell do I know. You got any ideas?"

"I might."

"Then let's hear them."

"Let's see what you do with it first."

It started to come through then, even the bit with the blonde outside. "What was Tucker doing with it?" I asked them.

Trusky threw Reed a sidewards glance and when the attorney nodded he said, "There's been some speculation in higher quarters that your friend might have been engaged in some illegal activities."

"Like what?"

He shrugged again. "Florida's close to enough places to make a lot of illegal things practical if you don't mind getting killed for them." They stood up and Trusky said, "See you tomorrow. We're going through all of your friend's papers, private and business. Everything. You can lodge a complaint if you feel like it."

I gave him a grin that was all teeth. "Hell, why should I? Be my guest."

Chapter Two

THE WIRE SERVICES had never said much about it. Tucker had simply flown out in the Staggerwing Beech he had liked so well and never come back. He had told Charlie Traub, his chief mechanic, that he was going to do some preliminary work on an aerial survey job he was bidding on and headed for the southern tip of Florida. An hour after take-off, a line squall came up. It was supposed that Tuck tried to fly around it, couldn't get through and ditched in the ocean. An air-sea rescue unit located pieces of wreckage that were unmistakably from his plane.

You get old but never bold. It just didn't sound like Tuck.

Only the local paper played up the incident big. Tucker Stacy was a prominent character in Celada, a war hero who turned an old Air Force auxiliary field into the Capital K and promoted a couple of electronics plants to locate in the area. That, with a booming resort section, put Celada on the map and Tucker Stacy in the city council.

Old Tuck, how he had changed. He sure used to be the wild-assed one, ready to charge into anything. Nine confirmed kills on Me-109s. Tuck? Hey, remember that leave in London? That pair of Scot lassies! Crazy, man. What did they teach them on that farm? Remember? *Remember, hell. When you're dead you don't remember anything.*

I propped the scuffed jump boots on the end of the couch and looked at the ceiling. Across the room, the TV was giving the weather reports for tomorrow. Hot. Clear. Probably local thundershowers in the afternoon.

When the knock came I said, "Come on in," and didn't take my eyes off the ceiling. The door *snicked* shut. "I've been waiting for you," I said.

Lois Hays tilted her head and smiled. "Sure of yourself, aren't you?"

"Why not?"

She was prettier face to face than reflected in a plate glass window. Even though the suit was cut in an almost military fashion, she couldn't hide the full thrust of her breasts or the rich sweep of her hips and thighs.

"You got pretty legs," I said. "Pneumatic. Soft, cushiony."

"I don't know if I should thank you or not."

"Never mind that. Just make the pitch."

"What?"

"Honey," I said, "you made the point clear in the lounge. I dug the bit with the legs and all. I appreciate the generosity. Now let's hear the offer."

For a moment she poised there, motionless, then her face flushed and the anger tightened her mouth. But only for a second. The pink left her cheeks and she laughed deep in her throat. "I think you've known too many hotel rooms and too many..."

"Whores?" I added for her.

She didn't get mad. "Like you say, why not?"

I turned my head and grinned. I couldn't have made a pretty sight. I still hadn't shaved and the scar on my face always showed worse then. "Wrong, baby. I'm a funny sort of guy. I never buy it. It gets given to me or I take it."

"Should I be frightened?" She laughed again and sat down.

"Not tonight, kid. I'm tired. It's been a long day." I closed my eyes and settled back. "What do you want?"

"A story."

"Yeah, sure."

I could feel her smiling. "My name is Karen Morgan. I'm with Barrett Syndicated Features and I'd like to get some background on Tucker Stacy, and, of course, you and your plans. You may not know it, but Mr. Stacy's activities were of great interest statewide."

"Honey," I said, "cut the crap."

I opened my eyes and she was watching me, the softness gone from her face. She was steady, studying me, waiting. "I don't understand," she said.

"Tuck's death is only a local matter," I said.

Her tongue touched her lips. "All right, I'll come clean," she said. "There's been speculation."

"How about that."

"Aren't you interested?"

"Kid, Tuck and I faced death plenty of times. You're bound to get it someday anyway. I've had a plane torn apart under me in a storm."

"Have you checked the weather for the day he died? Several planes flew through that line squall without any difficulty."

"Sugar, inside a thunderhead..."

"There weren't any severe ones. I have verified pilot reports to that effect. So does Miami. The squall line was light. A Cessna 90 and two Tripacers passed through it."

"So?"

"So there's been some speculation..."

I twisted on the couch and propped my head in my hand. "What about?"

Her smile was almost disarming. "Were you ever a policeman?"

"No, but I've operated in their area of work."

"Very well. Mr. Stacy, it was rumored, was not above turning a dishonest dollar."

"With all his loot and his investment here it doesn't sound reasonable, honey. As an airport, the Capital K is a going concern. Try again."

She stood up quickly, frowning in concentration, and walked toward me. There was a "woman-with-a-mission" look spread right across her face. "A few years ago he had nothing except a few surplus airplanes. Somehow he managed all this. It came suddenly and expanded fast. The big question is why?"

"He was lucky, baby."

"All right. Then the big question is *how?*"

I shrugged. Tuck's business was no affair of mine. "Where do I come in?"

She found my eyes with hers. "Supposing he did have an illegal operation going somewhere, then the possibility of his having been killed would be increased, correct?"

I nodded noncommittally.

"And there's a possibility that he would have left some record of a sort."

I nodded again.

"If I could see his papers...or whatever effects he left...I might be able to come up with a story." She paused and gave an impatient toss of her head. Hair swirled across her shoulders like a golden wave. "You inherit his property. You could let me do this. Will you?"

"Maybe," I said. "What'll you give me?"

Her eyebrows raised. "What...do you want?"

"Try me and see."

For three full seconds she stood there, a curious smile toying with the edges of her mouth. Then her hands went to the buttons of her jacket and flipped them open. She dropped it to the floor, then did the same thing to her blouse. There was another minute pause before her fingers went to the hooks of the brassiere at her back. With a motion of her shoulders, she let it slip down her arms, dangled it a moment in her fingers, then dropped that, too.

The smile was gone now. In its place there was an intense, sultry look she couldn't conceal. Her breasts were magnificently full, seeming to pulsate with pressure that wanted to burst through the taut red nipples. Her breath was jerky and a shudder went through her shoulders to twist down into the supple, trim waist that flowed into her skirt.

I hadn't moved. I just watched her. It was something she had never done before and showed it, and the doing had turned her into a person she had tried hard to conceal. She swayed toward me and in another moment would have taken the step that would put her inside my reach. Already I could see her hand groping, feeling for the zipper at her side.

I got up quickly, walked to the door and turned around. "Nice act, Lois, but you'll never make the big time."

It was as if I had belted her. The longing disappeared and for a moment there was a hint of fear, then something else.

"Lois?" she said.

"We've met before, baby. You didn't get what you came after then, either."

Chapter Three

FROM THE AIR the runway system of Tuck's airport was shaped like a capital K, and that's how it got its name. It was built during the war as an auxiliary to nearby Martin AAFB, but not enough B-24s or 17s put down there to cave in the runways so it was in top shape. Tuck had erected a fine operations building, attached a lounge and restaurant, added a motel unit and a group of specialty shops built around a generous swimming pool. There was a golf course bordering the south edge of the field, several tennis courts, an adjacent highway and, at the far end of the field, away from the social center, the hangar area. Not a very military setup, but a profitable deal in these days of fly-in vacations. At night, each burning light read like a dollar sign. The motel units were filled, maintenance and repairs were going on around the clock in the hangars, and overhead was the sporadic drone of light planes coming into the pattern.

At 9 o'clock I got one of the kids who drove the caddy cars to take me to the hangars. Tuck had had his office there, where he liked it best...in the middle of engines and airframes. Sam Devin, Tuck's attorney, would have preferred his own office, but he was looking to please what might mean a new account, so he came where I asked him to.

Sam was a short, wiry guy with a gray crew-cut. He was probably pushing sixty but moved like thirty. His eyes gave him away. They had seen the inside of too many courtrooms and too much misery. We shook hands briefly, and Sam said, "Charlie Traub will be here in just a minute. Mind waiting?"

I said no, poured myself a beer from the cooler in the corner and sat down. Charlie Traub came in like a little fox terrier, introduced himself to me on the way to the cooler and pulled up a chair.

In one way he was like Sam. He had the stamp of the old-time flier all over him, from his stained white coveralls to the wrench scars on his knuckles. They were both about the same age until you read their eyes. There was still a lot of life left in Charlie's.

Sam spread his papers out on the desk. "Ready?"

Both of us nodded.

"Fine." He picked up the top sheet, glanced at it briefly and put it down. "Tucker's will provides for two persons. Charlie Traub here gets twenty thousand in cash, three airplanes specified here and a five percent participation in the profits of the Capital K. He is to remain here in his present position for one year before he can be fired."

"And to Cat Fallon here goes the entire rest of Tucker's estate. I haven't had time to itemize the assets, but to give you an idea, I'd say the cash value of his properties is about a million. On deposit is some two hundred thousand dollars."

"Anything else?" I asked.

"Just a personal letter to you, Mr. Fallon." Sam fingered an envelope and handed it across the desk to me. It was sealed and the note inside was undated. From what it said, it seemed neither important nor cryptic.

Dear Cat: Keep things going for me. There aren't too many of us left. A few maybe, but not many. Like Verdo and Cristy. Have fun. Don't choke on a banana.

I felt myself frowning at the note the second time I read it. Who the hell were Verdo and Cristy? The names sounded familiar enough, but I sure couldn't recall them. Back in the old days, Tuck knew everybody on the base and in town. Me, I didn't give a damn for any of them. Verdo and Cristy! Well, hello to them wherever they were. I folded the note and stuck it in my pocket.

Sam said, "Now for your immediate plans, Mr. Fallon..."

I waved him off. "Let's keep things running the way they are. Charlie knows the maintenance end and the rest of the staff must be on the ball. The Capital K has been making money. I'll take a look at Tuck's personal end and see how I can fit in. Hell, I got no place else to go anyway. Sound okay?"

"Fine with me," Charlie mused.

Sam stood up and began collecting his papers. "I'll have everything in final form in a few days," he said.

"Before you go," I said, "just one more thing. Between us."

Both of them glanced up sharply.

"Did Tuck have something going for him?"

They exchanged sharp looks, then Charlie squinted and looked at the ceiling. "Like what, Cat?"

"Let's cut it clean. Was he involved in anything illegal?"

"Why do you ask?"

"Because, Sam, the cops are already asking questions and I gave my approval for them to poke around Tuck's papers. How does that sound to you? Upset any applecarts?"

He didn't hesitate. "Nope. They can look all they want. If Tuck or anybody else were involved with an illegal operation to my knowledge...or even if I suspected it...I wouldn't be here."

"Good enough. How about you, Charlie?"

"As far as I know, nix. He made some smart deals, but legal right down the line. He never chiseled or stole and his credit was tops. He's flown out of here alone many a time without bothering to tell me where he was headed. I didn't check his flight plans or even know if he filed any. But hell, a guy's entitled to some time off. So maybe he went to Vegas or to one of those fancy fly-in fields where they have a cathouse

at the end of a runway. Okay?"

I thought it over and nodded. "Suits me. I just don't want my neck stuck out."

"You're the boss now," Charlie said. "Any orders?"

"Yeah. Fix me up with one of the motel units. I'll have my stuff sent over from the hotel. And run a hundred-hour check on the Mustang."

"No trouble. What about parts?"

"Trans-Florida Aviation over in Sarasota has a full stock of P-Fifty-One components. And since we have some loot in the bank, don't go scrimping. My instrument panel is outdated, so get the King Radio catalogue and mount me up. I want new tires and canopy on the baby and find a reticule for the gunsight."

"You got a K-fourteen on that thing?"

"Uh-huh."

"What for? You can bust your head if you..."

"I always wear the shoulder harness locked on landing, buddy. Besides, I might want to shoot somebody."

"Oh," he grinned, "a nostalgic."

"There aren't too many of us left," I said. Then I remembered it was what Tuck had written. I tried to remember who Verdo and Cristy were. There was some reason why I should remember them, but the reason was twenty years old and only a hazy recollection now.

The kind of circles I traveled in made it no trouble to enlarge my contacts. One call to Slim Upgate in New York put me through to a lead man in Celada named George Clinton, and with a clearance like Upgate he was glad to give me a run down on Tucker Stacy. Briefly, he told me, Tuck was a wheeler-dealer who operated on a comparatively small scale, liked what he had in Celada and decided to stick around. Clinton hinted that Tuck had some outside interests, but speculated that they lay somewhere between a man's normal attachments for girls and gambling. He didn't think it was anything in the rackets.

When I mentioned the cops, Clinton shrugged, but Del Reed's name brought a squint to his eyes and he made a couple of phone calls. After the last one he hung up, dragged on a cigar and told me Del Reed was the state man handling any of the operations involving the new Cuban setup, especially the anti-Cuban bunch in the Miami area.

"Where would Tuck fit into that picture?"

"I could guess," Clinton said.

"Then guess."

"He had planes, an airfield. Now you guess."

"Smuggling?" Clinton made a vague gesture. "No, that's

not logical," I continued. "He couldn't get into Cuba to start with. Besides, they come out in bunches. They commandeer boats generally."

"The big ones?"

"Aren't most of the big ones already here?"

Clinton studied his cigar a moment. "Yes, I'd say so." He looked up at me. "There's still a bunch operating in the mountains like Castro did."

"No dice, friend. Castro's was an army of poorly trained malcontents who were glad to see Batista go. It's not like that now. With Russian and Chinese Commies in there running things, whatever opposition shows its face will get smeared like a bug. The groups in the mountains are scattered little units. Any real opposition to Castro will come right out of the States."

"You never know what the Commies are going to pull," Clinton said. "Well, if there's anything else you want any help with, let me know."

"I will."

"You want me to pull the local fuzz off your neck?"

"That's a real power play, friend."

Clinton made another small gesture with his hands. "I'm a heavy contributor to certain campaign funds. Little favors I can get."

"Save them until we need them."

"Suit yourself," he said.

———

OUT OF HABIT, I checked the weather before I hit the pad. The latest out of Miami had a tropical disturbance building up. The weathermen had already named the hurricane Ingrid. It was enough to put a crimp in the traffic pattern even though the sky was clear and the wind a gentle five knots from the west.

Charlie Traub's crew had already started tearing down the Mustang, and after a cursory look around, I walked back to the end unit of the motel that had been Tuck's, stripped down, took a shower and flaked out on the bed.

For a while I lay there with my hands behind my head,

trying to get inside Tuck's mind. Damn, there wasn't one reason in the world outside of sentiment that would have made him leave me all his goodies. Big wheelers just don't have sentiment. I had known too many of them. If I had been an operator who could make a go out of what Tuck had built up, I could see a reason, but I wasn't an operator.

So maybe it *was* sentiment, like that reflection back to Verdo and Cristy. I'd have to look them up, whoever they were. Maybe a couple of late replacements from a repple-depple in '45. Tuck always did baby the new ones. Me, I watched out for me first.

Sentiment? No, there was another reason somewhere. Meanwhile, I had a half million bucks to play with and no sentiment involved. It was going to be a lot of fun. One big ball and to hell with everybody. When it was over and spent, I'd climb back in the rebuilt Mustang and find some more fresh sky to find a buck in.

That's how I fell asleep.

And when I woke up she was standing there in the moonlight with a gun in her hand pointing it at my head. Not a little girl-type rod, but a fat black musket that was a .38 police positive with a four-inch barrel. In the pale yellow glow from outside I could see the dull gray of the slugs in the cylinder.

She was only smaller than average in height. The rest of her was all magnificent woman that slacks and a sweater couldn't hide. Only the total black of her hair lightened her face by contrast. No sun-worshipper could have had a more luxurious tan.

She saw my eyes open. "Don't move, *señor*," she said.

"I could use a sheet over me."

"I've seen naked men before."

"Drop dead," I said, and flipped the sheet over myself.

"You almost *did*, Mr. Fallon. Don't move again."

I could see the expression on her face, a peculiar set to her eyes. She wasn't fooling. It had been close. Very slowly I settled back and folded my hands behind my head. Never trust a broad with a gun. If she could use it, that made it even worse.

"Your play, baby."

"Quite, Mr. Fallon." Her voice carried a soft Spanish inflection.

"Am I supposed to know you?"

I could see the tip of her tongue wet her lips indecisively. "Not necessarily. I am Sharon Ortiz."

"Cuban?"

She didn't hesitate. "My father was Spanish. We lived in Cuba. My mother was Irish." Her mouth smiled over beautiful white teeth, but there was no humor there at all. "But I am Cuban, *señor.*"

"And what do you want with me?"

"Right now I am to decide whether you would be better dead or alive."

"Great. How does it look?"

Her hand tightened around the .38. I hadn't figured out yet how I was going to take it away from her. "Don't be flippant, Mr. Fallon. This is not a toy."

I gave her words back to her. "I've seen guns before."

"Yes, I imagine you have."

"Then either use it or tell me what the hell you want."

Her eyes never wavered from mine. "You prefer to stay alive?"

"Sure."

"Then you are to stay here, out of sight. You are to see no one, talk to no one. You will give us...one other person and myself...authorization to inspect all of Tucker Stacy's personal belongings and this entire installation. Then you may live."

"Thanks. Now what are you after?"

"It isn't necessary for you to know."

"Sorry, baby," I said.

She was going to do it, damned if she wasn't. She thumbed the hammer back for single-action release and took one step toward the bed to be certain of her target and that's what happens when you send a girl out to do a man's job. When you shoot somebody you do it *then* and from where you stand. You don't take time to single-action a double-action gun or step into the target where a guy can kick the piece right out of your mitt with one foot and yank you into the sack with the other.

It doesn't take much to turn a tough broad into a soft one. You take all their defenses away when you grab them by the collar and rip the clothes off their back. I hooked my fingers in the waistband of her slacks and with one wrench tore them loose with the pink things underneath. The spitting, clawing tiger became a sobbing, frightened woman in seconds.

She was beautiful, a terrified, beautiful animal with black hair and tawny skin and big, round eyes filled with horror— not so much at what she thought was going to happen to her, but at the mistake she had made.

I said, "You could have caught more flies with honey than with vinegar, baby."

Then, instantly, the woman touch was there again and she saw her out. *Give a little, get a little,* she was thinking.

"But not this time, baby." I grabbed her by the arm, dragged her off the bed and hustled her to the door. I gave her a shove outside where the scream she started broke off into a gasp when she realized she was naked in the world.

I laughed, locked the door and went back inside. I found the .38, stuck it in my pants hanging on the back of a chair and sat on the edge of the bed. She'd be back. You don't do things like that to a broad who comes calling with a gun without her coming back.

Outside, the wind had picked up a little. It felt good rolling across my chest. I pulled the sheet up and went back to sleep grinning.

Hell of a thing. Two of them almost back-to-back, Lois and Sharon. I was throwing away more than most guys ever got.

Chapter Four

At 7:30, I had breakfast and went over to the operations building. Charlie Traub was already there with Del Reed and Lieutenant Trusky. When I nodded to Charlie he came over, both hands jammed in his coverall pockets.

"These clowns been poking around ever since dawn," he said.

"I told them they could."

"Not in my private office. They got two men over there now cleaning up the mess they made. I won't stand for that crap. You know what they're looking for?"

"How would I? Hell, let them look. The sooner they get done the sooner they're out of my hair."

"Sure, but you better talk to Trusky."

"Why?"

"You'll find out."

I told Charlie to get back to the hangars and walked to the files. Everything from them was spread across the counter while Del Reed fingered each sheet carefully.

"Find what you're looking for?" I asked.

Del Reed put down a folder. "Not yet, Mr. Fallon, but we will."

"If Tuck ever went to Cuba, I doubt if he'd file a flight plan."

This time both of them stopped at once and turned

toward me. "You seem to know a lot, Mr. Fallon," Del smiled. There was no friendliness there, just the smile of a lawyer baiting a witness.

It took Trusky to break through the ice. "Knock it off, Del. He's played too many of these games." His eyes glued themselves to mine. "Suppose you try talking a little bit, Fallon. Like where your information comes from."

"Back issues of the Miami papers," I lied. "Interesting articles about your partner here and his pet activities...the Cuban bit. That's all he touches...that's all he's assigned to. Right?"

"Go on."

"So it figures, Lieutenant. Tucker had planes and an airfield. He had an interest in politics. He's suddenly dead and the Cuban expert turns up to go through his records. Now let's tighten things up a little. Let's go into my office where you two can talk to me. If I like what you say, I won't throw up any roadblocks. You're here at my convenience, and I can crowd you out any time I like. Try subpoenaing anything and the story comes out. I don't think you want that just yet. Okay, now what do we do?"

Trusky looked at Reed. The little man glared at me and nodded.

"Clean up the mess first," I said, "then meet me in my office."

Later, over Reed's objections, Trusky laid it out. He said, "You know the background on the Cuban deal. Right now the ticklish part is that anti-Castro people ready for an armed attack are here in Florida. It's something that should be dealt with on a national level, but because of the peculiar circumstances and the proximity of Cuba, it's all centered in the end of one state. Our people have put up with it and are better qualified in most cases to deal with things.

"However, all the anti-Castro bunch aren't Cubans. Plenty of U.S. types are right there with them. We suspect your former buddy Tuck was one of them."

"So what?" I said. "I feel the same way. What's wrong with that?"

Del Reed stood up impatiently. "Wrong? I'll tell you what's wrong. If it's played out politically or economically that's one thing, but when it comes to any acts of violence it could touch off a hot war. Don't you realize the Reds are just waiting for us to make a move so they'll have some excuse to come to the aid of Castro? Don't you think they'd have a beautiful piece of propaganda going for them if one of our citizens got caught up in an international mess?"

Reed leaned on the desk, his face livid. "Tucker Stacy was reported to have made numerous unauthorized flights out of the country. He was reported seen in the company of several well-known anti-Castro people on several occasions."

"Reported," I reminded him, "not proven. And if you *do* prove it, what can you do? He's dead."

"Exactly." His face was bright with sweat now. "And supposing his death was not accidental and it gets out. Do you realize the stink our own people will make? You realize how much closer that can push us to all-out war?"

"Maybe it's about time," I said.

Del rubbed his hands together until he regained his composure. "Don't be stupid. Nobody wins with a war."

"Maybe not, but you could still be doing this wrong."

"Then *you* tell *us,*" Trusky said.

"Let it die. No harm is done."

Reed's face showed his contempt for my suggestion. "Unfortunately, the damage might already be done. Tucker Stacy was a brilliant promoter. There's no way of telling how far he went or what was involved. One thing we're sure of. Your friend was in the hottest juggling act that's come up so far. All we know is that something big was underway and he was part of it. We have to know what it was. Do we have your cooperation?"

"Sure," I said, "only you have a time limit. Three days. That ought to be cooperation enough."

"Well?" Trusky asked.

Del Reed nodded. "That will do it."

Before they could leave, there was a rap on the door. It swung open and Charlie Traub poked his head in. "Some broad here for you, Cat."

"Send her in."

The request was almost useless. Lois Hays came sweeping past Charlie before he could ask her. I grinned, waiting to see the malice in her face, but there was none. "Well, hello, sugar," I said. "Meet Mr. Reed and Lieutenant Trusky."

Something happened to Del's face. It seemed to freeze up. "We've met before, Mr. Fallon."

"Yes, in a courtroom, wasn't it?"

"Quite. Now, if you'll excuse us, Mr. Fallon, we'll get on with things." He nodded curtly to Lois and walked to the door with Trusky behind him. The cop's eyes were half closed, and I could sense his mind working. Halfway out, Reed paused and said over his shoulder, "I can expect a confidence between us, can't I?"

"I wouldn't worry," I told him.

Lois had seated herself behind the desk and was sucking gently on a cigarette. Her eyes were laughing at me now. She answered my question before I could ask it. "No, I'm not mad. In fact, I think you were kind of cute. Anybody else would have gone all the way."

"I've been there, baby, it's nothing new anymore."

"But I'm curious, Mr. Fallon..."

"Cat."

"All right. Cat. You said we had met before." She blew a cloud of silver smoke toward me. "Where?"

"Uh-uh. I like my advantage. Maybe some other time I'll tell you. Right now get on with your pitch. What's it this time?"

She waved one hand toward the closed door. "You had an important visitor. What's he doing here?"

I shrugged and slid off the desk. "The same thing you're doing."

Her eyebrows went up with mock curiosity.

"Come on, quit the games. I wasn't born yesterday, kid. He's a state rep engaged in political work dealing with the Cuban situation. You're a nosy legman for a political reporter. You both want the same thing."

"And what would that be, Cat?"

"Whatever you think Tucker Stacy was doing for the anti-Castro bunch."

"It would make a good story. It *is* my job, you know."

"Happy landings."

"Will you help me?"

"What for?"

"I could guarantee you certain rewards." She grinned impishly.

"Sex isn't a reward with me, baby. It's a functional necessity. Like lunch. Got any better offers?"

Lois snubbed out her cigarette in an ashtray, glanced at me and picked up her handbag. She smiled, cocked her head and said, "Give me time. I'll think of something."

I waited until she was almost out. "Lois..."

She looked back at me. "Yes?"

"What are you after?"

"Have you gone through your deceased friend's things yet?"

"Casually."

"Did he traffic in bananas?"

"Beats me."

She smiled again. "If you find out, I'm at the Jackson Hotel."

"Swell. I'll bring a bottle."

"Why waste time drinking?"

"Yeah," I said as she closed the door. *Bananas! Now it was bananas. What was it Tuck's letter said? ..."Don't choke on a banana."*

————

I GOT CHARLIE TRAUB, two of his assistants and three girls from the office. We spent the rest of the day going through every piece of paper in the files. There wasn't a thing mentioning bananas anywhere. I said the hell with it, went back to my motel unit to clean up for supper. The second I stepped inside the darkened room I knew I'd been had. The first solid *thwack* caught me rolling away but brought me to my knees. The second one did the job and was almost a relief. The sudden swell of unconsciousness blotted out the terribly explosive pain that seemed to be bottled up inside my skull, dulling it little by little until it was only a memory.

There were three of them there: two small dark men in

gray business suits and a taller, sardonic type who sat comfortably in a chair, watching me with mild amusement.

I lay on the floor at his feet, my legs drawn up behind me and taped to my wrists behind my back. A piece of the same adhesive had been plastered across my mouth so that the low moan of pain I let out seemed to come through my nose. Each eye was a separate ball of torture, the ache in my head seeming to be concentrated at the pupils. Every pulse beat was an individual torture.

Either the pain moderated or my tolerance to it increased, because I could see and hear again. There was wind, but it came from outside the building, gusts rattling the palm leaves and whistling as they twisted past the corners of the motel.

"Feeling better, Mr. Fallon?" His eyes danced again and the pencil-line mustache twisted as he smiled.

All I could do was glare at him.

"Don't try to talk. Until you fully understand your predicament, I merely want you to listen and understand. Then you may speak. Let me remind you—one attempt to draw attention here and you will regret it." He turned his head to the man beside him. "Juan..."

With a practiced move, the little guy flipped open a knife.

"It can be painful, Mr. Fallon."

He didn't have to point it out. I'd seen it all done before. I let my eyes wander past his face and take in the room. They had destroyed it pretty well. The one in the chair smiled again. He reached inside his coat and found an envelope. When he pulled out the letter, I saw it was the note Tucker had left for me.

"I'm going to remove the tape from your mouth, Mr. Fallon. I want you to explain something, and if it is satisfactory we will simply leave you here. Frankly, dead men can cause trouble. However, you can make me kill you, if you wish. Your life is a very impersonal matter. Do you understand?"

I nodded. I had done business with these types before.

"Take off the tape."

The man with the knife bent over, felt for the edge of

the adhesive like he was going to peel an apple, caught it and ripped it loose with a jerk. I felt the skin of my lips tear and I almost made a fatal mistake of trying to catch his nose with the top of my head. He grinned, realizing my intention, and squatted there with the knife, ready to slip it into my belly.

"You have control now?"

"I know the rules," I said.

"Good." He fingered the paper, holding it up so I could see it. "A carefully guarded note from your late friend, no?"

"No."

"Then why hide it where you did?"

"It wasn't hard to find. I just considered it personal, that's all."

"Perhaps. But I think you couldn't quite figure it out and kept it as a memorandum."

"Why?"

"Ah yes, why. We know that Tucker Stacy had little or no previous contact with you, so I agree that you have no knowledge or interest in his...let's say, ventures. However, as his inheritor, you do have now, and it is likely that you think to capitalize on *everything* he was involved in. Therefore you do not wish to let anything slip through your fingers. Reasonable?"

"Yeah, but not true," I grunted. "What the hell is this all about?"

"Who are Verdo and Cristy, Mr. Fallon?"

"I wish I knew."

"Ah, but you do."

"Sorry, buddy, but that's one thing you can't get from me. Whoever they are belongs to twenty years ago."

"Tucker Stacy seemed to think you would know them."

"He was wrong." It was the way I said it that made him frown.

"Yes, that could be, but there are ways of probing a man's mind to make him remember."

"So hypnotize me."

Very languidly, he screwed a cigarette into a holder. "You are in no position to be facetious, my friend."

"So go screw yourself then."

The little guy with the knife pricked the skin of my neck.
He was enjoying his work.

I said, "What's this all about?"

"It is better that you don't know. None of it is your
affair."

"Then you're at a dead end, buddy."

The tall one nodded and pulled at his cigarette, "If we
could be sure of that, your chances of survival would be
much improved."

There was a sudden shriek of metal and something
smashed against the window frame. Like a cat, the little guy
was at the light, snapped it off, then opened the door a crack
to peer out. He turned, closed the door and flipped the light
back on. "It is the window shutter, *Señor* Marcel. The
wind..."

His voice cut off at the look the tall guy gave him. I
faked a groan and laid my head back to cover the moment.
A name. At least I had a name now. Señor Marcel.

When I opened my eyes he was watching me. Then,
after a few seconds, he seemed to make his decision. I was a
nothing. I couldn't have caught his name. "This note, Mr.
Fallon...it mentions choking on a banana. Could you explain
that?"

Inside my head the pounding started again. Cramp
spasms were starting up my neck and all sensation was gone
in my fingers. "I don't know what the hell he meant. Get off
my back, will you?"

The knife touched me again. "Shall we try another way,
señor?"

Marcel pulled the cigarette butt from the holder and
dropped it into an ashtray. "No, not this time. I think our
friend here is telling the truth. It is quite possible that he
might learn something later. In that case we shall pay him
another visit." He stepped toward me and looked down at
me, his eyes cold little slips of ice. "You are a smart man, Mr.
Fallon?"

I didn't answer him.

"If you are, you will say nothing about this. We have
people around and if it is necessary to eliminate you I will
be more than happy to accommodate. If you even become a

nuisance, this will happen. You may, for instance, speculate on your friend Tucker Stacy."

Before I could grasp his meaning, he made a motion to the one with the knife, the tape was slapped on my mouth, and with a smile of pure pleasure he swung the sap at my head and the world was all dark, pinpricked with a million lights that went out one by one.

Chapter Five

I DIDN'T REALIZE I was awake until the beam of a light seared my eyes. I had been in a state of half consciousness when the flash beamed itself at my face, twisting a knife into my brain. A curiously lilting voice said, "Maybe this time I shall kill you, *señor*."

Sharon Ortiz.

It won't take much, I figured.

The light made a circuit of the moon, spotting the disorder and the strewn papers. "They found something," she accused. Then the light hit my face again. "You will tell me."

I was past the point of argument. I didn't care one way or another. There was a lot I wanted to tell her that could be summed up in two distinct words, but something always made me play the angles.

She leaned forward and caught the tape over my mouth by a corner. I squinted my eyes against what was to come, but unlike the others, she worked it loose carefully. "What was it?" she hissed.

"Bananas," I said. "That's all those damn fools wanted to know about."

Air whistled through her clenched teeth. "They know!"

"Nuts."

"Mr. Fallon!" I was looking right down the barrel of the .38 again.

I said, "He left me a note. He told me not to choke on a banana. Now drop dead. I'm sick and tired of being caught in the middle of all this."

Slowly, the gun dropped so that it pointed at the floor. The light bouncing off the tile threw a soft glow around her, making her hair shimmer like new coal. "Yes, I realize. You are typically American, *señor*. Nothing is of any importance to you except your dollar and yourself. You are making it so easy."

Sharon Ortiz knelt beside me and I felt her fingers at the tape behind my back. She stripped it off with a harsh, tearing sound, not trying to be gentle. Then she stood up to watch me writhe helplessly as the blood flowed back into my arms and legs.

"I don't think you are worth killing, *señor*. Maybe later, but not now."

"That's what everybody thinks."

"I hope your friend gave you good advice. Don't choke on a banana. If I were you I would not even look for one. Good night, *señor*."

For a half hour I lay there rubbing myself back to normal. When I could walk, I found a bottle of Four Roses in the kitchenette and mixed a drink. Damn Tuck and whatever he was up to. Why did he leave me trouble? I had enough on my own. Damn every one of them. I was tired of being kicked around like a stray dog. Well, the Capital K was mine now and I was going to run it. Nobody else. Just me and my way. You get one chance in life to cut out of the ditch and this was mine.

––––––

By MID-MORNING, Charlie Traub had the Mustang ready.

It was crouched in the hangar like the deadly, hungry thing it was, defanged now, but ready to scream back into the blue where it belonged. Charlie came over wiping his hands on a dirty rag, and when he looked at me his eyes narrowed.

He pointed out the hangar doors. "You going up? Wind's pretty stiff."

"Not enough to bother this bird."

"Ingrid is cutting in on Jamaica. Looks like she's coming this way. We ought to be tying down a lot of kites pretty soon."

"Good. Look, am I gassed up?"

"Ready to roll."

"Get her out on the ramp. I might want to take off in a hurry."

"Sure, Cat. Thought you wanted that jump seat installed, though."

"I'll tell you when. You see Trusky and Reed around?"

"Sure. Since six A.M. they've been asking everybody questions. What do you think they'll come up with?"

"What *do you* think, Charlie. You were closer to him than anyone else." I paused and studied him. "Was he involved with the Cubans?"

For ten seconds he stared out the door, then came back to me. "Sure he was, Cat. He was the contact man between Miami and the ones in Cuba trying to oust the Commies."

"How do you know, Charlie?"

"Like a maid who washes your clothes. She knows if you're clean or dirty. Some things you can't hide. Bullet holes in wing fabric, for instance. Sand in the fairings from beach landings. Certain fuel loadings and special harness rigs for cute drops and pickups. He had some good cover for what he was doing, but he didn't fool me none." He looked down at his hands and stuffed the rag in his back pocket.

"And whose side were you on, Charlie?"

His eyes bored into mine. "I hate that Commie bunch," he said.

I held out my hand. "I'm with you."

George Clinton was having lunch when I found him. He waved me over, put down his paper and offered me a cigar. He said, "I had a call from Slim Upgate to make sure you got what you needed. You got some big friends, buddy."

"I did him a favor once."

"Pays off. What can I do for you?"

"Any connections in Miami?"

"What kind?"

"Guns and ammo to the bunch in the mountains."

"You can check that through surplus sales."

"Not this time. The stuff would go through too many hands. Besides, a lot of arms dealers have held the stuff for years, waiting for something like this. It'll be strictly black market for these shipments. Our State Department isn't clearing anything through to Cuba the easy way."

"I know. They do everything bas-ackwards. Now they got real trouble on their hands."

"How about it?"

"Where can I reach you?"

"Suppose I call you. How long will it take?"

"Couple of hours."

"Where can I reach you?"

He jotted down a number on the back of a matchbook and handed it to me. "Keep your fingers crossed."

"Sure," I said. "And find out if anyone knows a guy named Marcel."

Clinton took the cigar out of his mouth slowly. "Andre Marcel?"

"Could be. Tall, thin guy with a mustache and an accent."

"You're asking for trouble, Fallon."

"That's all I been getting. Who is he?"

"If he were in the rackets, you'd call him an enforcer. He's a troubleshooter for any country with money to spend. The last I heard of Marcel he was operating in Panama. He was responsible for re-routing the drug traffic that used to come into the States from Algiers up through Italy and Spain. He saw to it that only the stuff out of China got in."

"So two birds got killed with one stone," I said.

"Right. The Red organization piled up loot and the moral breakdown was speeded up here with the influx of H."

I got up to leave.

"Fallon... How far is this going? Are we covered?"

"Nothing will involve you."

"Good. Let me know if you need a couple of hands. I know some boys who will be glad to do a favor for Slim, too."

I called Lois Hays from the lobby of the Jackson Hotel

and was invited right up. When I knocked, she opened the door and stood there smiling at some secret joke, waiting while I took my time to look at her.

The sheer black negligee was all she had on, carefully arranged so that the neckline plunged in a wide open V that laid bare half her breasts before it swept into a knotted belt.

"Like?" she asked.

"Neat, but not gaudy," I said.

She chuckled and led me into the room, quite conscious of the fact that the sun streaming through the window in the far wall did more than just silhouette her figure. It illuminated it with cleverly distorted shadows that were uncomfortable to watch. Sitting down was another contrived production designed to jolt the stability of any situation. Almost carelessly, she crossed her legs and let the flesh of her thighs sparkle through the slit in the gown.

I showed my appreciation and looked—like I was supposed to. The only trouble was that there was nothing new about it. But women never seem to take that into consideration.

"You said you'd bring a bottle."

"And you said why waste time."

"So?"

"You were right. There's more to do."

"And what's that supposed to mean?"

"Bananas. You asked me about them. So has everybody else."

I slid into a chair beside the phone and glanced at my watch. "You brought the bit up, so you must know something about it. You're in the news business. You're covering something to do with the Cuban situation. Whatever the bananas are, they're not quite a secret and since I'm involved I'd like to be let in a little bit more before I stick my neck out."

"And how far will that be, Mr. Fallon?"

I watched her a few moments, then I said, "All the way, kid. Somehow it revolves around me. I don't know how, but I intend to find out. I got the strange idea that without me the whole thing can't work."

"Possibly," she told me.

"Or something else."

She paused in the act of reaching for a cigarette. "And what might that be?"

"Maybe it's just necessary to be sure I *don't* know anything—because if I did I might want to follow through on what Tuck started."

"What do you intend doing?"

"I'm going to satisfy my curiosity, sugar."

"That's what killed the cat."

"Not this cat. Can I use the phone?" She waved her hand to go ahead. "Long distance?" I asked.

"It'll go on expenses." She snubbed the cigarette out and unfolded from the chair. "I'll get dressed."

The long-distance operator made a good missing persons tracer. She started with an obsolete number, but finally ran down Joe Conway operating a propeller rebuilding shop in south Jersey. He was another guy from the old 252nd Fighter Squadron whom I had seen on rare occasions since the war. He had put in a lot of pub time in London with us. Like Tuck, Joe had known practically everybody on the base.

For ten minutes, he rehashed the old days in a bubble of enthusiasm before he realized there was something I wanted. He had read of Tuck's death and didn't seem surprised at me inheriting his estate. All I told him was that Tuck mentioned two other guys and wanted me to look them up—Verdo and Christy.

After a moment's silence, Joe said, "Jeez, pal, those names are familiar, but I'll be damned if I remember who they are. You sure they were with our outfit?"

"They must have been. Think they were late replacements?"

"Could be, but I knew most of those, too. This real important?"

"Yeah."

"Tell you what. I see Whitey Thompson once in a while, and he has an album full of pictures of the old bunch. Suppose I go over what he has and see what I can do."

"I'd appreciate it, Joe."

"I'll get right on it. Keep your head out of the cockpit."

"You know me."

When I hung up, I dialed George Clinton to see if he had found anything out. "Cat Fallon, George. Find your man?"

There was a small hesitation, then, "Yeah, I got him."

"Well?"

"Your buddy Tucker Stacy was working against the Castro bunch, all right. He was making arms drops, but from what I gather it was more of a cover for something else. He was closer to the political situation."

"What do you mean?"

"He was hauling important people in and out of Cuba, working on the big end. Now listen, these people of mine have funny sources of information. It's damn reliable, and in their kind of work they have to be sure of the score. At the same time, they don't want to get involved. They come up with more stuff than the CIA. You know what happens if any of this leaks through you? Even Slim Upgate won't try to help you."

"I'm clued in, buddy."

"Okay then. Ever since the Bay of Pigs, something big has been in the works down in Cuba. Nobody seems to know what it really is, but it's mighty explosive. Our own agencies have been working on it and running up against a wall. Whenever someone gets inside the Castro outfit and learns something, they never show up again, so their counterespionage must be pretty good. Whatever's going on, Stacy was wise to it. He got so hot none of the boys would do business with him. They'll peddle guns, ammo, equipment—but nix on politics. They can be hit from both ends if they try."

"How about Andre Marcel?"

"A Castro boy. He doesn't give a damn about arms shipments because the Reds can out-supply anything the black market can send over from the U.S. He's strictly political. A rough guy. I'll tell you something else, too. Nobody seems to think Stacy died accidentally. He had some live cargo with him when he went down, somebody from the hills with proof of what was going on down there."

I said, "That's all?"

"That's all anybody will talk about. What comes next?"

"A trip to Miami. I want to find out a little more about that accident. And give me a contact there."

"Try Felix Ramsey at the Cable-Hurley Supplies Company. It's listed in the book. Felix runs the operation from behind the scenes. He'll go along with whatever you want as long as it's in line with policy."

"Got it. Thanks."

"Good luck. You want my boys?"

"I'll handle it."

When he hung up, I called Upgate in New York and passed on the word. Slim seemed pleased and wished me luck, too, without asking what I was doing. I cradled the phone and sat there thinking the thing through. But it still boiled down to just one thing...who were Cristy and Verdo?

"Do I look all right?" she said from the doorway.

Lois Hayes was sheathed in black, the sheen of a soft fabric clinging to the curves of her body. A wide belt nipped her in at the waist, giving the thrust of her breasts the look of aggressive jetpods on a Boeing 707. I had to laugh.

She frowned. "What's so funny?"

"Nothing. What's the outfit for?"

"I thought you'd take me with you."

"Why?"

"Because you're looking for something. So am I. It may be the same thing."

"What'll you do with it when you find it, kid?"

She took a few long-legged strides into the room so I could get the full effect. "I want to write about it. That's my job."

For an instant she had that dedicated look again, then she turned slowly and gave me the total charge of those deep blue eyes. "Will you take me?"

I shrugged. "Why not. Maybe you can pull some strings I can't. Only let's go now before I get sexy."

Chapter Six

HURRICANE INGRID HAD PICKED up speed since the last weather check. Miami had it at full strength with winds over the 100-mph mark and alerts going out all along the coast. So far the state was only tasting the far-reaching effects of scud and heavy gusts, but in a few more days Ingrid was going to tear things apart if she stayed on course. The patrol planes had it heading directly for Cuba, and if it followed the normal track, it would continue toward Florida.

Charlie Traub felt a little uneasy about me going out, but I filed a flight plan for Miami, made a visual check of the Mustang and helped Lois into the jump seat. She wasn't going to be comfortable and I didn't care, but there was no word of complaint from her at all. Installing that back seat knocked out the fuselage tank, but I didn't need the range much.

I started up, checked the mags at the end of the runway and got a tower clearance for take-off. Once in the air, I switched to the Miami frequency and stayed on a heading until the airfield was in sight.

Lois made my first contact for me, a local reporter named DeWitt who had written the original story of Tuck's disappearance—the one the wire services picked up. We met over coffee in a restaurant and he laid out a folder of clips on the incident. There were several pictures of Tuck beside a plane at the Capital K, one at a ground-breaking cere-

mony somewhere in Celada and another taken outside the
state capitol.

Most of the copy was devoted to his activities in helping
build Celada from a nothing town to a national tourist spot,
but because of the unknown factors surrounding his death,
the details mainly centered on the squall line he was supposedly caught up in, the extent of the search and the statement
of the helicopter pilots who spotted the wreckage and the
fisherman who collected a few fragments.

I jotted down the names of the pilots and the fisherman,
thanked DeWitt and got on the phone to the airbase.
Captain Rob Olsen was on alert but at his home, and when
I located him he said he'd meet me at the club in an hour.
This time I let Lois rent a U-Drive-It on her credit card and
drove on out to the field.

The captain's story was concise...it was a routine search
mission in a given area that extended no more than ten
miles offshore on the supposition that Tuck had simply tried
to skirt the storm and got caught up in it. He had pictures of
the pieces of flotsam from the Staggerwing Beech. Enlarged,
they showed a seat cushion, pieces of fabrics and a dented
GI gas can with a familiar white hand and a large K
beneath it. Twisted around the can were unmistakable parts
of aircraft framing and more fabric. Since his helicopter was
not equipped with floats, Captain Olsen had not made an
attempt at pickup, but radioed the location to his base. Then
a boat was sent out. However, before the patrol boat arrived,
the fisherman got there, attracted by the chopper, salvaged
the wreckage and later handed the remains over to the
government launch.

Before we left, I told Captain Olsen I was a pilot, briefed
him on my background and asked him what he thought of
the squall line.

"That's the funny part," he told me. "It wasn't that bad.
The Beech could have made it without any trouble, I'd say,
but you know thunderheads. Maybe he hit it at the wrong
spot."

"But it *could* have been torn up in the storm?"

"It could have been."

"Thanks, Captain."

Later Lois said, "What now?"

"I want to be certain of something."

"Do you mind telling me what you are really after?"

"I don't think you'd understand."

"Why not?"

"Because you aren't curious enough, honey. You sit and listen while I talk—like you knew all along what's going on and are just letting things stall out. You're supposed to be a reporter with a newsy nose. You gather facts for a political hack who is always after our government policy, but you aren't prying a bit."

She made a wry face. "All right, I know what you're after."

"Tell me."

"You want to know how Tucker Stacy died."

I grinned at her. "I know that, sugar. I want to know why."

"Go right ahead then. You're doing fine. You'll make a good story yourself if nothing comes of this one. If you have something more specific for me to do..."

"I have."

"What?"

"Miami is loaded with anti-Castro people. You know any of them?"

"There are some who have appealed to our government. There's their government-in-exile and..."

"Okay, try them. Get to the big ones and see what you can come up with on this bananas thing."

Her eyes darted to my face.

"You got it from someplace. Where?"

She licked her lips, then: "A rumor. The person who mentioned it was killed before he could testify before a Congressional committee."

"That Gonzales guy last week?" I asked.

"Uh-huh. He had come over in a small boat that had floundered halfway across and drifted for a week. He was near dead from exhaustion and exposure. I was there when they took him off the rescue boat. I heard him mention the word."

"So he was hungry."

"Could be."

"Suppose you find out. Think you know the right people?"

Lois nodded. "I can try. Shall we meet later?"

"There's a Paramount Motel across from where we rented the car. I'll stay there tonight."

She started to smile.

"Two rooms," I said.

The smile turned into a pout.

"Adjoining," I added.

"I'd like that," she said.

RATHER THAN HAVE DeWitt come out again, I went to the office and had him show me the editions of the paper that carried the account of Gonzales' death. When he didn't appear for the hearing, he was found choked to death in his rooming house near Washington—even though a police officer guarded the building. Investigation showed that the killer had gained entry by climbing a tree in the backyard, forcing a second-floor window and making his exit the same way. It was assumed the killer was a Castro fanatic.

DeWitt said, "That wasn't the first one of those."

"Oh?"

"This town is loaded with people from both sides. Hell, it's open warfare around here no matter whom you favor. Luckily for us, they keep it pretty much inside their own quarter, but the situation is going to blow someday. By the way, you know who this guy Gonzales was?"

"Nope."

He thumbed through some later editions and pulled one out on its rack. The story was on page four, a resume of the rescue and subsequent murder of Gonzales. It said he was formerly employed by one of the ousted American industries in Havana.

After I finished, I said, "What about it?"

"Nothing much," he shrugged. "Up until now they'd been playing the guy like he was a peasant climbing off the farm. Turns out he was a chemical engineer. What I'd like to know is what he wanted to spill to the Congressional committee."

"I don't think it would matter. They never seem to listen to anybody anyway."

"That's how it goes. Need anything else?"

"Where can I find that fisherman?"

"The one who picked up the plane wreckage?"

"Uh-huh."

He told me to wait, dug into some other files until he found what he wanted and handed me a slip of paper with a name and address on it.

Peter Claude Watworthy was a dried-up little guy who had spent too many years in the sun. His face, neck and hands were withered and brown, but toughened to a leathery consistency. He sat on the back of his trailer puffing a pipe, staring into the sunset with obvious pleasures and let me speak my piece.

Finally, he put the pipe down and propped his feet up on a crate. "I been wondering about that, too, son. Up to now, nobody's asked me—and I ain't about to be traipsing off tellin' what's none of my business anyway."

"Mind talking about it?"

He knocked the ashes out of his pipe and started stumping in a fresh load. "Not at all, son. Like to talk, matter of fact. Don't get much chance to anymore, seems like. You want to know about that airplane, huh?"

"Anything you can tell me."

"Well, I think the papers got it all wrong."

"How's that, Mr. Watworthy?"

"Peter Claude's the name."

"Sure."

"I been out three days fishing when it happened. Now I ain't saying I'm sure, y'hear? I'm saying what I *think.*"

"That's good enough."

"The night of that storm...after it was all over...I seen this flash in the sky. Could've been a rocket a long way off, could've been anything else. Anyway, there was just that one flash. Around here, you get so you take things into consideration. Nothin' I could do about it, and since nothin' came over the radio I just forgot about it. It wasn't until two days later I saw that there helicopter and went looking to see what the trouble was. That was when I found the stuff in the water and gave it to the government men when they come out.

"Peculiar thing was, if that plane went down in the storm, the stuff would've wound up on the shore by then. If it did come from the flash I seen, it was about in the right place."

Impatiently, I sat and made nothing out of it.

"Later, I got to thinking about something else I found," the old man went on. He eased off the seat and shuffled toward the cabin where he rummaged around in a box. When he came back he had the handle and part of a suitcase in his fingers.

I took it from him, examined the charred edges and the peculiar way the leather was shredded into its fibrous parts. One end of the handle broke loose and I saw where the brass clasp had been almost melted.

"Got that out a way, near where the flash was." He paused. "Ever see anything like that before?" he asked.

I nodded. "I've seen bomb damage do things like this to leather."

"Dynamite, son. I seen it happen, too. Now you know what I've been thinking?"

"I think you're right, Peter Claude." I handed the fragment back to him. "Hold on to this in case I need it."

"Trouble, son?"

"There's always trouble, Peter Claude."

"How right you are, son."

———

WHEN I REACHED the Paramount Motel, I picked a Coke out of the machine and stuck my key in the lock. I closed the door, flipped the light on and the Coke stopped halfway to my mouth. "What the hell..."

"Come right in, Mr. Fallon," Del Reed said. He pointed to the two sitting on opposite sides of the room, big men with bland faces that had the mark of government service stamped on them.

"Do you have a warrant, Reed?"

"Do we need one?"

"Okay, what do you want?" I glanced around the place. "How'd you find me here?"

"We've had a tail on you, friend. I'm glad you were truthful about your flight plan. We picked you up the minute you got here. You've been asking a lot of questions."

"Your business?"

"We're making it that. These gentlemen are federal agents. Mr. Smith and Mr. Jones. Improbable names, but theirs nevertheless."

"So what?"

"If you care to be inconvenienced, it can be done. It's your choice now."

"I don't get it," I said.

Jones, the heavy one, spoke, scarcely moving his month. "We've run a pretty thorough check on you, Fallon. You have a few things in your immediate past that might not stand a good investigation."

I put the Coke down and sat on the arm of a chair. "Kill it, buddies, I've had the con by the experts. This you'd do sure enough, except for one thing."

"And what would that be?" Jones asked.

"Time. You need time. You want to know something. Okay, so do I, so quit wasting time."

They passed a quick look between them and the other one nodded. Jones said, "Sometimes we have to take certain risks in this business. But first let me tell you some-thing...from this moment on, you'll be involved with national security. Break it and you've had it. Clear enough?"

"Clear enough," I repeated.

"You know what you're doing?" Del said angrily.

"Keep quiet, Reed," Jones told him. "It's out of your hands now." He leaned forward, staring at me. "When the Russians folded in Cuba, they shipped their missiles out. Aerial photos showed them lashed to the decks of ships, and information from our agents confirmed the fact up to a certain extent."

"Go on."

"Whether or not the nuclear warheads were removed

couldn't be proved. Let's suppose something, Mr. Fallon. Suppose one of those devices were installed in a ship and that ship headed for some strategic port here in the States and blown while it was docked."

He stopped there and sat back, waiting for me to digest it.

Finally, I said, "So that's what 'banana' is."

The look went between them again. "What's that, Mr. Fallon?"

"Banana. It's a boat. A ship."

"Where did you find that out?"

"Tucker Stacy mentioned it in passing."

"No jokes, Fallon."

"Is it a ship?" I asked softly.

"Yes. That isn't the name, but it's a ship. It's a code name the Cuban underground gave it."

I looked at the three of them. "Where is it?"

"Someplace at sea."

"You don't know?"

"We can't get inside the hurricane area to find out. It cleared Cuba to get away from the storm and that's all we know. But what we want is...what do *you* know, Mr. Fallon?"

"No more than you do, but Tuck knew about it."

"We knew he was involved with them. What else did he tell you?"

"Nothing, but it was obvious why he was killed."

Jones's eyes narrowed at the word. "That's right, he was murdered. Apparently he was bringing someone back from Cuba in the Beech and a dynamite bomb got loaded aboard with him. Somebody else had to get out fast with the information so Gonzales went. He got knocked off before he could talk too."

Jones grunted, "Stupid."

"Why?"

"We should have had him before the committee. They wanted him recovered from the trip. We could have gotten the information earlier. Damn amateurs." He took a heavy breath and settled back. "That isn't locating the ship, Fallon."

"You won't get it from me. That's all I know."

This time it was Smith who spoke. His voice was a hoarse growl that didn't go with his face. "We're beginning to wonder. You might have a personal angle."

"Like what?"

"The Hays woman. It could be a pay-off for a news story. It could be something else."

I just looked at him.

"You're looking for a kick in the teeth, boy."

"It's just a thought we'll keep in mind. I hope you don't plan on going anywhere soon."

"Why?"

"Because I'm going to be your closest companion until this thing gets settled. Someplace in your mind you got a bug. It says you got something we want to know. I've been in this business too long not to smell things like that—and sooner or later I'm going to get it out of you."

"Lots of luck."

He ignored the crack. "Tucker Stacy told you something else. You're still thinking about it. I want to be around when you find out what it is."

Jones and Del Reed got up then, but Smith didn't move. They weren't kidding anymore. They said good night pleasantly, opened the door and left. I looked at Smith and he grinned, then switched on the TV. A newscaster appeared. Hurricane Ingrid was a blaster. All ships were being warned out of the area and the local citizens were being warned to batten down. Ingrid was over Cuba, still on course, picking up speed and increasing in wind velocity.

I walked to the phone, told the switchboard operator to get me a direct line and take time and charges, then I dialed through to George Conway up in Jersey. I asked him if he had seen Whitey Thompson about his old squadron pictures.

"Got right to him, Cat. Look, we went over everything, but he couldn't remember anybody named Cristy and Verdo. He wanted to know, could it've been a squadron call name or anythin'? He remembers the names, but not who they belonged to."

"We were all color and animal calls, George. Red three and four, Tiger Two...you know."

"I'll keep working on it. You'll call me back?"

"Roger."

I hung up and went back to watching television. Verdo and Cristy! Who were they? What were they? They hung there in the past of 20 years ago, meaning something Tucker thought I'd understand without any trouble at all. Why? What made him think I'd get the angle? So we were fighter pilots. We flew Mustangs and escorted B-17s and B-24s in and out of Germany. We did some low-level strafing, a little photo-recon work, covered the invasion and horsed around London. What else? I couldn't figure it. I squatted down on the edge of the bed and gave up.

Lois Hays was due in. It was going to be a long night.

Maybe. The little gust of air on my neck turned me around.

Smith turned, too, and died before he ever saw who it was. The bullet from the silenced gun caught him right in the middle of his forehead.

Andre Marcel said, "You have been speaking to the wrong people, my friend. Now you will come with us. You will speak with us, too, and if you will speak well you will die quickly like your government friend there—not slowly like so many others have died before him."

Chapter Seven

IT WAS a small room filled with the smell of the sea, and I could hear the waves lashing at pilings beneath my feet. The wind was alternately shrill and sorrowful, building in strength.

They had me on a table, stripped to the skin, an overhead light blazing in my eyes. The hypo had worn off and I was fully awake. I could feel my heart pounding inside my chest. Andre stood above me, the two goons on either side. Very delicately he ran a finger over two scars on my body. "I've seen these marks before, Mr. Fallon. They were professionally inflicted."

"Algiers," I said. "I'm still here."

"Quite. They never had a chance to finish, did they?"

A shudder ran through me, I wasn't as brave as I thought. I strained at the ropes that held me spread-eagled. I was lucky the last time in Algiers. The French had come just in time. And I couldn't have talked because I had nothing to say. Still, the Wogs would have gone ahead with the job. It was that way now, too.

"You are familiar with Arab torture?"

I didn't answer him.

"Ah, I see you are. In that case, let us forego a few of the more basic steps and come quickly to those appliances that seem to guarantee results." He reached for something attached to the table and brought up a pair of insulated wires. On the end of each one was a battery clip that could carry a lot of amperage.

"In case you have forgotten, this is an unusual instrument. One end we attach like so..." Andre Marcel snagged the clip in my earlobe. I winced, but it was nothing compared to what was to come.

"The other end," he said, "will be attached to your testicles. At given intervals, a switch will be thrown and...ah, I see you realize what will happen. Not only is it most painful, but totally destructive. You would no longer be a man *if* you lived. You would never again know a woman or even want to. Most probably, however, you would die right here after hours of living with the pain centered in your vitals. Unpleasant to contemplate, isn't it, Fallon."

"You haven't got long to live, Marcel."

"So! You did catch my name." He looked at the guy beside him. "You see?"

The one he addressed twitched nervously. Mistakes could be fatal in his business.

"Still," Andre said with a humorless smile, "like you, I am still alive, but my chances of survival are better. Now, shall we proceed?"

"I can't tell you what I don't know."

"We shall see. First, what did you tell the government police?"

Sweat ran into my eyes and started to burn. I played it cagey and gave him facts. He would know them anyway. "They know Stacy was killed because he was trying to get information back about the nuclear warhead on the ship."

"What ship?"

"You call it *Banana.*"

Marcel nodded slowly. "Good. You are telling the truth. Where is that ship going?"

"I don't know."

He reached out and jammed the clip up between my legs and the teeth bit into me. I started to yell when he said, "The switch, please," and the yell rose into a wild scream that didn't sound like my own voice at all. When it stopped, the sweat poured down my face and my whole body jerked spasmodically for a moment before the pain came.

Marcel let me taste it fully, let me realize that it was only that of a second's duration, let me imagine what it would be like if it had continued longer. "Who are Verdo and Cristy, Mr. Fallon?"

I shook my head. I saw his nod toward the one at the switch and I tried to tell him that I didn't know anything—but my tongue seemed to bloat suddenly at the incredible sweep of pain that came over me like a tidal wave of liquid fire.

When I tried to talk, my lips couldn't form the words and my chest heaved convulsively. The sticky warmth of blood trickled down my wrists and ankles from where the ropes bit in when I strained against them. The sheer terror of knowing that there was nothing I could say turned my brain into a mad thing.

"You will have a minute to speculate, Fallon. Time to recover, time to reconsider, then we will begin again."

My mind raced with something to tell him. *Verdo and Cristy, Verdo and Cristy. They alone could break me loose from this. Who the hell were they? Who? WHO!*

"Very well, Fallon, once again, who are Verdo and Cristy?"

He was ready to nod again. Then I had it. I had Verdo and Cristy. Not who, *what!*

And I was going to tell him. The hell with them all. He could have it.

The blast from Sharon Ortiz's gun caught the guy at the switch full in the face. His head came apart in pieces, and before they could hit the floor she nailed the other one in the chest. He fell into Andre Marcel enough to ruin his aim and tumble him to the floor on one knee. I could see his expression as he looked up at her, the almost simpering grin of an idiot not knowing what to do yet knowing too what was coming. He started to make an imploring gesture when Sharon smiled back at him and almost casually pulled the trigger of the .38.

The first bullet hit Marcel in the stomach and he grabbed his gut as he doubled over. He looked up imploringly, holding his hand out, and the next one went through his palm into his chest. It slammed him back into the table where he coughed once and said something foul in Spanish. Then Sharon took deliberate aim and planted one right between the horns.

Very gently, she removed the clips attached to me. Then wiped the sweat from my face with her scarf. "You have not been hurt, *señor.* They had a long way to go before you were hurt."

"Get me loose," I breathed.

"First I must look at you."

"Damn you."

"Why, *señor?* I remember you looking at me like so not long ago. Can you imagine the things I could do to you now?"

I didn't answer her.

Then she smiled. "But they would not be unpleasant," she said.

In spite of what had just happened, I felt some crazy things go through my mind. "Stop it."

Deliberately, she did something, then grinned again and reached in the pocket of her coat and pulled out a small knife. It took only a second to cut me loose. My clothes were in the corner on a chair and I dressed while she watched, never without that damn smile. She didn't know it yet, but for this she was going to get fixed. Soon and good.

I said, "How long were you outside?"

"Long enough to know you wouldn't tell them anything, *señor.* "

She didn't know, I thought. *She was wrong, but she didn't know.*

Sharon changed then. The smile faded and a look of serious concern crossed her eyes. "I know whose side you are on now, *señor.* "

The shadows dancing across her face gave a different life to her beauty. Her hair was a deep midnight glow, her lips lushly ruby, the Irish and Spanish in her trying to come out at the same time. I felt the firm swell of her breasts brush against my forearm and I ran my hand up her shoulder. Beneath her suit coat, she was warm and a muscle under my fingers trembled.

"How did you find me, Sharon?"

"By following Andre Marcel. He is so smart as to be

stupid sometimes. He does not realize that our organization is also efficient. We are small, perhaps, but necessarily efficient. I knew he would keep contact with you. You are the key, *señor,* to all that we have."

"I know what the score is now, honey," I said. "The whole deal. I know about the ship you called *Banana.* "

"And where it is going?"

"Not yet."

Stark disappointment flooded her face.

"In a little while, kid, just a few minutes more. Look, where are we?"

"On a wharf in the south end."

"There's a phone nearby?"

"I know where one is."

"Good, let's find it."

I got Charlie Traub out of bed and asked him if Tucker had ever taped any of his plane-to-tower conversations.

He said, "Sure, whenever he wanted a permanent record the tower operators would cut in a tape. Why?"

"Back in the old days, Verdo and Cristy were wire recording devices we could call while in flight on photo-recon missions if we spotted something in a hurry and didn't have time to jot it down. It was a squadron deal our own intelligence officer installed. Tuck still used the system, but with tape. You have a recorder handy?"

"One in the tower."

"Okay, put me on that extension and get up there. Get out the tapes of Tuck's last day. He may have called in, and if it was an automatic setup the tower operator never knew what was on there and just filed the thing."

When he made the exchange of extensions, I held on and got the rest of the information from Sharon. They had definite information on the removal of the warheads and the installation in the ship, but Castro's security was so tight that's all they had. A top agent named Manuel Alvada was to come out with Tucker with documented evidence of the switch, but the plane had been sabotaged by Andre Marcel's men. Gonzales was a technician who had stayed on in Cuba deliberately with intent to buck Castro and the know-how to get inside their major operations. When he defected they knew why and waited for him to show up in the States, Marcel preceding him there. The one thing he didn't know, however, was where the ship was headed.

Charlie came on then.

"Ready on the tapes."

"Roll it."

I heard Tuck's voice then, the drone of the engine in the background. Very calmly he stated his position and the fact that he was flying out an anti-Castro agent with the story of *Banana*. He was taking no chances. In the event something happened before he could land he wanted the statement on record even if it wasn't documented.

Banana was a World War II Liberty ship named *Leona*. It was scheduled to sail for the Panama Canal where it would be blown up. It was to be quite a coup. In this day of the airlift and almost overnight reconstruction, the damage wouldn't be enough to impair our military or economic might. But that wasn't the intent of *Banana*. It was a propaganda program the Reds had set up that would work against us. With all the unrest in Central America, the *Leona* would blow and the Commies would say that it was a deliberate United States action to give us a chance to move directly into South American countries to "protect" them—thus offsetting a true people's movement against capitalistic governments. To back them up would be proof that the Panama Canal was an almost outdated project in these modern days of transportation, not even large enough to take modern carriers or battlewagons.

The cold war would become hot. The Reds had a live excuse of their own to move in militarily and the shooting would start. With the Red propaganda machine rolling, who would be on our side? Great!

Tuck's voice suddenly cut off. He had died.

I hung up and explained it to Sharon. I watched her pale. "It's too late, isn't it, *señor?*"

"Not now, not after all that's happened," I said. "It's never too late, Sharon." I looked up the number George Clinton gave me. I got the watchman at Cable-Hurley Supplies Company and he gave me Felix Ramsey's home number.

Ramsey didn't like me dragging him out of the sack, but when I mentioned Slim Upgate he was ready to do anything. I nailed it fast. I wanted two 500-pound demolition bombs to swing under the Mustang and I wanted them installed right away. He stuttered a little when I told him, but he said he'd have a truck out at the field in an hour.

I had one more call to make. This one was the big one. I got the man named Jones after three tries and told him to listen carefully and not bother tracing the call. I told him Smith was dead and so was the guy who killed him. I told him where they were. I also told him there was only one way the thing could be handled, and it was my way. If our government stepped in there would be hell to pay and the propaganda bit would go right on, but modified a little. The Reds would play up the attempt but capitalize on the fact that when they blew the whistle on the plot it was their men who were killed performing a public service and the U.S. who tried to destroy the evidence of it. It was all very neat and covered from every angle.

Calmly, Jones said, "Then how will it be done?"

"I'll do it. They'll never come back to me, brother."

"And you want what from me?"

"Get the reports from the planes patrolling the hurricane area. One of them might have spotted that ship. Can do?"

"Will do. How do I reach you?"

"I'll call you from another phone," I said and hung up.

The men were waiting by the Mustang with a truck. It didn't take long to swing the two bombs under the wing or to hook them up. When they were ready, the guys simply looked at me curiously and drove away.

I made the call to Jones. He had the information at hand, but his voice sounded shaky. He started, "Listen, Fallon..."

"No time, friend, this is it. When it's over I'll explain. Not now. What about that ship?"

"She was spotted. In fact, the planes directed her through the best section of the blow." He gave me the last coordinates and I wrote them down. "I know what you're planning, baby. You got me on a hook and I can't say a thing."

"Don't try."

She was waiting for me by the plane, her eyes shiny with tears. "You think you can do this thing?"

"I'm going to try like hell, baby."

"Then take my love with you, *señor.*" She reached up, her arms going around my neck and her mouth was a volcanic thing of sweetness and fire that said everything at once, promising everything, and I remembered what she did to save my life and felt a wild hunger for the woman she was, full and glossy, vibrant with a love she was giving to me.

When I took my mouth away from hers I said, "I'll be back, Sharon," then I climbed in the old 11-51 and went through the starting procedure.

The tower didn't want to clear me, but I never gave him a chance to tell me so. I headed into the wind and eased the throttle forward and fought the side gusts until I was off the ground. Then I climbed to 30,000 feet, over the storm, picked up my heading, held everything at max cruise and waited. The moon above made the rolling clouds of Ingrid look like gray snowbanks that gave way to the 60-mile width of the hurricane's eye before narrowing across its southeast quarter. Then I passed it.

Chapter Eight

I FOUND the *Leona* ten miles off her course estimate. To make sure, I swept in low with my landing lights on, wheels and flaps down. There was her name plastered across the stern in fading white paint. I got the gear retracted before the first bursts of gunfire winked at me from the decks. I picked up altitude and circled the ship below.

Two chances, that was all I had.

I made the first pass from the stern, dumping her over from 15,000 feet and releasing my bomb at 2000. Behind me came a shuddering *whump*, and when I looked back I could see the yellow glow of the burst and the lurch of the ship as she caught the near miss. There were lights on the deck now and in their beams I could see the ant-like figures of men running. A spot flicked on and tried to catch me, but there wasn't much chance of that. If they knew what they were carrying they'd be worrying about saving themselves, not killing me.

I took the Mustang up again and got set for another pass. I started to make a 180-degree turn into the run when I felt a sudden lightening of the ship, a quick uplift on the left wing and the insides wanted to drain out of me. Down below, the other bomb tore harmlessly into open water a half mile from the *Leona*.

It was too late after all.

For one second I thought of a suicide run, but I didn't

have the guts for it. In helpless anger I circled over the *Leona*, cursing that battered old hulk and wishing I still had the six .50s mounted that could at least tear some holes in her, damning the idiots that mounted the bomb, but mainly damning myself for not having checked everything out.

I took one last look below. This time there *was* something different. The ship had stopped. It had heeled over sharply to port and was low in the water. I took another chance and went in again with the gear down and the lights on. I saw what had happened.

The first bird had been a near miss, all right, but those rusted plates of the ship's bottom were too old to take the concussion. They had folded and I had won. Damn it, *we* had won!

I eased the stick over and got out of there, getting on a return heading. But I couldn't help looking back. I was far and high enough away to see it safely when it went off. No big flash. No mushroom cloud. The *Leona* must have been underwater when it happened. Just a beautiful, diffused glow that changed colors in a soft pattern that rippled out gently and just as gently receded.

Ingrid came into sight again, her eye and front quarter reaching out for Florida. I beat her in and taxied up to the hangar where Sharon was still waiting, the wind whipping the dress tight around her legs. The tower was trying hard to get me to get under cover and the lights of a truck were coming toward me. I waved the truck off, motioned that I was going up again and the guy yelled something unintelligible and swung around.

As he did, the motor coughed twice and began to run rough until I idled it at higher RPM's. The old trouble was back again, despite Charlie's work. I wouldn't be able to shut down and re-start now without getting into it—and I wanted to get the hell out of there.

I edged in close to the hangar doors where there was a windbreak, locked the breaks, hopped out and chocked the wheels.

It was a bad thing to do, but I had no alternative.

Sharon came into my arms with a rush, burying her face in my chest, sobs of joy coming from her like that of a happy puppy. I shouted over the roar of the engine behind me, "She's gone. It's all right now...we have it made."

"As long as I have you back, my big one..."

"Inside. I have one call to make."

I pushed her ahead of me through the door into the hangar and felt for the light. The place was empty; everybody had cleared out in advance of Ingrid. I picked the phone off the wall and dialed my number.

The voice in the doorway said, "Hang up, Fallon."

We both turned around.

Lois Hays stood there, her face a mask of pure hatred, the gun in her hand a cold, deadly thing. I put the phone back.

"Yes, I'm sure of it now, Lois, I knew how Del Reed, Jones and Smith could have found me, but not Andre Marcel. You were the only one who knew about the Paramount Motel."

"You're quite right. I told him."

Outside, the wind was a tearing shriek. Ingrid was here. So was death. I felt Sharon's hand grope for mine, find it and hold tight.

I said, "It's too late, Lois. The *Leona* is down, the bomb is gone. The propaganda is a dead issue."

"Is it? I think not."

Somehow, she had figured an angle and I knew I was sweating. Her smile was as deadly serious as the gun in her hand. I measured the distance to her and thought about Sharon's gun, but each time Lois Hays was following my thoughts as though she could read my mind.

"No," she told us both, "there is not one thing you can do before I kill you. Not one thing."

Trying to play for time, I said, "How can you make it, kid?"

"If you thought about it, you'd see. Tomorrow the papers will carry the story with Duncan Knight's byline and we'll still win. Pity you won't be able to see it."

"What story?"

"How an American citizen carried out an act of unprecedented violence—aided and abetted by authorized agents of this country—and destroyed a harmless Cuban vessel engaged in commerce with a neutral country. Don't you just see how the rest of the world will eat that story up? Oh, I know what you intended the world to think...that the *Leona* went down in the midst of a hurricane, and certainly it could be assumed that such an old ship would succumb to hurricane seas. But you're out of luck, Fallon. It will be my story."

"And us?"

"When accused of the act, you tried to take me captive and I had to shoot you both. Who would deny that possibility when they know of the three men lying dead on the wharf? Fallon, you're better off dead. And me, I'll live to work another day. I'll see that my story is well supported and I don't think the government will want to go into the matter any more than is necessary. They want no part of a shooting war."

She smiled again and raised the gun a little higher. "Outside, please. We might as well keep it clean. I don't want any shots heard—not just yet."

She stepped back through the door as we came toward her.

Tuck's words: *There are still some of us left.*

Yes, there were.

We stood in the fierce forefoot of Ingrid, with our clothes snapping around our legs, our faces stung by sand that was ripping by. I held Sharon as tightly as I could and kept walking. Lois was still backing up, almost ready to pull the trigger. We walked forward and kept on walking, the three of us that were left—two in the front and one behind and all the while the crazy scream of the wind was the only sound we could hear.

The gun came up, leveled on the last step Lois took, but in our faces she read that we had won after all. There were still some of us left like Tuck had said, two in front and one behind her.

She started to scream as she backed into the great churning blades of the prop on the Mustang and dissolved into a red, misty froth that was carried away in the gale.

The Gold Fever Tapes

The Gold Fever Tapes

THEY KILLED Squeaky Williams on the steps of the Criminal Courts Building with two beautifully placed slugs in the middle of his back and got away into traffic before anybody really knew what had happened.

But I knew what had happened and my guts felt all tight and dry just standing there looking at his scrawny, frozen face in the drawer of the morgue locker. One eye was still partly open and was staring at me.

"Identify him?" the attendant asked.

"He doesn't have to," the other voice said and I turned around.

Charlie Watts had made captain since I had seen him last, but ten years and a few promotions had only screwed tighter the force of hate he had for people like me.

"An old cellmate of yours, Fallon...isn't he?" Even his voice had that same grating quality like a file on a knife blade.

I nodded. "Six months' worth," I said.

"How'd you manage it, Fallon? What'd you have on the wheels to get paroled out like that? What bunch of suckers would let a damned crooked cop like you out after the bust you took?"

"Maybe they needed my room," I told him.

The drawer slammed shut and Squeaky went back into

the cold locker and the last I saw of him was that half open eye.

"And maybe you ought to come over and talk about this little hassle in more familiar surroundings," Watts told me.

"Why?"

"Because there might be something interesting to discuss when ex-cons get shot down on public property and old buddies show up to make sure he's dead."

"I came in to identify the body. As of this morning he wasn't I.D.'d."

"The picture in the paper wasn't all that good, Fallon."

"Not to you, maybe."

"Knock it off and let's go."

"Drop dead," I said and held out my open wallet.

After a few seconds he said, "Son-of-a-bitch. A reporter. An *effing* newspaper reporter. Now who the hell would give you a job as a reporter?"

"Orley News Service, Charlie. They believe that criminals can be rehabilitated. Ergo... I have a reason for being here since I can write a great personal piece on the deceased."

"Ergo shit," he said.

"If you want to check my credentials..."

"Go screw yourself and get out of here."

"Ease off. The past is behind us."

"Not as far as I'm concerned," he said. "You'll always be just a lousy cop who took a payoff and loused things up for the rest of us. It's too bad that con didn't kill you up at Sing."

"Squeaky took that knife for me," I reminded him.

"So pay your last respects and blow."

"My pleasure, Captain." I put my wallet back and walked across the room. At the door I stopped and looked back. "Your leg ever hurt when it rains?"

"I don't owe you any favors for deflecting a slug for me, Fallon. I've taken three since then."

"Too bad," I grinned, "that hole in my side still bugs me."

———

WHY SOME WOMEN look naked with their clothes on is beyond me, but with Cheryl I finally figured it out. She was what I called posture-naked. She always did those damn things that made a man look at her, like bending stiff-legged over the bottom drawer of the filing cabinet so that her mini-skirt hiked up to her hips, or leaning across my desk in those loose-fitting peasant blouses so that I forgot whatever she was trying to point out to me.

When I walked into the office Orley News Service had provided me with she was scratching her tail with the utter abandon of a little kid and I said, "Will you stop that!"

"I'm itchy."

"What've you got?"

Cheryl glared at me a second, then laughed. "Nothing. I'm peeling. I got my behind sunburned skinny dipping in my friend's pool."

"Great guys you go with."

"My friend is a girl I was in the chorus line with. She married a millionaire."

"Why didn't you do the same thing?"

"I have ambition."

"To be a typist?"

"Orley pays me as a secretary and researcher."

"They're wasting their money," I said.

She gave me that silly smirk of hers that irritated the hell out of me. "So I'm a sex object the brass likes to keep around."

"Yeah, but why around me?"

"Maybe you need help."

"Not that kind."

"That kind especially."

"Everybody was safer when you were a social worker."

"Parole officer."

"Same difference."

"Like hell," she said. Then her eyes went into that startling directness and she asked, "What happened this morning?"

"It was Squeaky. He's dead."

"Then write the story and stay out of it."

"Don't play parole officer with me, kiddo."

Her eyes wouldn't let me alone. "You know what your job is."

"Squeaky saved my ass for me," I said.

"And now he's dead." She studied my face for a long stretch of time, then caught her lower lip between her teeth. "You know why?"

I swung around in my chair and looked out the window over the Manhattan skyline. It wasn't very pretty anymore. Absolute cubism had taken over architectural design. The city used to be sexy. Now it was passing into its menopause. "No," I said.

"In the pig's ass you don't," Cheryl told me softly. "Don't forget what your job is. You stick your neck out and everybody gets hurt."

When the door shut to the outer office I pulled the little cassette tape from my pocket and shoved it into the recorder. I wanted to hear it again just to be sure.

And Squeaky sure had a hell of a story to tell in a matter of two and a half minutes.

———

HE HAD COME out of the big house after a six year stretch and opened a radio repair shop just off Seventh Avenue, made enough bread to consider marrying a chubby little streetwalker who lived in the next tenement and got himself killed before he got on the freebie list in exchange for marital security. But that part wasn't on the tape. That part I knew because we had kept in touch.

The tape was a recording of two voices, one wondering how the hell the Old Man was going to get eight hundred pounds of solid gold out of the country into Europe and the other telling him not to sweat it because anybody who could get it together could get it out and with the prices they were paying for the stuff over there it was all worth the risk even if five people had already been killed putting it into one lump. All they had to do was knock off the mechanic who had made it possible and they got their share and to hell with it.

The miserable little bastard, I thought. He had taken a cassette recorder with a built-in microphone into the restaurant to work on it during his lunch hour and picked up the conversation in the next booth. The trouble was he knew one of the guys by his voice and tried to put the bite on him for a lousy grand.

But they didn't call him Squeaky for nothing. His voice went across to the other end and he was staked out for a kill before he knew what was happening. All he could do was send me the tape and try to get into protective custody before they nailed him and he never did make the top steps of the Criminal Courts Building. Whoever was protecting eight hundred pounds of solid gold for overseas shipment had taken a chip off the lump and paid for a contract kill on my old cellblock buddy.

Peg it at one hundred bucks an ounce minimum and eight hundred pounds came to damn near a million and a quarter bucks. Less the cost of shipping and a few dead bodies. One was Squeaky's.

Little idiot. He was too hysterical trying to run out a few inches of tape to remember to identify the guys on the other segment. All I had was their voices and the single name, *the Old Man.*

I stuck the tape in the envelope with the graphic voice print pattern Eddie Connors had pulled for me and filed it in the back of the drawer with my bills and locked it shut. My stomach had that ugly feeling again and I was remembering how blood smelled when it was all spread out in a pool on hot pavement and that half open eye of Squeaky Williams was looking at me from under the frozen eyelid. I said something dirty under my breath and pulled the .45 out from the desk and stuck it in my belt.

Everything was going to hell and I couldn't care less. All I could remember was Squeaky stepping in front of that knife Water Head Ardmore had tried to shove into me just because I had been a cop.

———

A LOT of them wouldn't look at me because I had gone sour, but there were those who had done exactly what I had done without making the mistake of getting caught and the burly Lieutenant was one of them and couldn't take the chance of not meeting me without taking the chance of me pulling the string on him. He was as uncomfortable as hell because he had been forced into it, and even though he had cut himself loose, he had done it and damn well knew it.

We sat together in the back of the Chinese restaurant and over the chow mein I said, "Who's collecting gold, Al?"

"Who isn't?"

"I'm talking about a million and a quarter's worth."

"It's illegal," he said, "except for manufacturing purposes."

"Sure, and it's too heavy to ship. But that didn't stop them from forming it into aircraft seat brackets, phony partitions and faked machine parts."

Al Grossino forked up another mouthful of noodles and glared at me. "Look, I haven't heard of..."

"Don't crap me, Al. They've reopened the old mines since the price went up and technology advanced to the point where they can make them productive. Those companies are processing the stuff on the site to cut costs. It's all government supervised and if there has been any rumbles you're in the position to know it."

"Damn it, Fallon..."

"You make me push it and I will," I said.

He waited a few seconds, his eyes passing me to survey the rest of the place until he was satisfied. "Hell, you're always going to get the looters. Small time crap."

"What's the rumble?"

He gave a small shrug of resignation and said, "Two Nevada outfits and one in Arizona are hassling with the unions. They started missing stuff before it got to the ingot stage. So far nothing's showed up on the New York market."

"As far as you know anyway."

"Don't lip me, Fallon."

I grinned and waited.

Al Grossino said, "We got a wire to keep an eye out but

so far it doesn't look like anything. Those companies will use any excuse for a tax deduction."

"Horseshit."

"You that dumb that you don't know how the feds cover every grain of gold mined in this country?"

"You that dumb that you don't know the difference between the official price and the black market?" I said.

"Okay, so the speculators..."

"Crap on the speculators. Spell it out in hard language. Who are the biggest speculators over here? Who built Las Vegas? Who handles the narcotics traffic? Who..."

"The mob isn't moving into gold, Fallon," he snapped. "They're too damned smart to play around with currency."

"Why do they handle counterfeit?" I asked him with a nasty grin.

He threw his napkin down and swallowed the last of his cold tea. "Make your point and let me get out of here."

"Find out how much those companies think they're missing," I said.

"Why?"

"I'm a reporter, remember?"

"It's hard to picture you that way."

"Your time might come, Al. By the way, who's the *Old Man?*"

"Hell, you're not that stupid, Fallon. You were in the army. You were a cop. Anybody who runs anything is the *old man.*" He picked up his hat, stuck me with the check and left me sitting there.

———

I LOOKED at the cop on the door, showed my press card and took a handful of garbage from him until I spotted Lucas of the *News* inside and read him off with some language from the U.S. Constitution and walked into Charlie Watts running an interrogation scene on a weepy Marlene Peters. He was backed up by two detectives and an assistant D.A. But the chunky little street hustler who had been slated to marry Squeaky Williams had been busted too often not to know all the tricks and, now, she was turning on her ultimate weapon of salty tears. She had the guardians of civic virtue all shook up. Lucas was there ready to put it all down and I was wondering who had the warrant or did they get themselves invited in.

Apparently I was a welcome relief and my old commander said, "I was expecting to see you sooner or later."

"Which one is it?"

"Sooner," he said. "No doubt you know the lady."

"No doubt."

"Professionally?"

"I never paid for it yet, Charlie."

The D.A.'s man couldn't have been out of his twenties and made the mistake of saying, "What the hell are you doing here?"

I said, "I'm about to throw your ass out of here, kid. I mean physically and with blood all over the place unless you ease on out of here on your own. And take your friends with you."

Charlie Watts made a real grin hoping something would happen, but I was right about the warrant. They didn't have one. That's why they all got up and glanced at the red-faced D.A.'s man, and Lucas put his notes away with disgust, reading the whole thing right down to the button. I waited until the door was closed, then tossed my hat on the table and said, "How're you doing, Marlene?"

There weren't any tears now. She was dry-eyed and scared, but not because the cops had been there. Her tongue kept flicking over her lips and she couldn't keep her hands still at all. "Please, Fallon..."

"You worried about me?"

"No."

"You love Squeaky?"

"A little bit. He was the only guy who ever wanted to marry me."

"You know why he was killed?"

"Yes."

That crawly feeling went up my spine again. "Why?"

"He didn't tell me. He just knew something, that's all. He

said he could prove it and it would make us the big bundle that could get us the hell out of this town. He had a tape recording of something."

"Oh?"

She spun around, eyes as big as wrist watches. "But I don't have it! He sent it to somebody just before he went up to see that judge who sentenced him and told me to get out quick—and all of a sudden he was dead."

"Why didn't you go?"

"Are you kidding?" She covered her face with her hands and this time the tears were for real. "Why do you think the street's so empty for? They're outside waiting for me, that's why. Shit, I'm dead too. I'm as dead as Squeaky and I don't even know what for."

"You're not dead, Marlene."

"Go look out the window. There's a car on each end of the street. Oh, you won't see anybody. They're just waiting there for the right time and when you all leave I'm nothing more than a dead screwed-up whore who crossed up her pimp and got her throat cut for the trouble."

"So I won't leave." I pulled her hands away from her face. "Squeaky say anything at all? Come on, think about it?"

Marlene shook her head and pulled away from me. "Let me alone."

"That didn't answer the question."

"What difference does it make?"

"No sense dying, is there?"

The tone of my voice got her then and she turned around. "I'm not talking to any cops."

"I'm an ex-con," I said, "Squeaky's old roommate, remember?"

"He wanted to marry me. He really did."

"I know."

"I would have, too. He wasn't much, but nobody else ever asked me."

"Somebody will. What did he tell you?"

"Nothing. All he said was he knew who the rat was and this time he'd put him in his hole." She made a pathetic gesture with her hands and her eyes got wet again. "How am I going to get out of here?"

"I'll take you," I said.

So we went downstairs to the back of the landing and felt our way to the basement steps, inching our way past the garbage and the empty baby carriages until we made the crumbling concrete steps that led out to the rear court and the night and stood there long enough before we crossed to the rotted fence that separated her building from the one opposite, ducking under the hanging wash and skirting the crushed cartons and tipped-over garbage cans.

But they had been guarding the night longer than we had and their vision was adjusted to the dark so that when the first cough of a muted gun spit out all I saw was the flash and felt a slug breeze by. All I could do was shove her aside while I clawed at the .45 in my belt. The white spit came again, then another, but this time I had the big end of the Colt and the roar of the blast tore the night open whose only echo was a choking, gurgling gasp, until I heard the little whimper from my left and feet slamming away in front of me.

I said, "Marlene...?"

And the little whimper answered, "He really would have married me. You know that, don't you?"

I lit a match and looked into blank, dead eyes. "I know, kid," I said.

Windows were banging open and someplace a woman screamed. Some guy was swearing into the night and another nut had a flashlight trying to probe into the darkness but couldn't tell where it had all come from. I walked over to the fence, found the body and lit another match.

The guy didn't have much of a face left at all. But he did have a wallet in his right hip pocket and I put it in mine and got out just as the guy with the flashlight almost picked me out of the shadows.

Maybe my guts should have been all churned up again. Maybe that crawly feeling should have had my shoulders tight as hell. In an hour Charlie Watts would have an APB out on me and in two hours the papers would be running the old story on the front pages with my pictures in the centerfold or even splashed on page one and there wouldn't be any place at all for me to surface.

But for the first time in a long time I felt nice and easy.

I even wished I had Cheryl handy.

Fallon, you slob, I thought, *you got a real death desire.*

Somebody else did too...now. They had a man dead and knew this kind of an ex-con didn't let his old cellmate down. And wherever he was, the *Old Man* would be sweating because the possibility was there that a real live killer knew about all that gold just waiting to reach the European market.

————

MA CHRISTY WAS one of those old time New York pros with no eyes, ears or memory who ran a boarding house right close to the docks where the Cunards used to unload and all she did was point with her thumb and say, "The broad's in number two, Fallon."

I told her thanks and went up to where Cheryl was waiting in the dingy room with a hamburger in one fist and a copy of the *News* in the other. At least this time I was well on the inside pages and when she looked at me over the top of the sheet said, "You sure did it, boss man."

"Pull your skirt down. Ma thinks I rented the room for an assignation."

"It's too short. Besides, assignation sounds like a dirty word."

"There's only one 'ass' in it."

"A pity," she said.

I closed the door and locked it, then crossed the room and pulled the blinds closed. She still hadn't looked up from the paper. "What did you get?"

"You're wanted for murder," Cheryl told me.

"Great," I said.

"His name was Arthur Littleworth, alias Shim Little, alias Little Shim, alias Soho Little, alias..."

"I know."

"Contract killer out of Des Moines, Iowa. The .357

Magnum he carried was the same one used in two other hits, one in Los Angeles, one in New York."

"Which one in the city?"

"Your friend's. Squeaky's."

"They have an angle on it, don't they?"

"Sure. He was in the can with Squeaky before you were. They were enemies."

"I don't remember him."

"He got out before you got in. I checked the dates. Your hit was pure retribution." She put the paper down and watched me with those big round eyes of hers. "You're on everybody's kill list now."

"How about that?" I said.

"Why do you have to ask for it?"

"Screw it. What do you care?"

"You don't know much about women, do you?"

"Kitten, I've been there and back."

"Learn anything?"

"Enough to stay away from you sex objects," I told her.

"One phone call and you'd be busted."

"So would you, doll."

"I'm no virgin."

"But there are other ways and the busting hurts worse."

"Sounds interesting."

"Try me," I said.

"Maybe later."

"You're lucky. Right now I'm spooky of little typists with a sex drive."

I got that silly grin again. "You bastard," she said. "Why do I have to be torn between duty and schoolgirl love?"

"What do I look like to you?"

"A big ugly bum with a record. You don't even know how to dress properly. Ex-cop, ex-con, neophyte reporter, currently wanted criminal."

"Thanks," I said. "It's been a stinking two days."

"Can I help you out?"

"Feel like being an accessory?"

She looked at the half-made bed and grinned again. "Sometimes I wonder about myself."

"Ummm?"

"I talk better when I'm being loved," she said.

We lay there a little while afterwards and she said, "You haven't got any chance at all, you know that."

"Who ever did?"

"It was all decided a long time ago."

"No Kismet crap, baby."

"Face reality. Your whole future was based on programmed performance."

"Screw it, parole officer."

"It was an assigned risk." She was looking at the ceiling, deadly serious. "They thought it would be worth it."

"They forgot about the incidental factors," I said.

"He was only a person in the same cell."

"Try living in prison. See what the person in the upper bunk is like."

"Worth dying for?"

"Isn't everybody?"

"Us too?"

"All I'm doing is screwing...not saying 'I love you, sweetheart.'"

"Screwing's enough for a parole officer," she told me.

"Not for a typist," I said. "Now tell me what you found out."

"Charlie thinks you'd be better off dead."

"Nice."

"He's not the only one. There's a contract out on you."

"That's what I figured," I said, then turned over and wrapped my arm around all that lovely soft flesh and fell asleep. I still was feeling nice and easy. My last coherent thought was how far a doll would go for a guy.

———

THE THING they call gold fever is a thing you can't hide. Like giving the clap to your wife and the neighbor next door. So your wife won't squeal, but the neighbor will when she gives it to her husband and he's peeing red peppers in the bowl and hanging onto the rafters while he howls and he's ready to blow the whistle on everybody.

And gold sure makes them pee.

Loco Bene was so terrified of seeing a first-rate killer standing in front of his bed that he damned near browned out at the sight of the dirty end of a .45 and said, "No shit, Fallon, I never heard of nuthin' except what gets talked up on the street."

"Bene...you roomed with Shim Little." I was remembering what Cheryl had filled me in on.

"Yeah, yeah, I know. We wasn't no pals, though. Just because he had a couple of mob connections we were just crap to him."

"Okay, Loco, you've done your share of the delivery work in the narcotics rackets. How're the new routes set up?"

"Come on, come on! Like you're givin' me a choice between who knocks me off. If them routes get tapped, you think they won't know who was talking? Besides, they're all incoming tracks. I never ship outside."

"Loco, the word's out. There's gold going to be passed and you're a first-class route man. Don't tell me you haven't heard any buzz on it."

"Fallon..."

I thumbed the hammer back and the metallic snick sounded like thunder.

He swallowed first, then made a gesture with his shoulders. "Sure, I heard some talk. Like somebody wants to contact Gibbons only they don't know he's pullin' a stretch in a Mexican jail."

"Adrian Gibbons?"

"Sure. He used to handle heavy stuff, mostly expensive machine parts. He was an artist the way he could build them into cheap gizmos to fake out the inspectors. Never had a bust until he tried to rape that Mex chick."

"They won't ship gold like that," I said. "Who else are they looking for?"

"Nobody tells me...hell, the Chinaman turned down an offer because he's still hot from that picture deal he made with the museum. And anyway, he uses legit routes. But gold..."

"Who's the Mechanic, Loco?"

"Huh?"

"You heard me."

"Like for cars...or a card sharp?"

"Who would Shim Little call the Mechanic?"

His hands pulled at each other and he wet his lips down again. "Was a guy in the joint they called the Mechanic, only he used to set up cars to run hash and junk in from across the border."

"Remember his name?"

"Naw, but he had a double eight on the end of his number. He got out before me. Now how about laying off, Fallon? I gave you..."

I eased the hammer down on the rod and stuck it back in my belt. "Maybe I'll come around again, Loco," I said. "So keep your ears open."

———

THE TELEVISION and newspaper coverage I had gotten over that damned back yard shootout had turned me into a night person. Every cop in the department would be alerted and there weren't many of the street people you could afford to take a chance on. Not when you knew they wouldn't mind scoring a few brownie points with the cops by pointing a finger your way. But there were a few no better off than myself and these were the ones with the best antennae in the system because it was their best survival device and they had words to say.

Cheryl's information had been exact, all right. A fat, open contract was out on me and some new faces with old reputations had shown up in places I generally frequented. O'Malley, the doorman at my apartment building who was a real, solid buddy, was glad to hear from me and was pretty damn sure somebody had my place staked out. He was going to pack a change of clothes for me and leave them in his locker in the basement, with the private rear entrance key stashed over the doorsill. Long ago I had anticipated a possible tap on the office phone line and had arranged an alternate communication system with Cheryl. She was picking up the same information, going through repeated questioning by the police, the reporters and two of the D.A.'s men.

There was an irritated note in her voice when she said, "You're going to blow this one sure as hell, Fallon."

"It's too late now to cut out."

"You know better than that," she said.

"Sure," I told her. "I can prove self-defense and claim the gun was one of Squeaky's but who gets that contract lifted off me?"

"That's the odd part, isn't it?"

"Damn odd. It's too high a price to pay for an ex-con who knocked off a punk hit man, but when you're protecting somebody who's sitting on a big lump of gold, it's only like paying a nuisance tax."

"Okay, don't lecture me. Just tell me what to do."

What I wanted, I told her, was to find a guy they referred to as the Mechanic. I gave her the approximate dates of his stay in the joint and the last two digits of his number. She was to get those voice print patterns and the tape from my file, that Japanese mini recorder I had, and meet me at Ma Christy's at two A.M. That gave her just four hours.

Then I went back into the night again. Somebody had to know who the Mechanic was and if the *Old Man* was scheduling him for a kill too, the quickest way to flush him out was to put the word around. Whatever the Mechanic was doing would get jammed in a hurry if he knew the payoff was to be made with a bullet. All that gold was just too big and too heavy to be moved around without somebody getting wise, so it would have to be shipped in a pretty special way. Small parcels would involve just too many different operations, too many people and accumulated risks, so my bet was that it would go as a single unit directly to a market. All I had to know was where it was, who had it and how it was going. And what I was going to do about it if I ever found out.

Sure, I could lay the story on Charlie Watts and the good captain would dutifully process it, but if this were a possible mob operation there were always those pipelines into the bureaucratic maze of officialdom that would send out the warning signal and all that yellow metal would go right back into hiding until another time.

No, I wanted one shot at it myself first.

By midnight I had the story out in three different quarters and had picked up a little more on Shim Little. He was a loner who shuttled around between cheap midtown motels, never keeping a permanent address, always seemed to have enough money in his pocket and didn't have any regular friends anyone remembered. A few times he was seen with the same guy, a nondescript type who didn't talk much, but Paddy Abies, the night bartender at the Remote Grill, said he knew the guy packed a gun and the couple of times he saw him he had an out-of-state newspaper with him. He couldn't remember the name, but it had a big eagle in the mast-head. Paddy was pretty nervous talking to me, so I told him thanks and left.

Outside, a fine mist was blowing in from the river and you could smell the rain in the air.

I walked down Seventh Avenue to the cross street the builders hadn't gotten around to remodeling yet, sniffing at the acrid smells that were worn into the bricks like grease in an old frying pan, and turned west to the last address Shim Little had used. It was a decrepit hotel with rooms by the day or week but used mostly by the hour or minute by the jaded whores hitting the leftover trade from Broadway or the idiot tourists who thought getting clapped up or rolled in New York would make a great story to tell in the locker rooms back home.

The young kid with the dirty fingernails behind the desk made my type but not my face and was satisfied with a quick look at my press card and a five-buck tip to tell me that the cops had scoured Shim Little's room and came up with nothing but a suitcase of personal belongings and a portable radio. As far as he knew Little never had any guests and never said anything, either.

I asked, "How about dames?"

His eyes made a joke of it. "You kidding? What kind of a place you think this is?"

"So he didn't bring any in."

"All he had to do was knock on any door. This is a permanent H.Q. for two dozen three-way ten-buck hookers. A few even got super specialties if you're a weirdo."

I let him see another five and he flicked it out of my fingers. "What was he?"

He waved a thumb toward the tiny lobby. A chunky broad in a short tight dress was coming through the doors, her face grim with fatigue. "Ask Sophia there. She knew the guy." He made a motion with his head and when she spotted me the grim look disappeared like somebody turned a switch and the professional smile flashed across her face. She didn't even bother to be introduced. She simply hooked her arm into mine and took me up two flights to her room, unlocked the door and had her clothes off in half a minute. She turned around, held out her hand and said, "Ten bucks and take your pick."

I gave her a twenty and told her to put her clothes back on. Between the appendectomy slash, the caesarian scar, an ass full of striation marks and a shaved pussy red-flecked with pimples from a dull razor, she didn't exactly radiate my kind of sexuality.

But for the twenty she did what she was told. "You a freak?" she asked curiously. "I got some dresses if you like it with clothes on."

"Just a conversationalist," I told her.

This time her smile was tired and real. "Oh, great, mister." She flopped into a chair and yanked the black wig off her head. Her hair was a short mop of tight curls. "Tonight I'm glad to see you. It's been rough here. Now, you want dirty talk, the story of my sex life, some..."

"Information."

Her eyes narrowed down a little bit. "You can't be a cop because you already passed the bread."

"Reporter, Sophia."

"What the hell have I got to say? You doing a piece on whores? Hell, man, who needs to research that? All you have to do is..."

"Shim Little."

"Man, he's dead." Her face said that's about all she was going to say.

"I know," I told her. "I killed him."

She recognized me then. She was remembering the photos in the paper and was putting it all together and letting her imagination gouge horrible thoughts in her mind. "Mister..." her voice was hoarse and scared, "I only laid him twice. Just a straight job. He was...okay."

"He lived here for two weeks, kid. Don't tell me you don't know about your neighbors."

"So we talked a little bit. He wasn't much of a talker. In this business you're on and off if you want to make a buck."

"How much did he pay you?"

"Fifty...both times. He was a good tipper. You don't get many like that."

"With him you'd spend a little extra time the second time around."

"Why not?"

I grinned at her and it scared her again. "Where'd he get his loot?"

"Honest, mister...hell, we just..."

My grin got bigger and she wiped the back of her mouth with her hand. "He was...one of the boys. Not very big. He wanted me to think so but I could tell. He said he had a nice safe job now and laughed when he said it. Yeah, he really laughed at that, but I didn't go asking any nosy damn fool questions. He was the kind who could get mean as hell and he had that crazy gun with him all the time. He even put it on the other pillow while we were screwing."

"No names?"

"Just that it was the safest job he ever had. He kept laughing about it."

"How about friends?"

"Not around here. I saw him on Eighth Avenue once with some guy, that's all."

I got up and she shrunk back into her chair. "I don't have to remind you to forget about making any telephone calls, do I?"

"Mister," she said. "You got your conversation, I got my bread, now just let's forget it."

"Good enough." I looked at my watch. It was quarter to two.

———

CHERYL HAD BEATEN me to Ma Christy's by five minutes and had a bag of hamburgers and a container of coffee ready for me when I got there. She had deliberately dressed as sloppily as she could, using no makeup at all with a hairpiece I hated pegged to her head, but even the attempt at disguise couldn't quite hide all that woman if you looked hard enough.

I said, "Hello, gorgeous."

"Two detectives were covering my apartment. They were expecting a ravishing creature."

"No trouble?"

"They're still back watching out for Miss Ravishing. I exited through the building next door just to be sure."

"Bring the stuff?"

"Yeah but eat first."

I had forgotten how hungry I was and wolfed down the chow. When I finished I pulled the notes from the manila envelope she had brought and spread them out on the bed. The contacts had come through and it was all there.

The guy they called the Mechanic was one Henry Borden, fifty-nine years old, arrested for possession and selling of narcotics, suspected of reworking car bodies for transportation of illegal items. By trade he was a tool and die man, sheet metal worker and was currently employed in an aluminum casting foundry in Brooklyn. His current address was down in the Village.

Little things were beginning to tie in now. The connecting link was *metal.*

I took the package, slid it under the rickety dresser without disturbing any of the dust and said, "Let's take a ride."

"Now?"

"Now," I told her.

"You look like you could use some rest," she said impishly.

"No. I have to keep what strength I have."

Downstairs we picked up a cab on the corner and gave an address two blocks from Henry Borden's and walked the rest of the way. The drizzle had started and we had the empty street to ourselves. We found the house number and the basement apartment Borden occupied and didn't have any trouble getting in at all because whoever had been there before us didn't bother to lock up on the way out.

He had just left the Mechanic lying there with his throat cut almost all the way through in a huge glob of blood that was draining toward the back of the room on the warped floor.

The apartment was too small to take long to search, but the frisk had been efficient enough. Everything was turned inside out, including the pockets of everything he owned with an empty billfold lying in plain sight to give the earmarks of a robbery. Even the lining of Borden's work jacket had been torn loose and the zipper pocket yanked off. Still dangling from the flap were two ball point pens and a small clip-on screwdriver. I tugged them off, tossed the screwdriver on the chair and stuck the pens in my own pocket. Borden wasn't going to use them again.

In back of me, Cheryl was beginning to gag. I got her outside, walked her until she felt better, then grabbed a cab and got her back home. She went in through the other building and I went back to Ma Christy's. Nobody followed me.

For a little while I sat on the edge of the bed and listened to the tape again on the mini recorder. The voices were talking about knocking off the Mechanic, which completed the job and the stuff would be ready to ship. Well, now it was ready to go and I'd fall with it. I took out my pen and jotted down a few notes for tomorrow. It skipped on the paper so I put it down and used the other one. I finished what I was doing before I saw the printed name on the pen. It read, *Reading Associates, Rare Books, First Editions.* The address was on Madison Avenue in the lower fifties. I looked at the other pen. It was another cheap giveaway with *Macintosh and Stills, Aluminum Casting* printed on it. I shrugged and flopped back on the bed. I was asleep in a minute.

———

So THE OLD cop instinct comes out and you check all the possibilities, but the con instinct was there too and you do it as unobtrusively as possible because you know about the eyes that are watching and how fast it could end if you weren't careful.

I checked the papers, but the morning editions didn't have anything at all about the body down in the Village and unless somebody purposely checked in on Henry Borden he might not even be found until the odors of decomposition started to smell up the neighborhood.

At ten-thirty I took the elevator up to the fourth floor of the building that housed *Reading Associates*. It was a multi-office operation with a staff of a dozen or so and already getting some traffic from some elderly scholarly types. A few collegiate types were browsing through the racks and examining manuscripts in the glass-topped cases.

I wasn't much of an authority on rare books, but apparently the collectors were a breed apart and assumed anyone there had to be an enthusiast. A tiny old guy gave me a friendly nod and immediately wanted to know if I were going to exhibit at the show. I faked my way around the question and let him do the talking. He had already attended the one in Los Angeles, was going to be at the one here in New York next week, but unfortunately had to skip the one in London the end of the month. Of course, the main event would be the Chicago showing in six weeks where it was hoped some new finds would be put on display.

I even shook hands with Mr. Reading himself, an owlish man in his middle thirties with thick glasses and a bright smile who was in the middle of three conversations at once. The main topic seemed to be the surprise he was preparing for the Chicago exhibit.

When I broke loose I roamed around long enough to get a quick look into the offices, but there was nothing more than the crackle of papers coming from any of them. The door to Reading's office stood wide open, a book-lined room with a single antique desk stacked with papers and an archaic safe with the door swung out stuffed full of folders.

I was about to leave when a pair of magazine photographers I recognized came in and I squeezed back behind the shelves backing into a smudged-faced girl in a smock and knocking the waste basket out of her hands. She let out a startled, "Oh!"

I said, "Sorry, Miss," and bent down to put the junk back in the basket.

She laughed and brushed her hair out of her eyes. "Here, let me do that. You'll get your hands all dirty and you know what Mr. Reading thinks about that." She picked up the used carbons, stencils, wrapped a paper around the mimeograph ink cans and the two paint spray cans, dropped the empty beer bottle on top of the lot and edged around me.

The photographers were clustered around Reading, pointing out something in the cases, and when I had a clear field I went back to the corridor and punched the button for the elevator.

It was a good try, but that's all it was. A real, fat fizzle.

When I reached the street the rain had started again, but it gave me a good excuse for keeping my head tipped down under my hat. I went across town to the big newsstand that carried out-of-state papers and scanned the racks without finding any with the big eagle in the masthead. I tried one more and didn't make it there either. The later local editions were out, but there still wasn't any mention of Henry Borden's death.   .

Time was always on the side of the killer when these things happened. You can't just let them drop when you trip over them no matter what the score is. I found an empty booth in a Times Square cigar store, looked up Macintosh and Stills in Brooklyn and got an irritated manager on the other end. When I asked him if Borden had been in, he half-shouted, "That bastard hasn't shown all day and we're sitting here with an order ready to go out."

"Maybe something's wrong with him," I suggested.

"Sure. We let him use our tools to do a moonlight job and now he forgets where they belong. He's the only guy here who can handle this damn job, but if he doesn't get his ass in we'll damn well do without him."

"I'll go check on him."

"Somebody oughta," he said and hung up.

I checked by calling 911, the police emergency number,

and told them where to look for a mutilated corpse and didn't bother to leave my name. I made one more call to Al Grossino and arranged for a meet at nine o'clock. That was still a long way off and I didn't want to go prowling around the city in daylight. The answer was in a crummy little bar on Eighth Avenue that didn't believe in over lighting and didn't care how long you sipped at a beer as long as you kept them coming.

By six o'clock I was starting to feel bloated and was ready to cut out, but the TV news came on and the pre-show rundown made a big splash about another gruesome killing in Manhattan, so I called for another brew. It was great coverage, all right. They didn't show any body shots, but the announcer on the street was giving a running commentary on what the police had found after an anonymous tip. Half the residents in the neighborhood were gawking and waving into the camera or pointing at the rubber body bag being loaded into the morgue wagon, but by that time I had stopped listening and was watching the background, because there was one character there standing on his toes to look over the heads in front and folded in his pocket was a newspaper with a big, rangy eagle in the masthead. He walked out of camera range as I was leaving for the phone booth in the back of the room, and this time I didn't have to leave my name because Charlie Watts recognized my voice the second I said hello to him.

"You coming up, Fallon?"

"You want another commendation in your file, Charlie?"

"They don't give out medals for nailing people like you."

"How about that body with its throat cut?"

Charlie let a beat go by, then: "I'm listening."

"Your guy got himself on television tonight without realizing it. A real good shot, front face and profile. He's on the six o'clock news with a newspaper in his pocket...one with an eagle across the front."

"How do you know?"

"Check him out, buddy. You'll have his mug shots somewhere. If that's his hometown newspaper you can go through his local department. I got the feeling this guy's still got some of the amateur left in him. No pro is going back to make sure the body is growing cold."

"You ought to know."

"Get with the legwork, Charlie. You don't have to say thanks." I cradled the receiver before he could get a trace through, left a buck on the counter for the bartender and went out to join the rush hour crowd getting home. I had spent too much time in the same clothes and was getting sloppy and soggy looking. Right then I could smell myself and I didn't feel like getting tapped for being a bum, so I hustled up the avenue, turned east where the buildings partially kept the rain off me and headed toward the street that ran behind my building.

It took better than a half-hour and nobody was around to see the underground route I took to my own place. I crossed the yard behind Patsy's, pushed the boards in the fence out so I could squeeze through and went in the rear entrance to the service personnel's locker room.

O'Malley had left everything I needed, including a shaving kit and a towel. When I had showered and gotten the beard off my face I changed into my fresh clothes, packed the old stuff back into the locker and slid the .45 under my belt.

Outside the thunder rumbled and I slung my raincoat on. Something was bugging me and I couldn't quite reach out and touch it. Squeaky had handed it to me on a platter, but killing one lousy punk had thrown the whole thing out of kilter. All I had to do was sit through an interrogation by the cops and everything would have been blown sky high. Routine police work could have jammed the entire operation, but Squeaky had to go and try to take a bite out of it. Damn it, that nice little guy was a born loser and he went down the hard way, scared half out of his mind with no way out. He didn't even have sense enough to let somebody else make that call to Shim Little, and him with a voice you could spot like a snowball in a coal pile.

Now the operation had bought its time and I was the only one who could stop the clock. But I couldn't surface very easily and they'd know that too, so all the options were on their side.

That little bug inside kept nagging at me. It had a big grinning face like it knew all the answers and I did too, only I couldn't put it together like the bug did.

Darkness had finally settled in and I went into it grate-fully. I edged around the row of plastic garbage bags and headed for the fence, my hand feeling for the loose boards. I was halfway through when I realized how stupid I had been, because there were other people who thought like I did too.

But this one's stupidity was not putting the boards back the way I had left them and I had the bare second to dive and roll under the knife blade that hacked a huge sliver out of the post above my head and there wasn't a chance in the world of reaching for the gun I had buried under my clothes.

He didn't get a second chance with the blade because this was my kind of fight and my boot caught his elbow and the steel clattered against the concrete walkway. I had a fistful of hair, yanking his face into the dirt beside me, one fist driving into his ribs and he tried to let out a yell but the ground muffled it all.

For ten seconds he turned tiger, then I flipped him over, got my knee against his spine, my forearm locked under his chin and arched him like a bow until there was a sudden crack from inside him and he went death-limp in my hands.

He should have used the gun he kept in the shoulder sling, or maybe he just enjoyed the steel more. Or he never should have gotten into the pro ranks in the big town. There wasn't any wallet on him, or any keys, but he wouldn't be too hard to identify. The newspaper was still in his pocket, a three-day-old weekly from a small town in Florida.

What really was interesting came out of his side pocket. He had sixty bucks in tens and fives and ten one-hundreds. Only the C notes had been torn in half and somebody else was holding the other sections. I had to grin at that old dodge. It was a neat piece of insurance to make sure somebody got a job done and could prove it before he collected the other part of his loot. I took the sixty bucks, two of the torn bills and tucked them in my billfold.

I almost missed something else, but it flashed in the light

and I took that too and the little bug inside me grinned bigger.

AL GROSSINO HUDDLED behind the wheel of the car, filling the interior with foul smelling cigar smoke. He handed me two sheets of paper, but I said, "Just tell me, Al."

"Those companies keep up a constant weighing system. That gold got lost before it was poured into ingots. The Nevada bunch think they figured it out. It was siphoned off with the same vacuums they use to pick up the residue on the floor."

"Somebody would be checking the containers."

"They found a by-pass."

"Yeah?"

"Three guys walked off the job a month ago. Security ran checks on their job records and they were all phony."

"So it was engineered," I said.

Al wouldn't commit himself beside a shrug. "Could be. It's a federal case now."

"What was the final count?"

"About a thousand pounds."

"That's one hell of a bundle of loot."

He took another deep pull on the cigar and looked at me. "Who's got it, Fallon?"

"You want to be the hero?"

"Why not?"

"Let's make it some other time."

"You're getting to own me this time, buddy."

"Fine. I'll make you half-hero." I told him where to look to find a dead man and how he could play it if he were smart, then I backed out of the car and watched while he drove off.

When I called Cheryl from the booth on the corner I gave her the code message that meant an immediate meet and in twenty minutes I saw her coming toward me. She passed me in the doorway while I made sure she wasn't being followed, then when she crossed and doubled back, I went over to join her.

"Any trouble?"

"That car was still there."

"Charlie's men?"

"Department registration. I checked."

"What about the office?"

"They have a man there too."

"Any squawks from Orley?"

"I didn't want to give you the bad news," she said.

"So?"

"You, my friend, are under the boom. They're about to lower it."

"A hell of a way to end a career," I grinned at her.

"Well, if the worst comes to the worst, I'll support you." She kissed her fingertip and touched my mouth with it.

"I like it better the other way around. Maybe Orley will see it my way." Then I told her what had happened and even in the dim light from the street I could see her go pale.

She shook her head a little sadly. "They won't see anything now. You know how fast Charlie can work when he wants to. He'll pull out every stop just to nail your hide."

"But if I come up with the big package it won't hurt so bad." I gave her hand a squeeze. "Your training with parolees ever teach you anything?"

"Just to keep my skirt down and my blouse buttoned up with the ones fresh out."

"How about breaking and entering?"

"I've read up on the subject."

"Let's give it a try." I took out the two half-bills, scribbled a note across one and told her what to do. She repeated the instructions back to me, her mouth tight with worry, but she knew the score and she knew the alternatives and didn't question what I told her. The thing could go two ways now, but when you consider egos or fear or reprisals you could place your bets with the odds slightly in your favor and hope Lady Luck would give you the edge you needed. At least she seemed to frown on trivial stupidity and minor coincidences when they both locked hands to build a beautiful infield error.

I rang the night bell in the building and the sleepy-looking watchman unlocked the door and said, "Yeah? The place is closed up."

I showed him my press card and he shook his head. "That don't mean nothing."

Fifty of the sixty bucks I had taken from a corpse did mean something though and he agreed to a five-minute talk because his coffee would get cold.

"There been any night work going on here?" I asked him.

"Sure. Maintenance, cleaning...all the time."

"How about Reading Associates?"

"Night deliveries sometimes. They had their shelves reworked two months ago."

"I mean lately."

He thought for a moment, then nodded. "Some guy was let up to install new glass cases in the place, only Mr. Reading was with him most of the time."

"Use much equipment?"

This time I got a frown. "Yeah, a big toolbox and a small crate. Wooden one with steel bands around it. The day man said they had some welding bottles up there too. Why? They finished all that stuff the other day. Nobody's been here since."

"You like to make a hundred on top of that fifty?"

He started to get pictures in his mind then and his eyes got a flinty look in them. "Like hell, mister. You get your tail out of here like now. Come on, buddy, scram."

I took off my hat and let him see the edges of my teeth. "Take a good look, feller. You might have seen my picture in the paper recently." When I held my coat open, he saw the gun in my belt too and it all came through fast and he wore the same expression Loco and Sophia did when their mouths went suddenly dry.

I looked at my watch. "I won't be long. You'll get your hundred on the way out. But if I were you I'd stay right in the doorway where a buddy outside can see you, and if anybody comes in here you just ring that office once. Just once, understand?"

He couldn't talk. My reputation and the big story in the paper had put a knot in his belly and a lump in his throat. He nodded and I walked to the elevator, took it up to the floor I wanted and pushed the down button to get it back to the ground floor before I got out.

Getting into the office wasn't hard at all. It took two minutes with the picks and I was inside with all the musty paper smell and when my eyes were adjusted I went across to Reading's office and sat down behind his desk. If the schedule worked out I was twenty minutes early.

But the little Lady of the Luck was on my side for a change and I was only two minutes early, because the desk phone rang once and quit and I knew he was on the way up. I heard the keys work the lock, saw a single overhead light snap on and heard him come into his office. He had a gun in his hand, but it was dangling while mine was aiming for a spot right between those owlish eyes of his and he just stood there because a face-to-face shootout wasn't that end of his job at all. He had planned on an ambush and could have made it stick with me as a prowler but it hadn't worked out at all.

I said, "Drop it, Reading."

He let the gun clatter to the floor.

"Sit down. Over there."

"Listen, you came for a payoff. All right, I'll..."

"It's going to be more than the six hundred you offered your boy to wipe me out."

"Okay, we'll deal. How much?"

"All of it."

At first he didn't get what I meant, then the message went through, but a wily expression clouded his eyes and I knew he was thinking of his insurance policy. Too bad he didn't know about mine. "You're not very smart, Fallon."

"Cutting in on mob money isn't supposed to be, buddy. But neither is killing a guy's old pal very smart either. And I don't think organizing a few extra kills on your own without authority from higher headquarters is very bright thinking."

"You're out of your mind."

"Finding those torn bills under your door has made you pretty skittish, pal."

"What torn bills?"

"The ones you knew had to come from a dead man. But before that man was dead he talked to me and told me who gave them to him. That's what you thought. So it was just fine to meet with me right here and lay me out when I came in because the story would look good. Hell, man, you had me pegged when I came in today. Oh, you were cool about it, but you knew you had to work fast. There were others that saw me and could identify me as having looked over your collection and a heist of a few of those first editions of yours could net me a bundle in the right places. Yeah, it really would have looked good. And that hood you picked was a little smarter than I thought he was. He had the stakeouts pegged and knew I'd probably make a try to get back home some way. I was beginning to look too seedy to be roaming the streets anymore."

"Fallon..."

"Your own men blew it on you, kiddo." I was remembering what Shim Little had told the whore in the hotel. "But the big blooper was your own. You had those giveaway pens lying around and it's just natural for people to pick them up."

"Those pens are distributed in every bookstore in town."

"But they don't turn up in the pockets of odd people," I told him.

His smile was hard, going over the technicality, and he knew damn well it wouldn't stand up as evidence at all. He was still banking on his own insurance.

I said, "All of it, Reading. I want it all."

We both heard the door slam open and the pounding of feet on the floor. He let out a little laugh and said, "None of it, Fallon," then called out, "In here, officers."

They came through the doors in a rush and I nodded to Charlie Watts and the other three and laid the .45 on the top of the desk. "You took long enough to get here."

I was staring at all those police .38s and it wasn't a very pretty sight at all. "You're finally down, Fallon. You're finally going to get that great big fall."

When I smiled at him he didn't like it a bit. There was just too damn much confidence in it and he turned to tell Reading to shut up because he was cop enough to get a smell that wasn't supposed to be there at all. It hung in the room like smoke and he was the only one who could smell it.

"Read me my rights, then let's give it fifteen minutes and we'll do it all downtown like the old days. Later they'll give you and Al Grossino that new commendation and everybody will be happy."

I was thinking of what he was going to say when he heard the tapes, when they did voice prints from interrogation tapes on Shim Little and his dead buddy and tied in the dead Mechanic, then got a statement from little squat Sophia and tied it all in with the double-edged hook I was ready to throw.

So he gave me the fifteen minutes which was exactly the right amount of time for Cheryl to get there, escorted in by another patrolman.

Reading was still making noise, insisting I had called him under the pretense of blackmailing him for holding stolen rare books and like a good citizen had immediately called the police to intercept the action. The gun on the floor was his and he had a license to carry it, but I had gotten there first and was threatening his life.

Sure, it was true enough. It was what I had figured he'd do. I said to Charlie, "You get the rest of those torn bills from Al?"

The captain watched me a moment and nodded. "I have some more on me." I glanced over at Reading. "He has the other halves."

Once more I got that crafty look and he stated with indignant sincerity, "That's ridiculous!"

"Cheryl?"

"After I delivered the first two I watched through the window. He got an envelope out of his desk drawer and tossed it in the fireplace. He made one phone call then got out of there in a hurry. I went in through the window and pulled the envelope off the fire. It's under the rug in his den right now."

"Money doesn't burn very easily, Reading," I said.

"You're not planting evidence on me, Fallon. I demand..."

"Shut up," I said. "Charlie, come here."

My old commander walked across the room and I took out my wallet. I opened the back compartment and showed him something new. "For your eyes only, captain. Orley News Service is just a staged setup for this outfit. My being busted out of the department and doing that short stretch was all part of the staging."

I almost wanted to laugh because although he'd check it out in detail later he knew every part of it was true and he was hating himself for never having given me any benefit of doubt at all.

Reading was having a fit in front of the other officers, demanding to call a lawyer and I said nice and loud and clear, "He's holding the gold, Charlie. It was going to be shipped out of the country right along with him and his little prized book collection and when he gets ready to talk, you'll get all the names you want because Mr. Reading here doesn't want to get any contract put out for him for gross negligence in handling mob cash and prison walls are a lot thicker than the ones he has here."

But Reading was thinking he still held the trump card. I reached for the .45 on the desk and asked Charlie, "Mind?"

He didn't say anything, but the other cops were still holding hard on me. "Shim Little said he was on the safest job in the world. Let's see if he was right."

I thumbed the hammer of the .45 back and aimed it at the open door of the archaic safe and touched the trigger. The roar in the room was momentarily deafening and the stink of cordite was sharp.

Everybody had jerked back waiting to hear the whistle of a ricocheting slug bounce off the steel, but there wasn't any at all. There was just a neat hole punched in the door and under the dull black finish was the shiny yellow that only gold can reflect and over in the corner Reading slumped into the chair and began to choke on his own fear.

"Downtown now, Charlie?"

He smiled at me for the first time in years. "Yeah, you bastard."

"Let's keep it that way if we can. It's better for our business."

"The broad too?"

"She's one of us, buddy."

"I'll be damned."

Downstairs I paid the night watchman with a hundred bucks of Cheryl's money and we all went out to the cars together. I never thought it would happen again, but this time I got to ride in the front seat with my old commander. Just this once. Washington wouldn't approve of the fraternization after all the work they went through.

When we were getting in, Cheryl said, "We can't even hire a hotel room tonight, you slob. You took all my cash."

"There's always home," I told her.

She grinned and squeezed my hand. Like a little trap. And I was caught in it. But it felt good anyway.

Tonight I Die

A MIKE HAMMER STORY

Tonight I Die

YOU WALK DOWN the street at night. It's raining out. The only sound is that of your own feet. Then you hear another sound and you look across the street and see the blonde.

The blonde.

The woman you've been looking for, for two whole years. She's even blonder now. A little bit heavier but on her it's fine. And more beautiful than ever. The woman you've been looking for but never wanted to see again.

So you follow her for a little while, then out of force of habit, you cross the street and stay behind her. Yeah, even from there she hasn't changed. All the grace of a cat is in her walk and maybe some of their animal instincts too. Maybe she hears you.

Maybe she just feels you.

Her steps get slower and shorter, then she stops altogether and there she is – Helen.

Lovely, lovely Helen who you loved so much—but would kill in just another minute.

The gun in your pocket grown warm from your hand feels cold all of a sudden. Cold and almost too heavy to lift; but you get it out of your pocket and have it in front of you when you reach her. She still has those deep green-tinted eyes that could laugh at you even when you were dying, and now it is Helen who would be dying...but could she still laugh?

"Hello, baby."

A long pause. "Hello, Mike. Do I get it here?"

"That's right. Right here, Helen. Just like I said. The next time I ever saw you, wherever it was...and now it's here."

"All right, Mike."

"It won't hurt much, but what I want you to feel is right inside your mind. A slow, agonizing pain that wants to scream but you can't make a sound because it's trapped inside. It's life screaming because death is catching up with it...and all you'll be able to do is lay there listening to that silent screaming and the last thing you'll hear will be my feet walking away."

A twitch of smile. "Not even a goodbye kiss, Mike?"

"Not even a kiss goodbye. The last one was two years ago. That one will hold me... That was a real kiss...a real kiss of death. Remember it, Helen?"

Sure she remembered it. How could she ever forget it? The kiss of death. Hers. Two years ago was the night you died. But there was a time before that...the time we met.

————

THERE WAS A PARTY GOING ON. You know the kind...all the Broadway wheels spilling champagne, brittle laughter in the air and someplace in the background a soft piano setting the mood. A client invited me and even a private eye is a small businessman who has to make nice sometimes. So I said my hellos, but I didn't like the people I was being forced to associate with and was ready to leave when I saw her...

A loneliness clung to her, loneliness and something else...*fear.* The kind of fear that didn't belong at a party like this, with a crowd like this.

Then our eyes met over the heads of everybody and suddenly the room seemed to empty slowly until there was nobody there or even in the whole world except the two of us.

And that one unwanted companion: fear.

I walked over to her. Looked at her and could feel my spine get crawly.

"I came alone," I said.

"So did I."

"Then now you're with me."

I didn't expect the mist that flowed into her eyes. A wise-crack maybe, but anything except the mist.

"For how long?" she asked.

"However long you want."

She paused. "I think...I *wish* it could be...forever."

I reached for her. "Then we better get started. Let's get out of here."

Her scared cry overlapped my words: "*No!*"

My eyes went tight. "What's scaring you?"

That surprised her. "You...know?"

"Yeah, it shows, kid." I paused. "Look. Nobody'll bother you while I'm around. Trust me."

So we went, the two of us...and fear came too. Fear that was there when she told me her name was Helen Venn, fear that stayed like an invisible shroud when we walked through the park.

"It's...a beautiful night, Mike."

"You make it that."

She turned her head and looked at me, the swirl of her hair a golden waterfall in the moonlight.

"There's something wrong with your eyes, Mike."

"Yeah, I know. They don't look at you...they watch you. That what you mean?"

"That's right. What are they watching?"

"A kid in trouble. It's all over you. Why, Helen?"

"It's quite a story." She hesitated. "I think – *Mike!*"

Footsteps ran toward us, jostled into us, a beefy guy making a grab for her purse, but she yanked it back and the dark shape veered off, through the mess of shrubs. I ran after him, but he was gone.

"Got away," I said, breathing hard.

"Please don't go after him!"

"Don't worry. I couldn't find him in there anyway, not at night." I took her arm. "Let's go someplace and sit down. We'll hear some music and you can talk to me. Whatever it is you're in the middle of, I want to hear it – all of it."

So we went someplace and talked, a little place with soft lights—softer music, the kind of jazz that hangs onto the melody they were exploring. Then she told me.

"There isn't too much, Mike, but what there is...well, it's

deadly. Look at me. I've got what men want, all right...and I'm even educated. Some might say I'm lucky. But I'm not. I'm just one of thousands like me who are caught in this...rat trap of New York. Secretarial work didn't pay, but my legs got me on the chorus line at the Copa. Then I met a man. Who seemed like quite some kind of guy. Smooth, sharp, loaded. I went head over heels... Then he was killed. Shot. It was only then that I found out who Marty Wellman *really* was."

I leaned in. "Marty Wellman... *He* was your guy?... That slob was sitting at the top of the Syndicate."

"I know that now. Do you know *why* he was killed?"

I shrugged. "I know what they say. That someplace he had a couple of tax-free millions stashed away. It's a good reason for murder."

"*Now* do you know why I'm scared?"

"Tell me."

"They...or whoever the killer is...think I know where those millions are." She paused. "Mike...I'm tired of being afraid. I'm tired of walking down the street scared to look back and afraid to look ahead. I'm tired of looking at my front door night after night, waiting for it to open slowly until I see a killer standing there with a gun in his hand. Ready to torture a truth out of me that will only make him kill me all the sooner. Mike...I'm tired, do you understand? Tired of living...afraid of living anymore. Mike...it's got to where I *want* to die. I want to so bad I'm thinking of doing it myself. I'm – "

"Shut-up."

"It's what I've come to..."

"Shut-up, I said."

She did.

My turn. "We'll start with whoever killed Wellman. I'll find him for you, baby, and he'll never bother you again. He'll never bother *anybody* again."

Her eyes, big and blue, were filled with doubt. "The police...they never got anywhere with – "

"I'm not the police. And when I take your dead boyfriend's killer out, that'll send a message to the Syndicate that you're under my protection. And then they won't bother you, either."

———

SOMETIMES IT's good to be a guy who doesn't have to worry about the rules. You can learn things that are clubs to hold over somebody's head and you can prowl the night until you find the ferrets, the human animals who live by invading the dens of the rats.

But first I went to a rat.

He was dressed in gray from his head to his shoes. His hair was a mousy color and his eyes were the yellow kind you see peering out of holes along the bottom of a wall.

On his paper they called Sid Pollack a columnist, but to most of the world he was strictly a rat. He was living by night in a gin mill on Third Avenue that had taken on an air of respectability lately, the perfect place for a third-rate Winchell to pause on his way down. He even had his own booth. I slid in.

"Hiya, Sid."

"What do *you* want, Hammer?"

"Pearls of wisdom."

"Go jump."

"There was a court case recently," I said, just telling a story while the bartender brought me a beer and Sid another boilermaker. "There was a witness. There was a big lie told and a stinking murderer got off free." I paused. "There was a night a week later when the killer called on the witness and passed over an envelope with ten grand in it. And that's the kind of thing that can get a guy who's already on the slide good and fired."

His voice was hushed. "You dirty, lousy son of a bitch..."

"Don't hurt my feelings or I'll take what I know to Captain Chambers."

He licked his lips; poured booze into his gray face.

"What do you want, Hammer?"

"What else would I want from a famous reporter like you, Sid? News. Who runs the Syndicate since Marty Wellman got hit?"

"You don't know?"

"Would I be asking?"

"...You haven't heard? It's Carmen Rich."

I frowned. "How? He was down the ladder a couple rungs, wasn't he?"

"He moved up and in. Is there another way?"

"Not without an army, there isn't."

Sid smirked. "He's *got* an army."

"Since when?"

The reporter spoke slowly, with contempt. "You crazy fool. He imported that Buddy White psycho from Florida. So now he's got himself a kill-batty jerk who'll knock off all the competition in town if he says so. The Miami Kid is the fastest thing you ever saw with a rod. You stick your head out on this one, and I'll be giving you a two-line obituary in my column and happy to do it."

"Was he the trigger on the Wellman kill?"

"A prime candidate."

"Why haven't the cops tagged him then?"

He laughed. "The cops? The dirty ones don't care, and clean ones like your pal Chambers haven't got the evidence to hit him with, you jerk."

His tie was loose around his neck, so I snugged it up for him. Nice and tight. He was sputtering when I went out.

———

So I went to the place Marty Wellman used to run, a smooth bistro catering to the uptown trade, its back room a gambler's paradise and a sucker's grave. There was muted music and indirect lighting. The coatroom was jammed packed but there weren't a dozen people at the bar. The rest were digging their graves behind the curtain alongside the bandstand.

I walked up to the bar and sat.

"Yes, sir," the bartender said.

"Beer."

"Yes, sir."

He brought the beer and started to move away.

"Hey, feller. Come here a minute."

He came.

"How long have you been here?"

"About two years."

"You knew Marty Wellman then, didn't you?"

"Yeah, I knew Marty."

"*What* did you know about him?"

"Nothing."

"Don't walk away, pal."

He paused. "There's two ways this can go. If you're just a wise guy, walk yourself out before things take a bad turn. If you wanna play tough guy, I'll toss you out, personally. You know?"

I held my coat open just enough so he could see the leather of the sling that ran across my chest. I didn't have to show him the .45 that went with it.

"I'll tell you my name," I said. "Just once. Then we continue our conversation... understand? It's Mike...Mike Hammer."

His eyes got a little wider. "Yeah..."

"Who owns the place now?"

"Me... I do. There's my license on the wall."

"Swell. Who runs it?"

"Me... I—"

"Mac...you're going to be hurting awful bad with a slug in your leg."

"Ease off, will you, I'm trying to tell you..."

"Never mind, Joe," another voice said. "*We'll* tell him."

Whatever the guy behind me had in his pocket pressed hard against my back. The bartender tried to grin but it looked a little sick.

"Give you much trouble, Joe?" the guy asked.

"Not too much, Dave. But he's got a gun."

"He won't have it long. Get up slow, bud. You know where to go or should I steer you a little?"

That was a laugh. Go? I could find my way in this dump with my eyes closed. Sure, I went...nice and orderly, too, through the crowd at the wheels, around the dice tables, then up to the door marked *Private* and I didn't even have to knock.

There were four of them in the big backroom office, a

featureless modern space with a languid redhead on the couch for color. Of the four males, only one counted – the slick-haired, mustached guy behind the big desk.

Carmen Rich was a rising star in the world that lived at night. A health nut, they say, all his muscles wrapped up in a white dinner jacket, and his muscle boys in tuxes that were a laugh. The only one of those who counted was Buddy White, the towering gunslinger from Miami at Carmen's arm, all white teeth in a dumb tan pan. He was at my right.

"This the guy?" Carmen asked.

"Troublemaker at the bar," Dave said, jerking a thumb behind him.

Carmen shook his head wearily. "They never learn, do they?"

"Not until we teach them, Carmen."

Carmen's eyes were small and dark and fixed themselves on me. "Maybe you got a good idea of what's going to happen to you, friend. You want to speak up for yourself, do it now."

"You clowns aren't teaching me anything," I said. "But if you want a lesson, step up."

Carmen's sneer was only half-amused. "Go ahead, Buddy. Take him. Take him good."

"Yeah, take me," I said. I had a hood on either side of me and one behind. "But before you try, keep something in mind. Sure there's a gun at my back but there's one under my arm too and I can get it out a second before I die and in that one second I can plant a slug between your eyes and maybe the Miami boy too and if living is that cheap to you, have yourself a ball."

Nobody moved.

They just looked at me careful, and suddenly they knew. And it turned out nobody was in the mood to die.

Squinting now, Carmen said, "Hold it, friend... What's the angle?"

I said, "I just have a few questions about the former proprietor here. Marty Wellman. Like why did he die? Who killed him? *There's* your angle."

An eyebrow went up. "I'd pay for that information myself," Carmen said.

"When I get it, so will a killer."

The redhead on the couch was watching me, trying to decide whether she was in love or scared out of her mind.

My host settled back in his big swivel chair. Smiled. Tried to change the mood as he helped himself to a cigar in an inlaid box on the desk. "Have a Havana?"

"No thanks. I'll stick to my Luckies."

Carmen lighted up, clicked his lighter shut, puffed as he studied me. "Why'd you bring your questions here?"

"Because *you're* here, Carmen. The guy at the bar owns the joint, but *you* run it."

"That's right. Marty left a will."

I shook my head. "You don't leave a gambling concession in a will, Carmen."

"Ah. You know me."

"I know *of* you. And you know of me, too. Mike Hammer?"

Carmen's eyes got big for a moment. "Is *that* who you are? The trigger-happy hothead himself."

"You flatter me."

White lurched forward a step. "I hate these big-mouth characters. Let me take him, Carmen."

The boss chuckled. "I'd like to see you try it, Buddy – that would be good for a laugh. This is a guy would think nothing of risking his life on the chance to pump one into both of us."

"Balls," Buddy said.

"Buddy..." Carmen said, raising a cautionary palm. "If you try it...I'll put a bullet in you myself. I *know* this guy."

The cords in White's neck were standing out. "Know him, hell! He's running a bluff and – "

"*I'm* not bluffing, Buddy," Carmen said. "I've seen dead men he left behind."

"You heard my questions, Carmen," I said. "You have any answers for me?"

"You must know the story already," Carmen said with a shrug. "Some place Marty had money stashed away. Cash. Two million is a hell of a haul."

"Any idea where, Carmen?"

He gestured around him. "Would I bother running this joint if I did?"

"Okay," I said. "I was just figured this was a good place to start. Now I'll ask around some other places, and you'll know why when the word comes back to you. If you have secrets to share, we can clear the room."

"No secrets, Mr. Hammer."

"I find out otherwise? I'll be back."

"I have no doubt of that."

I turned quick and shoved the guy behind me on his ass. The redhead on the couch giggled. White and the other hood looked at each other and their boss and before any of that could turn into anything, I was gone.

IN MY RACKET, the cops are good boys to keep on the right side of. One in particular – Pat Chambers, Captain of Homicide. We were buddies, so I could speak to him. We were buddies, so he could speak to me.

"You know, Mike," Pat said, "if anybody but you asked me for information on Wellman, Rich or White, I'd hold them for questioning. What are you up to, anyway?"

"That isn't an answer." I was seated across from him. We both had smokes going, pretending not to study the other guy.

"First," he said, "*you* tell *me* things."

That was fair enough. "A woman is dying slow because a killer is loose. A woman I like, Pat."

He paused. "Not Helen Venn?"

I nodded.

He shook his head. "Be careful, Mike. She's got a target pasted on her pretty back."

"I know."

"We kept a tail on her after Marty's death. She's being watched by hoods from every mob faction in town. That missing two mil attracts a lot of bears to honey."

"And flies." I let some smoke drift lazily out. "The papers never said much about Marty catching it. Exactly how did it happen?"

Pat picked up a file folder on his desk and tossed it; the contents scattered. "There's what we have. A few pictures too. That one there is the last Marty Wellman ever had taken."

It was a police photo, a garish head-on shot of Marty Wellman, too handsome for his own good. Too big and broad-shouldered for anybody else's good either.

He looked pretty sharp sitting there at his desk in a dressing gown that was open to let his chest hair show through. His head was turned to one side and a cigar was tight in his pretty teeth. The only trouble was that he was pretty dead, too. The bullet hole showed right over his ear.

".38 slug did it," Pat said.

"He got it cold?"

"No...more like warm. The desk drawer was open and his right hand was resting on a snub-nosed rod. Notice his head. He's turned away from whoever shot him. Two people in the room, maybe."

"Did *they* get the two million, Pat?"

He chuckled. "I'll tell you something, kid, not for publication. We found out about that. The two million was a bluff. Wellman never had it. He called that bluff his insurance dough for retirement and used it to bank himself into control of the Syndicate's gambling set-up."

I thought about it. "Some use money...some use a bluff...and some use an army." Like Carmen Rich.

"What?"

"Nothing... Helen Venn. What about her?"

"Beautiful, but you know that. Lonely, but maybe you know that, too. Just another doll in the chorus line. Marty cultivated her."

"I'm don't mind him being dead."

"Oh, it wasn't all his fault, the jam he left her in. You know dames. If she hadn't been looking to get ahead, she wouldn't have hung out with the money boys. First, it was Ernie Haver. Then Salvy Slocum. Big Ed Smith got in line and finally it was Marty. She was quite a girl to get a yen for."

"Yeah."

"You say it funny, Mike."

"Was she *really* on the make, Pat?"

"No more than the next kid, blinded by the bright lights. These mob boys all got show biz connections. As for her background, she checked clean. Midwestern girl. College-educated. Rumor has it she handled Wellman's books."

"Swell. Now let's talk about the Syndicate."

"Like Carmen Rich?"

"Like Carmen Rich."

"No, Mike, we don't talk about that."

I bristled. "Why, Pat? Carmen too big to talk about?"

He scowled. "Let's stay friends, kid."

"Sorry," I said. And I meant it. Pat had always been the kind of cop who wouldn't help himself to an apple on the beat.

He gathered the papers and photos and stuffed them back in the file folder. "We don't talk because it's an investigation in progress. It's being worked on. I already gave you more than I should."

"Okay, Pat, thanks." I stood. "I'll dig around. Anything turns up, I'll buzz you."

"You better," he said.

I HAD ASKED RATS FIRST. They didn't know. Then the cops. They wouldn't talk. That left the ferrets – sharp-eyed little people who walked in the shadow of the rats and knew everything they did. All you had to do was get them to open their mouths.

On the Bowery I found my ferret.

He was sleeping in a doorway dreaming big dreams and living under a blue sky someplace that was warm and comfortable. Comfortable enough that he didn't like it too much when I shook him awake.

"Rise and shine, Jake."

"Hey...hey...cut it out!"

"It's me, kid—Mike Hammer."

He scrambled to his feet, scared, backing into the closed door. "Leave me alone!"

"What's the matter with you?"

"Look, leave me alone, Mike. Just leave me alone!"

I held his arm and hauled him in close until the sour whiskey smell of him was right under my nose.

"What's the matter with you?" I demanded. "You want a fin or a train ticket, I'm up for it, if you got what I want. I'm not too off-limits to speak to, am I?"

He groaned loudly. "Mike...look, let me say it fast – the word's out. They're gunning for you. You ain't healthy no more."

"*Who's* gunning for me?"

The rheumy eyes in the stubbly face got big. "Who knows? The word's out. Mike...lemme go."

"Sure, Jake. Just answer me something. Why did Marty Wellman die?"

A long hiss escaped his lips. He was scared.

"Why, Jake...*why?*"

"There's talk...it isn't loud talk because if it gets heard somebody gets killed. Marty, he *had* to die. He was in the way. You know, the king is dead. Long live the king. He got pushed out because somebody else wanted in."

"Carmen Rich?"

"You'd know that better than me, Mike. I just pick up bits and pieces. *You* gotta put 'em together, man."

"Okay, I won't push you. But the talk *I* heard had two million bucks in it. Then somebody else said that was the bunk."

"The bunk is right. Marty was flat. He borrowed fifty grand from the Chicago Outfit. Nowhere near two million, and it was a damn *debt* at that!"

"I hear you." I got out a wad of cash and gave him a fin. "Here—buy yourself a meal. Not entirely wet."

"Thanks."

And that was all the ferret had to say. But it had been enough: *the word was out.*

First somebody wanted Helen Venn. Now somebody wanted *me.*

"Don't move, pally," a voice said.

I wheeled around anyway and it was my boy Dave from Carmen's bar – and the second time he held a gun on me.

"You just *had* to nose around, didn't you?" he said, grinning nasty. "Come on, now. Play nice."

"Where?"

"There's a car over there."

"Suppose I don't go?"

"Try it and see."

"Okay!... Okay."

Somebody should've told him. But this is New York. You let them find out for themselves here. I stepped past him, turned with the .45 in hand, and the last little surprised sounds he made were blotted out by the roar of the rod which itself got swallowed by a honking horn followed by the complete silence that hung over the Bowery while a hundred eyes saw a kill that one hundred mouths would never speak of except among themselves.

But the dead man proved a point. I was important. Then I knew just *how* important....

Enough so for two more bully boys to be on top of me, and I never saw either one. But I did hear the swish and thud of the sap.

———

"WE CAN'T GO OUT to the Island," a voice was saying.

"Then use the park," another voice said. *"We can pull over, dump him, shoot his tail and blow."*

"Suppose somebody hears the shot?"

"For the kind of dough we're making, you don't take no damn chances?"

"Aw, shut-up."

"Here's the place. Pull over."

They carried me out, two of them; one was fat and wheezed a little. They dragged me through the bushes and around a jutting tooth of rock typical in Central Park, then they dumped me. The fat boy pulled the gun from his pocket, checked the shells, then flipped the cylinder back.

And I tackled him. But I still woozy and played it just a little too slow. The louse got me with the gun butt, but I'd spooked him and they ran off, while I went down again with my second concussion of the night. Damn!

But I wasn't too bad off. One dead man earlier would still tell the story when fools like these thought tangling with me was a good idea. I started to get up. Then my hand closed around a flat little something – a wallet!

I checked carefully – no ID, just a C-note, payment probably for a night's work.

I wrapped my handkerchief around the wallet, stuck it in my pocket and got to my feet. It wouldn't take long to reach the street or hire a messenger to run my package up to Pat's office.

That was enough for one night. I drove to Helen's apartment, where I'd told her to hole up and not answer the door for anybody but me.

She wrapped herself around me and her lips found mine.

"So good to feel you in my arms, Mike," she said.

She led me to a couch in her well-appointed apartment. The place was modern in a masculine way – this had been Wellman's pad. He had died here.

"Helen. You look different somehow."

"I...*feel different*, Mike. With you in my life, looking into this thing, I'm...I'm not afraid anymore."

"You'll never have to be afraid again, baby."

"But...*you* look different too, Mike."

"Somebody else told me that once, too. A woman who was in my life till recently. She said she could always tell when I killed somebody."

Her eyes went wide with alarm. "Mike! You *killed* somebody...?"

"Someone who thought pulling a gun on me was a good idea, yeah. Anyway, the pressure's off you now. They turned the heat my way." I hesitated. "You're beautiful, baby. But there's more to this than that. Why?"

"Why what, Mike?"

"Why did I fall so fast? What happens to a guy to make it happen so quick? *Why*, Helen? Why did a guy have to die tonight? And why is it I love you so damn much?"

Her fingers got tangled in my hair. "Maybe it's because you're easy to love, too, Mike. I thought I loved before...but it wasn't like this. Nothing like this at all. I

don't have to *work* to love you, Mike. It's just there. Like air
or sunshine or moonlight. It's something that makes you
and me the only two people in the world. It makes fear
seem so small and pitiful. When you love like this there
isn't any room left for fear at all. Mike...remember when
you said forever?"

"I remember."

"And I said I'd do anything in the world for you?"

"Yeah..."

"And you said forever had to start sometime?"

"So forever starts...?"

"Tonight, Mike."

She got up and gave me her hand and led me into the
bedroom. And I tried not to think of who she'd shared it
with before.

———

It's a day and a night later, and another day and a night
and all along the way voices whisper to you while you wait.

They're after you, Mike.

Hey Mike...watch it.

Pal...pal...a guy with a rod...he was here before...

And you listen without answering...but you listen. You
see them. You know their faces, faces that are all alike, the
faces of hunters. But you move too fast, and then you're
ready to move and you watch and wait for a long time
before you have him right in the gunsights of your eyes.

He comes out of a building finally, and for the first time
he's alone. No muscle boys to protect him.

"Hiya, Carmen."

Then he spins around and while the crazy fear is still on
his face and the scream in his throat, there's a crashing
thunder of a shot.

But it's not yours!

And Carmen Rich falls with a wild angry scarlet stream
spurting from his throat and you know the party isn't
over yet.

So you run and run until you're in the clear and stand
there panting your lungs out. Then another long day passes

holed up and then you begin to wonder and at least you get an idea.

And go to see Pat again.

He spoke slowly, softly: "Mike...all I know is what the brass upstairs *lets* me know. Carmen is dead...but you knew that. They all die sooner or later, the big shots, some in bed, some in barber's chairs, some with their face in the clams and linguini. But there's always somebody ready to fill in. No matter what the papers or the politicians say, we can't stop the Syndicate from operating."

"Who's filling in for Carmen, Pat?"

"I wish I knew, buddy. I wish I knew."

"So guess."

"Somebody who's already on the scene. A million-dollar corporation doesn't go without a president for long. But who? I don't know yet—give me time. By the way...the prints we lifted from that wallet you found. They belong to a guy named Ben Liter. Small-time hood. Mostly petty raps. What's the pitch?"

I snorted.

"Something?" he asked.

"No," I said. "No, nothing, Pat."

———

NOTHING. All over town, nothing. Even the voices that whispered told me nothing. In a way it was funny, all of it, from a bartender who owned a bar worth a fortune but didn't run the business to guys trying to make me dead, to an imaginary two million bucks that paved the way to a new top man. Lift your glass in a toast, everybody. The king is dead. Long live the king.

Or maybe...the queen?

So I went back to her apartment. It was quiet, dark, and late. And then there he was, about to go into the same building I was...

"*Buddy!*" I yelled.

The Miami Kid twirled and took two off-balance shots at me and ran off while I clawed my .45 out from under my arm and took pursuit.

And there we were, alone in the darkness, the back fences of the alleys crowding us, the rain a muffler that blanked out sound but we each knew the other was there and someplace where I could hear him breathing was the new king who'd been going to join his queen.

"Buddy...you won't get out alive."

"You're kidding yourself, Hammer. You think you're on top of this? Do you *know* who did it to Carmen? You know *why?*"

"Yeah," I said.

He told me anyway, a voice out of the darkness we shared. "Carmen was too big too long. I been small long enough, first in Miami and now up here. Well, it's my turn at the top now. And I got everything I ever wanted. *Everything.* Nobody stops me or gets in my way even. Not you. Not anybody."

"Big dreams, Buddy," I said, "from such a puny mind. Toss your gun out and we'll go to Chambers. Otherwise, man, you've had it."

"No," he said. "*You'll* get it. You and *anybody* in my way."

There was just that muzzle flash like lightning before came the exploding pain in my belly that smashed me into the ground...hard, wet and the breath was gone for long seconds. There was that fuzzy feeling that I had known once, a long time ago in the stinking jungles of a Pacific Island...but even then it hadn't been this bad...and then the king stood over me to put the final one in my head so I didn't have die slow, gut-shot. He shouldn't have been so gracious.

His laugh was a whisper as he came over and he was still laughing when I shot him.

YOU COULD HEAR SIRENS SOMEPLACE. They faded as I stood up, stopped altogether as I walked and all the sound I could hear was the rushing waterfall in my ears. Yet somehow I got up to her apartment, opened it with the key she had given me and staggered in.

My blonde queen was beautiful...so beautiful...standing

there in a single lamp's light, the blue eyes lit from within. Beautiful. And mine.

Only I was dying...

"Mike?" Her voice was querulous.

Blood was seeping through my fingers where I clutched the wound; there was no going for the .45 with my hands holding in my guts. "They're dead, Helen. All the players, including me. It's one way of stopping the fear."

"All...dead?"

"Carmen Rich...Buddy White." I paused. "Yeah, Buddy's dead, too, Helen, but I'm the only one who knows. You'll never have to be afraid of anything again. I'm the only one who knows."

"Knows...?"

"The death photo of Marty Wellman. He had his hand ready to go for a gun, so he was afraid of a killer. But his head was turned to look at something else. *Someone* else. Even with a killer in front of him, you'd be the only one he'd look at. The only thing he'd take his eyes off a killer for. And one other thing. It was small and wouldn't mean much except to me. One of the guys who tried to take me out was a small-timer. Dropped a wallet with no ID but his prints told the tale. So did the C-note. A guy with services for rent...but not to a big organization like the Syndicate, Helen. To you, maybe, but not the Syndicate."

Her chin came up and there was a new defiance in her voice. "Yes...that was me, Mike. Marty wouldn't cut me in on what I earned. *I was the brains behind him.* He *had* to die. And Carmen?" She shook her head. "He wasn't the strong one I needed. I wanted someone who could act...quickly, decisively. Someone who could respond to my...charms...without anyone knowing it. Someone ready to do whatever I asked him to...no questioning...nothing." She shrugged. "That was Buddy White. The Miami Kid, they called him."

"Forget them all, honey," I said. "There's only you and me now...for a few minutes at least."

"Mike...there's not even a few minutes. I'm scared again. I wanted so much. I almost had it...then I did have it...for a little bit. Mike...I'm going to have it for all time. I'm going to

MICKEY SPILLANE

have the world at the snap of my fingers. Not a little
bit...*everything!* Buddy killed Carmen for me." She laughed
shortly. "He was going to kill you too, Mike...here's how it is.
Buddy and I planned Marty's kill and did it together. But
Buddy had ambitions and as long as I knew his part of the
murder, I was in his way. So it had to be either Buddy or me.
One of us had to die and I don't like to kill anybody
myself...so I chose *you*, Mike, for my protector..."

"And I fell for you, Helen."

"And now you have to die, Mike. I can't even let you
have those few minutes to speak to the police when they
come...and they *will* come, you know."

"I know."

The knife was in her hand, a long slim little thing that
came close slowly. It came ever closer and I couldn't move
out of the way at all.

"Mike...believe something. In my way, I really did love
you."

My words were a raspy whisper. "Better do a good job of
it, baby. Otherwise, don't count on living too long. Someplace we might meet again...in Hell maybe. But no matter
where it is, you'll die too, Helen."

"It will never happen that way, Mike." She sighed.
"Mike...I truly am sorry."

She thrust the blade.

———

THAT WAS the night I died, all right. It wasn't my skin and
bones. No, my flesh had to live even though I didn't want
it to.

But something else had died that night. Something more
important than what you see when you look in the mirror.

———

YOUR THUMB FINDS the hammer and pulls it back.

"Really here...Mike?"

"Really here, Helen."

"Not even a goodbye kiss, Mike?"

"Not even a kiss goodbye. The last one was two years ago. That one will hold me. That was a real kiss. A kiss of death. Remember it, Helen?"

She remembers it, all right. Comes closer, with her arms reaching out for you and you're not supposed to see that same sliver of steel she used before.

"I really love you, Mike."

"And I really love you, Helen."

And then the only sound you hear is the gunshot, and her cry. And the sound of your own feet, in the rain, walking down the street at night.

If you enjoyed this, you may also like:
The Menace

BY MICKEY SPILLANE AND MAX ALLAN
COLLINS

BEST-SELLING AUTHOR MICKEY SPILLANE'S MOST TERRIFYING NOVEL.

In touristy Peachtree Heights, Georgia, a string of presumably accidental deaths of area physicians rouses the suspicions of Police Chief Blake Cutter. But the former big-city cop's attempts to warn Dr. Roy Ryan are viewed by his estranged wife as an attempt to muddy the waters of a custody battle over the couple's young son, Richie.

Too late to do anything more, a small, incredibly powerful creature emerges from the night to brave the walls of the doctor's compound, terrorizing the family and any and all police guarding them. The menace is suddenly real, and those physicians' deaths are anything but accidental.

And when young Richie's archeologist uncle gives the boy a grisly birthday present—an actual Aztec mummy!—the child begins to think the long-dead corpse is his friend, one who is still-breathing …

Mickey Spillane was the best-selling American mystery writer of the 20th Century. From an unproduced Spillane screenplay, his chosen successor, Max Allan Collins, has fashioned this compelling thriller.

AVAILABLE NOW

About Mickey Spillane

Mickey Spillane was the best-selling American mystery writer of the 20th century. He introduced Mike Hammer in *I, the Jury* (1947), which sold in the millions, as did the six tough mysteries that soon followed. The controversial P.I. has been the subject of a radio show, comic strip, and several television series, starring Darren McGavin in the 1950s and Stacy Keach in the '80s and '90s. Numerous gritty movies have been made from Spillane novels, notably director Robert Aldrich's seminal film noir, *Kiss Me Deadly* (1955), and *The Girl Hunters* (1963), in which the writer played his own famous hero.

Only a handful of writers in the genre have achieved such superstar status. Spillane's position was unique—reviled by many mainstream critics, despised and envied by a number of his contemporaries in the very field he'd revitalized; but the creator of Mike Hammer had an impact not just on mystery and suspense fiction but popular culture in general.

The success of the reprint editions of his startlingly violent and sexy novels jump-started the paperback original, and his redefinition of the action hero as a tough guy who mercilessly executed villains and who slept with beautiful, willing women remains influential to this day.

The Day the Sea Rolled Back, his first novel for young people, was a Junior Literary Guild Selection. That book, its sequel *The Ship That Never Was*, and a previously unpublished Josh and Larry adventure have been collected by Rough Edges Press as *The Shrinking Island*, offering further proof of Spillane's marvelous ability to hold readers of any age spellbound.

About Max Allan Collins

Max Allan Collins was named a Grand Master in 2017 by the Mystery Writers of America. He is a three-time winner of the Private Eye Writers of America "Shamus" award, receiving the PWA "Eye" for Life Achievement (2006) and their "Hammer" award for making a major contribution to the private eye genre with the Nathan Heller saga (2012).

His graphic novel *Road to Perdition* (1998) became the Academy Award-winning Tom Hanks film, followed by prose sequels and several graphic novels. His other comics credits include the syndicated strip *Dick Tracy*, *Batman*, and his own *Ms. Tree* and *Wild Dog*.

His innovative Quarry novels were adapted as a 2016 TV series by Cinemax. His other suspense series include Eliot Ness, Krista Larson, Reeder and Rogers, and the *Disaster* novels. He has completed twelve Mike Hammer novels begun by the late Mickey Spillane; his audio novel, *Mike Hammer: The Little Death* with Stacy Keach, won a 2011 Audie.

For five years, he was sole licensing writer for TV's *CSI: Crime Scene Investigation* (and its spin-offs), writing best-selling novels, graphic novels, and video games. His tie-in books have appeared on the USA TODAY and *New York Times* bestseller lists, including *Saving Private Ryan*, *Air Force One*, and *American Gangster*.

Collins has written and directed four features and two documentaries, including the Lifetime movie *Mommy* (1996) and *Mike Hammer's Mickey Spillane* (1998); he scripted *The Expert*, a 1995 HBO World Premiere, and *The Last Lullaby* (2009) from his novel *The Last Quarry*. His Edgar-nominated play *Eliot Ness: An Untouchable Life* (2004) became a PBS special, and he has co-authored two non-fiction books on

Ness, *Scarface and the Untouchable* (2018) and *Eliot Ness and the Mad Butcher* (2020).

Collins and his wife, writer Barbara Collins, live in Iowa. As "Barbara Allan," they have collaborated on eighteen novels, including the *Trash 'n' Treasures* mystery, *Antiques Flee Market* (2008), winning the Romantic Times Best Humorous Mystery Novel award of 2009. Their son Nathan has translated numerous novels into English from Japanese, as well as video games and manga.